APHRODITE *in* PIECES

TITLES BY LAUREN J. A. BEAR

Medusa's Sisters
Mother of Rome
Aphrodite in Pieces

APHRODITE *in* PIECES

Lauren J. A. Bear

ACE
NEW YORK

ACE
Published by Berkley
An imprint of Penguin Random House LLC
1745 Broadway, New York, NY 10019
penguinrandomhouse.com

Book design by Alison Cnockaert

Library of Congress Cataloging-in-Publication Data

Names: Bear, Lauren J. A. author
Title: Aphrodite in pieces / Lauren J. A. Bear.
Description: New York : Ace, 2026.
Identifiers: LCCN 2025043334 (print) | LCCN 2025043335 (ebook) |
ISBN 9780593638972 hardcover | ISBN 9780593638989 ebook
Subjects: LCSH: Aphrodite (Greek deity)—Fiction |
LCGFT: Mythological fiction | Novels | Fiction
Classification: LCC PS3602.E2477 A86 2026 (print) | LCC PS3602.E2477 (ebook)
LC record available at https://lccn.loc.gov/2025043334
LC ebook record available at https://lccn.loc.gov/2025043335

Printed in the United States of America
1st Printing

The authorized representative in the EU for product safety and compliance is Penguin Random House Ireland, Morrison Chambers, 32 Nassau Street, Dublin D02 YH68, Ireland, https://eu-contact.penguin.ie.

For Dan.
Duh.

"Hear anew the voice! O hear and listen!"

—Sappho, "Ode to Aphrodite"
(translated by W. E. Leonard)

"Now are you sure you want a piece of me?"

—Britney Spears, "Piece of Me"

APHRODITE
in
PIECES

1

MILOS
Second Century BCE

JUST AS SHE was born, the visitor arrives upon the sea, riding the wave-begotten mist to shore. When her sandals touch sand, she pauses to adjust the golden cloak about her shoulders. Her hands continue, traveling down her arms, brushing the tops of her thighs. Checking. Confirming.

All is perfectly dry, all perfectly in order.

All perfect, really.

Entrances matter. She learned that a long time ago.

Standing on the beach, the visitor inhales through her mouth, tasting the air's delicious salt on her tongue, the alchemical combination of light and water and rock. She breathes, her heart beats, a response and recognition. Her soul is also an island, and she has tarried too long on the mainland. Though the ocean is not her domain, it claims her like a childhood home. *Do all forms of life internalize their birthplace?* she wonders. *Do we ever truly leave the place where we were made?*

Questions for later. There would be time. For those like her, there always is.

Hood raised, she moves inward, away from the water and toward the town, passing from shadow to shadow, forging a dark and silent path. Her famous face, her infamous body complicate even the simplest of tasks. Yes, even centuries later, her appearance remains an issue, and she cannot be recognized tonight.

There is too much to do.

Too much to say.

If he does not listen, she will have to leave and find another.

She knows the route to her destination because she has done her research. This is no random happenstance, no whimsical decision. She is far more meticulous than others realize. For someone so passionate, she is also intentional. Calculated, her enemies call it, and there are many.

She will speak of them tonight, too.

She quickens her pace.

HE, WHO HAS less time and does not know of her approach, considers the stone. It arrived only that morning, hauled from port by a yoked team of beasts, entering his home to a cacophony of creaking wheels and snorts and swearing.

And now, with the sweating animals and porters departed, silence. Just him and the stone—not for constructing a pool or building a tomb, but for art.

His previous commission, a statue of the goddess Artemis, had been completed to little fanfare. It hurt to witness a piece he'd obsessed over with the passion and attention of a lover received with a half smile. Didn't the priestess see all the ways he'd made his Artemis distinct? The right arm—her bow arm—more muscled, the respective breast flatter. The calluses on the edges of her draw fingers. Frustrated, he began to enumerate, only to be cut off with a polite nod.

The temple paid its concluding fee without complaint, for the goddess's likeness was serviceable, and it isn't a popular temple. These days, the people of Milos care more about harvesting tuna and the wars between the Roman Republic and Macedonia than worship.

For most artists, completing a piece means celebration. Expensive wine. Cheap lovers. But instead of using the temple's coin to repair the roof or expand his stores, he almost immediately purchases more stone.

"Who are you?" he asks that morning's delivery. "What might you be?"

Will you be as good as the last one? And then, what he cannot say aloud: *Could you be my masterpiece?*

These questions trouble him during the day, plague him at night. How will he know when he has achieved his best? And could it have already occurred? Might he be on a downward path already, passing his peak to little notice? Are masterpieces claimed in the moment or only in retrospect? If he knew other artists, he would ask, but he has few friends as it is.

He *had* Timon once.

And with that name he lapses into a melancholic malaise. Art provokes the extremes in him—euphoria and depression, hope and angst—pushing him this way and that, sometimes with only a breath or two of respite between emotions. Volatile, his mother calls it, but that isn't quite right. To him, volatile implies anger. He doesn't feel irate, he feels *everything*, which subsequently makes him feel beyond understanding.

He is not naturally garrulous like his father, so he speaks through his art. Explaining himself in the choices he makes.

Yet no one listens.

Was he born different? An egg that rolled into the wrong nest? For nobody in this fishing town seems to share his observations or reactions, his penchant for dreaming. Back home, his family used to belittle him for doing nothing—*Get up! Eat something! Stop napping!*—but his mind was ever at work. Imagining and interrogating.

That night, as an intruder lands on the beach, he lays his cheek against the marble, sending his body heat into its pores, waiting until his warmth is accepted and shared and he feels its returning embrace on his face. To be an artist is to romance the stone—to love it enough to uncover its beauty. This is the first step.

It is a commitment, made firm by an idea. That is the second.

And loving the medium is easier than knowing what to do with it.

Sometimes inspiration is summoned, the fire prodded, the palm sliced and blood drained. Other times, it arrives through careful meditation or prayer, in blessing. And in the most singular circumstances, it knocks at the front door.

Rap, rap, rap.

Three percussive beats. Not timid, but hardly aggressive. Curt, but not rude.

He startles, drawing back from the stone. Nobody visits him. Does he owe the mason more coin? A neighbor checking in? Hardly. He does not dare to hope it is Timon; the disappointment would hurt too much.

But when he opens the door, a woman waits outside, and she is certainly no kin of his.

"Alexandros. Of Antioch on the Maeander."

Her voice is light and breathy, inviting him to lean closer, and when he does, he catches the scent of rose water.

No, not just the essence of a rose, an entire garden. A heady floral universe in every shade: yellow and white, all the pink petals on the path to red. And he thinks, *She is springtime.*

She stares at him, bemused, for he does not respond, lost as he is in sensory wonder.

"Yes," he stumbles, finally. "Yes, I am him."

"Magnificent."

The woman enters his simple one-room home without invitation, sauntering past the low bed with slow, swaying hips. Her movements linger like a fermata. With preternatural grace, she removes her cloak and tosses it on the worktable, unbothered by the indignant outburst of dust. She is marble, too, formed from alabastrine skin without blemish, uncreased by sun or age. The color of her hair is unique to the natural world, unable to be replicated in dye. He knows because he has tried. What would he call it? Strawberry wine? Crushed coral?

And she is decorated in precious metals. Orichalcum necklaces around her delicate throat and golden bracelets twisting up her arms. Two earrings in each lobe. Although he is a man uninterested in what meets between her legs, he is an artist first and foremost. It is his life's work to notice shadow and form, texture and angle. Her body's softness, the way mauve cloth melts over curve of breast and hip and thigh.

"My timing is impeccable," she purrs, running her ageless hands across the pristine marble, and he wonders which is more perfect. "Parian?"

"Yes."

Only the island of Paros boasts stone this fine-grain, so semitranslucent and pure.

She turns and regards him. Her eyes are striking, an uncanny lavender, framed by feathery dark lashes and set beneath arched brows. "Are you, what they call, a man of few words?" she wonders.

"No." Then he self-corrects. "Maybe."

"Do not be ashamed. Most men talk too much."

He agrees.

She seems to take in everything with those lilac eyes, sweeping and lifting as they itemize his life. The rumpled blankets. The tools necessary to carve stone—clawed chisels and pointed ones, flat chisels and rounded, abrasive powders, and hammers. He considers himself from her point of view. Worn and thin; in truth, gaunt. His tunic a size too big. He does not eat well nor sleep consistently when he's working. He longs to sneak a whiff of himself but is too embarrassed.

"For an artist," she comments, "there is very little beauty in this room."

"The beauty is in here," he counters, tapping at his temple.

"I appreciate that, but"—she sighs—"I *do* adore lovely things. A few vases, a rug, would make considerable difference."

He should defend his space, but he accepts the truth. He places very little priority on his own convenience, to his detriment, as he has been told. So he shrugs. "I was not expecting a guest."

"Taking care of yourself shouldn't be for others," she chides him, not unkindly. And then: "Can you guess why I am here?"

He shakes his head.

"For art, of course!"

"Art?"

She smiles. "That is what you do, correct? Why you left Antioch on the Maeander?"

Yes, that is why he left. Years have come and gone since he crossed the sea from Anatolia, but the pang of that farewell persists. A tender sore, still open to poke or prod in moments of self-loathing. His sisters' tears, his parents' frustration. They could not comprehend why he would forfeit their comfortable life, but he had to go, to seek style, to observe and expand and suffer.

For art.

"Yes," he replies.

"Magnificent." She claps her hands once and holds them clasped together over her heart. "I so admired your sculpture of Croesus."

That bust, commissioned by the titular aristocrat, was one of his earliest works. He frowns. "Croesus was not a beautiful man."

"Not at all," she agrees. "And you could have made the nose smaller, the jawline more pronounced. It would have improved his face, and yet, you did neither."

"That wasn't who he was."

"You let him be imperfect." She sighs again and does not disguise her longing. "Would you do the same for me?"

He nearly scoffs. "But you are flawless."

She laughs in paradox, light in volume, heavy in tone. "Do not confuse symmetry with perfection. Look again."

So he does. Anew. Inspecting her from crown to toe, removing her accessories with his mind, but also her colors, her aura. And with that focus on the bare, the exposed beneath, he finds it.

"May I?" he asks, stepping forward.

She nods, and he takes her delicate right hand in his calloused one.

His thumb traces the nearly invisible line scarring the top. "There," he murmurs.

"Yes," she whispers back, delighted, and she is gazing at him so intently, in such immediate proximity, that he flushes, dropping her hand and moving backward.

"I am not threatened or insulted by your touch, Alexandros of Antioch, for I know you do not desire me."

His cheeks warm. "No, I—"

"And thus," she continues, more gently, "you have no interest in domination or possession, of hiding me or exploiting me or changing me into what most makes you feel like a man. You will reconstruct me as I am."

"Well, I would try."

She beams, a dawn's ray of light—later he would learn how she loathed such comparison, but in that moment, she was the sun—and he might be halfway in love with her regardless of his inclinations, so pleased he is to have pleased her.

"Honesty is the greatest intimacy," she says.

"And you want me to sculpt you," he asks slowly—stupidly—desperate for clarity, "without worship?"

"Yes."

He swallows. "But if I err, or deviate from your vision, will you kill me?"

She raises an eyebrow. "Ah, then you have deduced my identity."

Almost immediately. When she stood at the threshold, he had felt her name in his core, its four syllables like the beat of a drum, invoking images of wet pearls and unmade beds, flowers opening, petals falling. Curses. Tears. Adonis and apples. Golden arrows. Ares.

Everything love, endless beauty.

But he only nods.

"Since you know who I am, you must also understand that you have no control over what happens next. It's decided. I picked you."

Should he be honored or horrified? Both, but also undeserving.

Who is he to take on such a commission? An itinerant artist of no real acclaim.

And *her*?

And yet . . .

Is this how it feels when the Muses sing to you? Do those others feel they have no choice but to answer their call?

The idea—*she*—has arrived.

His next piece will be Aphrodite.

WE BEGIN IMMEDIATELY. Do I pay you now or at the piece's completion?"

The absurdity of his situation strikes him, and he nearly laughs. That an extraordinary Olympian stands before him asking the most prosaic of questions is nearly unfathomable. "Whichever is more convenient for you."

A pile of coin appears at Alexandros's feet. Luminous lucre.

"Will that be sufficient?" she inquires, tilting her head. "I've never taken the time to understand mortal money. I find it quite dull."

There is no need to count the pieces to know she's provided him a fortune, far more than required for his standard of life. Enough to keep him in the finest stone for years and years.

"I have a golden apple you can have, if you'd prefer." Aphrodite's lips press together. "It caused quite a stir a few years back."

Somehow, he manages to decline.

"I will also give you one night," she adds, "this night. And I will reveal my complete self to you. Then, you will immortalize all my faults in stone."

He swallows tightly.

"Do not fret, Alexandros of Antioch. It is not such an unreasonable demand. I am uglier than my face and body appear. After I shed my story, you will see me differently."

But he has his doubts.

She scans the room. "Where would you like me?"

"Standing here, preferably, where there is the most space." He stumbles as he clears away the accumulated mess of a single man's artistic life. All the while, she observes him with those keen violet eyes. Their gaze penetrating his skin. He pulls forward a short stool. "For when you tire."

"I am perfectly capable of remaining on my feet."

He nods, feeling foolish. *Of course she is. She is immortal.* He gestures to her dress. "And this is what you will wear?"

"Clothes? Yes. Shocking, I know. If you've heard the gossip, you'd think I never wore any."

Mortification burns his cheeks.

"I was only naked at my birth, in the bath, and when I loved." She raises an eyebrow. "Yet my image has been stripped. How many frescoes in how many brothels depict me reclining on a couch, waiting to be enjoyed? Despite what so many painters believe, I do not walk around clutching my bare breasts."

Aphrodite moves to the open window. The moon over the island casts her in its milky light. He remembers when Timon told him of jellyfish that glow within the deep. To communicate, but also when pressed to fight.

"You know Praxiteles made his own version of me."

Everyone knows of Praxiteles, master sculptor of Attica, and his *Aphrodite of Knidos*, the first life-size female nude. *A masterpiece*, his acolytes proclaimed, and when word passed over the mainland to the isles, Alexandros could hardly rest, so consumed with intrigue and jealousy. Against the best interests of his finances, he traveled to Athens to view it himself, and yet, when the moment came, Alexandros couldn't look.

Why?

Fear.

What if the statue merited its brilliant reputation? What if it was, indeed, *perfect*? How could he, Alexandros, continue to create in its wake; what would be the point? So instead, he walked past the celebrated studio and straight into a tavern, where he drank low-quality, unfiltered wine until he lost consciousness and woke in an alley with unaccounted-for bruises. He overpaid for the next available boat home and never spoke of the trip to anyone. Not even Timon.

And he will not mention it tonight either. He simply nods.

"Then you may also know what Praxiteles said of my naked body?" Bitterness sours her dulcet tone.

"'I have made her as Ares would have wanted,'" he replies solemnly.

"Ares would have his tongue if I wanted. Even now." She turns away from the window, toward Alexandros, and her beautiful mouth is hard, violent. "Praxiteles is a presumptuous fool. He based my likeness on his favorite courtesan but had the audacity to say I saw the sculpture and exclaimed, 'Oh! But where did Praxiteles see me naked?'" She scowls. "Audacity is only attractive when it's free of arrogance. I'm partial to bold men, it's true, but I detest those who *lie*."

"Is that why you are here with me?" He has to ask. "Because of Praxiteles?"

"Our piece must outshine his! You will learn this about me soon enough, Alexandros of Antioch, but I adore petty vengeance."

Maybe he does, too.

"I have never sat for an artist before," she continues. "The idea of me has gotten so much bigger than I am. How could the flesh-and-bone Aphrodite ever live up to her image? But then Praxiteles's pride annoyed me, and I realized that I do not need another statue of myself covering my loins."

"No, you don't."

"All bodies return to the earth eventually; it imbues mortal life with meaning. But because mine will not die, I need to give something else. My story." Her palm touches the marble. "I want you to receive my bruised heart and place it in here."

He can almost feel the echo of her outstretched hand on his own chest.

"Can you love me enough, Alexandros, to tell the truth about who I am?"

Is it possible? Alexandros wonders. Can the divine, the inexplicable and impossible, be re-created in a finite medium? Can beauty herself? Despite his doubts, he has the source before him, willing to bare herself for one night, so that he might achieve his own dream of rendering reality in art. It is more than anyone else has been offered. It would be insane not to try.

"Yes," he finally replies, and he is proud.

"Then you are very brave." She steps away from the stone and spins, slowly, her hands flexed at her sides. "Shall I move like this? Or stay still? What do you want from me?"

"Tonight, I will make sketches of your body"—he swallows uncomfortably, his mouth dry—"but how you pose, the clothes you wear or don't wear, the props you carry, are all your choice."

"I like to be offered choices. Typically, I must fight for them." She laughs suddenly, and it is gorgeous. "Already I am revealing myself to you. Do others share so easily? Are you the kind of person that naturally invites confidence?"

"Sometimes people who pose say nothing at all, other times everything."

It still surprises him what people will let slip if he doesn't press. Some people need to fill the quiet, but not him. He has never minded talking within his own head. Even now, he knows the longer he takes to assemble his supplies, the more likely she is to continue.

"If you could ask me a question, any question, what would it be?" She has one arm wrapped beneath her chest, the other propped up, fingers resting beneath her chin, lips slightly parted, in a pose so suggestive he understands why she has consumed the collective imagination these thousand years.

"I think what we will hold dear speaks more to who we are than the curve of a breast or the line of a jaw." His sketching instruments lie ready, charcoal and thin wooden panels, clay tablets and stylus. Fully settled, he sits upon a low stool. "So, my question would be this: Aphrodite, what do you carry in your hands?"

Part I

A SHELL

Aphrodite Urania, the heavenly
Aphrodite, risen from the foam
Aphrodite Paphian, of Paphos
Cypris, lady of Cyprus
Sea-spawned

2

CYPRUS

Fifteen Hundred Years Earlier . . .

ARE YOU AFRAID of love, Alexandros?

A question for a question, forgive me, but I have learned the hard way that I inspire fear.

I despise weapons. I don't like to run, can't properly make a fist.

Yet I can ruin a man.

Does my presence here cause you panic?

Though I am neither innocent nor a pacifist; I have destroyed my share of souls. But I am blamed for far more disasters than I have caused. I relate to the Sirens in this way. *We didn't crash into the rocks! Our steering is perfect.* She *made me do it.*

The eponymous *she.*

The monstrous women, the lovely ones. It doesn't matter. We are all *she.*

I haven't slept with nearly as many men as I've been accused, but I remain Olympus's whore. Men worship this myth of me. The sunset version, alighted with promise. Aphrodite at night and all that entails. But come morning, when I'm just a woman? Or worse, when I express needs, too? When I don't exist simply to please?

I disappoint.

But I am not an idea. I am real.

I've tried to alter my appearance—to build muscle like Artemis, lower my voice like Athena, darken my locks like Hera. If I cut my hair, it immediately grows back. Dyes fade almost instantly. My skin will not tan. I could starve myself, but my breasts won't shrink.

I am as I am.

Not the first beauty, but the greatest.

Most life stories begin with childhood, but I had none. I wasn't born so much as made, materializing fully grown from the sea-foam, more unnatural than supernatural. Have you heard of my gruesome provenance? Gaea, the earth goddess, exhausted by her lascivious husband, Uranus, begged her son for aid. "Cronus!" she cried. "I am so tired! Let me tend to the life I have already created and engender no more!" The Titan grabbed his sickle and castrated his sky father, tossing the severed genitals into the sea. From the drops of blood came the Furies and giants, the ash tree nymphs. And in the resounding splash of shooting semen, I appeared.

I am kin to the lusty sprays of adolescent boys, the splatter hitting walls in a brothel. These castoffs, these motherless wipe-aways, are my siblings. I began my life as a joke between men.

But I also arrived upon mankind's most insidious and inherent fears: emasculation and replacement.

Uranus, Cronus, Zeus, all preoccupied with their seed, with succession.

Oh, Alexandros, there is so much more to being a man!

Nobody came for me. No hands reached into the ocean, pulling me to safety. No one called out, *Are you alive? Are you all right?*

Because I have no real parents, I have no mother to compete with or cry with. No father to protect or ignore me. I am missing both the good and the bad of all a family can do to you—an absence, like a missing molar, not seen by others, but touched upon constantly with my own tongue. Or perhaps an abscess, filled with rot. What kind of girl might I have been? An obedient one at her loom? The dreamy one amid the flowers? But this body and its curves were always awaiting me. I would have ended here, regardless.

(This is what I tell myself, what I must believe, when I regret the scholar, the healer, the inventor I might have become.)

I remember the waves, their froth, and my confusion. I was swimming in open sea, struggling against wild currents. I could not catch my breath before another cascade pushed me under. I recall my arms flailing, my legs kicking, breaking the surface to gulps of air, desperately searching for aid. I soon realized the stormy cause. Giants circling me, roaring with new life, fists raised. Nymphs already racing away, light as air upon the surface of the water. The Furies followed, a trio of dark angels, wings whipping around with cries of cruel delight. A discordant entrance, elemental and raw and fraught.

This is living, I thought. *It will be brutal.*

I had no wings, no great size. It is a miracle I did not drown. A shell rose beside me, a beneficence from some elemental divinity, and I climbed inside, guided solely by my instinct for survival, and I rode it across the sea. I was not standing, resplendent, but huddled and naked, sopping wet. An overgrown newborn, bereft and alone. With no destination and no guidance, I let myself be carried in and out of days, past parts unknown. Did I wonder at the creatures below me, worry about the danger ahead? Honestly, I cannot remember.

Existence and experience develop emotion. I had neither. I just *was.*

And then, finally, I was lifted upon one final wave and propelled forward faster: my shell skidding across the beach, and me, tumbling into the sand.

An inglorious arrival, to be sure.

I stood on two shaky legs for the first time and walked onto the island, moving inland, away from the water. It was so long ago, I cannot recollect my intentions, but I must have been searching. Exploring. Just testing out what it meant to be alive.

I had landed at Cyprus, what would become my beloved isle, my favorite home. Have you been there, Alexandros? It is a true paradise, more so than Olympus or the Garden of the Hesperides or any man-made temple or acropolis. Poets adore the word *cerulean*, don't they?

But it is an inadequate description for Cypriot blue. Cerulean is blue like the sky, but Cypriot blue is water. It's layered, dense and dynamic. Vibrating, fluctuating with shades of life.

I skirted the salt marshes. I met flamingos. I dipped my fingers into lotus ponds, where frogs and toads croaked their hellos. Everywhere I stepped, flowers popped open to welcome me, lifting at the tread of my foot. I smelled each one, admired these natural beauties I could not yet label. Later I would call them rose and violet, lily and poppy, and identify them within the full spectrum of color. But then, I only knew they made me feel happy.

I did not understand my nudity, nor did I comprehend the passage of time. I wandered alone. When I was hungry or thirsty, I ate from the trees, apple and quince and pomegranate, and drank from the pools of waterfalls. When I tired, I slept on the beach, bed and blanket outside my realm of comprehension. Because I had nothing to compare it to, I felt no sadness in my loneliness, but I did wonder what became of the giants and the Furies and the ash tree nymphs. Those other souls who shared my initial memory. Where did they go? Were they together? Why did they not come for me?

But then I made my first companions.

Three women, all lovely and nearly identical. Before I knew them better, I could distinguish them only by their distinct hair. Aglaia with her straight white locks, black-tressed Euphrosyne, and Thalia, whose dark brown curls tumbled down her back. They greeted me with song, a crown of myrtle, and good cheer.

"You are so beautiful," sighed Thalia.

"We are here to assist you," explained Euphrosyne.

I did not know I needed help, but it felt nice to be wrapped in their arms and doted upon. The trio presented me with a dress, and then, most importantly of all, they gave me a name.

"Aphrodite," announced Aglaia. "For you arose, shining, from the sea-foam."

Of all they did for me, this might be the most significant. To be named is to matter. To belong to somewhere and something.

They were the Charites, known as the Graces. Goddesses of joy and mirth, dance, song and banquet, but also relaxation and harmony. I thought they might take me somewhere new, but they insisted we remain on the island.

"It is safer for you here," Thalia told me.

"Safer? From what?" But nobody clarified.

Though they possessed lesser magics than the others I would come to know—and possess myself—the Graces brought forth a home from the earth itself. One with a hearth and roof, two luxuries I'd yet to encounter. Nevertheless, we spent that first night together outside on a hilltop, lying on our backs beside a campfire, watching the stars. I was astounded by the Graces' knowledge, for they seemed to know everything about the ruling forces of our shared world: the primordial entities that fashioned the Titans, who then produced another generation of immortals, and so on. The Graces taught me the words *mother* and *father*; they explained to me where I came from.

"It was bad of Cronus to attack his own father," I reasoned, "but it was also bad of Uranus to abuse his wife."

They nodded. *Yes, yes, you are understanding.*

"Cronus, the Titan—my brother?—is good, then."

They shook their heads. *No, no, the story continues.*

"Cronus became increasingly paranoid of his own legacy. What if his own children did as he had done and castrated him?"

"So he ate them."

I laughed, sure that they jested, but Euphrosyne stopped me. "Six babies," she contended solemnly. "Swallowed whole."

"But one survived through a trick of Cronus's wife, Rhea."

"And he was raised by nymphs."

"To return one day and seek vengeance and his throne."

Bewildered, I asked, "But how do you know this son lives?"

The Graces shared a sly smile. "Because he is *our* father!"

And then they divulged his name, before he became so many things to me and everyone:

"Zeus."

One word, one sibilant syllable. As I repeated it aloud, the blade of my tongue moved toward my teeth like a snake. His is a name that vibrates. I felt it then, just as I do now.

I contemplated all I had heard. "Do daughters do the same to their mothers?"

"No."

"Never."

"Women make life. Men make war."

"And what is war?"

Thalia shuddered. "It is what comes."

It is what comes for me.

I flinched at this strange assertion in my own mind. Here I was, presented with an entirely foreign concept, yet to be defined, and still it felt inevitable. I have reflected upon this conversation many times since. *When did you know he was the one for you?* people ask me now. Perhaps it was then, in that moment, when I began to hunger for more.

"That's not an explanation," I argued, and so Aglaia spoke of objectives, of sides and lines, of combat and its demand for bodies.

"War is desire made bloody," she concluded.

"Surely there are other ways to settle matters."

Euphrosyne shook her head sadly, black hair swishing along either side of her solemn face. "It is the only way for Zeus to be king."

I frowned.

"Power is never passed peacefully," agreed Thalia.

"It must be taken!" explained Aglaia, clasping her hands together. "And gripped tightly."

Power must be scarce, I thought, *to be so valuable.*

For I was dreadfully naive—to the subjectivity of power, to so many things.

"One day, Zeus will fight the Titans," I said, attempting to summarize. "And I am a Titan."

The Graces hushed me with frantic hands.

"No, no, no!"

"Say nothing yet!"

"Our mother is a Titan," confided Thalia, noticing my skepticism. "Yet she has sided with our father."

"Why?"

"Because she believes Zeus offers her the most assured future."

"To survive in this world as a woman," Euphrosyne added, "you must make yourself amenable to the strongest men."

"I'm not sure I will be amenable to any men," I quipped, and Aglaia laughed.

"You will," she murmured, in an aside that pricked me like a warning.

Our early days together passed like an eternal spring, similar in their effulgence and simple sylvan pleasures. We played games—the Graces loved dice—and while Aglaia composed melodies on her flute, Euphrosyne sang and choreographed dances. Every afternoon we rested, napping in the sun like happy cats. Over many tranquil hours, Thalia taught me more about our world—the plants and animals and cycles—but also about what I was: a woman and a goddess.

Blood arrived between my legs.

"You will bear children," the Graces exclaimed, excited for my future though I clutched my stomach in pain, far less certain.

"Your fertility will attract a mate," added Thalia.

These two concepts—fertility and mating—seemed to trail me, in conversation and environment. I had long since noticed how my presence made things multiply. After my arrival on Cyprus, the trees sprouted more fruit, the animals more litters. Rabbits bounded beneath trees filled with chirping baby birds. Warblers nested in bushes, and I counted their speckled eggs. Fawns and kits and cubs dashed and tumbled through the woods.

Because the Graces had explained to me that immortals manifest a natural proclivity, a predisposition toward one aspect of the world, I thought I had found mine.

"Babies," I announced one day, only to be met with three blank faces. "My domain," I clarified, flustered.

Thalia wrinkled her nose. "No, I don't think you are the goddess of babies."

"Maybe making them," giggled Euphrosyne.

I knew what that meant, for I had watched turtles together, and even two wolves, once. I had yet to attempt such an act myself, for there were no men on our island. But I felt urges. Sometimes at night, Aglaia, who slept in the place beside me, would sneak her fingers through mine. And sometimes her lips found me, too. I did not mind. I enjoyed her affection while still acknowledging a missing element. Though my body responded in kind, my heart craved *more*.

The Graces were a unit, a trio, and though they were never anything but generous with me, I was not their fourth. So many evenings I spent with my feet in the ocean water, salty, windswept hair flying behind me, staring outward, searching for my own partner in the infinite blue.

"What is your purpose?" I asked my friends, for they always seemed so gratified—happy to accompany me, to follow our routines, re-creating the daily bliss.

"It is our joy to bring joy!" exclaimed Euphrosyne.

"Our honor is to elevate others."

"We were sent by Zeus to care for you, Aphrodite."

"But what do you want for yourselves?" I insisted, frustrated by their lack of understanding.

"Ambition is not a delight," replied Thalia on a frown.

If ambition meant to want more, then I sensed ambition in myself. Besides the Graces and the birds, I spoke to no one. Our days centered upon me, my needs and whims, as my friends did all they could to keep me content while they kept me *safe*. Yet I sensed an absence, a lack of meaning. My life was an idyll, but also an interlude—a respite both idealized and unsustainable. Immersed in this pleasantness bordering on ennui, I awaited a contrast to the cosseting, the opposing force that might give pleasure its substance.

Danger, perhaps.

I was not looking for pain, but like love, it found me anyway.

3

CYPRUS

THERE ARE SO many stories of my lovers, but I doubt you know the first one. I would wager you've never heard his name. He was called Nerites, and as the sole brother of fifty sea nymphs, the Nereids, he was both exceptional and inconsequential. Where you come from matters in whom you become.

Maybe that is why I am so self-centered.

The Graces liked to frolic about the beach, but kept to the sand, rarely wading into the sea past their knees. But the water called to me, and when I tired of their constant glee, felt their obsequiousness too tedious, or simply wanted to scare them, I would swim out to the deep waters.

I can be dreadfully contrary—even then, when I was still innocent and inexperienced.

And on one such day, as Euphrosyne hummed and Thalia collected red algae to make face paint, a spirit of mischief possessed me. I pulled off my dress and ran into the sea, giddy and naked.

"Come back, Aphrodite!" shrieked Thalia. "Awful beasts will eat you up!"

"What if you are swept away from us?" added Euphrosyne, clutching her sister.

I laughed lightly at their dismay, shouting back. "I cannot die!"

"There are torments worse than death!" Aglaia warned.

The water temperature plummeted and the Graces' squeals grew fainter as I moved farther from the island. My form was atrocious; I paddled like some inelegant four-legged creature and swallowed mouthfuls of salt water. But though it stung my eyes and throat, I persisted, turning to look back over my shoulder periodically to check my progress.

The Graces gradually disappeared, blending into the rocky beach, until Cyprus itself was only a shape in the distance. I paused, treading water in my terrible way, to appreciate my journey, when I felt something brush against my bare leg. I stiffened, sure that Thalia's beast had found me, but the creature who surfaced was neither monster nor dolphin. It was a man, with wet hair both gold and green, who gleamed beneath the midday sun, luminescent, like the inside of an abalone shell.

"Hello," he said.

"Do you bite?" I asked warily.

He smiled. His teeth were square and flat.

I brought Nerites back with me, convinced I had found exactly what I needed. The Graces greeted him courteously, but I knew them better by now. Aglaia shoved the dress I'd thrown off before my swim into my chest. "Cover yourself," she huffed. I did, but took my time, making a proper fuss with wringing my hair and waiting for my skin to dry.

I liked Nerites's eyes on me, especially since it caused the others discomfort.

"Your father is Nereus?" asked Thalia, filling the silence with a compelled politeness.

"Yes."

"Ah," commented Aglaia, raising her eyebrows, "the illustrious god of . . . fish."

Nerites only beamed. "And my mother is a sea goddess, as well."

I made a face at Aglaia. "It would *please* me," I said pointedly, "to show Nerites this island myself. It would make me *happy* to see you later tonight."

"Of course," murmured Euphrosyne.

"Enjoy the tour," offered Thalia.

The antithetical Aphrodite reveled in their resistance, at this crack in their good-natured facade. They proceeded up the island as if leading a funeral cortege. Aglaia's head and shoulders bent forward, carrying her reservations like a heavy load. Had I become a physical burden? And I watched them walk away, wondering why they cared so much. Why was my independence a cause for concern? Did they worry Nerites would hurt me? Or that I would hurt him?

"They are nice," Nerites said.

"They are," I agreed.

"And you are very beautiful."

"Am I?"

"More than any woman I've ever seen."

I was not being purposefully ignorant, Alexandros. In those early days, I truly did not know. He made me feel special.

While we walked Cyprus's perimeter, Nerites spoke candidly of his family, the sisters he adored and his doting parents. When I had little to share in return, he showed me how to throw stones across still water and make them jump, how to whistle on a piece of grass. We climbed a cliff jutting over the sea and leapt off, holding hands as we hit the water. When we emerged, laughing, he grabbed the back of my head and kissed me. His lips were drier than Aglaia's, but his tongue wiggled against mine, soft as a clam, awakening a force at the core of me.

With our lips fumbling across each other's faces, Nerites and I kicked toward the beach, settling beside each other in wet sand partially submerged.

When I finally pulled away, I took in his flushed cheeks, his brightened eyes. "Are you ill?" I asked, worried.

"No, it's just that touching you makes me feel . . . unusual."

"Is that a compliment?"

"It is." He grinned and shook his head. "You're so very beautiful, Aphrodite."

"You said that already."

"It bears repeating."

And then he asked for permission to visit me. I told him he must come again, for I was enamored of his sleek muscles and boyish charm. I wanted to keep kissing him.

I arrived home late that night, and the Graces regarded my tousled hair and swollen lips with wrinkled noses. Annoyed by their sniffs and snorts, I went to the dovecote Aglaia had built when I expressed a liking for birds.

"Are you cross with me, as well?" I asked my turtledoves. A particularly dainty white bird hopped into my hand, turr-turring in its darling way. I brought it close to my mouth and pressed my lips to the top of his head. "I'll tell you alone the truth, dear one," I whispered. "I don't care."

For I sensed this was only the beginning of others being angry at me.

NERITES RETURNED THE next day.

"I am going to teach you to swim," he announced, hands on his hips.

"I swim," I bristled.

"You don't drown," he teased, "but you lack style."

He was the first to tell me such, Alexandros. I ensured he was the last.

Nerites introduced me to formal technique, pontificating on the coordination of arm strokes and head positions, kicks and counting. I found it all somewhat droll, but I was determined to show him I could do it, and our lessons continued, regardless of the weather or how much wine I had drunk with the Graces over the previous night. I learned to float on my back and tread water on days both mild and severe. To hold my breath, to dive from heights great and small. It was perhaps the most physically active period of my life, but Nerites made it enjoyable, engaging my natural curiosity for the teeming life below the surface. He taught me about the turtles and octopuses, urchins, eels and slugs and fish in almost unfathomable sizes and colors. I found this—the endlessly creative capacities of the living—infinitely more amazing than the mechanics of floating.

Of course, I practiced other things with him, too.

I put my mouth and hands all over his body, causing him to pant and groan. Knowing just how and where to touch him came so naturally to me, and his reactions made me feel formidable.

He was pleased with me. I pleased him.

And I was so desperate for connection, I told myself this was enough.

He gave me a necklace, a pierced scallop shell strung with a leather cord. Horribly ugly, juvenile really, but it remained around my neck.

The Graces hated it.

"Why don't you warm to him?" I asked. "Has he slighted any of you in some way?"

"No," replied Thalia. "But he is not worthy of who you will be."

"I am more concerned with who I am now," I snipped. "And Nerites is fun."

Aglaia scoffed. "Fun? Aphrodite, you are destined to become unforgettable. And he is a sardine."

"Hush, Aglaia," scolded Euphrosyne. "That is indecorous."

"He has *gills*," Aglaia hissed back.

"We care about your safety," explained Thalia, "that of your body *and* heart."

There it was again, that word. I clenched my fists. "Nerites is no more a predator than a wild sheep."

"He is a male. That is sufficient."

"Just let him go, Aphrodite," urged gentle Euphrosyne.

"No, *I* will go."

I left the house in a fury, storming toward a cave at the waterline, where I sat cross-legged and sulked. I hurled a rock into the water below, not a graceful skim and bounce, but a flat, angry *plop!*

I have always had a temper.

But then Nerites arose from the sea, rubbing his head. "Ow!" He grinned. "That was a solid throw."

My spirits lifted as he pulled himself up over the rock ledge and came to sit beside me.

"Your face is sad," he said, brushing hair back over my shoulder.

"Why don't you ever spend the night with me?"

I hadn't intended to blurt out such a question, this was hardly the reason for my foul mood, but it *was* a concern. Ours was a daylight relationship. Sun and sand. Even now, seeing him in the evening, was unusual.

"This is not my place," he explained, even as his arm slid around me. "It's too far from the water."

"It's an island, Nerites," I retorted, all the while wondering why I couldn't be his place. And though I glared at him, he seemed only somber, resigned.

"And it's a good island. Peaceful. It's where I come to escape. At home . . ." Nerites exhaled deeply. "At home, it is stressful. Zeus and Cronus have both amassed forces. They will fight soon, and nothing will be as it was."

I sighed, exasperated, for this was the Graces' favorite conversation, as well: Zeus freeing his magical siblings from their sire's gut and everything that entailed. I was weary of it all and could not comprehend why it should affect Nerites and me.

"That is them, this is us."

"For now," he added cryptically.

"Stop worrying about what will be. No more pushing me away. Stay with me until morning, Nerites"—and I softened my voice, my face, myself—"while we still know peace."

Finally, he surrendered.

Within those rock walls, upon that earthen ground, we came together fully. He began on top of me, but I soon realized I could create more pleasure for myself with him on his back. I flipped us over and finished that way, Nerites gazing up at me with adoration and awe.

And maybe a bit of alarm.

Afterward, we lay on our backs, sweating, connected by the edges of our arms.

"Who am I?" I murmured. "What am I?"

"You are beauty, Aphrodite." His fingers lightly stroked the side of my thigh. "But now, after this, I think you might be something more."

His words should have warmed my body in the night air, but I shivered.

"The Graces imagine some glorious future for me."

"I see it, too." And Nerites did not hold me in his arms when he said, "But I will be the first to say, 'I love you, Aphrodite.'"

I turned onto my side to look at him. "Do you, Nerites? Do you, truly?"

"Yes."

"And I love you, as well."

We slept beside each other that night, and I thought I had everything. We were connected; we were in love.

We were, in a sense, but we were also neither.

The story of a life is often a journey, Alexandros, and mine has been a quest for definition.

The lexicon of "love" feels infinite. Even after a millennium, I continue to hear it used in distinct ways for distinct purposes. The word can be a lie, a manipulation, an exaggeration. Often, its use and meaning are dependent upon circumstance.

Love, to so many, is a relative term. And back then, it was for me, too.

Nerites, love, life itself—all novel. The Aphrodite who fell for Nerites had never worn precious stones or seen kingdoms burn. She knew nothing of kings or greed or conflict. I was ignorant enough to be satisfied by a good-looking, green-haired boy.

Now? He would bore me to tears.

I have been ruined by passion and ecstasy and sacrifice and the anguish that grinds your bones to dust. I've been bewildered by love, half-mad with a need that exceeds desire, as strong as any survival instinct.

I cannot resist my own impulses.

And while I do not regret what I have done in love's name, I have paid the price in blood.

With retrospect comes perspective and knowledge. I feel a fondness for that girl on the beach with her sea nymph because she—*I*—was happy in the moment, blissfully unaware of another love that awaited.

A love that could never be described in relative terms, for it is incomparable.

4

CYPRUS

THE CLASH BETWEEN fathers and sons arrived as promised, generations of gods and their monstrous allies in open war. The Titan army, led by Cronus, battled Zeus and his newly released siblings, on every terrain, in all conditions. A battle between such forces is like nothing a human can conceive: white lightning and green flames, seismic waves, mountains cleaving and erupting, islands coated in falling ash. Giants with one eye and hundreds of arms rose amid primordial forces of every omnipotence in a clamor of claws and fangs and fire, the world itself in open revolt.

The rage of broken families is a unique kind of anger.

I watched the rampaging and ransacking from Cyprus's highest point, hair curling behind me in the fraught breeze, brazenly bearing witness. When the ground shook, the animals cowered, the birds hid in their trees, and the fish darted into the crevices of coral and rock. Even the flowers tucked behind their petals. And all the while my heart and mind asked each other the same question: *Should the war come to this island, which side will you choose?*

Honestly, I did not care who won.

Neither side had ever bothered about me.

The Graces shared none of my hesitation, pledging their full support to Zeus—not just because he was their patriarch, but because they genuinely believed in a new order. They were zealots and gathered updates from the front like they were sweet summer berries.

"You must align with Zeus," Thalia pressed. "He has vision."

I shrugged. "I do not know him."

"Cronus would keep life as it is, whereas Zeus aspires for more!"

"More of what?" I asked, but nobody had an answer.

"He sent us to you," replied Aglaia instead, "the moment he knew of your birth. He cares."

Yes, yes. I'd heard this countless times. But why Zeus, a complete stranger, prioritized my pleasure and protection still made no sense. Nerites spoke often of my appearance. Could that be the cause of Zeus's interest? Was Zeus saving me from hardship, or just saving me for later?

These were unsettling questions, to say the least.

Visits from Nerites became increasingly sporadic, and I worried for him, for us.

"Will you be called to fight?" I asked, for I wondered how long he could remain, like me, on the periphery of the turmoil.

"My family prefers I remain below the surface."

"But your mother and father are Titans," I pointed out.

"They call my father the 'Old Man of the Sea' for his wisdom. He has held discussions that will protect us, either way."

I narrowed my eyes. "What does that mean?"

And Nerites told me how Nereus bartered the pick of his lovely virgin daughters to whichever side prevailed. Zeus's brother Poseidon particularly admired the nymph Amphitrite.

I bristled. "And your sisters don't mind being used in such a way?"

"They will do what is necessary to preserve our home."

Nerites did not take kindly to any criticism of his kin, and his hypersensitivity irked me. Why should any of his sisters sacrifice themselves while their father and brother sat by unscathed? The injustice upset my stomach, and I stood.

"I must attend to my birds," I announced. A lazy and obvious excuse.

Nerites hung his head. "My family belongs in the sea, Aphrodite," he began, without looking up. "We will do anything to stay there, and we are united on this."

I took a roundabout path home, one that brought me along the beach where the monk seals gave birth. I liked to sit and watch the mothers nursing their fluffy black pups. There were no babies that day, it was only the start of their breeding season, but I did sense a disturbance that gave me pause.

Just off the shore, two male seals fought—one I recognized by his scars, the other was new to this area. They dived and flipped, biting and slamming into each other. Barking aggressively as their mingled blood lifted into the white of the cresting waves.

Male monk seals, Nerites explained to me once, mated with all the females in their territory. When another, stronger male, came and replaced him, the females then belonged to the usurper. From birth to death, these poor creatures existed within an endless cycle of possession.

How had this knowledge not made me angrier before?

I picked up two large stones from the sand and rushed to the water's edge, chucking the rocks at the fighting seals.

"I hope you both die!" I yelled.

Then I crumpled into the sand, arms around my knees, head lowered.

Alexandros, I was confounded, craving clarity. Involute thoughts spun inside my head while my emotions wrestled in tiresome conflict. I was irritated by the Graces' loyalty to Zeus yet disgusted by Nerites's self-centered neutrality. What did I expect from them; what did I expect from myself? I would never cut a deal like the sea nymphs, nor would I offer blind fealty to an unknown entity. But when this war had reached its conclusion, what might become of me?

Ah yes, the eternal struggle of "me."

Who am I? What am I?

I challenged myself to an exercise, to describe myself with one certitude. I wouldn't leave the beach until I had it.

I am Aphrodite. I live on the isle of Cyprus.

I love . . .

(Nerites? The Graces? What could I confirm with confidence?)

. . . the sea.

But these were almost platitudes, a shallow understanding. My hands lowered to my navel and pressed down. What about here? Aphrodite in her depths?

A fighter.

The response—not yet a realization—shocked me. I held up my arms, inspecting their softness, and shook my head.

And yet—

Within me, I sensed it. A force, a fierceness, awaiting its cause.

TEN YEARS OF watching and waiting, swimming and spreading flowers, making love to Nerites, listening to the Graces sing.

Ten years of blessed anonymity.

And then, one otherwise unremarkable day, it was done.

"It is over! Aphrodite, the war is over!"

In the garden outside our home, the Graces dropped their garlands. The shouts came from the beach, and we waited, frozen, as Nerites ran toward us, green hair falling into his face.

"Who won?" cried Thalia, face ashen.

"The usurper." Nerites paused, hands resting on his knees as he bent forward and caught his breath. "Zeus."

Screams ensued.

"Father, you have done it!"

"I will compose hymns of praise! A paean for the ages!"

The Graces raised their arms in gratitude. Tears streamed down Aglaia's face. I thought of monk seals. Whom did we belong to now?

While the sisters clung to one another, giggling and sobbing, Nerites pulled me from their celebration.

"Zeus gave Poseidon the sea as his provenance. He will marry my sister Amphitrite. Our home is secure."

He seemed relieved if not jubilant, and I could understand. There would be no more battles, no more uncertainty. But what he did not say told me so much.

Never, in an entire decade, had Nerites once worried for *my* place.

"And what of me?" I asked slowly, riding my rising temper.

He caught the change and held out a beseeching hand. "I do not mean to offend, Aphrodite, but you are so powerful."

"Powerful." I laughed.

"You will see," he insisted under his breath, for the Graces had joined us.

"They will come for you soon," said Thalia, her excitement palpable.

I recoiled. "Me?"

"We will accompany you, of course."

"To where?"

I looked to Nerites in urgency, for any explanation, but he kept his lips pressed together in a tight line. Lips I had kissed thousands of times now silent, stymied, when I most needed his support.

"You will join the new gods, Aphrodite!" explained Euphrosyne. "On Mount Olympus."

"What if I don't want to leave?" I folded my arms across my chest.

Euphrosyne and Thalia exchanged glances.

"If I am as omnificent as you all seem to think, who is Zeus to tell me what to do?"

"He is the king of the gods now, and this has always been his plan." Aglaia beseeched Nerites for help. "Tell her, Nerites. Tell her it would be foolish to anger him. Tell her it is an honor to be summoned."

"Beautiful Aphrodite," Nerites said gently, his hand at my elbow, leading me away from the mounting frustration. "Let us simply enjoy what time remains."

But how could I continue as before with this looming threat? I shrugged off Nerites, telling him I preferred to be alone, and walked for a long time, to the rocky peaks along the northern coast. From there, as I caught my breath in the shade of a carob tree, I spied a whale's spout of warm air blasting upward. The creature was impossibly long and slender, its ridged back ending in a small, hooked fin that cut through the sea, and it moved with a liberty I envied.

I, who had lived a life almost entirely unconfined, was not as free as I thought. Without access to a vessel and with limited information of the world beyond, I was fettered to this island prison hidden in the distraction of paradise.

But no—the island and I were both innocents. I would not lay blame with the prison or prisoner but with the captor.

"I will return," I promised, to nobody, to everything. And when I came back, it would be of my own volition.

Yes, I would enjoy the days that remained, because this island had never been dull; it was perfect, and it was mine. But I could no longer abide my own naivete. I would prepare for my imminent departure by learning everything I could about Zeus and his allies.

No more swimming, no more bird-watching. Not until I made myself ready.

When I faced Olympus, I wouldn't just be pretty.

THE GRACES' COLLECTIVE attitude toward Nerites completely reversed, now that our sojourn on Cyprus neared its finish and Nerites brought valuable gossip from afar. In fact, they hung on his every word. Though I pretended disinterest, I listened attentively as he spoke of fantastical palaces, constructed at miraculous speeds, for Zeus's court. I collected names, then interrogated the Graces later.

"Who is Hera? Who are Demeter and Hestia?"

"Zeus's sisters."

And from there, I learned of his brothers, Poseidon and Hades, and the children he had sired on multiple mothers.

Another monk seal.

Within this family were gods and goddesses of water and the dead, hearth fire and harvest, wisdom and war and healing. Real things, important ones. And I still did not understand what I had to offer. How could I compare or compete?

I wondered if Nerites would ask me to run away with him under the sea, but though he continued to thrust himself into me at night, with the solemn determination of a man who knows his time is fleeting, he never said those words.

Only "I was the first to say 'I love you,'" muttered into my neck between grunts.

Nobody was going to abet my escape.

I was sitting atop the highest rock in the sea stack along the shore when a golden-helmeted man flew down, sending the sun's rays refracting in every direction. He carried a strange staff along with my fate. When I hopped down and approached him, his eyes roamed up and down my body as he whistled.

"Despite everything I heard," he said and smirked, "I was not prepared for you."

I scowled.

"Brother!" exclaimed Thalia, rushing into his arms, with the other Graces in tow.

"Hermes!" cried Aglaia.

I recognized this name, one of the many scions of Zeus. I returned the same inspection he'd given me, taking in his high cheekbones and sharp chin, his dark brown curls. Hermes was thin, like a sapling, and not much taller than me. There would be no returning whistle; I wasn't impressed.

"Aphrodite," began Hermes, "Zeus has commanded I express to

you his most ardent admiration. He is so pleased with your development."

"He does not know me."

"He knows enough to be excited."

How? I wondered, my stomach rolling over. Were the Graces reporting about me? What information might they have relayed?

"Anyway," continued Hermes, "you should be falling over yourself in gratitude that you dodged all that dreadful battle business and—"

"Why?" I interrupted. "Why was I kept apart?"

He chuckled. "You think Zeus would've risked the Titans scooping you up? Besides, you are a treat, my girl, a promise for good behavior." Hermes's mouth twisted in cruel mirth. "Think of it this way: How do you get young ones to eat their dinner? You promise them dessert."

I despised him. It was a new sensation for me.

"You are needed at home, Aphrodite."

But I was not going to make this easy for him. "Cyprus is my home."

Hermes sighed. "It is very pretty, very quaint. Very blue. But you are expected at court. It's time to assume your throne."

My lips were dry. I moistened them with my tongue, stalling for just a heartbeat before asking the essential question: "As what?"

He cocked his head, perplexed, then responded as if it were so obvious, I must surely be teasing: "The goddess of love and beauty."

And there it was, finally. My domain. Though it seemed too straightforward, too anticlimactic, I felt a resounding pulse at the core of me. A recognition and an awakening, myself, in this moment, joining with my destiny.

Love and beauty. Spinning, swirling around my body, soaring up and outward.

Love and beauty. Casting life in amber light, making the whole world more luminous.

Yes.

"Tell Zeus I am flattered but refuse his offer."

Behind me, the Graces gasped.

Hermes shook his head. "No, I refuse to deliver that message. You may tell him yourself, but on Mount Olympus."

I was losing options like dandelion fuzz in a spring wind. "Unfortunately, I have already professed my love for another and cannot leave Cyprus without him."

Hermes closed his eyes, muttering invectives under his breath, then whirled on the Graces. "Get the nymph boy here. Now."

The sisters squealed and dashed into the waves. While they summoned Nerites through the ocean channels available to our immortal kind, Hermes and I glared at each other.

"You are very difficult."

"Thank you."

"He won't like that."

"That hardly seems important."

Hermes sighed. "You have been sheltered here, with indulgent attendants and your bland boy, and now you are spoiled. It is different on Olympus. Zeus will be up in arms—again—if you defy him and deny his charity. The other gods and goddesses are already bitter that you did not have to fight and still earned a throne."

I raised an eyebrow. "The others or you?"

"Should I be honest?"

"It hardly matters. I won't trust anything you say."

"That, at least, is a wise decision. Your first so far."

It has been so long and so much has changed, Alexandros, that I can be candid in a way I wouldn't allow myself to be that day. Here is the truth: Part of me longed to leave with him. I was so curious about the world beyond Cyprus, about the others who might be like me. Genuine excitement was an unfamiliar emotion. I hadn't been thrilled by anything in such a long time, if ever.

But I did not want to do what I was told. It felt too much like a concession. If I left—when I left—I'd rather it be of my own accord.

The Graces returned with Nerites, rescuing me from my internal and external debates. He wrapped me in his arms, and I molded into the slender, toned body I'd come to adore.

"Nerites," I murmured, "come with me."

He kissed both my cheeks, but when he pulled back, I met his devastation. "I cannot leave my family. I have no influence outside of them. I will become nothing but your accessory on Olympus, and you will tire of me."

"Why must you doubt yourself? What reason have I ever given you?"

"Aphrodite, I am saying no. Do not force me as they have forced you."

And though my chest jolted, heart stung by self-inflicted hypocrisy, I couldn't help but wonder, Why was he allowed to refuse when I could not?

"I will remain on Cyprus," I told Hermes, chin jutted defiantly. "The Graces will represent me at court."

Hermes rolled his eyes skyward. "Oh, I tire of this melodrama!"

Before I could anticipate his actions or prepare a proper defense, Hermes lowered the point of his staff at Nerites. A terrifying burst of aureate energy shot my lover from my arms. I watched, horrified, as Nerites transformed, shrinking, screaming, until his face collapsed inward and his spine shriveled, his bronze limbs retracted. The hair I ran my fingers through lay in undignified clumps upon the sand, like seaweed cast ashore, beside all that was left of Nerites.

A scallop shell. A living replica of the one strung around my neck.

Beside me, Thalia sank to her knees and Euphrosyne retched.

"There," said Hermes, relieved. "Now we can get out of here."

5

MOUNT OLYMPUS

"YOU KILLED HIM!" I raged.

"I changed him," corrected Hermes. "He's quite alive."

I slapped the smug god across the face, his expression going from amused to livid with remarkable speed. Ambivalence might have been his reflex, but it was feigned. I saw the flash of rage underneath, the buried fury, and stored that information in my mind.

"Change him back."

"I will, once you assume your seat on Mount Olympus."

I raised my hand to slap him a second time, but Euphrosyne gripped my arm. "Don't, Aphrodite," she warned. "If you are going to battle, you must learn to choose them better."

It might be the best advice she ever gave me.

Hermes smirked.

I carried Nerites carefully to the sea. Before placing him below water, I murmured into his fan-shaped shell: "You were the first. I will not forget." I stood back and watched him bury himself beneath the sand. Then a larger wave came, and he disappeared completely.

I lost him.

No tears spilled down my cheeks but, Alexandros, do not imagine I wasn't distraught. I was stunned, horrified; however, I rarely react the way people expect, particularly if there's an audience. Wouldn't my cries only satisfy Hermes? Why would I give him that?

"Come, Aphrodite," entreated Aglaia. "We must ready ourselves."

From the house, we collected our scant valuables—musical instruments and dresses—but abandoned everything else. "We will have no need of these things where we are going," Thalia effused. "Everything will be much finer."

I opened the dovecote to release my birds, the turtledoves and sparrows and swallows. As they ascended, I held up my arms, eyes closed, as their wings whipped the air around me, and I felt the ecstatic beat of their deliverance with wonder and jealousy.

Hermes exhaled loudly, studying the declining sun above us. "Perhaps we'll make it to Olympus in time for the next war."

"Do not rush me, errand boy," I warned.

He only grinned.

Past time to embark, we each put a hand on Hermes—me, with reluctance and an overstated show of disdain—and his enchanted sandals lifted the five of us into the air. My first time flying was a wild sensation, but I refused to flinch or falter, even when Hermes dipped and swerved with puckish glee. I kept Cyprus in my sight for as long as possible as we rose higher and higher and it grew smaller and smaller. When it disappeared, I did not wish it farewell, for I had already vowed to return.

I will keep my promises, I thought. *If not to others, at least to myself.*

The sun set and rose again as we headed northwest, over lands that would one day be mapped and marked in infamy—Persia and Troy—to the border of Thessaly and Macedonia, where the heralded—and dreaded—Olympic mount reigned supreme.

"Oh, Father," the Graces murmured, awed, as Zeus's compound came into view. "Look what you have done!"

Their veneration was certainly consistent—particularly in the way it galled me—but I was not blind. Though I played apathetic, I, too, was astounded.

Consider the provincial I was. In my life to that point, I knew only our island cottage. I had seen no other buildings. Zeus's home, at the mountain's peak, was the palace of all palaces, of any before and all that would come after. Since that day, I've encountered hundreds of attempts at imitation; none compare. There were stone pillars of such extraordinary dimension, they must have been transported by giants. Gates, thrice my height, molded from pure gold. Endless verandas and ivy-covered gardens, scented pools. Palm trees and peacocks and fruits and flowers.

And those were just his premises. Spread across the summit were dozens more in a similar, albeit less grand, fashion.

I did not hate it.

"Welcome to Olympus," Hermes said with a wink.

We landed in a spacious courtyard, and while the Graces fawned and flattered, I kept a sharp eye on our periphery. I would not be caught unawares should Zeus present himself.

But he never showed, leaving me both relieved and disappointed.

Colorful servants arrived in his stead, ushering me inward at a hurried clip.

"We cannot risk anyone seeing you before the ceremony!" an attendant with green skin and tendril-like hair explained.

"You are truly beautiful."

"So beautiful!"

"What ceremony?" I demanded, but they disregarded my question, practically pushing me forward.

"Oh, there is so much to be done!"

These were the royal handmaidens of Hera, Olympus's queen, on loan for my arrival, and they were moving me too quickly. Fearful and fighting the fast pace, I grasped the Graces' hands, and we linked together in a chain of arms and fingers.

"We will not leave you," Aglaia promised. "There is nothing to fear."

"I'm never afraid," I muttered.

She smiled kindly.

We were led into a guest wing of the main palace, and the door was promptly barred. Again, I caught Aglaia's eye, and she gave a slight nod. I took a deep breath.

I am . . . a fighter.

Around me, bodies whirled into action, lighting fires and plucking petals, opening trunks and clay jars. "We must prepare you for tomorrow's presentation."

"And if I choose not to attend?"

Euphrosyne laid her weary head in her hands as the handmaidens stared, flabbergasted.

"The king does not issue invitations," murmured one.

The green servant touched my face. "Beauty like yours deserves to be shared."

I wasn't convinced. Is a sunset any less lovely because nobody stops to watch? Or a flower, fully bloomed, in the most uninhabited forest? Are they not beautiful, even if they are unseen?

But nobody in that room would debate with me, and I surrendered to the situation, my opulent cell.

Hera's attendants introduced me to novelties like heated baths and body oils, skin scrubs and perfumes. I drank ambrosial wine from a silver goblet while they brushed out my hair.

I loved it all.

Alexandros, as you are already aware, I was not born to such luxuries. And if needed, I could live without them again. But that does not diminish my appreciation of comfort and extravagance.

"Presents from Zeus!" the servants proclaimed, anxious and hopeful, as they presented a chest filled with my new wardrobe. Diaphanous linens as fine as cobweb. Jewels the size of bird eggs. A finely wrought golden crown, decorated in palmettes. Would I accept such treasure now, without understanding its terms? Never. But I was a novice to political games. I still believed gifts could be freely given.

And they were so lovely.

"You will turn every head in this," declared an attendant, holding up a sheer lavender dress.

"The men will be drooling!"

"Falling over themselves to get to you!"

"Hard as rocks!"

The attendants giggled, but the Graces knew better.

I accepted the garment and fingered the fabric. "Tell me more of this event."

"Tomorrow, the royal court will be officially presented in the Hall of the Gods."

"How many of us are there?"

"Twelve, including Zeus."

That is what I expected. I'd spent many hours considering how our king would construct his caucus, ordering and reordering the names of strangers who had become familiar.

"Everyone is so eager to meet you!" interceded Thalia, hoping for levity.

"And to learn who you will marry!" added the green servant.

I dropped the dress to the floor. "Marry?"

Everyone in the room shared wide-eyed looks, and the one who'd misspoken turned chartreuse, a wan shade of green. I grabbed her upper arm, fingers digging into her flesh. "Who speaks of marrying me?"

She mumbled an answer I couldn't make out, and I yanked her closer. "Who?"

"The gods," she replied, miserably.

"Which one?"

"All of them."

I shoved her away and ran to the window. The room rested at a decent height, and I considered the pain from such a fall.

It won't kill you, Aphrodite.

A snapped bone would heal. I climbed up onto the sill.

Euphrosyne rushed forward, hands steepled before her. “Please, don’t jump!” she begged.

Thalia, already crying, joined her sister’s plea. “I cannot bear to see you hurt!”

“You won’t get far on broken legs,” counseled Aglaia, quickly and quietly, “and nobody will dare offer assistance. You’ll have to drag yourself down that mountain on fractured feet.”

“A temporary discomfort.” But I shivered. My experience with injuries extended to nothing greater than scraped knees and jellyfish stings.

Aglaia continued, undeterred. “Zeus might allow you a head start before he calls his hunters, but they will catch you, Aphrodite, and drag you back in ropes.”

“I lost my lover this morning,” I shot back, even as I lowered my body from the window.

“It was yesterday,” muttered Thalia.

I did not justify her correction with a response, for the makings of a better plan were already assembling in my mind.

“Hera, Demeter, Hestia, Athena, Artemis,” I recited, listing the names of the other female Olympians on my fingers while making eye contact with each of the servants. “Ask them to meet me here.”

They nodded, wide-eyed, and dashed into the halls I was ordered to avoid.

If running away was not an option, I could at least ask for advice. These goddesses understood more about this mountain and its inhabitants than my Graces did, and we were all to be a part of Zeus’s court. These were my future allies, my potential sisterhood. Surely, they would help me navigate this troublesome course.

While I waited, I paced across the room, pausing only to refill my goblet with wine. Though racked with nerves, I was eager to meet these undoubtedly incredible women. How much we might learn from one another! My imagination went a bit wild picturing new friendships, momentous possibility. What might we create or achieve with our forces combined?

But the servants returned with bowed heads.

"Hera is, unfortunately, occupied."

"Athena sends her regrets."

And so on, down the line. All five goddesses were busy, indisposed, otherwise engaged.

I turned to Thalia. "You said everyone wanted to meet me. Did you mean only the men?"

"No, Aphrodite," she insisted, her face pale. "Why would you think that?"

The others shook their heads, placated me with noncommittal turns of phrase, but not one of them met my eyes.

They were lying.

Stomach roiling, I lifted my goblet and drank deeply.

DESPITE THE PLUSH bed, I slept terribly that night, turning and tossing, kicking out, consumed with anxiety. At the top of my mind was Nerites, an innocent, punished for my attitude. I imagined his mother's reaction when he never came home, his inconsolable sisters. After all the handshakes and wartime maneuvering to preserve their family, *I* was the one to ruin it.

And then there was the matter of a husband.

Zeus and Poseidon were already married, but would they demand me as a mistress? I nearly gagged. The third brother, Hades, king of the underworld, was unwed, but a life among shades and demons? I couldn't fathom it.

Which left Zeus's sons. I wouldn't be able to tolerate Hermes over any long period of time, so Apollo? Hephaestus? And all this positing assumed Zeus would match me within his court. There were countless others in the pantheon and its extension. To which old gods and monsters might he barter me to settle a debt, to be owed a favor? I pictured myself in bed with one of the Hecatoncheires, groped by their hundred hands, fifty open mouths coming for mine.

I rolled over, shoving my face into the pillow.

Shouldn't the goddess of love be granted the right to love?

I flipped over onto my back and stared at the ceiling.

And the other goddesses who denied my invitation.

Did they hate me? How? We had never even met.

With so many problems, I worried I might suffocate. I sat up in bed and, careful not to wake the Graces, who shared my room, snuck on the tips of my bare feet to the door. I paused at the threshold and, when nobody stirred, removed the wooden latch that locked me in, and slipped into the hallway.

Outside it was mostly dark. Only a few torches lit the corridors as I crept forward, barely breathing. I was a nocturnal predator in a nightdress, hunting answers.

Mostly I found empty or quiet rooms.

But as luck would have it, just as I had decided to turn back, I heard the low reverberation of male voices ahead. Instantly alert, I slinked toward the noise and held my body in the shadows of an entryway.

Inside, men sprawled on couches. This must be Zeus's andrōn, where he entertained his male guests. I didn't dare peek long enough to determine identities. My heart beat so loudly, I covered it with my hand.

". . . I wanted to," one was saying, "but Hera would have been apoplectic."

Ah, Zeus.

"Our sister is none too pleased that she's within these walls right now."

"She's always been the jealous type."

"You don't need to tell me!"

Laughter followed.

"And Hera's oblivious to what Poseidon learned! If she heard what Aphrodite can do to a man with her fingers and mouth . . ."

Somebody groaned.

Fiery shame, hot and rancid, rose up my neck and into my face. "A woman that sensual can't be trusted. That's why I won't pick her for a wife. Give her to a young buck."

"I disagree. If I had known then what I know now, I'd never have settled for Amphitrite. She's too slender. Aphrodite's got hips and a backside."

"Who told you again?"

"My wife's brother. He broke her in. Lucky bastard."

I could not stomach any more and fled from that vile hall, back to the room where I had still enjoyed blissful ignorance. I managed to relatch the door with shaking hands and crawled back into the bed beside Aglaia. I pulled the blankets all the way up to my chin, covering my entire body—clinging to a modesty that had been ripped from me.

Nerites. My first betrayal.

I wish it weren't true, but there would be many more. And they would hurt much worse.

Tomorrow. I will handle it all tomorrow.

This is what I told myself, what I wanted to believe, so that I could survive this deep breach of trust, of decency and intimacy.

But nothing would be handled tomorrow, for I would meet another man, one who would sweep my heart clean of Nerites entirely, who would occupy my mind so completely that I lost all reason.

I would also meet my husband.

6

MOUNT OLYMPUS

I RECEIVED THE NEXT day with melancholy.

"What ails you?" murmured Euphrosyne as preparations commenced. "How can I help?"

She tried to embrace me, but I shrugged off her touch. "There is nothing you can do."

My face and hair and body were attacked with brushes and pearl combs, powders and paint and floral fragrance. I selected a dress the color of sea-foam and sandals braided with strands of gold and silver, because otherwise they would be chosen for me. The Graces swooned; I tried to scrounge some delight in the sheer artistry of the items but failed.

"Aphrodite," coaxed Thalia. "Look." And together, she and Aglaia raised a polished bronze mirror. In it, I witnessed my reflection for the first time.

Yes, I had seen my face in the ripples of a pond, but this was all of me, in stark clarity.

What was it that others found so attractive?

My eyes were strange, my breasts a bit too large. I longed to be taller, thinner. My hair was sufficient, my face satisfactory. I met my own gaze with detachment, not exactly disappointed but unmoved. If this was beauty, shouldn't it feel like something? Otherwise, what was the point?

My hand drifted to my collar, where the scallop shell necklace once rested. It had gone missing. Nobody would confess to taking it.

"We will find it," reassured Thalia, "but in the meantime, wear one of these." She opened the box of treasures, and I selected two pearl bracelets and an aquamarine ring.

I didn't tell her I only wanted the shell necklace so I could destroy it.

Nerites had divulged the private things we did together, the most tender acts of love, to men who weren't even his friends.

After a dozen internal replays of the late-night conversation I'd overheard, I was nearly positive there were only three participants. Zeus and his brothers, Poseidon and Hades. Was it a relief that only a small group discussed me in such a violating manner? Not at all. That trio sat at the top of the Olympian hierarchy. What they thought, what they said, would only trickle down.

Was this a common male practice, to dissect a woman's body with such cutting disrespect?

If so, I found it repulsive.

Shouldn't the other goddesses feel the same? Why the disdain for me, when I had been wronged? If they would only speak with me, I could explain that I had not come to Olympus with the intention of seducing their men. Part of me longed to confess all to the Graces, but I was too embarrassed to repeat what had been said, even to them.

Already I felt so misunderstood, so alone.

And dispassionate time, the great arbiter, would not commiserate. Events moved forward despite my self-pity, whether I was ready or not. A winged messenger from Zeus's extensive retinue arrived with my summons.

"Aphrodite is allowed to leave. She may join the others."

The window beckoned. The jump might be worth it. But Aglaia

anticipated my flight and clasped my hand. "Think of Cyprus," she said. "Waves break and fall, but resume. So shall you."

Whether her counsel stemmed from clairvoyance or our accumulated years together hardly mattered; she knew precisely what words I needed.

I echoed, "So shall I."

We left the room, joining the herald, and commenced our procession—the Graces following at a respectable distance and the handmaidens after them. Oh, Alexandros, I have behaved brazenly for so many ages, it can be difficult to remember what emotions are true and which I assume. That day, which began with such apprehension, evolved along that hallway, for every movement constructed a shield, hiding my shyness and projecting my strength. Maybe, to those who observed, all I did was walk, but wasn't I, with each step forward, catching myself from falling?

I was the sea, its waves touching ground and rebounding upward, a miracle of resilience.

And when we reached the end of the passage, after one deep inhale through my nose, I entered with fortitude.

Lips pursed and shoulders back.

It was a circular room, lined in columns of freshly cut stone that supported a domed roof, and enormous. Large enough to fit every denizen of Olympus with space to spare. Situated along the circumference were twelve thrones, nine of which were occupied.

Eighteen piercing, probing eyes penetrated me as I made my way inside. Though these gods and goddesses kept their judgment tight and taciturn, the general audience let their fascination loose.

"It's her!"

"Those eyes!"

"Such hair!"

"That body!"

While their commentary escalated, I studied the faces and

postures before me, those of the other Olympians, and experienced a heady mix of umbrage, indignation, caution.

And beneath it all?

Lust. Always lust.

I did not allow my chest to deflate.

Zeus's brothers, Hades and Poseidon, were easily recognizable in their regalia, black robes and a trident. They occupied secondary positions on each side of the vacant central throne, which was raised on a dais and fit for a king. Zeus's sisters and children spread out from that trinity. A sneering woman in a helmet must be Athena. The man with a lyre in his lap, Apollo. A dark-haired woman wearing a diadem glared at me with open hostility.

Hera, I guessed. Zeus's wife.

I sensed their suspense. They hoped they intimidated me; they wanted to see what I would do. Would I cower? Could they make me squirm?

No. Never.

For I had made a decision that day, Alexandros, one begun in my dressing room and finished in the Hall. One whose repercussions have trailed me ever since.

The other Olympians wanted me to take my place, but instead, I assumed my power.

I smiled at Hera, smiled at all of them, then spun toward the assembly, waving, blowing kisses into the crowd. They received my attention with titters and sighs.

Is she kind? Is she coy?

Let them wonder.

Regardless, I was beauty, I was love.

Besides the seat reserved for Zeus, two others remained empty. It was glaringly obvious which one was mine.

A throne with a back shaped like a shell, the very same that had rescued me at birth. Stepping closer, I noted all the details etched in silver filigree, running the tip of my finger along outlines of bees and apples and sparrows, all studded with beryl and lapis lazuli. The seat was covered in swans' down, a softening touch.

I sat with a flourish and slight spin, intentionally swirling the bottom of my dress.

Hera's nostrils flared.

Nobody spoke to me. No one introduced themselves or said hello. But I had lived in absolute solitude on Cyprus before the Graces; I could shoulder their exclusion.

I kept my eyes up and straight ahead, locked upon the empty throne directly across the room. It was built of brass and covered in skulls. Wild boar tusks decorated the edges, shooting out at sharp angles, and decorations of red paint and red stones—tiger's eye and jasper—descended the legs, giving the impression of . . . and it took me a moment to understand . . . *dripping blood.*

It was ghastly; I shuddered.

Meanwhile, the goddess to my right conversed with the god on her other side, and though my face betrayed nothing but serene ambivalence, I strained to listen in.

"I told you he wouldn't come," she muttered.

"He will."

"Bet?"

"Terms?"

"I'll give you a golden stag antler. You give me a sunstone."

"Deal."

They did not shake but lightly touched fingertips.

This duo must be Zeus's twins, Artemis and Apollo, and clearly, they were similarly preoccupied with the empty throne.

The hall, filled with standing spectators, fell eerily quiet the longer we waited. And as even the whispers died out, the energy of the room tingled in visceral expectancy.

I stared at the blood throne.

As did Hera. She caught me looking, then conferred discreetly with Poseidon, speaking behind her hand though a tapping foot betrayed her impatience. The sea god nodded. Athena, in her ostentatious armor, stood and joined their discourse.

"Athena's offering to track him down," observed Apollo, in an aside to his sister that was loud enough for me to hear. I wondered if he suspected my eavesdropping and was sparing me the inconvenience.

An act of consideration seemed doubtful among my new peers.

But before any search commenced, a man burst into the hall with a brisk stride. At first, I thought this might be Zeus, but he was far too young. He wore a dark gray tunic, belted, and leather bracelets on both wrists—so different from the rest of us with our pomp and props. He did not make eye contact with any of the others as he assumed his seat, but when he raised his head, he saw me.

No, that's not right. We saw each other.

I startled and, I believe, so did he.

Oh, my heart said.

Booming footsteps severed the moment. The man's gaze dropped, and Zeus appeared.

It was almost surreal to encounter Zeus in the flesh after years of stories, and my expectations were both met and unmet. I knew all the lore—I thought I knew him, too—but now I wasn't so certain.

He commanded a massive presence, with a chest as wide as a wine barrel and thick legs like the trunk of a chestnut tree. His hair, once brown, was already run through with lightning streaks of silver. I couldn't determine much shape to the face under his beard, but his sky-like eyes fluctuated like the weather. Calm to chaos and back.

Yes, there was an undeniable force to him, and I already understood why he had surpassed his brothers, one somber and the other slimy.

Before he assumed his grand throne, he found me, raising an eyebrow and nodding once.

I did not return the gesture. There would be no smiles for Zeus, but neither would I glare. If he wanted a reaction, I would give him nothing. Let him believe he could not affect me, even if his callous words had kept me up half the night.

I know, Alexandros. Such pride! I had always felt its tremors within myself but didn't comprehend its magnitude until Olympus.

Zeus cleared his throat. The audience, already silent, went still.

"This is my family," Zeus announced, opening both arms, gesturing to us gods and goddesses on either side of him. "Together, for the first time. We are all descendants of Uranus. His son, Cronus—my father—was a despot. A lover of mayhem. He ruled by himself, for himself, with no vision for progress or respect for community. I am different."

His voice prickled my flesh, lifted the hair on my arms and neck. Confirmation I'd heard it before. *What she can do to a man with her fingers and mouth.* I suppressed a shiver.

"My family is my court, and with our combined affinities, we will support and sustain a better world, for the living and the dead, the mortal and immortal, the flora and fauna, land and sea.

"There will be humans, made in our image. To build their homes and cities, they will need wisdom and communication, music. Structures like government and marriage. They will go to war, but they will also love." At this point, Zeus broke countenance, face cracking open with a wide smile. "Oh yes, in the generations to come, we will become quite dependent upon acts of love."

The room's focus shifted toward me, foreigner and newcomer. Me, who belonged to this family only by the most inclusive definition, who had shunned their war. I lowered my gaze beneath my lashes but placed a hand lightly upon my chest.

Winsome Aphrodite, the coquette. My creation. Coming to life before all these witnesses.

Sighs abounded.

"Already, our power is significant," proclaimed Zeus. "Enough to defeat the Titans, to imprison them in the deepest pits of Tartarus!"

The crowd cheered, and Zeus raised a fist. His solemn act forgotten, the faux humility slipped as he glowed with undeniable glee. He had achieved it, he was king, and he was thrilled by all of it. First the success in the war, but now, here, us. The spoils. Hierarchy. Absolute authority. *What fun this will be!*

"In my future, our powers will grow exponentially as humans, our lesser cousins, erect temples to our majesty. With their worship, their offerings and sacrifice, we will initiate an unprecedented era!"

The crowd could not contain their enthusiasm. In the roar of applause, I noted every reaction to Zeus's proclamation, committed every tic—the physical giveaways of honesty—to memory.

Apollo's yawn.

The throbbing vein at Poseidon's temple, so incongruous with his ready smirk.

Hera's anxiety, her blatant need.

But it was the man directly across from me that I tracked most closely, intrigued by his apartness. He wore his hair and beard shortly cropped; while the rest of us veritably glowed, his were dark features on pale skin. And he slouched a bit in his seat, curved into himself, but tense, toned. A coiled snake.

"There is no charm in him."

I flinched, surprised by the clandestine comment from the goddess beside me.

"Who?"

Artemis nodded her chin across the floor. "Ares."

"I wasn't looking."

"You were. I have a good eye for the hunt." Then she returned her attention to her father's speech, as if we had never conversed.

I'll admit, I was thrown off-balance, unused to such astute company. It was a reminder to be more conscientious.

All the while, Zeus prattled on.

"Here, on this mount, I declare us Olympians for the first time. Tonight, as a sign of my benevolence, I present each member of my court with a home. Together, *here*, we will lead the realm to glory!"

The crowd gasped at our king's magnanimity, but I bit back a frown. This arrangement felt no different than Zeus keeping me "safe" on Cyprus for so many years. For I saw the cage beneath the shiny gilded exterior. Zeus would keep us as hostages, in thrall to our keeper. Another Cronus, but far more cunning. He would not eat us, but include us in his mock government, a dictatorship disguised by a counsel. And we would be watched. Our minor thrones and palaces were debts to be paid in obsequiousness.

And a space that is gifted can just as easily be retracted.

Was it as obvious to the others?

The speech concluded, and everyone dispersed into the succeeding party. Attendants carried innumerable platters of food, everything saturated in honey, and the fountains ran with wine instead of water. We mingled, gods and goddesses, nymphs and satyrs. There were Titans present, as well. Those who had betrayed their kind for the upstart, who'd gambled correctly.

When the musicians took up their instruments, I retreated to the periphery. Sipping my wine, scoping the room. Hera kept a vigilant hand or eye on her husband, who gravitated mostly toward his brothers or sour-faced Athena. Apollo and Artemis huddled together. Demeter lingered by the doors, biding her time until she could politely excuse herself. Hermes glided deftly through the party, offering glib remarks.

Hermes. Should I demand he return Nerites to his original form? That had been my intention yesterday, but things changed quickly on Olympus. With my broken faith came a weakened resolve. Could Nerites's transgression justify my inaction? And did his punishment fit the crime?

Before I could make up my mind, however, I was impeded by another god—bearded and small with incongruously muscled arms—holding an overelaborate walking stick.

"I heard you were lovely," he began, winking, "but gems are lovely. Molten gold does not shine like you."

I nodded, accepting the compliment without thanks. Already I had tired of being acknowledged first and foremost upon my looks.

"I am Hephaestus," he continued, oblivious to my disinterest. "A son of Zeus and Hera. My father has bequeathed me a forge at the base of his mountain. I would be honored to show you some of my work, now that you will be joining us on Olympus."

"I am sure it is exquisite," I demurred half-heartedly, for I'd decided I *should* speak with Hermes on Nerites's behalf, but I'd lost sight of him. He had been flirting with one of the Muses, and now, I could find no trace of either. While Hephaestus blathered on about iron and fire, I scanned the party, exasperated.

And then, as if the crowds had parted just for us, I saw *him* staring back at me.

Not Hermes, but Ares.

Again, that *Oh*.

Almost frozen, as if we were alone, I held the intensity of his attention, took in the entirety of his face. That low brow and small mouth, the slight furrow to his forehead—such touching points of contrast, soft features on a hard-seeming man.

And then the thump of my own heart, ever beating, jolted me out of the moment.

I inhaled.

Ares promptly turned and strode away.

No doubt Hephaestus was still speaking, but I couldn't be sure. "Excuse me," I murmured as I rushed off, pushing a path through the partygoers. I'm not embarrassed to admit I chased after Ares. Patience is no strength of mine, and I needed to understand why my heart reacted to him in such a way.

Maybe I'm more embarrassed that this would become a pattern of ours.

Me, impetuous. Him, reserved. One always pursuing, the other retreating.

I searched every shadowy alcove, found more than one guest sleeping, couples kissing, others crying. But then I spotted Thalia.

"Have you seen Ares?"

Confusion wrinkled her nose. "Ares, are you sure? He's the mean-looking one, Aphrodite."

"Yes."

"And he is the god of *war*." She whispered his provenance like it was taboo.

"I'm aware."

Thalia's eyebrows lifted. "Well, then, he left." She led me to the balcony and pointed. "He went down that way."

The stables.

"Thank you."

I flew in that direction.

"Aphrodite!" Thalia called. "Wait!"

I whipped back around. "What is it?" I demanded, hands on my hips. "I don't care how he looks."

Her expression saddened. "No, Aphrodite. I only wanted to say, be careful."

THE SOLES OF my sandals clipped against the marble floors as I hurried outside the palace, so worried that I would be too late, that I would find him cuddled up with some pretty nymph in the hay.

When I set foot in the stables, the horses broke into a racket. I lacked the language for the din then—the neighs and whinnies were just snorts and screams—but I hushed them, nonetheless. One large brown beast stuck his nose at me over the door, nostrils flaring and lips quivering, showing enormous yellow teeth.

I recoiled. "No," I told it firmly.

At the sound of my voice, Ares appeared from out of the farthest stall. He saw me in the aisle and tensed.

"Why are you here?"

It was my first time hearing his voice. Low and understated. A thrilling surprise.

I lifted a shoulder. "For fresh air?"

He frowned, gestured to the manure on the floor, then crossed his arms over his chest.

"You've caught me." I gave him my most kittenish smile. "Perhaps I was just curious why *you* were here."

Ares snapped his fingers, and a massive wolflike creature came to heel at his side. It had scarred skin and mottled fur. One ear was missing. Its mouth opened enough that I saw fangs twisted and far too long.

I reeled. "What *is* that?"

"My dog."

"Oh." I cursed myself. "Of course."

"Graegus is not allowed in the palace."

"Because he's so ugly?"

"Because he growls at pretenders."

It resonated the ether between us, what went unsaid, for the dog hadn't growled at me; in fact, it seemed to grin in its dilapidated way, a thick line of drool spilling from its open mouth.

I typically preferred birds to other animals, but this one, hideous though he may be, had potential.

"I am Aphrodite—"

"I know who you are."

"—and I don't have any friends here—"

"Friends are gratuitous."

I stepped closer. "Only because you've never been friends with me."

It was exhilarating, this boldness.

"Go back to the party, Aphrodite."

"I'd rather we get to know each other."

His mouth tightened. "No." And he shook his head. "I'm not interested."

"In what?"

"In you. In what I see in your eyes."

I could barely breathe, could hardly make the words, let alone affect a tone of lightheartedness as I took another brave step forward. "What is it you see?"

I was so present, so alive and aware of my own pulse and breath. Of his body, impossibly strong and achingly close.

"Eternity."

Before I could clutch him, the god of war turned on his heel and fled.

7

MILOS

Second Century BCE

SHE STOPS SPEAKING and the artist knows, *She is remembering him.* He lets her, casting his eyes away, hoping to give her privacy. As they pause, the pieces of her story settle into the space between them, lying like stepping stones on the path they are building toward each other.

"Our meeting," she finally says. "Our first day. I haven't thought of it in so very long."

"Firsts are important," he replies simply, recalling some of his own.

"We invented love, he and I. Not the poets or playwrights. Us." She closes her eyes. "Ares and I have experienced every first you can imagine."

"I do not doubt it."

And he does imagine. He pictures the earth as it was before love and war entwined, then what it became afterward. The unstoppable creative energy, but also the inevitable collapse. The force of two such passions in union is its own confusing alchemy, inspiration and violence, art and death.

Such a love could both destroy and remake the world.

"Nobody wanted us together. No one understood. Ares is all the things people say about him, and he is none of them."

So are you, Alexandros thinks.

He considers the silhouette of his preliminary sketch, adds an arm lifting, hand to ear. "You could hold a shell," he offers, and stands, demonstrating. "Like this. As if you're listening for the ocean within its chambers."

She mimics his pose, but her movements are so graceful, so inherently sensual, that to be in duplicate beside her is almost unbearable. He flushes and drops his arm.

"It could be the clam shell you rode to Cyprus. Or the scallop Nerites became?"

He mentions her former lover carefully, voice tilting upward in question.

Aphrodite sighs. She wrings her hands as though they are wet and ambles toward the window. "Poor Nerites. He, who was once my everything, became so easy to forget. You must think me cruel."

"I don't." And it is the truth. Love is no sport for the softer hearts.

"I shouldn't hold a shell."

With a wet rag, he smudges away the arms on his drawing.

She inhales deeply. "You need a better garden. It smells like a single man in here."

Alexandros winces. "I haven't the time to maintain it."

"You just don't want to," she replies, admonishing him in her playful way. "We make time for the things we truly want, don't we?"

"I suppose we do."

"I said to Ares once, 'A house is not a home without flowers.'"

"And did he listen? Did he change?"

Aphrodite laughs lightly. "We aren't there yet."

As the goddess remains, stationed at his window, something shifts. First, an aroma rising, then the accompanying flowers, creeping up from the earth until they graze the windowsill. Vines climb into the rooms, spreading across the walls. Buds burst open in delightful color.

The breath catches in his throat at the magic of it all. The wonder of his home in a veritable spring.

Aphrodite leans out the window, fiddling with the fresh growth below. When she returns to the room, she holds a blush-colored rose before her lips.

"Maybe this is better. Flowers are love, after all."

Aphrodite sits on the stool.

"Love can take a thousand shapes, can wind any number of ways. This is where ours went."

The artist and his model begin again.

Part II

THE ROSE

Aphrodite Philommeides, laughter-loving
Aphrodite Automata, spontaneous love
Aphrodite Potnia, mistress

8

MOUNT OLYMPUS

I SETTLED INTO LIFE on Olympus by re-creating Cyprus as best I could. Together, the Graces and I decorated my palatial home in petals and wings. We installed ornate cages of doves beside vibrant rose gardens. Grew sweet myrtle trees around lotus ponds. Lavender plants attracted bees, and ivory swans roamed freely among fountains. It was a space rich in scent and sound, the gentle babbling of naturally perfumed water beneath a choir of birds.

Thalia, Euphrosyne, and Aglaia kept their word: They did not abandon me. By caring for me on Cyprus and ensuring my delivery to Olympus, they had fulfilled their obligations to Zeus, but still, they stayed. Perhaps we had become dependent upon one another; despite the myriad ways our personalities differed, we maintained a balance. Emotional Euphrosyne and steadfast Thalia. Myself, the dreamer to Aglaia's pragmatist. The four of us were bonded by our time together, and they were my closest understanding of family.

While we personalized my palace, I dreamed of Ares. So, too, when I rested. Awake or asleep, it hardly mattered; I was obsessed. I could not find him in the Hall of the Gods. He did not walk the meandering paths of Olympus.

Eternity, he had said. *He saw* eternity *in my eyes, in* me. How could you say such a thing to a woman and then just disappear?

Love demands proximity. Because Ares was physically gone, I kept his image within me. I fantasized about him grabbing me in that stable, lifting me against the wall, the ends of my dress in his clutched fists as we made furious love. Other times I pictured him courting me, arriving at my palace with outrageous gifts, desperate for one glimpse of my face.

Neither could be further from the truth.

And so I wallowed. I moaned. I threw myself dramatically from one couch to another while the Graces watched helplessly, eyes wide and wary.

"What is wrong with her?"

"She's never been like this before."

"Is she lovesick?"

"It is the war god," Thalia theorized. "She hasn't been the same since she met him."

"Ares?" Euphrosyne squealed, more than a little mortified. "But he never smiles!"

"He is terrifying." Thalia nodded, and Euphrosyne shuddered.

"You don't know him," I sniffed.

"Neither do you," countered Aglaia.

"He's a son of Zeus and Hera; you cannot fault his pedigree."

They conceded me that point, at least.

"Hades, Hephaestus, Hermes, Apollo," said Aglaia, ticking them off on her fingers. "Four Olympians without a wife. If you revealed even a hint of interest, they would come grovel at your feet."

"Yes!" Euphrosyne clapped. "Choose Apollo! He is everything Ares isn't."

My arms crossed over my chest. "I don't want Apollo or any of them! I only want Ares."

Aglaia groaned. "Why?"

It was a fair question. I was behaving irrationally, insanely. The Graces weren't the only ones unable to understand my cathexis. I'm not certain I did either. Apollo was more handsome, Hermes more diverting. Hephaestus possessed the most wealth and Hades the most power. Was I so simple that I wanted Ares solely because he did not want me back?

No, not quite.

Was it because of his reputation, some perverse attraction to his ruthlessness? For I collected stories of him, hoarded them, retelling them to myself at night. He had been ostracized as a youth, sent away to live with wild beasts because his mother considered him too violent, too uncouth. Thus, the stories of his childhood were sparse. Most of what I gathered involved his skill in combat. Ares could decimate an entire army with a proper sword or spear. He could land a throwing ax between a buck's eyes from across a field, explode a man's heart with one focused punch. He was half-wild; wrestled lions for fun, drank a mother bear's milk to break his fast each morning. This information, whether exaggerated or not, should have repulsed me. Was I enamored of danger?

No, it wasn't that either.

Maybe it was because he loved that disgusting dog.

It was all these reasons combined beneath one overarching suspicion—a feeling that we might be similarly misunderstood. I'm a very instinctual creature, Alexandros, and I sensed an identical struggle within both of us, even in those few moments we shared.

Love and war: intrinsically involved in society, but too unpredictable to be anything but outcasts.

We toed the line of madness.

I sighed. "What must I do to garner his attention?"

"Bring him wine and food. Men think with their bellies."

"Naked," emphasized Thalia. "Because men think with their . . ."

Though I joined the Graces in laughter, I knew such brash acts wouldn't impress him. He'd more likely close the door in my face.

"Ask him to teach you something so he can feel important," suggested Euphrosyne.

"Men love that."

"Yes! Like the bow and arrow."

"He would have to put his arms around me," I mused, tingling as I imagined my back pressed up against that body of his. His intense attention fixed solely on me. "But how do I guarantee he'll accept?"

"He only obeys Zeus. The order must come from him."

I threw my head back, sighing. "I cannot involve Zeus."

"You can't," replied Thalia slowly, "but we can."

I leaned forward as she continued, my sweet, devious accomplice.

"Zeus would never believe any of us want to fight, but ride horses? That's within our nature. If we requested help, he would send one of our brothers to teach us."

"Hephaestus is always busy in the forge," noted Euphrosyne slyly.

"And Apollo's hands are too precious," Aglaia added.

"Hermes has no need to ride since receiving those sandals."

"He will choose Ares," concluded Thalia.

"Thalia, you are a genius," I exclaimed.

She nodded, pleased.

"And when he arrives for the lesson, thinking it will be one of you . . ." I held out my arms. "Surprise!"

Thalia giggled.

"Ares will be so angry!" Euphrosyne winced, covering her eyes. "I cannot be a part of this."

"Oh, neither will I," said Thalia.

"It was your idea!"

"Yes, but I'm no fool."

"Please!" I begged. "I need to see him again. Please, you must help me!"

"I'll ask Zeus," volunteered Aglaia, albeit reluctantly. "For I'd rather face the wrath of my bloodthirsty half brother than suffer your pitiful moping a moment longer."

ON THE APPOINTED day of my subterfuge, I needed to appear impeccable, but I didn't know Ares's preferences. Pink dress or blue? Hair up or down? Would he prefer a fresh face or dark, seductive eyes? In my volatile mood, I tossed my belongings around the room and snapped at the attendants assigned to my toilette. Someone must have complained to the Graces, for Thalia came and took my hands in hers. "Breathe, Aphrodite. He's just a man. And you are everything."

Just a man.

My heartbeat settled.

I arrived late to the stables, hoping that if Ares had already prepped the horses, he was less likely to walk out. And when I entered, he had two horses fully tacked.

When Ares saw me, his fists tightened on the leather lead rope. I caught the brief flare of his nostrils, the hunch of his shoulders. I'd made him mad, but this only delighted me.

I waved. His atrocious dog barked cheerfully in greeting.

"Where is Aglaia?"

"She's indisposed at the moment. Too many figs." I pulled my shoulders back, just the slightest bit, the suggestion of an arch. So shameless. "But I am here in her place. Your time will not be wasted."

"I don't like tricks."

My hands met my hips. "I am desperate to learn about horses."

He narrowed his eyes. "Horses are dirty. You seem very . . ." He paused and gestured to my immaculate outfit. "Clean."

"You are judged by your name and appearance. I'd ask you not do the same to me."

Ares seemed to hesitate. He ran a hand along the darker horse's withers.

"Well?" I pressed. "Will you teach me to ride?"

"I was ordered."

I bit back a smile. "Magnificent."

Ares did not speak to me again unless it was to issue instructions: *Sit back, outside rein, elbows down, less leg, more leg, I said sit back!* It was miserable. My horse smelled, and I was soon covered in a gritty mixture of dust and loose hair. I rubbed it from my eyes, spit it out of my mouth. By the time I'd accomplished a passable trot, I was sweaty and irritable, my dress all but ruined.

Ares swung down from his saddle like he was born to such maneuvers, while I slid off awkwardly on my stomach. I could barely stand on my sore legs.

"Tomorrow then," he said, taking my horse's reins.

"That's it?" I called to his retreating back. "Your instructional methods are truly motivating."

Day after day, he met me at the stables. I learned that if I came early enough, I could watch him work his own horses in the arena. There were four dark stallions, all spirited and tall and terrifying. Their hooves sent sparks flying when they hit the ground. Ares would lunge them without a rope, just a crop, and I worried they would trample him, but though they bucked and reared, he kept them under control with just his voice and his arm.

The first time one of them snorted actual fire, however, I nearly shrieked.

Ares leapt upon the offending horse's back and rode him hard until the flames were nought but wisps of smoke.

If I get too hot, Ares, will you ride me?

Anticipating his reaction, I laughed out loud.

Though I devised ways for him to touch me—pretending to trip, requiring assistance to mount the horses I despised—his hands upon my body were perfunctory. Practical. He seemed as desirous to be rid of me as I was desirous for more of him.

"I will not burn you, Ares," I teased, my frustration evident.

His lips tightened.

Alexandros, here is another secret: I am often underestimated, but extremely capable. I mastered the rhythm of riding early in our lessons, but faked incompetence to delay our parting. The longer I struggled, the longer I held him in my proximity. I was certainly no closer to winning his affection, maybe even further from it, but my dreams of him were only getting more salacious.

What would he do if I told him what I actually thought about during our rides?

And one day, so preoccupied with visions of him between my legs instead of the damned horse, I forgot to fake my uselessness. It was only as I was making to dismount—after a perfect halt—that I realized my mistake; he hadn't needed to correct me once. Ares watched me, a satisfied smirk on his face, triumphant.

So I did what any goddess of love and beauty would do.

I fell.

"Ow!"

My ankle twisted as I hit the ground, and it hurt—genuinely. I clutched it between my hands, gritting my teeth. I didn't doubt it would heal by dawn, but for the time being, it could not bear weight.

Ares looked down from the saddle, stone-faced. "Let me guess, you can't walk."

I beamed.

ARES LEFT OUR horses with Zeus's grooms and carried me back to my palace, one arm around my shoulders and the other beneath my knees. I abused his generosity, leaning my head against his chest, luxuriating in our closeness. I wet my lips just below his ear, made little sighs and moans of pain into his neck.

"Ares, my hero," I cooed.

"Stop it."

"You rescued me."

"Enough."

I cuddled closer.

Ares stormed into my home, sending the servants scurrying. I directed him toward my room, and he deposited me upon my bed.

"I'm certain you'll feel better soon."

I held my bottom lip between my teeth as I gazed up at him, but he immediately spun on his heel to leave.

"Stay!" I cried out, one arm reaching for him. "Oh, please stay."

I stripped the artifice from my voice, exposing myself—my honesty—though I remained fully clothed. The breath left his body, and his shoulders slouched. When he turned back toward me, it was with resignation.

"Don't you feel it?" I demanded. "Since we met, there's been a hook, right here, tugging us together." I laid both my hands upon my navel.

"You are love. I am war."

I refused to accept his nonanswer. "That's not what either of us are."

"It is what we do. And we do not belong together."

"Why? Give me one good reason!"

"I am too brutal, Aphrodite."

"So am I!" I slammed my fists into the bed. "Our power shares the same source, Ares. There is agony in battle and in love, but there is also ecstasy." I softened my pleading. "Let me show you."

It was too much, to speak of such matters, with him, alone in my private rooms. I didn't care that his hands were filthy, I wanted them on me.

He exhaled, groaning almost, as he rubbed the back of his neck. "Choose another man, Aphrodite. Be happy."

"I can't, I won't."

"Why?"

"Because," I retorted, in an almost accusatory way, "you're the only one who didn't comment on my beauty the moment we met."

He came toward me like some kind of panther, the lines of his body made lethal in motion. Despite my assertion that I feared no man, it took all my courage not to recoil. How had I disregarded the danger in him, despite all the warnings?

"Is that what you need to hear to let me go?" He spoke quietly but I heard a tremble. "How I think of little else besides your mouth? Not just your perfect smile, but your words." His hand reached forward, cupping my chin, and his thumb pulled at my lower lip. "I never know what you will say next."

"Taste me."

His face lowered at my challenge, and I waited, heart and hope rising, but he dropped his hand with a strangled sort of sound and thundered from the room. I sank back into my pillows, chest heaving, heart beating like the drum in a galley ship, the rhythm of oars hitting water at ramming speed.

Speeding toward my own destruction.

I had never wanted anything so badly in my life.

I was the goddess of love; shouldn't I be able to make him love me?

The next day, my healed ankle and I waited expectantly at the stables, but Ares never showed.

9

MOUNT OLYMPUS

A PROCESSION OF GIFTS began to arrive at my door, a new one each morning. A golden swan for my garden. A sword etched in flowers. Sets of copper goblets, silver platters. Anklets and earrings.

I know what you're thinking, Alexandros, but sadly for me, these were not from Ares, but his brother, Hephaestus.

There were notes, as well, praising my enchanting looks and asking for my attendance at dinner.

I tossed each one into the hearth fire.

"You need to thank him," admonished Aglaia, admiring my treasures.

"At least acknowledge his largesse," agreed Thalia.

"And perhaps reply to his invitation?" Euphrosyne suggested.

I grimaced. Not only was I disappointed in the gifts' provenance, but I had little interest in any interaction with the blacksmith god.

"I'd rather eat nails."

"But maybe it will make Ares jealous."

I considered Aglaia's point. I hadn't seen Ares since I'd offered myself to him, a humiliation that still prickled and panged. "All right," I replied, brushing the memory away like a biting insect. "Tell me what you know of Hephaestus."

The Graces exchanged puckish glances. Nothing tickled them more than relaying gossip with a touch of piquancy.

"His is a sad story," began Euphrosyne. "For when Hera first held him as a baby, she was dismayed by his size. 'A runt!' she exclaimed. 'He's hardly worth the milk.' And she threw him from the window."

My mouth fell open. "That's despicable," I said, and truly, I was sickened by the thought. I already disliked Hera, but with this information, I lost respect for her, too.

"It was our mother, Eurynome, who rescued him. She nursed Hephaestus until he was old enough to make his own way. He went to the isle of Lemnos and learned his craft with the wild Sintians."

"When he returned home, a master of metalwork, Zeus welcomed him back with gratitude," added Thalia. "Hephaestus works relentlessly at the bellows, despite the pain, equipping Olympus with everything we need."

"Pain?"

"From his fall."

I remembered the elegant walking stick I'd seen in his hand.

"I think his strength is commendable," continued Aglaia, "but Hera hates that he survived and earned Zeus's favor."

"Because she made a mistake?"

"No, although that's certainly a reason. Around that same time, Zeus's mistress delivered the twins, Apollo and Artemis. Apollo is gorgeous and joyful, a child to celebrate," explained Aglaia. "Hephaestus is a physical reminder of Hera's failure as a wife."

"Yes, but she also gave birth to Ares," I replied defensively. "Who is gorgeous, as well."

Thalia and Euphrosyne exchanged a look.

"She doesn't like him either," Aglaia said. "Ares was too unruly a child. Hera couldn't handle his tantrums and sent him away."

"The queen's sons are war and fire. Hera would much rather have a child of festivity."

My heart ached for Hephaestus and Ares. I was denied a mother but not denied *by* my mother, and even I knew there was a difference. I wondered how such trauma altered a person who was still taking shape.

"I'll eat a meal with Hephaestus," I relented, "but only so that this siege of gifts relents. I don't know where to put them all, and it's upsetting the decor."

Thalia smiled.

Truthfully, with Ares vanishing for a second time, I had little else to occupy my days. My decision originated less in altruism and more out of boredom.

And perhaps Ares would hear of his brother courting me and feel some impetus to act. Could I elicit envy in him? It was doubtful, but I would certainly try.

HEPHAESTUS PREPARED HIMSELF for our evening together with the same extravagance he put into his gifts. He wore ostentatious clothing, thick bracelets and rings around his calloused hands, and a golden headband over long, lank hair. I put far less energy into my own appearance, opting for a high-necked, conservative dress with minimal accessories. I wore my waist-length hair in a tight bun. If he had seen how I arranged myself for horse riding, then he would understand the message I wished to relay.

We could be acquaintances. Perhaps friends.

Hephaestus welcomed me inside with a grin that did not falter and led me toward a long dining table, rambling all the way. He blinked often while he talked, his eyelids emphasizing his sentences like punctuation marks.

He was an odd man.

And his home was odder still, decorated in a superfluity of metal. Bronze statues. Gold and silver ornaments. Everything in excess, embellished with electrum and orichalcum. I searched for fresh flowers, a potted plant, anything of the natural world that hadn't been processed or adulterated, but found nothing.

And then I nearly leapt from my seat when the first dish arrived, carried by a strange automaton of scrap metal, conjoined and animated by magic.

"My goodness!" I exclaimed, hand to my chest. "That was unexpected!"

"Aren't they exquisite?"

"Hmm." I took a timely sip of wine.

"I am their lord, they respond only to my command, and to those I favor." Hephaestus inclined his head.

"You don't find them . . ." My voice trailed off as I searched for the right euphemism. "Unsettling?"

The automatons, though shaped in a familiar bipedal form, had no faces, no mouths or eyes. They were mute and blind, the figures of nightmares.

"They cannot spy on or speak of me—intentional, of course. A clever man protects himself. I would never employ a flesh-and-blood servant."

I murmured some sort of ambivalent sound and continued to move food about my plate. Oblivious, Hephaestus resumed speaking at me about his forge, and the fire he always kept aflame.

"It is an unnatural fire, unlike any other, and can only be handled by me. I use it to cast Zeus's lightning bolts."

"It sounds quite dangerous."

"It is."

"And you are never afraid?"

"I do not fear anything I can control."

He seemed pleased with the direction of our conversation, and I worried that he thought I was flirting with him. After that, I became painstakingly careful with my language, ensuring that no stray remark might accidentally imply I was intrigued by him or enamored of his hearth of horrors. And those copper creatures brought course after course, as hushed as the dead, sending gooseflesh down my arms. I shivered.

"You are cold!" he exclaimed, and he briefly exited, only to return with a luxurious robe. As he draped it over my shoulders, his hands grazed the exposed skin from my shoulders to my elbows.

"So soft," he warbled.

"It's only olive oil and sea salt," I replied, shaking off his touch as I tightened the robe about me.

"No, it's you. It's all you."

Oh, Alexandros, he was the antithesis of Ares. I tried not to compare everything Hephaestus said or did to his handsome, ascetic soldier of a brother, but it was inevitable. And when I mentioned their relationship, Hephaestus grimaced.

"Are you close?" I asked, guessing the answer but relishing any opportunity to speak of Ares.

"No closer than I would be with a dog. Decent enough company for hunting, but not much else."

"I have yet to meet a dog who can lead an army," I quipped instead.

Hephaestus scoffed. "Ares may fight on the front line, Aphrodite, but I win the battles. I supply the swords and shields and chariots. In reality, *I* am the god of war."

It was a stunning proclamation, and my face clearly mirrored my shock, for Hephaestus, flustered, quickly amended his statement.

"I only mean that I take my responsibilities very seriously."

"Of course."

"I have worked very hard," he explained. "All my life. Yet I've come to the realization that I am lacking in one achievement." Hephaestus paused, slipping into a shy smile. "And that is a wife."

I nearly choked.

"A man is not whole without a woman at his side."

"It is not a woman's responsibility to fulfill a man," I countered demurely.

Hephaestus chuckled. "Every man wants love and beauty. When he acquires both, he has accomplished everything."

"Love is not accomplished. Women are not acquired."

"Oh, don't do that!" he exclaimed, spearing a bite of meat with his fork. "Don't twist my words into something oppressive. I am a good man."

I thought I could smile through anything, but my face would not obey. I was done with this dinner, this conversation, this obtuse, oblivious man. I rose from my seat.

"This has been an illuminating evening."

Hephaestus asked me to stay, and I knew, with a deep lurch in my stomach, that he meant in his bed.

He thinks you will sleep with him. This is what they all think of you.

"No," I replied, mind racing for a suitable excuse only to repeat myself. "No."

His shoulders drooped in disappointment as he led me toward the entryway.

"Another night," he insisted, taking my hand. "I've heard so much about you, Aphrodite. Maybe you can thank me for all the gifts with a few of your own."

He thought he was being charming, but I was repulsed. As Hephaestus kissed my hand, he yanked me closer, and I crashed against him. I stiffened—he reeked of iron, of bloody meat and the forge—but he would not release my body.

I hated that he was stronger than me.

"Your hands have an excellent grip," I commented smoothly, and he loosened his hold. "That should serve you well tonight."

And then I escaped, slipping through his arms and out the front door.

I nearly tripped in my haste to be rid of him, rushing toward the path that circled the summit. Alone at last, I shuddered, rubbing my palms against the gooseflesh dotting my upper arms.

Except I wasn't alone.

"Aphrodite?" called a voice from behind. I froze, panic tightening my throat, as footsteps jogged toward me. "May I walk with you?"

Be calm, I told myself. *It isn't Hephaestus.*

And I discovered, with much relief, that the speaker was Apollo.

"I would very much appreciate your company."

He settled into step beside me, and I watched him out of the corner of my eye. By the rubescent glow of his cheeks, the free and easy way he walked, I knew he had come from someplace far more diverting than I had. "Where were you?" I couldn't help asking.

"At Hermes's palace. He throws a worthy party. We drink, play dice."

"Oh. That sounds nice."

"It is, though tonight Athena and Ares played against Hermes and me, and we lost."

At the mention of Ares, my foolish heart skipped a beat.

"I like to drink wine. I like to play dice."

He studied me with a curious, sideways look. "Is Aphrodite fishing for an invitation?"

"Never." I shrugged a shoulder. "But if I were on your team, you would have won."

Apollo grinned. "I don't doubt it. I'm only surprised you'd be interested."

"Why?" I didn't mean to be defensive, but I heard it in my voice, unmistakable.

"Because I've seen you in the Hall of the Gods. You are there but barely present. You look perfect, of course, behave perfectly. Smile when it's expected, laugh at the right places, but you don't participate. Not really."

Astute Apollo. I hardly thought anyone noticed my behavior, as long as I played the role I'd been given.

"I am not afforded the same luxuries as you. Not when every man I meet is trying to bed me or wed me."

"You'd be surprised how many are trying to bed me, too." Apollo winked and I laughed. A genuine laugh that came from deep in my core. It was the best I'd felt in days.

Until Apollo asked: "So, where were *you* tonight?"

"Dinner."

When I didn't offer any additional details, we continued in silence.

Apollo escorted me all the way to the Cypriot-blue door of my home. "We have forever ahead of us, Aphrodite," he said solemnly. "It will be better with friends."

"Thank you," I replied.

For the company. For the advice.

He nodded, and I watched him walk away. Returned his wave when he looked back over his shoulder. I trusted no one on Olympus, but Apollo seemed decent. I hoped he would remain that way.

10

MOUNT OLYMPUS

IN THE TIME I spent obsessively pining over a man who didn't want me, and dodging the one who did, the world below Olympus changed. Humans arrived, as Zeus had promised, and their spectacular, perplexing cities and temples seemed to erect overnight. Mortals move with such haste! It's almost exhausting to observe.

Personally, I've never been one to hurry.

With their worship, our power grew. I felt a new energy in my chest and at my center. My hands had a stronger grip upon the threads of love and beauty winding through the world. When the humans called upon my services, I answered, tugging and weaving.

Sweet Aphrodite, grant me beauty!

Oh, Aphrodite, I love her!

I love him!

I love them!

Help me, help us!

You might wonder, Alexandros, about my capabilities. How did I respond to my supplicants and their urgency? What can a goddess of love and beauty provide? Here is what I always say: Love cannot be manufactured. Not real love, anyway. No matter how often or how ardently I am asked, I do not provide love potions. I tried, at the outset, but love spells against nature only become obsessions or infatuations, never ending well. If there is possibility, I can enhance and quicken the potential. Same with beauty. I do not remake mortals anew, but I emphasize the beauty they already possess. I like to think of myself as an immortal polisher. I add a bit of shine.

In the beginning, the other Olympians regarded the humans with disdain, chatting and jesting about their inferiority, but I admired the mortals' resilience. I found the women especially strong, considering the lives forced upon them, and tried to provide them with loving connection and moments of beauty when I could.

I visited my shrines and sanctuaries, accepted my offerings. I listened to the prayers.

And sometimes, I would simply close my eyes and whisper *Yes!* into the wind, sending my goodwill to any and all who needed me.

In those days, before I was married, I imagined lovers of all ages receiving everything I wanted: affection requited and hot passion. I was so hopeful.

While the other goddesses buzzed about Olympus like gnats, in a tizzy over errands and appointments, I spent my free time at home, daydreaming. I'm far shyer than people realize, craving deep, intense connections over a bounty of friends.

I may be famous, but I've never been popular.

My imagination was—and is—a comfort; I enjoy wandering the maze of my own mind. It keeps me occupied, keeps me awake to possibility—of all that I might have in this life. Back then, I loved lounging upon one of the couches that dotted my garden, sipping water with lavender and lemon, beside my medley of birds.

Summer days beneath palm fronds, I'd drift often into buzzy, blissful sleep.

On one exceptional occasion, I woke to a warm body beside mine.

My eyes shot open; my body snapped upright. But no man lay beside me; my intruder was a beast.

"Graegus, you pest!" I exclaimed, exasperated. "Go home!"

But Ares's dog did not move. He lay comfortably on his side, his wagging tail thumping against the couch. Thick lines of drool slipped between his crooked teeth onto my cushions, and I grimaced. I pointed in the direction of *Away!* Gave him a half-hearted shove. Nothing registered.

I sighed. "Even the flowers cannot cover your smell! Does your master ever bathe you?"

He sneezed, viscous globs shooting from his nostrils.

"Ugh."

But my revulsion was quickly replaced with an idea. Excited, I called for the Graces. "Come outside! Bring all the combs from my room!"

We giggled as we administered to Graegus with brushes and salves, picking out burs, cutting free tangled knots, hanging woven garlands around his neck. Euphrosyne sang while we worked, the dog's eyes closed and his mouth opened, panting in a lazy canine smile.

"Has he ever been groomed before?" wondered Thalia, nose wrinkled.

"I doubt it," answered Aglaia. "We've all seen his owner."

I sniffed. "I'm sure he's well-groomed in all the places that matter."

Euphrosyne covered her ears.

"He's going to be so angry with us," warned Thalia, trimming Graegus's nails.

"I'm fully prepared to bear the blame," I said.

However, the consequences arrived sooner than expected.

He didn't need to shout or clear his throat; I sensed his presence immediately. Ares stood at the edge of the courtyard, glowering, angry brown eyes gone black. I could see why his appearance on the battlefield caused mortal men to cower.

Thankfully, I was no mortal man.

"You stole my dog." His steely voice sliced through our harmony.

"Your dog ran away." I scratched the sacred spot behind Graegus's ears, and his back leg twitched. "Poor dear was in desperate need of affection."

"Graegus is a war dog. I've seen him rip off a man's hand and eat it."

Thalia flinched.

"He seems to enjoy my hands," I replied airily. "And I'm more than happy to show you what they can do."

The Graces blushed. Aglaia nudged each of her sisters, and they left me, bowing slightly to Ares as they scurried past him.

"He didn't sneak into your courtyard for a backrub; he's hiding from punishment."

"I'm sure whatever he's done is entirely justifiable."

"He bit Poseidon."

"Exactly." I patted the top of Graegus's head. "Good boy."

Ares exhaled; one hand rubbed at his short beard.

"I don't see you at the stables anymore," I lamented.

"There's no need. You know how to ride; you just need practice."

"Practice?" I perked up. "On you, perhaps?"

But he met my teasing with stony resistance. "No, Aphrodite. None of this."

"Of what?"

"The posing and purring. You are not a cat. If you want my attention, say something real."

His dismissal stung, but so did accepting my complicity. I *did* flirt and flounce, especially since I'd relocated to Olympus, but Ares failed to understand that my kittenish ways were armor, not a weakness. Behavior is an observable aspect of personality—it is what I do, but not why I do it. That why, that foundation of me, remained protected, safe beneath an arch exterior.

Ares was a hypocrite. Why should I drop my shields while he remained guarded?

But even a dare from him was a chance I would not waste, and I had a lot to say.

I lifted my chin and told the truth.

"I worry that since everybody thinks they love me, nobody ever will. I fear that my beauty doesn't mean anything and maybe I don't either." He listened, head down, in a pose that would become familiar, so I continued, riding my momentum. "Am I a water well, Ares? Are you conducting a depth test? Let me save you the effort. Some days I am reserved and thoughtful, while others I am shallow and unbothered. I ache and I question. I'm lazy. I like drinking wine until I'm drunk and wearing fine clothes, and I have no interest in matching your insufferable intensity."

Silence.

Not one tic or reflex or indication whatsoever that I'd angered him or impressed him, or that he had even heard what I said.

Ares did nothing, and it was infuriating.

"I don't believe anyone is ever good enough for you," I concluded, "and I am tired of trying to be. Take your adorably ugly dog and go."

But he didn't.

Instead, Ares came toward me. Graegus immediately jumped down from the couch, and Ares replaced him, shocking me by sitting with his leg so voluntarily close to mine. "If I thought you were nothing more than a perfect face, Aphrodite, we would have enjoyed my bed a long time ago."

I nearly laughed. "That's your response?"

"I've never doubted your depth. I've always known you to be infinitely more interesting than me."

"And yet I do not seem to interest you."

He scoffed, shaking his head. "No, it's not that . . . It's those violet eyes of yours." Ares met my gaze and did not waver. "They put strange ideas in my head, ones unsuitable for a man at constant war."

He doesn't believe he deserves love.

I felt triumphant, as if I'd solved a Sphinx's riddle or untied some impossible knot. But how could I change his mind? How could I convince him of his worth?

"You run away from me, but never from battle."

"Because you are a fight I cannot win."

The urge to kiss him had me discomposed. "I would let you win," I whispered. "Sometimes."

A corner of his mouth lifted into a half smile. "My responsibilities below this mountain are . . . far-reaching."

"I know," I sighed. "Human men enjoy killing each other."

"Yes, but I also care for another."

Damn it all to Hades, I thought, sinking. *He has a mortal lover, and I am going to curl up right here and die.*

"I have a dragon."

A dragon? A dragon! I brightened; my instantaneous death averted. "Oh!"

"I call him Drakon, and keep him hidden near a spring that is sacred to me, away from mortals who would hunt him."

"You should train him to pull your chariot."

Ares shrugged. "I already have four fire-breathing horses."

"I saw."

"I wanted you to see."

I raised a brow. "To intimidate me?"

And his eyes shifted away from me when he said, "To impress you."

Alexandros, you could have knocked me over with a peacock feather.

"How fares your ankle?" he asked.

I lifted my leg, placing my bare foot in his lap. Ares took it in his hands, the pads of his thumb massaging its length as he inspected its wellness. I thrilled at his touch, at the dark leather bracelets he wore, the blunt edges of his fingernails. I noticed every detail.

"Even your feet are precious," he murmured.

"My second toe is longer than the big one."

"Then that is the ideal."

I smiled.

Ares stood and proffered his forearm. I gladly accepted. We strolled the perimeter of the courtyard, weaving between the trees and meandering around the pools. Graegus trailed behind for a time, then dozed off in a flower bed. I didn't even scold him for trampling my lilies.

"Your landscaping is beautiful," he commented, "but imperfect."

"In what way?"

Ares gestured to a cluster of purple, star-shaped flowers. "You're growing deadly nightshade beside your roses."

"Indeed." I reached forward, brushed a petal with the tip of my finger. "I prefer to keep my girls in wild company. Some flowers aren't meant to be tamed."

His mouth twisted, hiding his smile.

"And in your gardens?" I asked. "You enforce military discipline?"

"I grow nothing."

Ares did not elaborate, and because I sensed his sadness, I did not press.

Instead, I led him toward my birds. I opened the dove cage, and one landed upon my outstretched palm, cooing as I stroked its tiny head with my finger.

"Doves mate for life," I informed him.

"What's life to a dove? Five years?"

I narrowed my eyes. "Up to fifteen."

"Humans associate me with vultures," he said grimly. "Battlefield birds, those that feast on the dead and decaying."

"You are not the god of death, Ares. The point of war is the peace at the end."

I took his hand with my free one and carefully passed him the small white bird. He held it so gently, and I stepped back, marveling at this intersection of fragile and hard.

"My mother sent me away when I was barely a toddler," he began, keeping his eyes on the dove instead of me. "She says I threw too many fits, that I was aggressive. I only remember wanting her to hold me. The wilderness, she said, would be a better home for someone like me.

"For a while, I lived in a den with a family of bears. During the day, I brawled with the cubs, and at night, I climbed upon the mother's back, clutching her fur for purchase. She was so warm, and her heartbeat, her steady rise and fall, lulled me to sleep."

The bird became restless, pecking at Ares's fingers in search of seed. I scooped some from a clay storage jar and sprinkled it lightly into his palm. If I kept the bird sated, occupied, I hoped he would continue his story.

It worked.

"After the bears, I joined a pack of wolves. Everyone is wrong about wolves, Aphrodite. There is no dominant male leader; they are a community. They exist in cooperation, not competition, raising each other's pups and caring for the elderly and sick. They share knowledge and defend each other."

The muscles around Ares's jaw tightened. "The other Olympians call me an animal. This is what I learned from animals."

He stilled, cleared his throat. I waited patiently for him to speak again, but he seemed to reconsider. Ares returned the dove to its cage and commented, "The day is nearly done."

I looked above at the purpling sky, a ripe plum. "Yes, that is apparent."

"What I mean to say is I have overstayed."

"Not at all," I replied softly. "I had hoped you would—"

"Aphrodite!" We both fell silent as Aglaia came dashing into the courtyard, face as pale as her white hair. "A messenger from Zeus is here!"

Hermes, that loathsome leech, followed, sporting his usual affected air.

"Ares," he remarked coolly. "I have exhausted myself in pursuit of you."

"You shouldn't have," I demurred.

"Alas, our father demands his presence."

In Ares's frown I caught a flash of reluctance. He didn't want to leave. My heart lifted in my chest; I thought I might float away if I didn't gain purchase on something substantial.

Meanwhile, Hermes's eye flickered between us, a telltale crease to his forehead. "I trust I wasn't interrupting."

"Aren't you always?" retorted Ares stiffly.

"Be wise, brother," Hermes said with a smirk. "Her last lover ended up in a shell."

I inhaled sharply, seething.

Hermes winked at me. "Did you forget the boy nymph already? Oh, the queen of love is heartless!"

"Continue to interfere in my life, Hermes," I warned, "and I may have to interfere in yours."

"Also unwise." He cocked his head, considering. "Perhaps you two have more in common than I thought."

I flicked my hand in his direction. "Fly away, pest, before I use my power indecently."

"Sounds like my kind of night."

"You talk too much, Hermes," cut in Ares, intercepting my retaliation. "It grows wearisome." He snapped his fingers and Graegus came to heel. To me, he said, "Thank you for watching my dog."

"I hope he doesn't bite Hermes. That would be terrible."

And they left, neither looking back at me as they answered the call of their king.

I ENTERED AN EMPTY home. Where were the Graces? In their absence, I indulged myself in my favorite activity: climbing into bed and recounting every moment of my encounter with Ares. I fell asleep, for Thalia, Euphrosyne, and Aglaia startled me awake later with a plate of food.

"Your dinner is untouched."

I had forgotten.

"Is it morning?"

"No, the middle of the night."

The Graces lit candles and stayed with me as I picked at the food. They were cagey, avoiding my eyes and conversing with unnatural levity.

"What is it?" I demanded. "What do you know that I do not? Where have you been?"

Euphrosyne sighed. "At our father's palace."

"With Ares?"

"He was there." Thalia exchanged a hesitant look with her sisters.

"What happened?" When nobody responded, I asked again, louder: "*What happened?*"

"There has been a . . . disturbance . . . in the family," answered Thalia, looking wretched.

"There have been many before and will be many again."

Euphrosyne's face twisted. "This time is different."

"Hephaestus has abducted his mother," explained Aglaia.

No wonder Ares had been called.

"Why would he do such a foolhardy thing?"

"A while ago," disclosed Aglaia, "Hephaestus went to Hera for help. He thought she could arrange a betrothal."

"She is the goddess of marriage," I replied evenly.

"Yes, but she laughed in his face."

I winced.

"Hephaestus became very angry and told her she's the reason for all his pain," said Euphrosyne.

"They spoke such nasty words to each other," added Thalia somberly.

"Days later, a throne arrived at Zeus and Hera's door, one of unprecedented craftsmanship. It was a gift from Hephaestus to his mother in apology for his outburst."

"But the moment Hera assumed her seat, she was magicked away."

I gasped.

"Hephaestus has her in his forge below the mountain, fettered to that throne, surrounded by traps of fire. He will not release her."

"He says it's apt punishment, and he will let her free when she apologizes for the way she has treated him."

"She never will," I stressed.

"No," agreed Aglaia. "Nor will Zeus engage on her behalf. Though he is aggravated by Hephaestus's disrespect, he depends upon his son's work. He is rallying others to rescue Hera in his stead."

"Hephaestus manipulates immortal fire," I said. "Whoever ventures below will be scalded, ruined."

Euphrosyne sniffled, turning uncertainly to the others, who nodded her on. "Hermes suggested that Zeus offer a prize for the safe retrieval of Hera, an incentive for volunteers."

My stomach plummeted. "What is the prize?" I managed to ask, barely recognizing my own voice.

But I knew. I had always known.

"You, Aphrodite," answered Aglaia. "Marriage to you."

I closed my eyes. "Zeus must call off this competition. Hephaestus is unbeatable in his den of iniquity. Once he hears of the terms, he will return Hera and claim me for his own."

"That was Hermes's thinking, as well," said Thalia. "But . . ."

"There was a volunteer . . ."

"To enter the mountain and end this madness."

They wrung their hands as my trepidation grew.

Let it be him. Please don't let it be him.

"Ares has gone to the forge."

11

MOUNT OLYMPUS

I LOCKED MYSELF IN my bedroom with a chamber pot and retched, ignoring the knocks and pleas, for I would not allow anyone to see me this way, chest heaving until I had nothing left to give. I wiped the detritus of sick from my mouth with the back of my hand and slumped against the wall.

While I sat there, shattered and useless, Ares was undoubtedly being burned beyond recognition, trapped and tortured by his brother's soulless automatons. And my life, my happiness were being bartered by men, for men.

Worse. I was bait. No better than fish guts or a lump of meat.

I had never experienced such rage and disgust. I'd known anger, but never to the point of becoming physically sick.

So this is hate.

I wondered if hate was the opposite of love, if I had discovered the inverse of my power. But there is either love or no love. Hate is another force entirely. It has nothing to do with my domain.

"You have a visitor," came Thalia's voice through the door.

"If it's Hermes, tell him to—" Oh, Alexandros, I do have a mouth on me sometimes. Suffice to say I spoke some invectives that aren't pleasant to repeat.

"No. It's Graegus."

I opened the door, let Graegus in, and succinctly slammed it shut again. Only Ares's hideous dog could understand my sorrow. I led him into my bed, where he nestled his head in my lap.

"You worry for your master," I said, running my hands over the nape of his neck. "Shall I lie to you? Do you want to hear that everything will be fine?" I held him steady, took in his large, sad eyes. "Or should I confess that I am afraid for him, too."

Why had Ares gone into the forge?

His sense of honor would compel him. Though Hera had never spared him a single kindness, he would feel it his duty to save his mother. And there's no debate that Zeus would expect him to volunteer. But a small, stupid part of me hoped he went for the reward. Would Ares actually marry me, should he somehow succeed? It seemed inconceivable; he barely tolerated my presence.

"What was he thinking?" I demanded of Graegus, but he could only whimper in reply.

EVENTUALLY, GRAEGUS AND I left my room. He needed to relieve himself and I needed wine.

"Is there any news?" I asked the Graces.

They shook their heads, despondent.

"Ares will return," insisted Euphrosyne. "Hephaestus's quarrel isn't with his brother; he will release him eventually."

But that supposition did little to soothe me. Ares would survive, but in what form and at what cost? After suffering excruciating pain? His body deformed by immortal fire, that stoic face ravaged? All before I'd gotten the chance to properly love him.

"One of you must go to Zeus's palace and wait for word."

Aglaia volunteered.

"Come back immediately if you hear anything."

She nodded, then departed.

Time spent waiting is difficult to quantify. In the moment, it felt interminable, but of course, it passed no differently than any other period. The dutiful sun rose again and set, rose and set, while I stood vigil, incapable of rest while my fate was being determined by others.

I've had plenty of years to consider how these events spiraled out of control, and how I could have better maneuvered them to my advantage. I should have entered the forge and negotiated with Hephaestus myself. Ares's brawn was never going to defeat Hephaestus's traps, but my wiles might have matched his cunning. Unfortunately, it didn't even enter my mind then. I was young still, my planning limited by experience.

Thinking in retrospect can be precarious. For every decision, every action—or inaction—there is a hypothetical counter. The mind can lose itself in labyrinths of what-ifs, traversing eternal paths of possibility. I cannot go there. Regret is an insidious foe, known to cause madness in its victims. To stay sane, I must focus on the course ahead.

Which is why, Alexandros, what we discuss tonight is so notable.

Eventually, Aglaia returned from the Hall of the Gods and I nearly leapt upon her.

"It's over," she announced, face drawn and ashen, eyes swollen.

"What does that mean?

"Everyone has returned," she explained. "Hera, Hephaestus . . ."

"And Ares?"

"Yes. Aphrodite, but he was . . . injured." She shuddered.

My chest constricted. "Tell me everything."

Aglaia collapsed into a chair and the three of us settled around her. "There is only one way into Hephaestus's forge," she began, exhausted but committed, "and he has it outfitted against trespassers with tricks and snares. Ares fought his way out of one after another and almost made it to Hera, but then the floor gave way. He fell into a metal tomb, and Hephaestus locked him inside." Aglaia swallowed tightly. "Every time Hephaestus ordered his brother to surrender, and Ares refused, Hephaestus shot blue fire through holes in the ceiling."

Hephaestus has gone mad, I thought.

"Eventually, Hermes descended with word of Zeus's challenge. He advised Hephaestus to return the queen and claim . . . the prize . . . for himself." She forced a hopeful smile. "So, Ares and his mother are free. I saw Hephaestus lead them into the throne room."

"You were there when Hephaestus and Zeus spoke?"

Aglaia nodded, her eyes downcast.

"Am I to be given to Hephaestus?"

"Yes," she answered faintly.

My pulse hammered in my throat. "Did you say anything in my defense? Did anyone?"

"I did speak with my father, Aphrodite, but . . . I didn't . . . I tried to . . ." She stumbled, steadied herself with a deep breath. "Zeus is going to do what Zeus wants to do."

What about what I wanted?

I stood. "Come along, Graegus."

"Where are you going?" Euphrosyne exclaimed.

"Oh, Aphrodite, please do nothing rash!" pleaded Thalia.

"I will do nothing but defend myself," I retorted, and Thalia sighed.

Aglaia joined me as I tied a cloak around my shoulders. "Remember our conversations in the first days here? You can jump from the window, but you will still end up where he wants you to be." She grabbed my hand. "I don't expect you to delight in a marriage with Hephaestus, but your energy is better spent accepting it than fighting it."

I shook off her grasp.

"Please, Aphrodite. I'm trying to help."

"You and your sisters may be able to force happiness, but I can't. Marrying a man I do not love will break my heart."

"We don't force happiness," she countered, "we find it."

But I would not argue semantics with Aglaia, not when time

was so precious. Without responding further, I departed, Graegus at my side.

THE ROYAL ATTENDANTS forbade Graegus from entering the palace. Though my unlikely connection to the mutt bolstered my confidence, I was forced to send him away.

"Go home!" I commanded.

It took a few more tries for my message to land. Tail between his legs, Graegus trod dejectedly across the mountain. I watched him trot out of sight, and then, steeling my resolve, resumed my mission.

"Bring me to Zeus."

A servant led me into the Hall of the Gods, where Zeus and Hera were seated.

"Aphrodite!" greeted Zeus. "How appropriate! You have been the topic of much conversation of late."

Hera sat beside him, looking worn.

"Welcome back," I told her curtly. Her expression hardened.

"You have saved my messenger a trip and allowed me the great honor of announcing my congratulations personally." Zeus spread his large arms wide. "Tomorrow we will gather in celebration as you wed my son."

"Which son?" I quipped. "You have so many."

"Our son," he amended, an admonition. "Hephaestus."

I smiled. "Oh, I am not going to do that."

Zeus's brows snapped together, but I only had eyes for the queen. Although Hera was no friend of mine, she was still my best chance at leniency. As a woman, she would empathize with my situation. She didn't care for Hephaestus either.

"Hera," I appealed, "you are the goddess of marriage, I am the goddess of love. Let us combine our intentions as allies. Consider what we can do for others and each other! Do not commit me to a loveless marriage with Hephaestus."

"If you understood anything about matrimony," she said in rebuke, "you would know I support my husband's decisions unconditionally."

My mouth fell slightly open as I stared, stunned and repelled by this woman who would rather waste her power, would rather idle uselessly on the side of men, than help another.

Your husband did not save you! I longed to scream. *He sacrificed* nothing *for your rescue!*

There are too many women like her, Alexandros, who choose men that don't choose them in return. Who choose security over sisterhood.

She got to her feet. "Now if you will excuse me, I require rest after my ordeal."

Zeus patted her backside as she walked past him, chuckling when I pulled a face.

"You can protest, Aphrodite. You can even fight me." He lowered his voice, even though his wife was out of earshot. "Some women do, and I don't hate it. But I always win."

"Do not underestimate the force of love in this world," I countered. "I would not make an enemy of me."

The skies changed. Thunder rocked the foundations of the palace. Lightning cracked and limestone shards dropped like daggers. My arms covered my head as stone pelted down around me.

"You will marry Hephaestus, or I will destroy your temples," boomed Zeus over the din. "I will strike down all the trees on Cyprus until it resembles a lonely bonfire."

"Please do," I shot back, lowering my hands. "Show the world your tyranny. It will spare me the effort of telling everyone."

"I will chain the Graces beside Prometheus and send my eagles to eat their throats out every night."

"Your own daughters? The Furies will plague you all your days."

Zeus licked his lips and leaned forward. "I have discovered who you love, Aphrodite, and I will trap him beneath the fires of Mount Etna beside the monster Typhon."

"Impossible. You know nothing of me."

His eyes glinted, sharp and ready. "You think Ares went into the forge to rescue you." His rollicking laughter shook my bones. "My son is battle hardened and was raised on hate. We fed him blood as a baby, not sweet milk. He did not burn himself for your love but because I ordered him to save his mother."

"Ares is not my beloved."

"No, he's not. In Sparta they keep his statue in chains. He is nobody's beloved."

Did I reel then? Did Zeus notice when doubt bowled me over?

"What matters is that you love him. I received a confession from one who will not lie to me. You will marry Hephaestus, as I command, or I will condemn Ares to a life darker than death."

Aglaia told him. It had to be. It wasn't tiredness that weighed her down, but guilt.

Oh, Aglaia. What have you done?

"I defeated the Titans," continued Zeus. "I imprisoned my own father in Tartarus. You are nothing in comparison, a pretty plaything to keep my son happy while he forges what I need."

He towered over me on the dais, but I did not quaver.

"We are still strangers to each other, Zeus, but I recognize the fool you are. You chose the sky as your domain because it made you feel big, but the heavens speak of love and beauty, not intimidation."

"Do you know what women do in war, Aphrodite?" He shook his head, chuckling. "No, you don't, because I protected you. I preserved you. Did I err? Should I have made you a camp whore, warming the beds of me and my brothers? Because that's all you are. A body. For us. For men."

And then, the last thing he told me before I ran from the hall:

"Be grateful I gave you to Hephaestus and not a brothel."

12

MOUNT OLYMPUS

ZEUS HAD DONE it, Alexandros.

He had scared me.

I dashed through the palace with no clear aim besides *away* until I was properly lost. Stopping, I laid my forehead against the cool stone wall, eyes closed and chest heaving, cataloging the many threats I'd just received.

My island burned and broken. The Graces tortured. Ares imprisoned. Me, a royal whore.

My head spun. I felt dizzy, weightless and insubstantial, my pulse quickening.

But before I succumbed to full hyperventilation, I caught a sound of syncopated breath. A door stood partially open, just down the hall, and I crept closer, curious. Peeking inside, I saw a trio of nude figures reclined on a bed: Hermes and two nymphs, sound asleep, damp sheets and clothing in jumbles upon the floor.

And there, beside his sandals, Hermes's helmet—the one that made him invisible.

I needed it. For an idea not yet solid, but a desire fully formed.

Manifesting the quiet of an owl, that noiseless hunter who flies on muffled wingbeats, I slid into the room. When I neared the bed, Hermes coughed, waking the red-haired nymph. I stilled, but she saw me, and as her lips parted, I placed a pleading finger over my own. *Please,* I begged, already anticipating her betrayal.

In my experience, women on Olympus didn't tend to support one another.

But this nymph only smirked and rolled over, turning her back on my mischief. I retrieved the helmet, conjured a deep crimson rose to leave in its place, and snuck out of that hateful place.

MY MIND WHIRLED with plans. Already it was evening, and Zeus said I would marry Hephaestus on the morrow. There was so much to be done before then.

First, I had to enlist help.

Apollo, god of medicine as well as music, lived on an estate surrounded by bay laurels. I announced myself to his servants, then paced the vestibule, wringing my hands and muttering to myself like a lunatic. Finally, Apollo appeared, iridescent with beauty despite the bewilderment lining his face.

"I need a salve," I blurted out. "For burns."

His mouth twisted. "From what kind of fire?"

"You know exactly what kind."

"Why do you assist Ares?" he hissed, pulling me inside his home and closing the door behind us. "It won't make your new husband happy."

"You think I care what Hephaestus thinks?"

"No, I don't, but you should."

I ignored his counsel. "You possess a golden stag's antlers. Don't they have healing properties?"

Apollo raised an eyebrow. "You don't miss much, do you?"

I remembered him and his twin betting on Ares at our first meeting—her antlers for his sunstone. "Observations are their own arsenal."

He sighed. "I'll make you a medicine if you keep my involvement discreet."

"Of course."

"Ares is a brute, but doesn't deserve our father's abuse."

"He's no more brutish than the others, but thank you."

"You really love him, then?" Apollo made a low whistle beneath his breath, shaking his head. "The war god and the fairest. Never would I have put you two together."

"But we are so alike," I countered. "Both demand a touch of insanity."

"I'll concede you that."

While I waited in Apollo's andrōn, a servant brought me a glass of wine, which I accepted with gratitude. "He said you could use this," explained the man.

"He is correct."

By the time I'd finished my drink, Apollo returned, carrying a small basket. "Here," he said, shoving it into my arms as if eager to be rid of it. I peeked inside and saw a clay jar full of a thick, gleaming ointment.

"Apply it generously and directly to the wound," he instructed.

I clutched the basket and its precious treasure to my chest.

"I am in your debt, Apollo."

"Should I need a favor, I'd prefer you do it out of friendship, not obligation."

His words touched me, and as I returned to the night, a glimmer of hope—for me, for all us Olympians, cursed as we certainly were—lit my heart.

WITH APOLLO'S BASKET in one hand and Hermes's helmet in the other, I continued my journey, stopping only briefly within a cluster of pine trees to remove my dress and sandals. I hid them beneath a fallen bough, then inspected my body. It was clean enough, I supposed, for what I was about to do, but I wished I had more time to prepare.

I placed my cloak back over my shoulders, then the helmet atop my head. Immediately, I disappeared, even to myself. Such delightful magic! No prying eyes would catch me now.

Zeus had spies everywhere; it would be inane to believe otherwise.

Ares occupied the palace farthest from Zeus's own, on the outskirts of the royal complex, shaded by tree and hill. Nobody guarded the front door—who would dare attack the god of war?—so I entered without effort. I stepped down the halls, soundless on my bare feet, unsurprised to discover a home with no color, no decoration, and barely any furniture.

Graegus awoke from his slumber and growled at my strange presence, but I hushed him with my voice. "It's me, you asinine animal." Confused but consoled, the dog settled.

But where is your master?

I continued my silent search and eventually found Ares sitting on a bench beside a bathing pool, clothed only from the waist down. Invisibility granted me the privilege of staring at him with impunity. The skin across his back bubbled, a map of destruction, pain marked in red and purple blisters, swollen with heat. It was appalling to behold, but my stomach churned most at all the white, the parts of him that had been fully charred.

I removed the helmet, tossed it to the side. Its metal crashed and clanged against the stone.

Ares turned. The left side of his face echoed the massacre on his shoulders.

"Do you still find me beautiful, Aphrodite?"

If this was a test, I would not fail. I would not gasp or cry. But, oh, Alexandros, how the sight of him destroyed me.

"I do."

He scoffed, but I walked closer with a confidence I did not necessarily feel. I opened the jar from Apollo and dipped my fingers into its cool moisture. "I got this from Apollo. He says it will help, but it might hurt. I can't be sure."

"I will bear it," he said, but those severe eyes of his, concentrated on my own, made me hesitate. "Do it." My fingers trembled as I applied that first application of salve to the devastated skin on his back. Ares's muscles tensed, his shoulder blades constricted, and I could not continue.

I could not bear to hurt him further.

"Don't stop," he growled through gritted teeth.

I am no nurse, Alexandros. I do not tend to injuries with any regularity. But I understand how people need to be touched. I know when to be firm, when to be soft and tender. That night, I was both. I coated the remaining blisters with my right hand while the other rubbed soothing circles into an unscathed section of Ares's neck.

"The next part will be worse," I warned quietly, eyeing the exposed tendons and bone while managing my own composure. His head bobbed once, a quick nod, and I placed a large portion of Apollo's cream in the worst of the wound.

Ares roared.

It frightened me.

It also delighted me.

I was a mess for him.

But the medicine was working. I watched, awed, as the golden balm seeped into Ares's back, repairing the skin, sealing the wounds in miraculous renewal. There would forever be a faint discoloration to that skin, but no significant scars. My appreciation for Apollo grew infinitely.

"Will you allow me to touch your face?"

He did not answer immediately, but I was forbearing. Finally, a soft "Yes."

Ares turned toward me.

I brought my salve-coated fingers to his cheekbone. He did not shudder at the searing pain, only closed his eyes. I continued, and his lips moved as he forced himself through steady breaths.

This proximity, this vulnerability, was true intimacy.

And I thought I had him memorized, but here were new treasures: the arch in his left eyebrow, but not the right. The circular dip where his neck met chest, the perfect size for my tongue.

Focus, I scolded myself.

Eyes still shuttered, Ares began to speak.

"I was nearly there. Hephaestus's creatures were not difficult to destroy, but then I fell. He enclosed me in a chamber where flaming metal rained down from the ceiling. My shield melted."

Hair rose on the back of my neck.

"Just when my body recovered enough, the fire returned. I was burned and reburned over and over again."

I applied a second coat, running my fingers up from his chin.

"Hephaestus would not fight me, but neither would he release me. Not until Hermes arrived and told him . . ."

"Told him what?"

"Told him about you." Ares's voice, always so still, so serious, cracked slightly. "That he could have you."

I watched his face heal, and knew I had only moments before he returned to himself and his dogged apartness. "You did not make it to Hera, so I do not come to you as a prize, but as a person." When he began to step back, I grabbed his hand.

"It is the night before your wedding."

"*His* wedding. Allow me one kindness. Just one kiss."

I untied the loose knot holding my cloak together, and emerged, liberated of all cover. I shook back my hair, and the muscles in his jaw twitched. Ares swallowed tightly as his gaze roamed over my naked body.

"You are my brother's wife," he answered roughly.

"Not yet."

I would not be dismissed or deterred—not now, not on my final night of freedom—so I murmured his name.

"Ares, please."

And then Ares was closing the distance between us, clutching the back of my head, and pulling his open mouth to mine. Our bare chests met, our tongues, our skin. Hands grabbing whatever they could, fingers spelling out *finally* on each other's bodies. Ares lifted me so easily, and my legs wrapped around his waist, ankles locked, as he carried me to his private rooms.

He threw me onto his bed, and I reached for him greedily, bringing him down toward me, and then his head was nestled in the cradle of my hips, his short beard rubbing against the inside of my thighs, and I was arching, begging.

Deep strokes, in and out, the dream to the reality and back.

Us, like this, after long last.

Even that first time, we were so good together.

Afterward, I did not want to sleep, but it was inevitable. When I woke, I kissed the length of him, claiming what was mine with my mouth. He roused and loved me all over again.

And we continued in this way throughout the night. Reaching for each other, releasing, resting just enough.

"I went there for you," he murmured into my hair.

Eternity, I thought as morning broke and Ares slumbered soundly upon my stomach. *This* and *him*.

For eternity.

And then I got out of bed without waking my lover, retrieved my cloak and Hermes's helmet, and walked home barefoot to marry his brother.

13

MOUNT OLYMPUS

THE DAY OF my wedding I got drunk.

Properly, disastrously drunk.

I started pouring glasses of wine once the Graces woke me from the couch where I'd collapsed that morning.

"Aphrodite, wake up! It's your wedding day."

"You smell terrible," exclaimed Thalia, wrinkling her nose.

"Magnificent," I replied, rising and stretching.

The Graces and the nine Muses had come to dress me. A bath was prepared, and the women sang and chattered, a flock of birds, the frivolous, incongruous accompaniment to my despair.

Thalia, however, noted my torpor and took my hand. "It could be worse, Aphrodite. What if Zeus matched you to someone far away, and you had to leave Olympus?"

Poor Thalia, I frightened her with my riotous laughter.

"You are a dear," I soothed, patting her arm. "But will you do me one favor?"

"Oh, anything!"

I had her return Hermes's helmet to Zeus's palace. She tossed it in a bush outside a window. Maybe Hermes would think it was thrown violently aside in his frenetic orgy. Maybe he'd notice the rose I'd left and suspect foul play.

Let him wonder. Dealing with him would be the least of my troubles.

The bridal gown, one of two wedding gifts from Hephaestus, was exquisite. It flowed in gossamer layers of dazzling blue and purple fabric, highlighted with silver and pearls and precious gems. When I moved, I shimmered like the sea under a summer sky. Underneath, I wore his second gift. A girdle that brought my waist into an impossibly narrow circle. A crown of white roses held my veil, which covered the strawberry waves of hair down my back.

"You are radiant!" sighed the girls. Euphrosyne wiped tears from her eyes.

I chugged my wine and poured another.

"Aglaia," I called out. "Goddess of joy, do I seem happy enough for you?" Her sisters didn't understand, and the alcohol made me brash. I opened my arms and spun. "This is the happiness for which you betrayed me to Zeus! Is it all you imagined it to be?"

"He is my father and my king," Aglaia replied haltingly. "I answered his questions. I never intended to cause you pain."

"You told him my secrets!" I hissed. "You gave him information to use against me."

"Please don't do this," cried Euphrosyne, coming to stand between Aglaia and me. "Not on your wedding day, and with you looking so lovely."

The Muses, especially Melpomene, watched us with wide-eyed fascination.

"He asked me who you loved, and I was honest," added Aglaia almost inaudibly, speaking for my ears only. "Sometimes telling the truth is courageous, and other times, it makes the teller a traitor. It is not always obvious which it will be until the act is done."

"Then let me settle that debate," I seethed. "You are a traitor."

Aglaia blinked, battling her emotions. "A traitor would not care about you as I do." She lowered her voice yet again. "There is no future for you in war."

"You are no prophet, Aglaia."

"But I am practical. You and Ares make as much sense as a lamb and a lion."

Oh, but I am a lion, too.

"Zeus threatened to chain you and your sisters to the rocks beside Prometheus if I didn't comply. Maybe I should've shown you the same loyalty you showed me."

Aglaia's lower lip quivered. It was a cruel thing to say, especially since Thalia and Euphrosyne overheard. The Graces shied from me, huddling together, deserting me—deservedly—in my moment of most need.

Since nobody would comfort me, I was left to console myself.

A marriage only means what you put into it, Aphrodite. Give this one nothing.

THE GATHERING AT Zeus's palace was less of an invitational and more of an injunction, but regardless of the motivation, the Hall of the Gods was, once again, packed wall-to-wall with the extremes of our pantheon. The crowds parted as the Graces and Muses proceeded toward Zeus's central throne. I followed, losing my footing more than once on the hem of my dress.

"It's her!"

"Those eyes!"

"Such hair!"

"That body!"

Hephaestus waited for me at the end of the aisle in his finest attire, smiling widely, and the jugs of wine I'd imbibed hit me with staggering force. Where he and Zeus once stood, I saw only a void. A stygian hole. I would fall into it, I would disappear, I would be consumed.

I halted, terrified, searching for Ares on either side of me in a panic, but the onlookers cheered and pushed me forward.

"The bashful bride!" they jested.

"Not Aphrodite worried for her wedding night!"

"Get up there, girl, and give Hephaestus what he won!"

I remember the following ceremony only in fuzzy, mute images: Zeus with his faux nobility, Hephaestus's glee, my own hands clutching a sprig of white lilies, Hera's favorite. Did I speak? Did I vow to respect and obey? Did anyone ask for my consent? And then my veil was lifted, Hephaestus's dry lips met mine, and my hearing returned; the roar of applause made me flinch.

My new husband gripped me in those deceptively strong arms.

"You are overcome, wife."

Wife.

I despised the word.

The wedding feast commenced. Hephaestus and I sat between Zeus and Hera, and Poseidon and his sea nymph, Amphitrite. While the men dined on the flesh of the sacrificed bull, oblivious, their wives glared at me.

I guess they had reason.

For me, Hera had been humiliated by her unwanted son.

Because of me, Amphitrite's brother was a scallop.

I needed to find Ares. To merely see him would provide succor.

Finally, I located him across the hall, dipping bread into olive oil beside the dawn goddess, Aurora. I watched their every move and motion like an eagle. He poured her drink. She laughed. He nodded as she spoke. My stomach soured. I thought of Ares's knowing hands the night before, the way he positioned himself inside me, and realized that came from experience. Lots of it. Why hadn't I considered this? How many before me? Who?

I would find them all and kill them. Starting with Aurora.

I excused myself from the table of honor and stumbled their way, wine sloshing over the rim of my cup. I made to sit in Ares's lap, but he shot to his feet, greeting me with a look of warning. I took his seat and leaned toward Aurora, who was blond and winged, wearing a saffron-colored mantle, and annoyingly pretty.

"My sincerest congratulations on your wedding," Aurora chirped. A little yellow bird.

"His dog bites," I returned. Bewilderment crossed her sweet face.

"They are calling for you, Aphrodite," said Ares, as his hand closed around my upper arm, and he yanked me to my feet.

"Liar," I breathed, though I did not resist him. Instead, I relished his closeness as he dragged me through the party. His smell, which recalled his sheets from the previous night, excited me.

I longed to kiss him.

"I'm dying, Ares," I moaned into his ear. "I will die from this."

"You will not," he maintained. "You are too strong and far too stubborn."

"You did nothing. You stood there and clapped while they took me!"

He reeled; his eyes flickered with hurt. "Have you already forgotten that Hephaestus kept me entombed in a pit of liquid metal for days on end? What would he do to you if you embarrassed him?"

But I was in no mood for rationality. "If she touches you again," I replied, redirecting, "I will cut off her hand and slap her with it."

When Ares tracked down Thalia, he practically shoved me into her arms. "She cannot have any more wine," he ordered, and I cursed, kicking out at him. Thalia held me back.

My hair, unwashed, was still coated in his sweat, yet he pushed me away like nothing had happened, nothing had changed?

"He is hateful," I spit.

"He is keeping you from harm, Aphrodite. Everyone watches. Show more care!"

I rested my head on her shoulder. "I am just so sad, Thalia."

She kissed each of my cheeks, my earlier transgressions forgiven. "I know."

Thalia did not release me from her sight until I drank an entire jug of water.

It was for the best, as I was considerably more sober when the howling began. The men, shepherded by Zeus, started to herd Hephaestus and me together, barking and chanting for us to consummate our marriage.

All those faces, red with drink and lust, circled me like a pack of wolves, activating my primal instinct for flight. Aggressive men can make any woman, even a goddess, feel like prey. Once again, I searched for Ares in the melee but found only Zeus's dark glee, cutting straight through me, relishing my torment. Poseidon and Hades hefted Hephaestus up onto their shoulders; the remaining mob yelled my name. I turned and ran, colliding with Apollo.

"I have you," he said, his voice true and strong. "Aphrodite, I have you."

And because I trusted him, I allowed the old god Pan to help lift me onto Apollo's shoulders, and we followed the trail of flashing torches across the mountain to Hephaestus's palace. The singing got louder and cruder, a gut-wrenching symphony of lewd jests, male bragging, and bluster.

It felt too absurd to be real. Here I was, being carted off like the spoils of war and deposited before my enemy. And where was Ares? After the night we'd shared, how could he be so unfeeling?

Too soon, Apollo and Pan set me on the ground.

"Do not cry," advised Pan. "Too many in this crowd will enjoy that."

I blanched, and Apollo leaned closer, speaking straight into my ear: "Remember, nothing in our world is eternal."

He was correct. Immortals were prone to boredom, to upheaval. We might live forever, but we sought constant change.

My eyes locked with Apollo's, and I nodded.

"Bring forth my wife!"

With a deep breath, I joined Hephaestus under the portico of his palace, holding myself with a feigned impassiveness. I would not be dragged over the threshold, screaming, but enter with dignity. Unbothered by the chaos, unaffected by this temporary imposition. And that's when I felt him watching me. That uncanny, telltale whisper brushing the back of my neck, the communication of two souls that have touched.

Ares was here.

I spotted him, leaning against a tree trunk, arms crossed tightly over his chest, far from the frenzy.

What did he think of all this? Were we lost to each other? Did he share my agony?

Oh, but I am most alive with him, even if it hurts.

The guffawing, jeering crowd quieted for Hephaestus's final benediction.

"Tonight, I am the luckiest man on Olympus for the most beautiful woman in the world will call me 'husband.' I welcome your envy!" Those assembled bantered back and Hephaestus chuckled, delighting in the attention. He lifted his arms and his reedy voice: "Now away with you all! I have a bride to enjoy!"

Clapping hands, raised fists. I could hardly bear it. I had to say something.

"Just don't come back tomorrow morning expecting a stained sheet," I drawled, raising a shoulder. "This bride hasn't been a maiden for a very long time."

The men loved it, whistling their approval, but Hephaestus's face sagged. He might have strong armed the king into issuing this mar riage, but Hephaestus would not be deflowering any meek or mild virgin tonight.

I was a woman, lest he forget.

Thrilled by my little triumph, I looked again for Ares, but he was gone.

I felt cold as Hephaestus ushered me into his home. His metallic servants closed the doors, shutting us off from the spectators, and Hephaestus gave me a tight smile.

"I know you will be safe and comfortable in my home."

Not our home. His.

And that word again. *Safe.* Too many kept offering it when I wasn't asking.

Hephaestus was agitated, uneasy, as he brought me to his private chambers. Despite his eagerness, I think he was nervous for what came next. Beyond the sculpted ivory doors waited Hephaestus's third gift, this one for himself. A bed composed from gold so pure that its shine in the light of the overhanging chandelier hurt my eyes.

I might have delayed the inevitable and fought Hephaestus off me that first night. Blamed my nerves or illness or my courses. But what did it matter? He was my husband, ordained by Zeus and ensured by a dozen threats. It would happen eventually, and with all the wine coursing through me, I felt numb and resigned. My detractors say I never gave Hephaestus his due because he wasn't as attractive as me. Truthfully, that part didn't bother me at all. It was his slyness I despised. His sneaky, underhanded cunning.

I would never forgive him for the way he hurt Ares.

I lay down. The act was over quickly, thank the stars.

Once he caught his breath, Hephaestus spoke: "Since my mother tossed me away, I have worked twice as hard as any to earn my place here. But tonight, now that I have you, I belong."

I listened but offered no reaction.

"I will spoil you, Aphrodite, and as you grow to admire and appreciate me, so will you come to love me. I have it all planned."

"Hmm."

But my mind was reeling. *He does not love me, either, despite all the antics.* Hephaestus only coveted me, just as he would any precious object. Both Nerites and Hephaestus cared for themselves first and foremost—their security, their reputation. Was true, reciprocal love even possible?

I drank long gulps of water from the bedside table as a burgeoning headache spread its noxious hold on my skull. And what of Ares?

Would he ever love me—did he? Could he? Was ours just a connection of two bodies?

I was a good time, a beautiful object, a physical pleasure. Nothing more.

Poor Aphrodite, the loveless goddess of love.

Beside me, Hephaestus snored.

14

MOUNT OLYMPUS AND BEYOND

I WAS AN AGREEABLE but indifferent wife. I avoided Hephaestus as much as possible but understood that being in his esteem made my life easier. We slept beside each other nearly every night, and on the occasions I allowed him to enjoy my body, I made sure to douse myself afterward with the necessary herbs and ointments.

I would sooner castrate the Nemean lion than carry his child in my belly.

Hephaestus spent long days in his forge beneath the mountain, and while he was away, I was relatively free. Though the Graces remained in my palace, running it as I wished, I visited only to enjoy my birds and tend to my garden. With the women I was polite but aloof. Thalia and Euphrosyne had done nothing wrong, but my fractured relationship with Aglaia complicated our previous serenity. I could no longer trust her and struggled to forgive.

When I desired companionship, I now went to Apollo.

Sometimes he and I drank and played games. Other times we walked the mountain, arms threaded together, trading scandals.

"Zeus has three more mortal sons," gossiped Apollo, wiggling his eyebrow. "How many does that make?"

"I don't have enough appendages to count upon," I replied dryly. "Who is their mother?"

"The girl Europa. The one he seduced as a bull."

I forced us to a halt. "Not seduced, Apollo. Abducted."

Apollo inclined his head, ceding my correction. "And one of my sister's virginal followers, Callisto. Zeus . . . forced a pregnancy upon her."

"Does Hera know?"

"She transformed Callisto into a bear."

My stomach flipped and turned. These stories made me sick. "I know he is your father, Apollo, but—"

"He's addicted to love."

"That isn't love," I countered quietly.

Apollo and I were still new friends. Would he countenance criticism of Zeus?

"It isn't," he finally agreed. "It is power."

He pulled me tighter against him and we resumed walking.

ONE PARTICULARLY WARM day, we sat beneath a lemon tree eating. Apollo, half naked and bronzed, laid his head in my lap while I finger combed his long blond hair. I thought him asleep until he asked, "How is Hephaestus in bed?"

"Dull."

He sighed. "I guessed as much. But is he harsh with you?"

"No," I replied truthfully. "He never raises his voice. Pampers me, even." I nibbled at my bottom lip. "But I remember Ares's body after the forge. Despite the soft way Hephaestus defers to me at home, I know there is violence in him."

Apollo considered. "I don't disagree." And then, more gently: "You still think of Ares?"

Every day. Every night.

But I had not seen or spoken to Ares since my wedding. Nobody had. Whether at Zeus's orders or of his own accord, Ares had gone missing. Alexandros, it had become a frustrating pattern with him, to disappear. Was he at war? With Aurora? In the wilderness, licking his wounds? I couldn't begin to guess.

I wrote undeliverable messages to Ares in my mind. *Where have you gone? Have you found someone else to hold? Do you still think of my mouth?*

Though I admitted none of this aloud, Apollo seemed to understand. He sat up. "I know a way to forget him."

"Tell me."

"I can't. I have to show you."

We boarded his golden chariot, and Apollo flew us to an island far west. We landed on the cliffs of its southern cape. Standing above the sea, whipped by wind, Apollo explained why he had brought me here.

"This is Leukas," he said. "And while I do not understand the origin of its magic, I know that if you leap from these white rocks, you will be freed from love."

I reeled at this revelation. "How do you know?"

"This is where Zeus comes, to rid his mind of Hera, so that he may enjoy others."

I peered over the edge of the promontory at the impassioned, ungovernable waves crashing so far below.

"Have you ever jumped?"

Apollo shook his head.

I would do it, just to prove I wasn't afraid of the fall, and life would certainly be easier without this agonizing unknown, but did I want to end my longing? Release my memories?

Ares on horseback, Ares cradling a dove. His fists in my hair, lips hovering above mine. If leaping meant losing all of that, it wasn't worth it.

"There is also my oracle in Delphi," offered Apollo, sensing my reticence. "She might be able to see your future."

Another tempting proposition. Who wouldn't want to know how it all turns out? "But if I already know what is to come," I protested, "is there any point in rising from my bed?"

"Yes, of course. To experience it. Perhaps to change it."

"No, Apollo. I appreciate your help but let us return to Olympus."

We rose into the air, and my eyes remained on the cliffs as I wondered if I'd made a mistake. Hundreds of years later, a mortal woman would do what I couldn't that day and fling herself from the white rock of Leukas, too lovesick to continue. An artist like you, Alexandros, named Sappho.

OF COURSE, HEPHAESTUS wasn't the only god with responsibilities. And without the distraction of Ares, I tended more diligently to my temples, journeying into the human cities to visit my worshippers and hear their prayers directly.

The Muses, who served as inspiration for mortals, lived closer to humanity than many of us. They occupied Mount Helicon, in the land called Boeotia, and because I appreciated the level on which they conversed, I called upon them frequently. Sometimes Apollo joined me—I think he slept with all nine of the goddesses at one point or another—and we discussed poetry and history and drama, with great introspection and profundity. I enjoyed the mental diversion; it gave me something to think about later, in the hours I lay awake in Hephaestus's bed, staring at my reflection in the gilded ceiling.

From Helicon, I would descend into the city-state of Thespiae, a place I found particularly diverting for its theater and its brothels.

It was there, among the celebration for a debut performance, that I first heard word of Ares's dragon.

"It is dead!" proclaimed an actor, flushed with wine and story.

"But who could slay a dragon?" asked the porne in his lap.

"A young prince called Cadmus."

I pushed the girl aside, and she toppled to the floor with a yelp. The man, scared of me, swerved, but I grabbed his chin. "Tell me everything, from the beginning."

The story marked the onset of legend, the nascent age of heroes. Cadmus, instructed by the Oracle of Delphi, followed a cow marked by a half-moon to the spot where he would build his city. As he made ready to sacrifice the heifer to Athena, his retinue retrieved water from the spring of the River Ismenus, sacred to Ares, and guarded by the dragon, Drakon.

"The Ismenian dragon killed the prince's companions for entering its master's hallowed ground. Cadmus returned carrying a stone and the determination of the vengeful. He killed the beast with one fortunate strike."

"And Ares?"

"The bellicose one mourns," concluded the actor, appropriately dramatic.

"I heard he guards the corpse," piped up another in the company. "So that no mortal man may claim a trophy."

One of the pornai pulled me aside. "The river isn't far, my lady. You can reach it on foot."

"Truly?"

"Oh, yes. It's just east of here. Half a day's walk."

I pulled a bracelet from my wrist and placed it in her hand. "For pointing me in the right direction."

I left Thespiae immediately, hoping with each stride that I wouldn't be too late, that Ares wouldn't be gone by the time I arrived. This was the first I'd heard of his location in so very long; I couldn't believe we were this close. The thought of seeing him again made my chest pound, my breath erratic.

I knew he needed me. I refused to believe otherwise.

The walk wasn't strenuous, the weather was pleasant, but I hardly noticed or cared. I would have trod through bog and brimstone to comfort him. By dusk, at last, I had followed the stream to a secluded pool guarded on all sides by towering sycamores. Though Ares was not there, his helm, shield, and spear lay upon on the bank beside a pile of clothes. Wherever he was, he would return for his belongings, so I waited.

Stars shimmered in the gloaming, and then Ares was swimming

toward me in their reflection, his dark head, his long arms emerging from the water in strokes forceful but unhurried. When his feet hit the sandy bottom, he strode toward me through the water, exposing his body bit by bit. First his bare chest, then his navel, then . . .

"I am unclothed," he said.

"I have seen it all before."

He wanted to smile—I saw a fleeting happiness lift his face—but the sadness overpowered him. When he came to shore and sat beside me, I wrapped his cloak around his shoulders.

"I am surprised to see you here."

"Surprised that I knew where to find you?"

"Surprised that you still care."

My mouth opened, but I could not rally the right words. He doubted me? How was that possible?

"At the wedding, you were angry that I hadn't stopped it, but you left that morning, Aphrodite, without waking me, without a word, and married him."

"Was there another plan I wasn't privy to?" I spluttered. "I don't remember discussing our options."

We had discussed nothing that night. In fact, we'd barely spoken at all once we entered his bed.

I sensed him hardening against me, the muscles in his back tightening.

"I came for you and Drakon," I reiterated. "Not to pass blame."

"Drakon is dead," he said bitterly, "and some boy boasts of murdering the war god's monster."

"Then find him, Ares. And silence him."

"Even you see me as a killer."

I sighed. "That's not what I said."

"It's what you meant."

This was hardly how I imagined our reunion, arguing, at each other's throats, once again.

"Punish Cadmus. Force him to atone and—"

"I am their death god," he interjected. "They sacrifice humans at my altar, Aphrodite."

"Did you ask them to?" I snapped, and his lips clamped shut. "No, of course you didn't. Just as I have never asked any man to force himself upon a woman. Yet they claim they do it for me. They misinterpret and misunderstand both of us, Ares."

"There are sundry reasons for war. Territory and resources, grievance and righteousness. But men like Cadmus kill for glory. With joy." His expression hardened. "There will be more heroes like him, the valid and the questionable, the aspiring and the prepossessed, all ravenous for quests. And these would-be saviors will bathe the earth in blood."

I shivered, then placed a finger across his lips. "Hush, Ares. Mourn the loss in front of you, not what may be."

"The loss of Drakon or the loss of you?"

He pulled my finger into his mouth with his teeth, applying a gentle pressure, and my other hand stroked his thinly cropped beard. And then I was straddling his lap, he was tugging up my dress, and I was shifting to fit him. We were kissing, rocking and kissing. My head thrown back, his hands on my hips, our shallow breaths.

We finished together and I collapsed against his shoulder, panting.

There was a pause, for the unsaid things between us.

"Does it feel like this with others?" I finally asked.

His eyes were still shut. "Not once. Not even close."

I knew it in my heart, but it was a relief to hear him say so aloud.

"Ares, I cannot return to a life with him if you are not in it, too."

His hand slipped through my hair, and he brought our sweaty foreheads together.

"I cannot be your dove, Aphrodite."

Monogamous. Committed. Paired for life.

"Then let us be something different."

What were we then, Alexandros? What did we become? Metaphors are for the comparable, and Ares and I were beyond that. Sometimes, even now, my heart is a fist. Other times it is the sun or a bloody star. So, too, can love be many things. A bridge, a weight, a balm.

But if love is a song, then Ares is its refrain, the best part, the one I come back to over and over again.

AFTER THE SPRING, my life changed in two irrevocable ways. The first was that I became thoroughly, almost uncontrollably, committed to an extramarital affair with Ares.

The second was that I gave birth to a little girl named Harmonia.

15

MOUNT OLYMPUS AND BEYOND

I PROTECT LOVE, NOT the sanctity of its institutions. It can be difficult for some to comprehend, but I felt no guilt with Ares. With him, I was choosing joy. It was an act of resistance.

I wanted Ares all the time, but as Mount Olympus was too dangerous, we met in the only place where we could ensure privacy: my old home on Cyprus.

To escape Hephaestus, I explained to him that my presence was required at my most sacred temple on my most sacred day, the fourth of every month.

"Dear husband, what is one day and one night when forever awaits us?" I stroked the side of his face with the back of my hand. "When I attend, I not only express my gratitude but also secure their continued worship. Respect matters to you, so it matters to me! I must be ever vigilant that my reputation as an Olympian matches your own!"

Hephaestus could never resist flattery.

On the morning of every fourth day, I flew to Cyprus, sometimes riding sidesaddle upon a white goose, other times driving the swan-led chariot Hephaestus designed for me. I spent all the daylight hours at the temple in Paphos, the mortal city, complimenting the priests and priestesses on their good work, receiving supplicants and granting boons, before excusing myself to my private residence.

"These nights I spend in prayer, reconnecting with my humble beginnings and reflecting upon my blessed rise to Olympus."

Nobody contested my ritual. The islanders wouldn't dare, but also, they were proud of their association with me. The sun fell, and I was left alone to worship love in the ways I desired.

I never knew whether I would see Ares or not. We had no fail-safe method of communication. He knew that I would always be in the old house on the fourth night of the month, and if he was able to get away from wherever he was stationed, he would meet me there. Often, he could not abandon his soldiers or position, and I would sit alone, until sunrise, despondent, hoping that the following month would be different.

But when Ares did come?

Bliss.

Is pleasure an escape from reality or a consolation for it? Ours was both; it was transcendent. And I was never sated. After each time, I only craved him more. For there is poetry in a rough man's tenderness. In the way Ares's knuckles skimmed the skin from my shoulder to elbow as we lay on our sides and he placed reverent kisses along the back of my neck.

Not that we were always gentle. Sometimes he walked through that door and had me up against the wall before I—

Oh, Alexandros, am I making you blush?

We tried not to speak of it, but neither of us practiced celibacy when we were apart. Sometimes, especially on the nights he did not show, I pictured him with others until I made myself sick. Especially Aurora. The image of her with Ares at my wedding haunted me like a specter. I consoled myself with daydreams where I clawed out her lovestruck doe eyes and tossed them into my pond as fish food.

The closest Ares and I came to ending our clandestine arrangement occurred when I brought him a gift.

Back on Olympus, Hephaestus had constructed a set of throwing knives, unparalleled in their perfection of balance, shape, and durability. I overheard him boasting to Artemis. "They will not lose their point, no matter how many times they are thrown."

At the first opportunity, I stole one for Ares.

It was simple enough to conceal my crime.

"Hephaestus!" I moaned as he returned one evening. "I must make an embarrassing confession!"

And I told him how I took the knives to try them myself, but—alas!—silly woman that I am, lost one to the woods. Though he was irritated by my carelessness, he wasn't angry, for he expected such behavior from me. Hephaestus, so intelligent with ore, was ignorant when it came to people. My husband equated beauty with weakness; he spent too much time in the forge.

Step into the wilds. Admire the fragrant, pink clusters of oleander, the white-belled lily of the valley, but only from afar. Both beautiful, both toxic.

Just like my garden, just like me.

I wrapped the knife in a scarf and hid it in the bottom of a basket. On the fourth day of that month, Hephaestus didn't spare a single thought as I walked with it out the front door.

The temple services seemed to drag longer than ever in my excitement. At their conclusion, I hurried through my farewells and rushed to the cottage, where I paced the floor, hoping Ares would arrive. I had never given him a present before.

When he came through the door, covered in battlefield, I should have known it was the wrong night.

Ares would not kiss me.

"I am filth, Aphrodite."

I drew him a bath, removed his armor and sandals, the stained and splattered tunic. He climbed into the stone basin, closing his eyes as I scrubbed away the grime and gore. The clear spring water quickly turned brackish. He did not speak, but I hummed lightly as I worked, scratching his scalp, ladling clean water over his shoulders.

Alexandros, I loved taking care of him.

Afterward, I wrapped him in a fresh towel and kissed his forehead. "Good as new," I proclaimed. "I have something for you."

He sat on the bed while I retrieved the knife.

I watched eagerly as Ares unwrapped the scarf and took the knife in his hand. It whirled through his fingers, then he tossed it upward, deftly catching it by the handle after multiple flips through the air.

"I have never seen its like," he admitted. "Where did you get it?"

"I stole it from Hephaestus," I announced proudly, stupidly.

Ares set it down like the blade burned. "Then I don't want it."

"Why?"

"Because every time I see it or hold it, I will think of you and him."

I scoffed. "Ares, it's just a knife."

"That your husband made. The man you share your life and body with."

"Do not speak to me of sharing bodies. I did not choose to be married, yet you choose to sleep with other women." My temper flared. "Who warms the cot in your war tent? Some mortal girl? Aurora?"

Ares rubbed his hands over his head and down his neck. "You are obsessed with Aurora. It is unhealthy."

"Then you don't find her attractive? She doesn't lie down for you?"

"You lie down for him and he tortured me! He gets to be with you each day, place his arm around you at every event, while I skulk around like some stray dog, happy with scraps."

"We both decided this arrangement was better than nothing."

And because I was correct, Ares adjusted his attack. "I'm shocked you'd think I would accept such a gift."

Enraged, I grabbed the knife and tossed it out the window. "Now there's nothing to accept."

We shared a bed that night, but back to back, mulish and fuming. Just before dawn, we broke, apologizing and forgiving through furious, desperate connection.

It was my first experience with Ares's jealousy. It would not be my last.

THERE IS LITTLE doubt I would have been reckless in my affair if it weren't for my daughter.

Harmonia.

She is still difficult to discuss, though hundreds of years have passed.

Yes, caring for Harmonia kept me grounded—and busy—for as the fruit of two immortals, she grew quickly. Hephaestus did not seem to note her resemblance to his brother, but neither did he notice the tonics and treatments I administered to myself after our cursory couplings. He was too complacent in his acquisitions: a lovely wife and charming child.

And she was a precious one.

Ares knew better, of course, but maintained a cautious distance, admiring Harmonia from afar. Was it enough for him that I loved our daughter and did the best I could?

It had to be.

Because I had no mother of my own to emulate, and had never been a child myself, I treated Harmonia like any other companion. She was my dear little bird. I would marvel at the size of her hands in mine, their light, tiny fingers, like the bodies of butterflies. Curious and emotionally intelligent, she trod delicately through our world, asking searching questions and accepting both answers and new questions with calm contentment.

I puzzled at her providence, that such a sweet soul could issue from Ares and me.

"Did your egg roll into the wrong nest?" I would murmur while she slept, awed by her perfection.

Despite our long lives and prodigious sexual appetites, immortals give birth only rarely, thus Harmonia was special. One of the rare, precious children of Olympus. She enjoyed free rein of the mountain, and I constantly lost track of her. I often found her listening to music with Apollo or tending to abandoned baby animals with Artemis. She baked bread with Demeter, worked the loom beside Athena. I encouraged Harmonia to pursue her interests, to absorb the wisdom of those who would teach her.

"I want to be beautiful like you when I grow up, Mama," my little girl often said.

"No, chickadee, be more. Be curious. Be brave."

We played together, taking turns creating games and characters. She liked to pretend she was the mother and I was the child. I liked us to be dolphins, agile and smart and without bounds.

The older she got, the more I worried, for she was so pretty and pleasant and girls like her were targeted by men. When Ares was next on Olympus, I brought my innocent girl to him and demanded assistance.

"She must know how to defend herself."

He did not disagree.

Ares showed Harmonia the right way to make a fist, where to kick a man who seeks to hurt you, how to hold a sword. My heart thrilled at the sight of them together, practicing. Ares patient and Harmonia adoring.

"Mama!" called my daughter, brandishing a spear. "You must try!"

"Your mother is far too lazy."

Indeed, I watched their drills from beneath a canopy I'd had Hephaestus's servants erect. Graegus lounged beside me.

"I'm conserving my energy for a different sort of combat," I replied slyly, reclining farther into the pillows. It was the third day of the month.

Ares laughed, and I was euphoric. Anytime I broke his intense countenance was a triumph. Harmonia was none the wiser.

Was it audacious to bring them together? Was I daring to be caught? Yes. Maybe. I had been lulled into a false sense of stability. I thought myself invincible.

But a life suspended upon a lie is a fragile one at best.

And one night over our dinner table, everything fell apart.

"Papa," said Harmonia, "did you know that I hold a sword with the same arm as Ares? Does this mean I will also be a mighty warrior?"

I jolted at the mention of my lover's name but smiled. "You will be proficient at anything if you dedicate yourself to practice, Harmonia."

"And, Papa, did you know the dog Graegus likes me? He lets me lie my head on his belly. Ares says I'm the only person he tolerates besides Mama."

Hephaestus stiffened. "You two spend an unseemly amount of time with my degenerate brother."

"We visit him no more nor less than any of our other family," I replied smoothly.

Harmonia, oblivious, beamed at both of us.

But after she went to bed, Hephaestus summoned me. He waited in a straight-backed chair. I poured myself a glass of wine, then folded into the couch across from him. Even after so many years together, there was no spark between us. Did Hephaestus not notice, or did he not mind?

"You let her run wild, Aphrodite."

I disagreed. "No. Wild is how I lived on Cyprus."

"You should be preparing her for the future."

"I am."

Hephaestus snorted. "Not her future in the sparring rings or symposium! Her future as a wife."

Harmonia, married. Harmonia, in a life like mine—trapped in a passionless marriage, choosing duplicity as a way to salvage my soul. I couldn't bear that for her.

"Perhaps Harmonia will have no husband," I retorted. "Marriage isn't for everyone."

"Harmonia will do as I say. I am her father."

I rolled my eyes.

"I have been too lenient with both of you."

I bristled at the piteous tone in his voice. "You're questioning everything because I let Harmonia hold a sword? There is no harm in her embracing what the other Olympians have to offer."

"Other Olympians or other *men*?"

"Men, women, whatever."

"Apollo is effeminate, and Ares is a brute. I forbid Harmonia to visit either."

"And me?" My voice trilled at the thrill of possible confrontation. "Will you dare to ban me, a goddess of Olympus, from my brethren?"

"Would I have justifiable cause?"

His black eyes held mine, and I saw the fire behind them, two burning coals.

"Say what you mean, Hephaestus," I dared.

"There are rumors, Aphrodite, about you now, about you before."

Rumors didn't spread on Olympus, they scurried like insects, carrying plague, infecting opinion. Still, I tossed back my hair and sipped my wine, savored the sourness coating my tongue. "Paranoia does not become you."

"You will not speak down to me in my own home. I am master here."

"Love has no master."

His brows came together in a deep crevice. "I have treated you with propriety, spoiled you even, and you refuse to show me the respect I deserve. Why?"

"Is your memory so limited that you forget *why* we were married, Hephaestus?" I slammed my cup down upon a low table, and wine sloshed over the edge. "Do you recall what you did to bring me here?"

Both his face and shoulders seemed to droop. "You could have forgiven me, you might have loved me, but you are too willful and petty."

He was right in every way but one: I could never have loved him.

I sighed. "This is about Harmonia, not me."

"And I forbid her to see Ares or Apollo without my permission or a *suitable* chaperone."

It required significant self-control not to lash out at his implication.

"It is impossible to keep Harmonia from the other immortals unless I lock her in a cage."

"A cage, yes . . ." Something indiscernible crossed his face, and he stood. "I must rest, think . . ."

He wandered away, still muttering to himself, leaving our conversation unfinished. I was frustrated by this abrupt dismissal, but more so relieved, for despite his threats, I assumed I had dodged discovery. Hephaestus remained unaware of my affair. Yes, he had banned Harmonia from Ares, but I would handle that.

I did not take my husband seriously, and for that, I was a fool.

AFTER OUR ARGUMENT, Hephaestus spent even more time beneath the mountain, working on what he declared to be his "most consequential invention yet." I thought little of it because I thought little of him. My world did not require another shield or automaton.

Instead, I brought Harmonia to my palace on Olympus for voice lessons with the Graces. They taught her breath and pitch and rhythm, vocal harmony and range. I didn't want her to simply sing prettily but learn the theory of song.

At first, it was just the five of us, but then servants began to arrive. New ones, every day, tending the plants, sweeping the floors, dusting the furniture.

"Did you arrange this?" I asked Thalia, but she shook her head, as bewildered as me.

Suspicion coursed through me. I cornered one of the younger servants in the storeroom, barring the exit.

"Who sent you here?"

"I was hired from the village," he stammered.

"By whom?"

He trembled as he shook his head. "I do not know his name."

"But you are paid? Where do you receive it?"

He peeked upward, daring a direct look at my face. "In a cave at the base of the mountain. I give my report and receive coin."

Right by Hephaestus's forge.

"You do not see his face?"

"No. I speak into the shadows."

"And you tell him of me?"

"Yes, and the girl."

Harmonia.

I did not punish the servant. Instead, I gave him a pearl from my collection. "For your discretion," I explained. "Do not repeat this conversation."

He would have agreed to anything in his gratitude. I could've had his head.

Or his heart.

My husband, who employed automatons that couldn't speak or see in his own house, had sent spies into mine. Now that my eyes were open, I saw them everywhere: shadowing Harmonia and me on our daily walks, watching my actions and encounters in the Hall of the Gods. I was never truly alone. I hesitated to bathe, worried that someone lurked nearby, watching.

It was the most disturbing, invasive period of my life. Even now, it gives me shivers.

I anxiously awaited the fourth of the month until I realized, somewhat belatedly, I'll admit, that Hephaestus would have infiltrated Paphos as well. My husband was thorough, exhaustive in his need for control. Someone with his meticulous attention to detail missed little.

Knowing that Hephaestus and I headed toward some precipice made me restless. I began to keep odd hours, finding relaxation impossible, and spent many nights in the courtyard, staring at the sky.

I have always felt a certain kinship with the stars, a force older than myself. I am grateful for their companionship, distant though it may be, as we share this piece of eternity together. Mountains erode, the mightiest trees fall, but the stars and I remain.

"Do you see what I see?" I asked, lying on my back.

A twinkle, an acknowledgment.

Hephaestus roused me one morning from the bench where I'd fallen asleep, scowling at the empty wine jug by my feet.

"Prepare Harmonia. She will accompany me to the forge."

"A forge is no place for a child," I replied blearily, yawning.

"Neither is chaperoning her mother while she flirts with my brothers."

I groaned. "Hephaestus, it is too early for—"

"I want her beside me as I complete my masterpiece. I aim to have it finished by dawn tomorrow."

"You would take her into the mountain all day and all night?"

"Yes. She will assist me. Someone needs to show my daughter the value of hard, honest work."

I hated the thought of Harmonia in his den of horrors, but Hephaestus would not harm her, and she had an inquisitive mind. She might even enjoy the experience.

And I was just beginning to comprehend the inadvertent gift I had received: a whole night alone in this house, with only automatons, no spies or servants.

"I'm sure she will be honored," I responded dryly. If Hephaestus doubted my sincerity, I hardly cared.

I dressed Harmonia in clothing that protected her skin and braided her hair into a crown around her head.

"What will I see today, Mama?"

"Marvels, my chickadee."

"I will know so many things when I come back!"

"Yes, and you will tell me all, or I will be jealous of the new ideas that get to rest in your beautiful mind!"

"Father says he works twenty bellows at a time."

"Yes, and they are very hot. You must promise to be careful."

"I will, Mama. But you must be careful, too."

My Harmonia, as precocious as she was kind.

I kissed her face too many times, but she bore it with a humored wrinkle of her nose.

I should have kissed her more, but no number of kisses would have been enough.

Hephaestus rode to work in a winged chair of his own creation. He waited in the contraption, impatient, as I placed Harmonia on his lap.

"Hold her tightly," I told him.

"It is my responsibility to keep her from evil."

It was an odd response. I wavered though I waved them off.

Alexandros, I never should have let her go.

Afterward, I went directly to the stables. If Ares was on Olympus, he would be there, for he always put Zeus's horses through their paces in the first part of the day.

A woman carrying a water bucket, ostensibly on her way to a well, followed me at a distance.

I found Ares grooming a gray stallion in the crossties, both equally damp with sweat from their ride. He paused when he saw me, but only for a moment. He continued his administrations and offered a formal greeting. "Good day, Aphrodite."

"Good day to you," I answered, matching his tone, but then, as I moved to the horse's other side, in a hushed voice: "Ares, he's watching me, everywhere I go, even Cyprus."

His shoulders tensed, and he frowned as he ran a brush through the horse's mane.

I scratched the horse's belly, eliciting nickers that would cover my voice. "He will no longer allow Harmonia in your company."

Ares's head snapped up. "Fuck him."

"No, fuck me," I whispered, with the words I knew drove him mad. "In my husband's bed. He has taken Harmonia into the forge until morning."

Ares groaned, rubbed at his beard, the back of his head. "Not in his house."

"Nobody will know, Ares. Please. I cannot meet you on the fourth. And I miss you."

I reiterated my assurances, the precautions I would take.

But it was all empty words, meaningless action. A farce.

Because soon enough, everybody would know.

16

MOUNT OLYMPUS

I HAD GREAT FUN preparing for my tryst with Ares, transforming Hephaestus's bedroom with sensory, sensual attention. I lit candles and sconces, laid platters of pomegranate seeds and oysters. Tied silk scarves to the bedpost. Arranged abundant aromatic flowers. I wore the girdle that shaped my body in impossible proportions, to the peak of redolence, under a sheer robe, and tied up my hair, freeing a few curls to fall evocatively—strategically—over my face and neck.

Small gestures I never made for my husband.

Hephaestus considered me petty? He had no idea.

I didn't worry about Ares dodging spies. This was a man accustomed to battlefields; he could enter a home unnoticed. And just after the sunset, my hardened warrior climbed through a window like a lovestruck adolescent. It made me giggle, and he grinned.

I couldn't wait to touch him and embraced him in the windowsill.

Oh, the gorgeous insanity of being in love!

He leapt down, and as we shuttered every window, Ares told me where all Hephaestus's lookouts were stationed. It was quick work for him.

"I planted my own watch," he told me. "Alectryon stands guard. He'll signal when Helios approaches. We will not miss the dawn."

Alectryon, one of Ares's favorite soldiers, was as devoted to him as Graegus. I relaxed, and took Ares's hand, leading him to the golden bedchamber. He took in the massive bed, the lacquered walls and ceilings, with grim admiration.

"Hephaestus is talented," Ares admitted.

"Not in here, he's not."

Ares's mouth curved as he tucked a stray piece of hair behind my ear. He cradled my face with both his hands and kissed me.

Alexandros, the way that man can kiss. Every woman deserves to experience it at least once. Every man, too.

I stepped backward, untying my robe and beckoning him forward. "Now give me what this room has been missing."

WE'VE REACHED THE wound.

Mine. And Ares's.

Most pain heals, scarring with space, with forgetting and forgiving.

But not all pain.

There is hurt that stays, that absorbs into who you are, organs and bone and blood rearranging to fit. This is the wound at the core of me. Mostly quiescent but always festering.

Seeping. Weeping.

This is also the moment in my story where I lose whatever reputation I had. Where my name transformed from one spoken with awe to one uttered with derision. I did not change. I was behaving in the way my domain was intended, celebrating what I was born to be and do. But not in the way others wanted.

I thought my beauty and my love were mine to give away, but I was wrong.

It was this exact night when I lost control of the narrative, and I became the whore.

ARES WAS ABOVE me when the net dropped.

He fell forward, crushing me under his full weight, and I yelled, confused. But then we were being lifted, tangled together, and rising toward the ceiling. Ares fought to remain upright, struggling for balance or purchase as he tore at the bindings that held us.

But we were not ensnared by any common rope; this was a net woven with unbreakable, magical chain.

My husband's masterpiece.

Panic began its insidious spread through my body, my heart beating frenetically against my bare chest. I was a goddess no longer, but something small and insignificant.

Ares gnashed his teeth, raging within our confines. I worried he would tear the muscles in his arms and chest. "Stop it!" I cried. "You will hurt yourself."

"There must be an opening somewhere. If I can at least get you out . . ."

"How did Hephaestus know we were here? What time is it, Ares? Is it dawn? Where is Alectryon?"

"Asleep."

I stilled at the sound of that reedy voice trilling toward us. Hephaestus stood in the bedchamber below, glaring upward. I caught his eyes through the net and saw, so clearly, both his victory and his heartbreak.

"You may have skirted my spies, Ares, but they still spotted your man. You should rethink your training regimen. Alectryon accepted wine from a stranger, on duty, with no qualms. In his defense, he did not know it contained a sleeping tonic."

"Ares," I moaned, searching for his hand in our tumble of limbs. I couldn't find it.

"Your fool missed Helios's ascent upon Olympus, Ares. Unfortunate, because the sun god is an ally of mine, I've repaired his chariot a time or two." Hephaestus gestured to the walls. "I noticed you shuttered the windows. Maybe that prevents prying eyes, but not the rays of the sun himself. He saw . . . you together and informed me immediately."

Hephaestus, angry as he was, couldn't keep the tremor from his voice. He was shaking. I watched him reach for his walking stick.

I exhaled, long and hard. "And now you know." This was a messy conclusion to our failed marriage, but an end, nonetheless, and despite my current predicament, I felt some relief. "Let us down, Hephaestus. This is insanity."

"I'm insane? My brother ruts with my wife in my bed, but I am remiss?"

"Let us discuss this properly," insisted Ares in a forced calm. "On the ground. And with clothing."

"You forget that I've seen her naked, too. And now everyone will." Hephaestus clapped his hands, and the ivory doors opened on command. "Come Zeus, come all, and behold what Ares and I have enjoyed!"

Now Ares's hand found mine and gripped me tightly as the gods of Olympus proceeded into the room: Zeus and Poseidon, Hermes and Hades, minor gods like Kratos and Zelos and Momus, and even Apollo at the rear.

No women, only men.

Frantically, I pulled my hair over my breasts, positioned my hands between my legs, but I was exposed. Ares did his best to cover me, but it was impossible, entwined as we were.

Hermes was the first to laugh. "Ares might be the quicker brother, fleeter of foot, but he was caught fast enough by the runt!"

The others howled.

"Ares has plowed the Elysian Fields!"

"Spread like honey!"

"I want a lick!"

"Not while she tastes of Ares."

"Is he still inside her?!"

"Love and war? How stupid could they be!"

"I told you, Zeus. Women that sensual are always promiscuous."

I had never been so disgusted, and I wish my revulsion were directed toward them because they were in the wrong, but I mostly hated myself. And it was not lost on me that most of the jeers came at my expense, not Ares's.

Only Apollo kept silent.

"Oh, but there is one more who must bear witness," snarled Hephaestus, surly and threatening, nearly unrecognizable.

He left, only to return with my daughter by the hand.

I bit my fist to keep from keening.

"And this is the most important lesson of all, Harmonia," he began, pointing upward. When she didn't immediately look, Hephaestus grabbed her head and forced her. "Do you see what your mother does, who she is, when we are away? She is unworthy of this family."

Harmonia began to cry.

"Chickadee!" I implored. "Do not sorrow, my girl. I will explain everything to you."

Ares reacted with a madness I'd never experienced. "I will tear you apart, Hephaestus! I will rip off your head and eat it!"

Hephaestus chortled. "This is what your mother prefers, Harmonia. Beasts."

Apollo stepped forward and scooped Harmonia into his arms. "Yes, Hephaestus. Beasts lust, beasts rage. But beasts are not malicious." To Zeus, he added. "I've seen enough." Holding my sobbing daughter against his chest, Apollo exited the bedchamber.

His departure sobered up the group like a jug of cold water dumped on a drunkard's head. They lingered, awkward and uncertain.

"Ares must pay me the adulterer's penalty," insisted Hephaestus, desperate to reclaim his moral authority.

A human practice, and yet another one of Hephaestus's traps.

"Ares has no wealth," chided Hades drolly, almost bored.

"Then they will remain," answered my husband, as stubborn as a young child.

"Hephaestus, release us now, or I'll expose every detail of our couplings so that your family may know of your . . . interests and abilities." I sharpened my tongue: "And understand why I sought alternative means of satisfaction."

Hephaestus's sallow face burned as red as the supernatural fire he manipulated, and Ares scolded me under his breath. "Don't."

I thought—incorrectly—I had nothing left to lose. Hephaestus had defamed me before my daughter; there could be no greater penalty. For truly, I've never suffered from modesty. The gods viewing me without my clothes was nothing compared to losing Harmonia's esteem.

"She is a vile, unnatural woman," hissed Hephaestus. "A harlot."

"Your point has been made, Hephaestus," interceded Poseidon. "And we tire of this marital squabble. You have been wronged, and I will pay the adulterer's fine for my nephew."

Hephaestus slammed his walking stick upon the tile. "It must be the culprit!"

Poseidon appealed to Zeus. "Your cuckolded son has lost all reason."

Zeus agreed. "I declare this matter settled. Poseidon will handle Ares's penalty. Hephaestus, release the offenders."

The net crashed unceremoniously to the ground, and I winced. Ares put out a hand to help me up, but I ignored it, standing on my own and shaking the silvery chains from my body.

Zeus examined both of us, as amused as he was angry. "Get dressed and report to my palace immediately."

Head lifted, and naked as the day of my ocean birth, I walked out of that bedchamber for the last time.

ARES AND I were brought before the king and queen in the Hall of the Gods. We were provided no opportunity to speak beforehand. He presented himself as the model soldier—stolid, severe—but I burned with rage. If anyone expected me to grovel, they would be sorely disappointed.

I wasn't sorry.

"I paid your dowry!" bellowed Zeus, without preamble. "And this is how you repay me?"

"I never asked that of you," I replied coolly, which only riled him more.

"You have no father, and it is customary."

Ares interceded. "Aphrodite is grateful for all you've done for her—and all of us."

"Do not speak for me, Ares," I snipped. Then to Hera and Zeus: "I came here the day before my wedding and begged you to reconsider. This is as much your responsibility as mine."

Hera gasped.

"Please . . ." Ares muttered.

"Marriage between two Olympians is a privilege," Zeus stormed. "It is a most hallowed rite!"

I couldn't help myself; I laughed.

"I amuse you, Aphrodite." A question without interrogative force. A statement that declared, that precipitated, only one acceptable response. Here was my opportunity to stop this. I could apologize, we could all go on pretending, but I was passionate in more ways than one.

"Hypocrisy can be amusing when it's so ironic," I explained.

"I am no hypocrite."

"Yet you would lecture *me* on marriage? On *fidelity*?"

Zeus might have been astounded by my gall, but Hera was incensed. "It is you, Aphrodite, who stands on pretense. You are the goddess of adultery, not love. Nastiness, not beauty. You have ruined my family with your foul magic!"

I gaped, momentarily lost for words, as Hera stewed in her hatred for me.

"You have pitted brother against brother and turned my husband away from me."

"I have cast no spells on either of your sons. I have—"

But Hera interrupted, pointed a beringed finger in my direction. "We were better before you, Aphrodite. You hurt people—"

"I do not—"

"You infect men's minds, foment their baser natures, and lead them to ruin. Europa. Callisto. All these maidens seducing our husbands are your fault!"

I was fuming, skin tingling. "You will not blame me—or wine or ale, lotus or poppy, what the girl wore or how she carried herself, what she didn't say or what you think she meant—for the violence of men."

"You are a man-hating witch, and you've cast a spell on Ares. You have poisoned him. Return him to who he was before!"

I reeled as if slapped, astounded by Hera's harsh appraisal but also by Ares's arrant lack of defense. He stood beside me, speechless.

"I am guilty of honoring my heart," I confessed, "but that is all. And I still believe my vices are less problematic than your virtues."

"Enough!" roared Zeus. "My head hurts worse than when Athena lived inside it! I would send you back to your husband, Aphrodite, to live out your days in repentance, but he doesn't want you anymore. Until the scandal fades, and my anger has abated, you and Ares are both exiled from Olympus," Zeus rubbed his temples. "Harmonia, however, is a daughter of this mountain, and she will remain here until she comes of age and I find her a worthy match."

The world went soundless. I heard nothing but the gasping of my heart.

No.

Not my chickadee.

I cannot live without her.

I regretted my tone, my sass, my defiance. I would apologize, atone, anything. I brought my hands together before my chest in exhortation.

"I will leave—gladly—but allow me my daughter. She needs her mother."

"And what ilk of mother are you?" chastised Hera.

"A loving one!" And then I whirled upon Ares. "Say something! Our child belongs with me."

"*Our* child?" barked Zeus, hands gripping the armrests of his throne. "Does Hephaestus know?"

"I thought it common knowledge," I shot back, abandoning my humble pose already. "My lovely girl shares nothing with that fiend."

Zeus turned to his wife. "Hera, as the goddess who best embodies motherhood, I cede Harmonia's care to you."

Hera? The same mother who threw one son off a mountain and another to the wolves?

She will teach Harmonia that to be a woman is to obey and make no noise. To cede your own pleasure, your own mind.

She will turn Harmonia against me.

I hated Hera, but I would say anything to keep my daughter.

"Hera, please." I dropped to my knees. Hot tears, heated by my devastation, scalded the backs of my eyes. "Please. I will serve you all my days. Harmonia and I will move into your palace. Only do not separate us."

"You have broken my family . . ." she replied, and there was no need for her to finish the statement. Now she would break mine.

Zeus pointed to the doors. "Get out. Both of you. And do not return until you are invited back."

OUTSIDE THE PALACE, I slammed my fists against Ares's chest. "You said nothing! You did nothing! And now I've lost my child!"

"We also lost our integrity."

"Who cares about integrity right now?"

"I do!" he yelled. "We look like liars. We *are* liars."

"No. Don't allow their judgment inside your head. Nothing about us is untrue. It was you and I first, before Hephaestus."

"That doesn't matter."

"It should."

"There are rules, Aphrodite. Wives are faithful to their husbands. Men can cheat on their wives, but they cannot steal other men's wives."

"Those are horseshit rules, created by and for men." My hands dropped to my hips. "There are no rules in love."

"But there are rules for life."

No doubt our argument would have continued to escalate if not for an interruption. Alectryon, holding his helmet between his hands, his face as long as a summer day but without any of the joy.

"Ares, I am so very—"

"What was your assignment?" Ares cut in, fatally serious.

"To stay awake. To watch for Helios and knock on the door before he reached the house."

"And what happened?"

"I accepted a flask and felt so strange," muttered the miserable man. "I fell asleep and missed the morning call."

"And you will never miss it again."

Ares pulled a dagger from the belt at his waist and pressed its tip into Alectryon's chest. The man's mouth formed a large circle as Ares's militant magic traveled down the blade and attacked Alectryon's body. The soldier seized for a moment and then shrank.

A bird emerged from the useless pile of his clothing. Some sort of male chicken.

A rooster.

"Alectryon, I command you to cry the dawn's arrival for always."

Staring at that pathetic animal twisted my outrage into something sad and desperate. Ares and I were behaving in vindictive and self-loathing ways. This wasn't who we were, and it frightened me.

For if I could not have Harmonia, then I must have Ares. Otherwise, it had all been for naught. I would be fully alone. Again.

"Come with me," I pleaded. "To Cyprus."

"I cannot."

"You can. There's nothing stopping us anymore." I wrapped my arms around his neck, but he did not respond to my touch, holding himself stiff and still. "My marriage is over."

"And so are we. I need distance from you, Aphrodite. I cannot think straight when you are near." He pulled my arms from him and thrust me away, harder than he intended, for when I cried out, his eyes flickered with contrition.

"Do you think I coerced you into this, that I manipulate you with my power?"

His face hardened in a harrowing way. "I have been under your spell since the day we met."

"Ares, I would never do that to you!"

"Wouldn't or couldn't?"

I didn't respond.

He backed away from me. "We are bad for each other. Everyone is right. Love and war do not belong together."

He did not kiss me goodbye; he did not even wish me farewell. Ares, who'd seen eternity in my eyes, who'd inflamed my fantasies and enchanted my bed, both denied and discarded me. He strode away without once looking back.

Ares was wrong, everyone was wrong. For if we were not the same, then why did our power feel so similar? What else was war but desire at its bloodiest? Wasn't love a battle?

Passion is an act of violence. Heartbreak is a death.

Aphrodite, wife, was now Aphrodite, whore and witch. All my appellations. Given, not chosen.

But this I could promise: I would be no man's bride ever again.

Alexandros, that vow remains.

17

MILOS
Second Century BCE

SHE ABANDONS THE narrative with a sardonic smile. "Should I pull my dress down, Alexandros? Why cover up what I am, now that you know."

"I do not think less of you."

"You should. I became a woman so invested in my own affairs that it cost me my daughter. I entered dark days, truly doubting if there was substance to me at all. Was Hera's condemnation fair?"

The rose still rests in Aphrodite's hand, and she grips it tightly enough that the thorns enter her skin. She hardly reacts as blood leaks from between her fingers. It makes him uncomfortable; he wants to tell her to stop.

"Ares gave me ecstasy . . . and agony. Have you experienced such an ache, Alexandros?"

Of course he has, but he does not tell her of the person he hoped would be at his door that evening. Because in that story, he is the Ares. The one who leaves.

And he is mad at Ares, for how he treated his goddess, and thus, Alexandros is mad at himself.

She releases the rose, wet petals drifting to the floor.

"I've never thought flowers to be delicate little things," he says. "I find them strong."

She lights up, intrigued. "Tell me why."

Alexandros chooses his words with precision. He's a considerate person in many ways, in his art, his messaging. And he longs to impress her. "You said before that flowers are love, and I agree. Because they multiply, because they feed insects and animals and sustain life. Because they spread joy." She is staring at him now with a fresh fascination, a fixed concentration, as if he is the most brilliant man she's ever heard, and he understands once more why people fall for her. "But flowers are alive. They are resilient. Snow comes, as does rain or drought, yet they return. You are a pretty face, but you are also irrepressible."

"And flowers are not always beautiful," added Aphrodite. "I've seen them all. Some smell dreadful; others look like raw meat or some bloodthirsty creature from the deepest sea." She kicks away the rose petals at her feet. The wounds on her hand have dried, and the blood dissolves into her skin.

"I was blamed for so many ugly things I did not do. Every time an act of lust ended in regret or censure, 'Oh, I was led astray by Aphrodite! She made me do it!' Mortals and immortals alike considered me selfish, vain, and troublesome, so in my melancholy, I thought, 'If I'm going to bear this reputation I did not earn, why not enjoy it?'" She lowers her voice. "Alexandros, I became awful."

He puts the rose sketch into the discarded pile, beside the images of shells. Hurting hearts hurt others. He knows this because he's done it, too. The words he hurled at Timon the last time they met were proof.

You do not fulfill me like my work does. Our relationship is temporary; my art is forever.

"Perhaps love isn't the flower, but the bee," she says. "It produces sweetness but can fly away. Or sting."

"They also call some pornai 'honey traps,'" he adds.

"Indeed! Some of those girls are assassins in disguise." She seems pleased by the direction their conversation is taking. "There is a temple for me on Mount Eryx. They call those priestesses the 'melissae,' the bees, for I am *the* melissa, their queen bee. They believe the symmetry of the honeycomb is a sign of perfection, of the cosmos's great order. Aeneas went there, you know, on his way to Latium."

A beehive materializes in her lap, oblong and clay, the kind with a lid on both ends. "Maybe this is in my hands, Alexandros, or I am turning it over, letting all those wings and stings out into the world."

Aphrodite stands, taking a place under the skylight, beneath the moon's opalescent glow.

Alexandros reaches for another tablet.

Part III

AN OVERTURNED BEEHIVE

Aphrodite Melainis and Aphrodite Skotia, the dark one
Aphrodite Anosia, unholy
Aphrodite Androphonos, killer of men
Aphrodite Tymborychos, gravedigger

18

PAPHOS, CYPRUS

I RETURNED TO CYPRUS, shattered.

The island was no longer a haven, but my prison. Once these were beaches where I roamed free, ignorant of Olympus and its oppression. Once I had brought my war god here, to reclaim my heart and body with his. But the goddess who returned was jaded, hopeless.

I descended upon the isle in my swan-driven chariot, with only the belongings that fit inside the carriage. I abandoned everything else to Olympus. What Hephaestus did with my dresses and jewels was the least of my concerns.

At the sweet-smelling Paphian temple above the sea, I met with the head priests and priestesses and officially announced my homecoming. Then I gave two immediate orders.

"Destroy my home. Completely. I never want to see a single stone or plank of wood from its premises again."

They stared at me, aghast. "But you love it!"

"Love doesn't last," I spit. "Level it. Today."

The second, perhaps obvious, command was to build me a new residence. Until then, I would occupy the temple's back rooms, out of sight.

"Do not disturb me," I warned.

For I had no desire to hear prayers, felt no obligation to entertain adoration. I was not worthy of worship or even companionship. Do you ever grow weary of stone, Alexandros? For I had tired of love and beauty. I was sick of it all.

And I was pregnant, again.

I did not want another child. I wanted Harmonia.

I hid in my dark room, shuttering out friendship with the fresh air. Temple servants brought me food and clean water, laundered clothes and blankets, which I disregarded. If there had been a way for me to disintegrate or disappear, I might have taken it, and I cursed the immortality that kept me alive.

"I hate," my parched, cracked lips cantillated. Two words intoned, my newfound religion.

But what did I hate?

Me.

I had always been a dreamer, but I was plagued by a recurring pattern of nightmares. In the first, I am swimming, so happy, but when I open my mouth—to smile, to sing—I choke on a hook, stuck in my throat, pulling me out and up. I dangle, thrashing wildly, naked and hanging from a fishing pole held by Zeus. All the Olympians, all the Titans, all the nymphs and monsters and hybrids laugh. Then Hephaestus steps forward with a butchering knife, and Zeus auctions off my parts.

"Who wants a fillet? Who wants a loin? Anyone for the cheeks?"

He slaps my backside, and I can neither speak nor scream with my speared tongue.

The second dream is of Harmonia. We sit with our legs crossed in a meadow, playing our imaginary games.

"What shall we be today?" she asks brightly.

"Chickadees," I coo, brushing the hair from her sweet face. Her skin is silk beneath my fingertips. "And we can fly far, far away from here."

"No!" she cries. "I want a home! I want a family!"

I try to soothe her, but she is disconsolate. "I want my mother!"

"You have her, I'm here," I insist, but she swats me away.

"You're not my mama anymore! I want Hera!"

And in the third dream, the final movement of this cruel, chaotic symphony, I am with Ares. We are in bed together, and it feels so right to be back in his arms, but then he shoots to his feet, roaring with pain. The side of his face, the skin on his back, are melting away, dripping like molten lava.

"You did this to me!" he yells.

He hears none of my defense as he runs from me, and though I give chase, dodging the smoldering pieces of him he leaves behind, I cannot keep up.

Needless to say, I was getting very little sleep.

I was exhausted, dehydrated, and starving, but no matter how little I cared for myself, my stomach continued to grow. I felt larger and tighter than with Harmonia, stretched beyond measure, my outsides taut with strain and insides in conflict.

Unwelcome memories returned, unbidden. Ares's hands on my swollen belly, marveling at the flurries of her tiny kicks. He was enamored of my pregnant body, and on the handful of nights we could be together during those nine months, he would not stop touching me. Hephaestus, conversely, avoided me. Reproduction, which he considered a woman's issue, made him squeamish. I gave credence to his nervousness, let him believe I was fragile, even had him convinced I required my own bed to keep the baby safe. Oh, how I relished the reprieve!

Ares said we were liars. I realized now, in my depression, that he was correct. I lied to Harmonia about who she really was from the moment of her birth. I think I planned to confess everything eventually, but not until she was a proper adult. And then, because I loved her so much—which I did, truly—my temporary dishonesty wouldn't matter.

Well, she knew everything now, and my enemies controlled the story.

I hate. I hate. I hate.

Me.

Though I strove to keep my condition secret, someone at the temple discovered the truth and sent for assistance, because familiar voices called to me outside the barred door, and I groaned.

"Aphrodite, if you do not let us in, Aglaia brought an ax."

The Graces. We hadn't spoken since Harmonia's voice lessons, but I was lonely enough that I opened the door. Euphrosyne saw my sorry state and wept.

"It is true! Another baby! You must take better care of yourself."

"Get. Out."

"Eat!" Thalia pleaded, presenting me with warm bread and honey. "You need sunlight! A bath."

"I am not a plant," I snapped.

"No, you are an Olympian," retorted Aglaia, "and you are needed."

"Am I?"

For Hera's words continued to gnaw at me, like a termite in old wood, eroding my foundations: *You infect men's minds, foment their baser natures, and lead them to ruin . . . You hurt people.*

"Yes! Mobs assemble outside your temples. The people wonder why you have deserted them!"

"Lovers are fighting, flowers are wilting," added Euphrosyne morosely. "The birds are mute, their nests empty."

"Without you, hale and present, embracing your power, the world suffers."

But I could handle no more guilt. "I suffer when they invoke my name with their exploitations and savagery. Men, gods, none of them deserve me."

"We understand," murmured Euphrosyne.

"And it isn't fair," added Thalia.

But Aglaia narrowed her eyes. "Who are you hurting with your pride? Not just men and gods, but very real women who warrant some love and beauty in their lives. The Aphrodite I know will neither accept insults nor tolerate disrespect. She doesn't just disprove rumors, she demolishes them."

"I'm not sure I'm that woman anymore," I replied weakly.

"Yes, you are!" chirped Thalia. "Now, get out of bed and prove everyone wrong!"

It almost worked. I felt myself relenting, my resolve crumbling, but then the baby within kicked, and I remembered my miserable situation. I fell back into bed and pulled the blankets over my head.

"Go away."

This conversation happened over and over; the exact wording was flexible, but the ending was consistent. A tired melodrama. The Graces would depart in a murmur of worries and exasperations, and I would return to my dirty cot, arms folded over my stomach.

I. Hate. Me.

Construction of my new home concluded, and within days of relocating, my labor pains commenced. I alerted no one. With Harmonia, I had hot and cold baths, scented compresses, hands to hold. This time, I had only myself.

And furthermore, I bore three babies, not one.

Alexandros, it is impossible to nurse three infants, but even more so when two of them are vicious.

I named my sons Phobos, Deimos, and Eros. The naming of immortals is strange, for it's not a process of free will. The name comes to the namer through a divine channel, perhaps connected to the Muses, or imparted by the original energy that created the world. In the naming, the essence is revealed—hence my dulcet girl, Harmonia.

While adorable, curly-haired Eros reached for me, the other two rejected my administrations. They were their father in every sense. Dark and surly and stoic. They refused my milk and my comfort. Their tiny fists struck me—and Eros, as well—and they would not sleep. I tried everything. Bouncing and swaddling, singing, walking, rocking. I brought in ewe's milk, goat's milk. Nectar and ambrosia. I dipped rags in wine to offer them. Nothing soothed their cries.

Worst of all, I knew it was my fault. There hadn't been enough love in me while I was pregnant. All I possessed must have been directed into Eros; Phobos and Deimos received only my fear and terror, my bitterness and rage. And they hated me for it.

"Please," I begged them. "Please eat. I'm sorry. I'm so sorry."

Phobos and Deimos screamed even louder. Eros whimpered.

Beyond frustrated—and frightened they would starve to death—I surrendered to my dire circumstances and convened the Graces.

"I am without hope," I began, battling tears. "These babies are miserable."

Euphrosyne attempted to hold Phobos, but he clamped his toothless mouth down on her finger—hard. She shrieked. Already, Deimos had a lock of Thalia's white hair in his tiny hand, yanked from her scalp. He waved his fists, and I gaped at the bloody ends.

"They were born for war," I explained. "Please, take them to Ares, appeal to Zeus if you must, but these boys belong with their father."

You are not Hera, I told myself, over and over, as the Graces packed up the babies' scant belongings. *She tossed her boys out like garbage. You are sending them to family.*

And weren't they Ares's responsibility as much as mine?

But it was another defeat—one of many, maybe my greatest—and I despaired to see them go.

I'd lost Harmonia, failed Phobos and Deimos. Eros became my only child.

And Eros was my duplicate.

My boy, passionate from his first breath, needed only to be held and kissed and coddled. "Cuddle my whole body," he would demand, once he had language, and I would oblige, delighted to hold him. He was more "me" than Harmonia had been, for she was an empath, generous in her affection, and Eros and I were both selfish. I let him sleep in my bed, and he'd dig his little feet into my body, waking me repeatedly with his kneading toes. I didn't mind. I joked that Eros would surely burrow back inside my womb at night if he could. I tied him to my chest in silk cloths and brought him with me everywhere, even when he could walk on his own.

And did I mention fly? For my Eros had wings.

He learned from the birds who answered my call. I would watch my son in their midst, flying in flocks of turtledoves and sparrows, intersecting wings in sweet euphoria.

And he was sensual. I would find him curled up, naked, in my furs.

As my boy grew, I retraced the steps of my own youth: I taught him to swim in the clear, shallow waters of my favorite white-sand beaches, eating figs while we dried in the sun. He memorized the creatures of the tide pools, learned the patterns of moon and ocean. Our life was painted in shades of turquoise and gold. We sat among the pine trees on the cliffs, or in the sea caves and coves, and I told Eros stories of Olympus, talking often of beauty and love.

"There are as many kinds of beauty as there are love, for I am not beautiful in the same way as an anemone, nor do I love you, Mama, in the same way I love a dolphin."

My bright boy, already wiser than most of his elders.

But he was mischievous, too. He would become famous for it later, but in those early days, it manifested as a zeal for pranks and jest. He kept a herd of rabbits that followed him about, bouncing and nibbling, and Eros set them loose during temple services more than once. He stole offerings, freed the beasts set aside for sacrifice, removed the wicks from every candle. The poor priests and priestesses were at wit's end, but I would hear no slander against my child and refused to discipline him. I found his antics amusing, and Eros would do anything to make me laugh.

I didn't receive many visitors from Olympus during my exile besides the Graces and Apollo. He taught Eros to play the flute, and my son would fly about the island to music of his own making. I came to associate his arrival with a merry arpeggio. And to the mortals, it was a warning that Aphrodite's rakish young son was on his way.

Whenever Apollo was on Cyprus, I went to war with myself, torn between wanting to ask for news of Ares and not wanting to know. Finally, Apollo, who understood me better than I realized, said: "I have noticed there is a name we do not speak, Aphrodite. I will let you say it first, when you are ready."

I kissed Apollo's face, but my lips refused to shape that name. It was a stubbornness stronger than anything Hephaestus could concoct in his forge—I was proud, I was *fine*—but it was also self-preservation. Ares's words and actions had hurt me more than Zeus's decree or Hephaestus's trap. The man for whom I would have dived into the mouth of Etna didn't defend us, and then he denied me.

We are bad for each other.

The harshest words, a rejection of what we were, our extraordinary magnetism, something I revered.

And then he pushed me away.

Elements of Ares showed in Eros—the athleticism, the sharp eye and quick feet—but my son exhibited little interest in learning about his father. He was content having me to himself.

My son and I didn't need anyone but each other.

Eros adored the Graces, and they doted on him. Especially Thalia, who was so joyful. They showered him with gifts and implored that I seek amends with Zeus so my child and I could return to Olympus.

"He belongs with us," insisted Euphrosyne. "A child this divine!"

But I was adamant; I would not share him. Eros was mine. Without him, I might have wasted away in mourning. He brought me back to life.

Because of Eros, I cautiously stepped back into my responsibilities as a goddess. I inhaled the petitions and prayers, breathed out beauty and blessings. Because of Eros, I remembered that love could be good, and good people deserved it.

It was a lot of pressure to place on his young back. I'd understand later, when my son betrayed me, too.

IN ALL THOSE years, there was no communication between Zeus, Hera, and me. A boon. But neither did I hear from Harmonia.

Not until the eve of her own marriage.

Whether it be fate or free will, the interference of the gods or the independence of humanity, the world works in peculiar ways. Harmonia, who was conceived in the days after a prince named Cadmus killed Drakon, was now to wed that same man and become the queen of Thebes.

"Ares will never allow this," I insisted to the Graces, breaking my vow to never speak his name. "Drakon's death devastated him."

"Cadmus served Ares for eight years to earn his forgiveness," answered Thalia. "He already gave their union his blessing."

"Oh." I forced a smile. "Magnificent."

So Ares had met our daughter's future husband, but I never had? I tried to swallow the sudden uprush of envy.

"The wedding will be momentous," added Euphrosyne. "Harmonia has an open heart, Aphrodite, and is cherished by all."

I was proud, but also sad, for she was these things despite me.

"Did she ask for me specifically?" I pressed. "Tell me precisely the words she used."

"She insisted *both* her parents be invited," Thalia said. "Zeus has lifted the exile for the wedding."

In all our years apart, I had sent her no message, assuming she wouldn't want to hear from her disgraced mother. I was a slut, a joke, unfit. Harmonia was better off without me and my notoriety shadowing her. But I should have been braver. I should have tried harder.

Alexandros, consider the number of regrets you hold in your mortal lifetime. Now imagine mine.

I poured myself a glass of wine as I prepared to pack, took a fortifying sip—perhaps a gulp—as anxiety swirled about my stomach and chest. Did the other Olympians still despise me? Did I still despise them? But these questions had to contend with so many competing emotions: anticipation and trepidation, dread and—dare I say it?—*hope*.

I was going to see Harmonia—and Ares—again.

I shoved my best dresses into a trunk.

Eros, who had never visited the famed mountain, could barely contain his excitement. He flew beside my chariot, in flips and a flurry, giddy with glee, heedless of my inner turmoil.

And then, too soon, we were landing. My yearslong absence blown away in an instant.

It was all the same.

The Graces had kept my palace in fine form, and I walked over its threshold as if stepping back in time. The roses swayed; the doves shook their cages with furious flapping. Even the potted plants sighed in relief at my return. It was still mine; I was still me. My son squealed, running from room to room, dashing around pillars and leaping from fountains, splashing and laughing and causing a ruckus.

I was hardly settled before Harmonia came to call.

My girl, grown into a lady, lovely from the crown of her head to her fine foot. She was lithe where I curved, restrained, held together elegantly in all the ways I was wild. Harmonia embodied a safe form of beauty, the one I would see replicated in generations to come as the feminine ideal.

A proper lady. Hera's influence.

"Hello, Mother," she greeted me, kind but formal.

I wanted to clutch her, to kiss her cheeks, her hairline, the tip of her nose, but instead I offered her refreshment. I led her into my garden, and we rested by the pool.

Where to begin? *The weather is ideal? I like your sandals? My soul cried for you every day we were apart?*

"You seem quite relaxed," I told her. "I was hardly so composed the day before my wedding."

I was yelling at the king and running naked to another's man home.

"I am." She smiled shyly. "Cadmus is a noble man, and I am happy to be his bride."

"You will live in the mortal city? In Thebes?"

Harmonia nodded. "Yes, within the Cadmea."

"And you love him? An arranged marriage works for some; it did not for me."

"I do," she answered, but she was pensive, melancholic. "I wish it had been this way for you, too."

What if Ares and I had raised Harmonia together? I saw it for a moment, a different life, another time and place. She would ride horses with her father, sunbathe with me, chase her three exuberant brothers around, a wet rag in her hand, trying to clean their filthy faces. Would she still be marrying a human king?

"Harmonia," I hurried to say, because our afternoon was fading into night too quickly, "if I had known my relationship with Ares would take me from you, I would have ended it."

My daughter gave me a rueful half smile. "I'm not sure that's true. I remember how you were together." Still, she took my hand. "But I also remember our laughter. I remember when we sang songs and changed all the words to naughty ones. I remember eating sweets for supper, and you sleeping in my bed because I asked, even though Hephaestus said it would spoil me."

"I worried you would forget . . ."

"No. I never stopped thinking of you or praying that you would come back for me." Harmonia rose to her feet. "I must go. There is much to attend to before tomorrow."

"I could arrange your hair," I offered, and her smile slipped.

"I'm sorry, Mother. I already told Hera she could help me, but I will see you at the ceremony."

After Harmonia left, I could not move for a long while. I sat, my raw heart red and inflamed, and when I was ready to stand, I destroyed the courtyard, smashing pots against the wall, ripping out flowers, and screaming into the heavens.

I grabbed shears and sliced the hair from my head, throwing

the rose-gold strands into the pool. I clutched my shorn skull and sobbed.

By morning, it had grown back.

AS THE GODDESS of love, not marriage, I am no fan of weddings. Too often the bride is unwilling. Too often the pomp and ritual strip the event of real emotion. But at this wedding, the bride and groom regarded each other in solemn-eyed appreciation, and the crowd tingled with the awareness that this was special, this was true, and we were all lucky to be a part of it. After the ceremony, I received my daughter and her new husband with open arms, as if we had never been forcibly estranged.

As if nobody knew we had been forcibly estranged.

When I kissed my daughter's cheek, I asked about the necklace around her neck. One of entwined emerald serpents, their open mouths residing at the center of her collar.

"Hephaestus designed it for me," she replied, her fingers tracing its design. "It is a treasure, is it not?"

I murmured my agreement but could not stymie my skepticism. I understood Hephaestus's spite and tricks better than most. No matter how he'd felt about her in her youth, once her actual father's identify became common knowledge, Harmonia was a living symbol of Hephaestus's humiliation. Was this a genuine gift, or was it revenge?

As Harmonia and Cadmus moved down the receiving line, Eros nudged me.

"Trouble, not treasure," he confirmed.

Later, it would be called the Necklace of Harmonia, and it would curse her entire family. I should have ripped the damned thing from her neck and thrown it off the mountain.

Hephaestus and I made cold eye contact once or twice throughout the event, but a single word did not pass between us. Because I would not embarrass my daughter, I didn't slap him senseless or stab him with a fork. I consider this an achievement.

I experienced a similarly frosty reception from the goddesses of Olympus. Hestia and Artemis muttered together, pointing at me, and Athena raised one supercilious eyebrow before turning her back. They hadn't been in the bedroom that day, but they'd heard enough to scorn me.

When Hera embraced Harmonia, I was the one who looked the other way.

And then there were the gods, most of whom had seen me naked and engaged in the most personal of acts, but I smiled and waved like one who has never known mortification. I had been humbled, no doubt, but presented myself without humility.

Aphrodite, she's so shameless.

Ares, on the other hand, was nowhere to be seen. He did not appear for the exchange of vows nor the succeeding festivities.

The Graces sang; the guests danced. Apollo and I stood together on the edges, observing the merriment and whispering about which couplings were the most random, who was getting the most drunk.

"Where is he?" I asked. It wasn't the name, but he knew exactly who I meant.

"He travels often," Apollo returned in a low voice. "The isle of Crete, but also the northern areas of Thrace and Scythia."

"With Phobos and Deimos?"

"Yes. He brings them to battle with him." My friend shot me a sideways glance, humor in his eyes. "They are insane."

I smirked. "I hope they give him endless grief."

"It has been tedious here without you, Aphrodite."

"The goddesses, particularly the maiden ones, don't seem thrilled by my return."

Apollo shrugged. "I love my sister, but she and her friends can be a bit sanctimonious."

I laced my fingers through his. "Dance with me?" I asked, one eyebrow raised. "Let's give them something to talk about. I want everyone to know I'm back."

AFTER HARMONIA AND her mortal husband were escorted to their home in Thebes, Zeus bade me to join him—not in the Hall of the Gods, but in one of his private rooms.

If he tries anything with me, I thought, *I will bite off his tongue.*

He awaited me in a cushioned chair, his legs spread wide.

"You have conducted yourself well today, Aphrodite," he condescended. "And for that, I have decided to lift your ban from Olympus."

I murmured some polite drivel and inclined my head.

"That son of yours though. Will he be a problem?"

"In what way?"

"He smiles too much."

"Hardly indecorous."

Zeus frowned. "And when you return, I will tolerate no more of this love and war business. I need Ares focused and ready for battle at all times."

"Since Ares is not here, I hardly think it's an issue."

"Hmm . . ." Zeus paused, lost in some thought, and I sought my exit, only to be called back. "There is one additional matter. Hephaestus is ready to remarry, and he has chosen wisely this time."

I ignored the slight. "I wish him well, and a willing bride *this time*."

"She is, and a dear companion of yours, as well. Hephaestus will wed Aglaia."

Alexandros, in all the centuries that have been—and all those still to come—I will continue to be shocked by Olympians. There are no guidelines to how we behave, no real precedence for our actions. We can still be entirely unpredictable.

"My Aglaia?"

"My daughter, Aglaia," revised Zeus. "It's a better match. Hephaestus prefers a more slender woman."

I barely stopped my arms from wrapping around my body in time.

"You will offer your congratulations and bless their union. I hope that she will make him happy."

"And I hope he will make her happy."

Zeus forced a smile. I forced one back.

Progress.

But as I returned to the party, visions of Aglaia and Hephaestus ran rampant through my mind.

Ugh.

But also:

Why?

Aglaia would sleep in the golden bedroom? Aglaia *wanted* to sleep in the golden bedroom?

Before I could find the Graces and pummel them with my questions, Hermes caught me in the hallway, carrying a wine jug and two cups.

"The only way to tolerate a wedding," he commented, lifting his wares.

"Though it pains me to agree with you, I can't disagree."

"The last time I saw you was a lot more fun," he drawled, eyes narrowing, "for you wore a lot less clothing."

"There are things I missed on Olympus," I returned. "You are not one of them."

He laughed.

"Come," he said, gesturing to a doorway. "Share a drink with me?"

"Luckily for you, Hermes, you've caught me at a moment of great thirst."

I may be a goddess, Alexandros, but sometimes I do dumb things.

I followed him into a room I remembered, the one where I'd stolen his helmet, and we settled across from each other at a small table.

Hermes poured wine into the two goblets and passed me one, which I accepted.

"I didn't think it possible, Aphrodite, but you are more beautiful than I remember."

I rolled my eyes toward the ceiling. "Spare me your flattery, Hermes. I hardly trust it."

"You, at least, had the decency to show up for your daughter. Where is your lover?"

"Former lover. And traveling in the north," I responded, inordinately glad I had an answer.

But Hermes shook his head. "A partial truth. Ares is most often in the east, riding the chariot called Firebright with a certain morning goddess."

Aurora.

I had suspected as much, but that didn't make the confirmation any less heart-wrenching. Since I'd left Olympus, I had taken no men to my bed. Naturally, I'd been lonely, had experienced longings, but I kept the flame of Ares and me alive. I had faith in our rekindling.

Ares and Aurora had extinguished all my beliefs.

I drained the wine in my goblet, and when I slammed it back upon the tabletop, Hermes watched me hungrily.

"She told her sister Selene that Ares might be the great love of her life."

"How endearing," I replied dryly.

"She's not as pretty as you, Aphrodite," he said, "but she's much nicer."

"I have little interest in nice."

"Neither do I."

His foot found mine, nudging, caressing, and despite my feelings for its owner, I liked how it felt. It had been a long while since anyone had touched me with any interest. This night should have been my reunion with Ares, but he wasn't coming, and here was Hermes, my sometimes nemesis, offering me something else.

And I was not in the mood to play nice.

Hephaestus and Aglaia. Ares and Aurora. True love meant nothing, might as well have fun.

"Take me to bed now, Hermes, before I change my mind."

He did not wear his winged sandals, but he certainly flew at me.

I made a mad kind of love to Hermes that night, biting his shoulder and clawing his back.

"Am I beautiful?" I asked, atop and astride him.

"The most," Hermes moaned.

"Could you fall in love with me?"

"Yes," he whispered.

If the bedroom is its own theater, this was my catharsis. I released all I had repressed, then left Hermes in a deep sleep, his mouth red and open.

I felt better than I had in years.

Until I imagined Ares doing the same things with Aurora.

And this, Alexandros, is why I despise my beauty being compared to the dawn. For I am far less temperate.

Aphrodite, in Direct Address

ALEXANDROS, I'VE BEEN lying to you.

But I was also lying to everyone—Zeus and Hera, Ares, Apollo, the Graces, and Harmonia.

Only Eros knew the truth.

I can cast love magic. And its reverse.

I can cause people to fall in love with trees or animals or stone. I can sever connections, cleave open hearts.

I can alter appearances, not permanently, but at least for a time.

I had always kept my abilities hidden because if others knew, I would be anathema. I wouldn't be trusted, nor would I trust others. Consider it, Alexandros. Consider me. Are you terrified to upset me? Do you wonder if you genuinely like me or if I've enchanted you?

I still hadn't healed from the hurt of Ares suspecting I'd bewitched him.

I have been under your spell since the day we met.

But Harmonia's wedding and my tryst with Hermes had changed me. I was disillusioned, jealous, and so angry. Ares was sleeping with Aurora and probably had been while we were together. He had made me feel crazy and obsessive when I brought her up, but my instincts were right.

She's not as pretty as you, Aphrodite, but she's much nicer.

Ares might be the great love of her life.

I returned to my palace on Olympus and excused every servant. With only Eros by my side, I brewed two necessary potions. These were concoctions of my own creation; it's my power, it requires no recipe. I made the first with rose petals, oysters and honey, strawberries and jasmine flower, and the second with the blood of a swan's heart. Both infused with intention.

It hurt me to kill the swan, but not as deeply as other things.

Eros possessed a bow and arrows, gifted to him by Apollo, and he would be my messenger. My rascally boy was more than happy to oblige. In his kit were two types of arrows: gold and lead. To the golden arrows, we applied my balm of love, and to the lead, heartbreak.

But I would not curse Aurora to hate Ares; I had a better idea.

"Travel Oceanus, my little bee," I told Eros. "Find the goddess of dawn and sting her with one of these golden arrows. Aim her love toward mortal men and away from the god of war."

"I will do anything you ask, Mama. And what of the lead arrows?"

"Keep them in your quiver. I'm sure we'll need them soon enough."

I sent our son off to sabotage his father's lover with no qualms or hesitation. Only a grim satisfaction.

If I had to ache like this, so did Ares, so did Aurora.

None of my benevolence was ever appreciated, and I was tired of feeling like I didn't matter. Nobody was going to disrespect my power or my beauty again.

If the world expected me to be bad, why not be worse?

19

THE KNOWN WORLD

MY WRATH, ONCE awoken, found no rest.

I laid curses like farmers laid seeds, spreading devastation far and wide.

My vengeance was a weed, noxious and impossible to contain.

After Aurora, I targeted Helios, for his part in revealing my affair to Hephaestus. With my son's help, we cursed him to a doomed affair with a princess of Persia.

But immortals weren't my only targets.

A human boy challenged me to a beauty contest. *Me*. For his hubris, I transformed him into a shark. The women on Lemnos refused to worship in my temple, so I cursed them with a horrific stench. When Narcissus, impossibly handsome and intolerably vain, continued to treat his admirers with disdain, I made him fall in love with his own reflection. He wasted away pining for himself.

Glaucus, a king of Corinth, refused to let his stallions mate, believing they pulled his chariot with greater speed when they were inflamed. I couldn't sleep at night for their braying and pacing—yes, anguished animals can pray to me, too, in their way. I commanded Eros to set the herd free. Was it my fault they stampeded over Glaucus? Maybe Glaucus should have treated them better if he didn't want to be trampled.

Once, as I traveled from my shrine on Cythera to Cyprus, I thought to stop at Rhodes and visit the Temple of Apollo on the acropolis. Imagine my indignation when a cadre of men waited on the beach, barring my entrance to the island. They were, I learned, the six sons of the sea nymph Halia.

"You are not welcome," they jeered, calling my name with its cruelest epithets.

"I was not seeking permission," I remarked, but when I made to move past them, the belligerent men forced me backward with strong arms and swords.

"You dare lay your hands upon a goddess?"

"You're only Ares's whore," they maintained. "And your kind is not allowed here. We are a decent city."

I tilted my head, one hand at my hip. "Your mother was Poseidon's mistress, no?"

"Do not speak of our mother!"

"I am a mother, as well."

"You are nothing like her."

"And yet, I'm certain we became mothers in the same way."

Blades lifted. Slurs flew in my direction. *Adulteress. Nymphomaniac. Cocksucker.*

Such disrespect could not be tolerated. The words themselves did not bother me as much as the hypocrisy. These men saw no problem in defaming another woman as long as it was not *their* woman. What a world we could enjoy if men treated all women like they were real people.

With one poignant clap of my hands, I brought hysteria down upon them. They went so berserk that Poseidon was forced to the scene to bury his manic sons beneath the sand.

"What will I tell Halia?" the sea god bellowed at me afterward, for I had remained on the beach to watch him deal with his insufferable spawn. It was an entertainment for me.

I shrugged. "That her children would have benefited from some manners."

"Aphrodite!"

But I was already walking away, waving over my shoulder. I had yet to see Apollo's temple.

Eros kept me apprised of Aurora, so I knew my spell worked. Already she had fallen for two mortal men. With Tithonus, a prince of Troy, she cast a spell for his immortality but failed to ascertain *at what age* he would become eternal.

Poor Ares. Rejected for an elderly man.

Such a pity. Often, I wondered if Ares heard of my exploits. I acquired a reputation for viciousness, but there was an undeniable method to my punishments, a sort of vigilantism. I believed in the justice of my actions. And since I'm finally revealing my truth, know this, Alexandros: I never instigated affairs between humans and animals or members of an immediate family. I find both to be despicable. I have been denounced for so much, my skin has thickened against the barbs, but these accusations still bother me.

I can still feel, despite all the years I carry.

Which brings me to Myrrha, a princess of Corinth.

When Myrrha came of age and into her beauty, her father, Cinyras, started to rape her. I refuse to call it anything else. Always when he drank too much wine and always calling her by a different name, pretending that she was a maid in his court. Myrrha prayed to me, not for love, but for an escape from her father's perversion of it. She called my name from her sanctuary among the rocky hills, her favorite place to sit and think. For she was a solitary soul, most herself when away and alone.

"Aphrodite, please. I need a different life, or I will end mine."

And because she held a dagger, I appeared at once.

"Child," I said tenderly, "it is your choice, and I will not judge, but is death truly what you want?"

She shook her miserable head, and I knelt beside her, taking the dagger into my own hands.

"What do you love?" I asked.

"This place. I love it here."

And so I changed her into a tree. She stood tall, overseeing the pine martens and lynx, providing shade and respite. In her boughs, nuthatches found asylum. Myrrha received the safety she'd always wanted, but also a community and a purpose within it. Wounded myrrh trees leak a resin that, when harvested, is ameliorative, curative. Used to purify air and body.

Isn't that just, Alexandros? Didn't I do well?

The rumormongers spun the story differently. In their version, I cursed Myrrha to pursue her own father. He was helpless against her charms; she was the seducer.

She was a child.

What about my character makes people believe that I would ever do such a vile thing?

A father-and-daughter coupling is salacious, it gets people salivating—the ones who hunger for disaster, for villains, for the sordid details of others' lives. It makes them feel better about their own failures and mishaps and dark secrets. Is gossip our oldest social ill? Did Pandora release it, or did it exist even before? I have my suspicions.

What I still don't understand is this: The true story is equally interesting; it didn't need to be changed. But stories are malleable. They adapt to the form of their teller and the times.

When men tell my story, I become the character they create.

But I am digressing, Alexandros, my apologies, for Myrrha's myth is not finished. In fact, it is this complication that changes this tale from ephemera to legend.

Unbeknownst to either of us, when Myrrha entered her tree body, she carried Cinyras's seed, which goes against all the laws of nature. After nine months, the tree expelled the baby, a true human child, with no leaf or root to be seen.

Eros heard the cries and collected Myrrha's newborn son from the wilds of Corinth. He brought him to me wrapped in a goatskin.

"Can we keep him?"

The baby cooed. He was truly adorable, and I was tempted.

"He's not a pet, Eros. I don't want another child; you've been enough work."

He beamed. Eros loved when I complimented his naughtiness.

"Then what shall we do with him?"

"He cannot return to Corinth. That wretched family doesn't deserve him, and it would be against Myrrha's wishes."

"Hera?" suggested Eros.

I leveled my hardest look at him. "I won't even respond to that."

He grinned, then offered Hades's wife, Persephone. "She is desperate for a child."

I considered my son's proposition. Persephone *was* a decent option. She seemed nice when we met—though I've already voiced my opinions on "nice"—but I wondered about sending a baby to the realm of the dead. Was a childhood in the underworld its own malediction? He would be raised in a palace, with every luxury, but also with ghosts.

A human childhood is the merest moment of time. The beat of a hummingbird wing in my forever. He would be a man soon enough, and in this world, whether above or below it, men can do as they please.

"Take the baby to Persephone as a gift from me." Then I helped Eros tie the baby to his chest in a sling—just as I once did with him. I kissed both their foreheads. "Remember Tartarus is not our domain. Do not dawdle."

"You will give yourself worry lines, Mama."

He and I both laughed.

Me. With wrinkles. Inconceivable.

Persephone accepted the child with open arms, naming him Adonis, and Eros returned to me laden with gifts. The queen of the dead could not thank me enough for my unexpected charity, and for eighteen years, I had one goddess firmly on my side.

Until I got Adonis killed, of course.

20

FORESTS OF PHOENICIA

I NEVER MEANT TO fall for a mortal.

After watching countless failed liaisons between my fellow immortals and our human counterparts, I'd developed a serious distaste for comingling. Our lifespans were incompatible, the power dynamics were disproportionate, and it never ended well. Zeus was the most prolific in disastrous affairs, but it also happened with my friend Apollo, who fell in love with mortal men and women with abandon.

And after what I'd done to Aurora, you might say it was my turn to be chastened.

In my existence, time is both everything and nothing. It defines who I am—an immortal, with all the days imaginable—and yet, by that definition, it is also meaningless. Eighteen years can pass without much consideration and so, in the case of Adonis, he grew into adulthood before I even gave him a second thought. It was Eros, who spied on everyone, who found him first. He told me Adonis was living in the forest of Phoenicia.

It took me a moment to place his name.

"Oh! The baby from the tree!"

"Not a baby anymore," said Eros emphatically, who himself had grown into a striking man. Muscular but slim, with curls and wings, and very little clothing, I understood exactly what women thought when they gazed upon him. And I admit, I was proud of my gorgeous troublemaker.

But his response struck my fancy. I felt a sort of proprietorship over Adonis, as his savior, and so I journeyed into Phoenicia to sate my curiosity.

I found him in the aromatic cedar woods of the highlands, in the midst of a solitary hunting camp—one tent, one blanket—sitting on an overturned log as he strung a bow. I landed my chariot at a distance and entered his site on foot, walking across the perimeter with my hands raised.

"Don't shoot," I teased.

Adonis looked up, slightly startled, and yes, I was struck by his handsomeness. The disheveled hair and bright, clear eyes.

He acknowledged my divinity with some hesitation. "Are you a friend of my mother's?"

"We are cordial."

I did not mention how I had known his human mother, for I could understand why Persephone might have kept this knowledge secret.

"Are you Hebe?" he asked.

The goddess of eternal youth. I must still appear in bloom! But Hebe is a lesser immortal. A cupbearer.

"Stars, no. I am Aphrodite."

His eyebrows shot up his forehead.

I gestured at his supplies. "You prepare for a hunt?"

"It is my first," he told me. "It took many conversations to convince my mother I could do it on my own."

"Hunts are dangerous," I replied. "Many fine heroes have fallen in similar woods. And you have no servant."

"I have no need for another to do all the work while I claim the prize." Adonis shrugged. "Though it is lonely out here, talking to the trees."

"I am sure they are wonderful listeners."

"The best, but the conversations tend to be a bit one-sided."

I conjured a wooden seat for myself, intricately carved from the cedar at hand. "I am quite adept at talking back."

Adonis laughed.

We spoke for the rest of the afternoon. I didn't even need to pour us wine, the conversation flowed so effortlessly. Adonis was unlike any of the men from my past; he had no intensity or smarm or shallowness. He was genial, gentle almost. And when Hesperus, the evening star, shone above, a warm hush lay between us.

"You could join me," said Adonis, before I had the chance to make a half-hearted exit.

"Me?" I gestured to our surroundings. "Here?"

He held out his hand.

An offer—in earnest—for my company. Ares had never once invited me to camp in the fields of war with him. Adonis had no bias toward me, no fear of my name or reputation. I had forgotten what it could be like to stand in the moment, judged only in the immediacy, not as an accumulation of sins and stories.

But hunt and camp? Me?

But also: Why not?

So I took his hand. I stayed.

I prefer ocean to forest. I don't enjoy climbing boulders or forging through bramble. But I did it for him. I shortened my dresses to make travel easier and kept my hair bound in a braid. Because I genuinely enjoyed his company, I endured otherwise unenjoyable tasks. I set traps. I helped Adonis weave nets and sharpen stone. I even attempted cooking over the fire, but Adonis quickly dismissed me from those duties after he tried my first meal and spent a night vomiting.

I hate cooking even more than I hate weddings.

Persephone had done well by him. Adonis was considerate, decorous, supporting me when we crossed rivers, pausing to check if I required food or rest. He asked me endless questions about myself, in ways that brought me to pause, for I'd never considered the answers.

What are you afraid of, Aphrodite?

How would you live differently if you could die?

Do you prefer new moons or full ones?

Kissing him was a true sweetness, and yes, though I was infinitely his elder, I made love to him.

I was his first.

I was softer with him.

We slept nestled together in lion pelts we carried in rolls across our backs, and I still associate the smell of tannin-rich bark, used to tan hides, with his body.

I had questions, as well. "After this season, where will you go?"

"The cities. Perhaps the Eleusis in Athens, where my grandmother, Demeter, is honored. Would you join me?"

A significant part of me longed to accept his offer, but Adonis brought out the better version of myself. The Aphrodite from before, the Aphrodite that could be selfless.

"Adonis, when the hunt is finished, so are we. If I keep you for myself, you will never enjoy a real life."

He went quiet, but he did not weep, nor did he protest. There was no anger in him.

"I will always miss you, I think."

My smile met his lips.

I have had so many years to miss him, Alexandros, and the greatest tragedy is not the years he and I lost, but what he might have been. Adonis could have been an artist; his sensitivity was his strength. Too many consider such a quality a weakness. They're wrong.

I would be more sensitive if I weren't so afraid.

ADONIS CAUGHT PHEASANTS, snared wild hares. He took down a deer with his bow and arrow. But never the elusive boar.

"Look at all these skins!" I declared. "You will return home with a bounty."

"My father won't be proud unless I kill large game."

Was it ego that hindered my young lover? Some unslakable ambition? Neither. He had no aspirations for fame; he only wanted his parents' pride—which he already had. That's something you only understand once you've become a parent yourself.

"Let me kill a leopard for you!"

"Aphrodite, no."

"Why? You'd prefer a bear?"

He laughed and pulled me into his chest. "Give me one more day and night."

If he weren't so adorable, I might have refused, but he brought his mouth to my neck, and I was convinced. I was just tugging at his belt when the boar appeared. Adonis stiffened.

"Hush," he breathed into my ear.

I should have known something was amiss by the size of the boar, its massive girth and height. Even at this distance, I could tell its flat, gray face would meet Adonis's shoulder. It was an unsightly beast—colored in gray and rust, greasy hairs sprouting from its thick skin—and it exuded violence. It watched us from the other side of the clearing, snorting and shaking. If fire had exhaled from its nostrils, I wouldn't have been surprised.

If you have never experienced a hunt, you might not be aware that boars run fast. They can jump and climb. The prominent tusks on their lower jaws are constantly sharpened by the upper teeth angling against them, creating natural sabers.

Wild boars are deadly. And terrifying.

"Aphrodite," murmured Adonis, "get behind me."

Adonis, for all his muscle, had never seemed so small, his arms so insubstantial. What was a sword and a spear against such a monster?

He drew his weapons, and the boar charged.

The attack was so fast, the collision so loud, I shook from the impact.

Before Adonis could even lower his blade, the boar rammed its head into my lover's bare chest, those prolific tusks entering his stomach. The boar swung its head, shredding skin, sending viscera flying.

It splattered against my tunic. I screamed.

The boar retreated as I dashed forward, dropping to my knees where Adonis lay on his back, his hands holding his intestines. His chest thrust upward in uneven, jerky movements as he struggled to breathe through the excruciating pain. My hands trembled as I placed them over his, slick, slippery gore coating both our fingers.

I could not fix this.

"I'll kill it," I promised him. "I'll bring its skin back to your father."

"Don't," he rasped. "That would be a lie."

Some people enjoy the comfort of lies, but not Adonis. And the usual death-side litany—*You're going to be all right*—would dishonor him. He wouldn't be all right; he had only a few racking breaths left to live. My tears descended upon his body, washing the blood into the ground, a holy mixture of life and love and death that sprouted crimson flowers. They circled his body in a protective wreath, the earth and my sorrow and the remnants of his blameless life in mutual commemoration.

"You are going home, dear one," I said, forcing steadiness to my voice. "Your parents await you there, and they will bring you to Elysium, to the peace of the virtuous. You will rest, released forever from this pain. And they will be so proud of you."

He tried to smile, for at this point, the blood filled his throat, and he could no longer speak. I hummed, I brushed the hair from his forehead, and I watched as his eyelids grew heavy, the light in his eyes dimming, rescinding farther and farther from me and this moment, and then he gasped, and his spirit was moving on, descending to the underworld to begin a journey I could not join.

Would never join.

"I think this might be my fault, Adonis," I whispered. "And I am so sorry."

I picked flowers from the new growth and made a large bouquet to cover his wound as best I could. I closed his eyes and kissed their lids, organized that messy hair. All the while, the boar remained nearby, watching my ministrations, unmoving and placid.

"It is you, Hermes?" I asked, letting the rage fill me, welcoming its return. "Did Zeus sense my happiness and send you here? Or are you Poseidon? Still upset over the bastards I punished?"

The boar changed, shrinking and stretching, teeth retracting. And then Ares stood in its place, blood around his mouth. He wiped it with the back of his hand.

I drew a sharp breath. I knew the boar was supernatural somehow, but not him. I never guessed it was him.

In every dream of our reunion, it was never like this. Both of us covered in an innocent boy's blood, glaring at each other.

"You didn't have to kill him," I finally managed to say. "I was going to let him go."

Ares stared at me, stony-eyed and still. "I could say the exact same about Aurora."

"Aurora is very much alive."

"By what definition? You've killed her spirit."

"It's not the same! He was a child."

"Pick your victims with more care, Aphrodite."

I regarded Ares, the body I had once held above all others. The familiarity of his cropped hair and hunched shoulders, the perpetually clenched fists. After my sojourn in the woods, I did not feel beautiful. Did he notice the dirt in my fingernails, the detritus in my hair? Surely my face was swollen with tears.

"You haven't changed at all," he commented, almost omnisciently. "Still selfish."

"Neither have you." And I chose the words that would cut. "Still death's dog, a killer without cause."

When he smiled in unspoken mirth, I lunged forward, my palms striking his chest.

"Leave! Let me mourn him!" I screamed. "Be gone, you murderer!"

Ares's hands clasped over mine, halting my attack and holding me in place. We were so close, I could see his jawline pulse as he gritted his teeth.

"This was no murder," he growled. "The boy was armed and trained. He wanted a boar; I gave him one."

"He never had a chance!"

"No." Ares's voice dropped. "He was bested by one stronger and infinitely more capable."

"I remember," I said, before I could think.

Ares's lips parted, the muscles in his arms contracted, and as my legs weakened, as I sank into him, his head leaned down toward me, hot breath brushing my cheek, and I was fearing and hoping. *He's going to kiss me.* But then Ares drew himself back in disgust and stalked off into the woods, leaving me forsaken and filthy.

I would lust for my lover's killer, within moments of his death? I was worse than the crudest, cruelest insults people spat at me.

With nothing left to hold myself together, I collapsed. Eyes closed, holding my knees, I rocked upon the forest floor.

I knew when Adonis's shade reached the underworld, for the earth seized with Persephone's keening.

21

BOEOTIA, MOSTLY

AFTER PHOENICIA, I was as fragile as a dandelion. Simply breathe too hard around me, and I might fall apart. The Graces did their best to provide me solace with their brand of musical companionship—even Aglaia, now married to Hephaestus, which we did not discuss—but I wanted only Eros.

"You are my other half," I told him. "My dearest friend. The only one I can depend upon."

I so overburdened him with my needs that it's really no surprise he began to keep secrets. My son knew I was in no state to accept the truth, that he was a grown man with his own life.

He was correct.

While I divided my time between Olympus and Paphos, mourning and moaning, damning Ares to Tartarus, wishing I had let Zeus send him there years ago, my son fell in love.

Eros, who had grown into his role as god of desire, was involved in countless love affairs, and I became accustomed to the constant stream of comely girls in and out of his room. I didn't mind, because they always went home. I convinced myself that Eros wasn't the type for a committed relationship—he didn't need one. He had me, and nobody could love him like his mother.

Word had reached me of yet another maiden whose beauty rivaled mine, a third-born daughter of some otherwise unnoteworthy king. These boasts had become monotonous, but this situation was different. People truly believed the girl was my chosen one, the human manifestation of all my gifts, whom I had sent to the world in my divine beneficence.

And while the mortals made pilgrimage to worship this common girl, my altars were left cold for want of fire, the garlands dried, wreaths died. I could feel my power weaken. It was an affront; it was insolence. I sent Eros to prick the princess with his arrows.

"Turn the upstart into a butterfly," I commanded, flicking a flippant hand. "Or commit her to a love affair with a mop."

"A mop? Not a broom?" Eros teased, fixing his golden curls in the hanging mirror.

"I leave it to your judgment."

"Yes, Mama. As you wish, as ever."

He kissed my forehead and departed. And I promptly forgot about this spare princess and my vindictive orders.

Around this time, Apollo was enamored with Chrysostomos, one of my priests at Paphos, so we spent considerable time on the island, throwing raucous parties. Over the years, my home had expanded into a veritable oasis, a menagerie of birds and flowers nearly on par with my Olympian palace. We were often joined there by Thalia, Euphrosyne, and the youngest god, Dionysus, god of wine.

I must speak for a moment on Dionysus.

He was Harmonia's grandson, the first Olympian that felt like my own kin. The path to his divine appointment was a convoluted one, and at the center of that knot?

Zeus.

My daughter and Cadmus had four children, and the youngest, the princess Semele, caught the eye of the sky god. Their torrid affair was discovered by Hera, and she tricked my granddaughter into asking Zeus to reveal himself to her in his full divinity. When he did, a lightning bolt struck Semele in the bed where they lay. She died instantly, their son in her belly. Out of some semblance of shame or guilt or duty, the old lecher retrieved their child from her smoking womb and brought him into our fold as a sort of tribute.

Yet another slight against his wife.

Dionysus and I got along well. He possessed a dark side, but in his brighter moments, he brought a debaucherous fun to our congregation. On Paphos, we lounged on couches in the lamplight, adding blue lotus to our wine and smoking opium from ivory pipes. We watched sylphlike dancers contort and commune to tambourine and cymbal, frame drum and hand drum. Apollo would accompany on his lyre, and sometimes Dionysus brought his wild maenads to perform. When Apollo and his priest left to enjoy each other privately, and my mind was properly nebulous, I would choose a priest or two of my own to take back to my rooms.

It was all diverting, dissolute. Unsustainable.

But it explains why I didn't notice that Eros never returned from punishing this third-born daughter of some otherwise unnoteworthy king. In my defense, my boy was prone to flights of fancy—literally and figuratively. It wasn't unusual for him to become distracted by some pretty person or find himself on a tangential mission for a friend or against a foe. He was so capable, I never feared for his safety.

And our bond was stronger than any metal forged by my former husband. My son always came home to me.

I was back on Olympus, pruning flowers with Thalia and Euphrosyne, when Eros came flying erratically over the walls and into the central courtyard, crashing unceremoniously into one of my pomegranate trees. Euphrosyne gasped. My son stood, but stumbled, falling into the topiary, and I rushed to his side.

"Eros! Are you wine drunk? What a preposterous entrance!"

"Love drunk, Mama," he bewailed. "Burned and betrayed."

His purple cloak covered his torso, but he opened it, showing the scalded skin across that taut, tanned chest.

"Oh no!" exclaimed Thalia.

And I was taken back to so many years prior. To Ares at his bath, anointing him with Apollo's balm and kissing him for the first time.

Stars, I missed him.

"Mama," Eros moaned, "it hurts so much."

But here was our son, needing me in a different way.

"Thalia," I said, snapping back into the present. "Run to Apollo and fetch his healing salve. Tell him the same as before."

"No, no," demurred Eros. "This is from the wax of a human fire, a simple candle. I hardly notice it." He pounded a fist against the center of his breastbone despondently. "It is my heart that tortures me."

His eyes were rimmed in red, the skin below puffed. Somebody had dared bring my son to tears? I would roast them slowly over a spit. Alive.

The two Graces and I shepherded Eros inside and laid him on his bed. Euphrosyne brought him lemon water and a bowl of grapes; Thalia fetched washcloths and a basin.

I sat beside Eros, brushing curls from his forehead. "My little bee, you must tell me all that happened, and I promise I will make it right."

Eros had indeed gone to find that princess—the one I'd assumed so inconsequential, I hadn't bothered to learn her name—but when he first gazed upon her, his mission, and my vendetta, flew straight from his head. For Psyche was blessed with not only a prepossessing face, but an even lovelier disposition. This was a girl who tended to the sick and elderly, who took in strays and runts. She gave away more than she had, much to her parents' chagrin. Psyche was so perfect, in fact, that though men journeyed far and wide to witness her beauty and kiss her hand, none offered her their own.

The points of pride among men are numerous and nonsensical; Psyche's goodness intimidated them. It illuminated their own deficiencies.

And thus, Psyche became an idol, set upon an altar, honored by the ardent, who crawled upon their knees but never touched her.

Psyche's two sisters despised her for myriad reasons, but their queen mother was a major factor. This was a woman who'd rather pit her daughters against one another than support their unity, encouraging competition and tricks. And the king not only turned a blind eye to his wife's intrigues, but forbade Psyche's sisters from marrying until Psyche was engaged. While the royal family coexisted, tangled together in their various tensions, Psyche cursed the looks that made her an object, a spectacle instead of a soul.

"Mama," lamented Eros, "I could have provided her a husband, pricked any one of those admirers with an arrow strong enough to inspire action, but I did not want her to end up with a man too cowardly to truly love her."

And Eros had fallen for Psyche himself.

The king, overwhelmed by the situation in his home, went to the Temple of Apollo for advice. But Eros got there first. He confessed his lovesickness to my friend, and they hatched a plan.

"Excuse me," I interrupted. "Apollo said nothing of this to me!"

"I begged him to keep it between us."

I replied with one injured word: "Why?"

Alexandros, should you ever have a child, I pray they never hide their truth from you. It is a unique and terrible misery.

"I did not want you to interfere." Eros's face fell. "I did not want you to force her to love me either."

And my son was afraid. He did not think someone as pure as Psyche would ever trust a man with his reputation, the amorous attendant of Aphrodite.

In their scheme, Apollo would send Psyche to Eros, who would keep his identity secret until they fell in love the honest way.

"Your youngest daughter will be married, but not to a mortal man," boomed Apollo as the king lay prostrate before the god's statue. "Her match has been willed by the divine. The bridegroom is nobly born, but a monster. Psyche must climb to the top of the windswept mountains, west of your kingdom, alone. From there, her husband will arrange transportation to his home."

Word spread and the people mourned, but Psyche was resigned to her fate. Her sisters could wed their betrotheds, and she would at last break this cycle of hope and heartbreak. She wished her family well, donned her cloak, and departed for the wilderness. At the apex of the designated mountain, Eros's longtime friend Zephyrus, god of the wind, picked the girl up and flew her to Eros's palace, the one he maintained in Thespiae.

During the daylight hours, Psyche had the grand home to herself, but after sunset, Eros arrived. He permitted no candles or lamps as they sat beside each other and talked. These vespertine conversations were an intimacy, and they felt their way toward each other, despite the darkness, with confidence and conviction.

"I will give you anything your heart desires," Eros told her, "but you cannot see my face."

"I do not need to see you to know you," she replied.

Their bodies joined, and my seasoned son was smitten.

"I do not believe that you are a fiend," Psyche professed, her fingers stroking his feathers.

"As long as you believe in me, we can continue to live like this."

They were happy.

But Psyche's sisters were not happy, for the girls corresponded frequently, and Psyche's marriage, mysterious as it was, far surpassed theirs. One sister had married a man whose riches were a ruse masking bottomless debt. The other husband was impotent. Psyche, with her resplendent home and amorous paramour, inflamed their envy.

They retaliated by poisoning Psyche's mind with doubt. Doubt, you see, is surreptitious but sadistic.

Most of her sisters' conspiracies were easy to ignore:

What if he's a ghost?

I assure you, he's quite corporeal.

What if he has a daytime wife?

Days are when he sleeps; he's up all night with me.

But at last, they hit a nerve:

Psyche, our precious, our baby, our sweet! If you become pregnant, which will happen soon based upon your prolific lovemaking, what kind of creature will you birth? A half-human, half-dragon monstrosity? Will it kill you to deliver such a creature? What horrors may you unleash upon the world?

Psyche had felt my son in every way, she did not believe him a beast, but had the intoxication of passion tricked her? In the euphoria of connection, had she missed horns? A tail? She knew he had wings, but she imagined them like a dove's. Were they black like a crow's? Was he an agent of death?

For their potential future child, Psyche had to know.

So, as Eros slept beside her in postcoital bless, she lit a treacherous candle and returned to the bedside. What she discovered took her traitorous breath away. Her husband was no creature at all. He was celestial. Luminescent. Glorious. As she stared, struck by Eros's face and body, melting wax dripped onto his chest. Eros awoke in a fury.

"What have you done?" he cried.

Psyche's hands clasped over her mouth. "You are Eros," she exclaimed.

"Yes," he replied bitterly. "And now everything is ruined."

"Why?"

"You will want me for my name alone. You will question the validity of your feelings, forever wonder if I pricked you with an arrow."

"I—"

"Can you deny it?" Eros yelled. "Can you deny my identity changes everything?"

"I don't know!" Psyche rejoined. "I must think. I am trying to understand!"

"I would have given you the world, and you could not give me this."

"I worried for our future children," she wept. "I feared they would be monsters."

Eros shot from their bed. "No, Psyche. They would have been the children of a god."

"Would have been?" Psyche gripped her face, beginning to comprehend her grievous mistake, as Eros donned his clothing. "You are still my husband."

But my boy, who had never known betrayal, refused her contrition. "Get out of my home."

"I'm so sorry, I— "

"Go!"

Psyche fled, taking only her cloak, and entered the wilderness for a second time, sobbing.

"I don't know where she went, Mama," Eros wept. "And I worry for her, still."

Eros lay on his side, wings folded behind him. "Rest, my dear boy," I said, rubbing his chest in circles like I did when he was but a baby. My son shook, body racked with grief.

"Why did she have to look? Why wasn't what we had enough?"

"You are more than enough, Eros."

"She wasn't like you and me, Mama. She was better."

I recoiled, stung. Did he think so little of me, of us? He was my everything; how dare some child make him question that!

I mixed him a hot drink with valerian root and made him sip until his cries subsided into whimpers. "Will I ever heal, Mama?"

I thought of Ares, of the open wound salted by Aurora and Adonis.

"Yes," I lied, and I stayed by his side until he slipped into tortured sleep.

My poor boy. He had learned nothing from my stories. Here he was, committing all my mistakes anew. Falling for a mortal. Trusting a lover and losing his power. In the days that followed, I did my best to pacify him, but he was taciturn, snapping at the servants and impatient with the animals. He was even rude to me, and he retreated into himself, refusing to speak or share his feelings.

Did he not trust me anymore? Would I lose him like I lost everything else, Harmonia and Ares, Phobos and Deimos and Aglaia?

I felt our growing distance with an agony that bordered on fury.

And it is a unique fury that consumes a mother when somebody hurts her child.

If I ever met this Psyche, I would make sure she knew that pain.

22

THE KNOWN WORLD . . . AND BELOW

I DID NOT FIND Psyche, she found me.

After Eros threw her from his home, she spent one entire day and night weeping in the forest, cursing her stupidity and lack of faith. In no way did she blame her sisters, for Psyche's decision to light the candle was all her own. Under the morning sun, she dried her tears. Pity, Psyche realized, would not win back her husband, and she was not giving up on their marriage.

Try as she might, however, the mortal girl could not retrace her steps to Eros's place. She hiked and climbed with zeal, appealed to Zephyrus for his guidance, but only traversed circles. For the building did not exist anymore but had disappeared with its master's abandonment. It sank back into the earth from which it had been wrought, like land subducted. A fallen tribute.

Exhausted but implacable, Psyche had another idea. A terrifying one, but her best remaining option. Psyche journeyed to my temple in Paphos. Straight to the motherland. If I weren't so irate, I might have admired the gall.

"She will not leave," the priestesses informed me in irritated whispers, "until she can speak with you directly."

"I will handle it."

Huddled at the base of my statue lay a haggard figure in a torn and tattered cloak. Stringy dark hair spilled out from the sides of the hood. Her hands were extended on the floor before her, nails broken and caked in dirt.

And she reeked. I wrinkled my nose.

This was the girl that had undermined my own worship and then broken my son?

But when she raised her head at my arrival, I understood Eros's attraction. It was the damned hopefulness shining through her eyes, this belief that she had a chance, that this world and its people were decent, and fairness would prevail. I had never encountered someone so blithesome, so guileless.

It was an enchanting effect, but one I had no problem brushing off.

"Aphrodite, good goddess, most beautiful and beloved! I am Psyche, and though I do not presume you would know my name, I was recently wed to your son, Eros."

"Oh, was there a wedding?"

I was being vindictive. We both knew there had been none.

Psyche colored but did not otherwise falter. "Our union was not recognized before an altar or with witnesses, but we called each other 'husband' and 'wife' and swore it upon our bodies."

I sniffed. "I have little doubt my son has sworn many things on many bodies."

She persisted. "I wronged him, and he is upset. His anger is justified. But I would atone, righteous Aphrodite, if only you might help me."

I stiffened at her use of *righteous*. Nobody had ever called me thus; was she being facetious? But Psyche did not seem to speak with any irony. What game did she play?

"Why would I condescend to help the fool who betrayed my son?" I snapped.

Her features softened. "Have you never made a mistake?"

"I am infallible," I lied, my own missteps running through my mind like a herd of deer, one bad idea after another.

"Of course, forgive me." Psyche bowed her head. Again, that earnestness. She was rife with it. "I only wonder . . . is he here? Will you tell him I came? That I will wait my whole life for him, if need be?"

As the goddess of love, I've heard these melodramatic proclamations more times than any mortal could ever count, and yet . . .

No, Aphrodite. Harden yourself. Do not be touched by this fervent performance.

She will take him away. You will be alone again.

"Do you know how many women would shoulder every tribulation to marry Eros? Not only is he the handsomest of all immortals, but nobody can love like he can."

"I know," she acquiesced. "You are right. But I will not give up. I will fight for him." And I watched, with some dismay, as determination strengthened her posture, her face, her very essence.

I pursed my lips.

"Prove it."

Psyche met my gaze. Her eyes were deep brown, wide and long lashed. Lovely but surprisingly fierce. Not a doe, but a fox.

"There is nothing I would not suffer to regain his trust."

Vengeance offered up on a silver platter. I thought of my son's agony and all the deliciously creative ways I could avenge him. Psyche would eat her words.

WHAT FOLLOWED WAS a series of impossible tasks, each designed for Psyche to fail. She had anticipated physical torture, that I would whip her, but I've never been prone to conventional violence. No, I sought to break her irritatingly indomitable spirit.

I brought the girl to the storeroom of my temple on Cythera. It was filled to the brim with offerings, bags and barrels and clay jars. Psyche took it all in warily.

"I will give you the rest of today and the entire night to sort and separate every grain and seed of wheat, barley, and poppy in this room."

Though it quivered, Psyche lifted her chin. "I will prove my devotion by whatever means necessary."

I smiled without showing my teeth. Then clapped my hands. Every bag and barrel and clay jar burst and tore open, hissing and rolling, spilling seemingly endless contents into one massive heap, taller than either of us, to a height brushing the ceiling.

Psyche hid her gasp behind her hands, but horror consumed her face.

"I shall see you in the morning, my dear."

I left, locking the door behind me with a chuckle. She would weep, she would fail, and she would go away. I would never tell Eros any of what transpired.

Psyche was just a fling. Eventually, my son would forget her, and we would return to the camaraderie we had always known.

But when I returned the next day at dawn, to my absolute displeasure, Psyche sat cross-legged beside three large piles of perfectly sorted wheat, barley, and poppy. She had the wherewithal not to gloat, but did greet me with a question:

"Now may I see my husband?"

It was implausible! How did she accomplish it? Stewing and steaming, I immediately threw down a second gauntlet.

"Silly girl, this was only the first trial. Come along, your second task awaits."

She did not complain. Psyche rose, though fatigue tugged at her eyes, and she followed me into the unknown.

This time I flew Psyche far into the fields of Thrinacia. "Do you see them?" I asked, pointing to a shimmering aura in the distance. "Down by the river graze Helios's flock of golden sheep. Bring me a tuft of their wool. They are unguarded; it should be quite straightforward."

Of course it wouldn't be. The dreadful beasts were vicious, their bites poisonous. Psyche would sooner be mauled than touch one by hand.

"I have until morning?" she confirmed, and I tried not to admire her resolve.

"Yes."

I would not stay and watch—I did not want to imply I found any of this worthy of my attention—so I guided my chariot away, searching for a secluded spot where I could wait, unnoticed.

I found a spring, so similar—too similar—to Ares's sacred space, and reined my chariot to a halt.

I stepped to the ground, removed my sandals, and remembered Ares after Drakon's death, as vulnerable as he'd ever been. We had cared for each other then. And it hurt even more to consider this: Would Ares attempt impossible tasks for me? Would I for him? Here was Psyche, some mortal princess of barely two decades, and nothing could deter her from my son.

There was a time when Ares and I fought for each other, as well. Why had we stopped?

"Where are you now, my love?" I whispered.

I sat beside the pool and considered my reflection. Had I become a landmark, something that remains the same while everything around it changes? For the first time, I wished my lived experience could reflect in my bearing, for it angered me to see the same stupid face when, inside, I was so different. And no matter the ugly things I'd done or would do, I would always be beautiful. I splashed the water's surface, letting my visage ripple and distort, better suiting the mess I had become.

An unfaithful wife, a spurned lover, a mother deeply jealous of her child's love.

For wasn't that what this was all about? My fear that Eros wouldn't need me if he had Psyche?

In the morning, I found Psyche standing exactly where I had left her, a handful of pure gold fluff ready to be presented.

"Now may I see my husband?"

Exasperated, I hurled the wool into the river. "All you have proven is that my tasks are too simple! What is Eros worth to you?"

"Everything," she replied steadily.

Why, girl? I longed to scream, to shake her thin shoulders. *Why do you believe it will work out for you when it never did for me?*

We boarded my chariot for a third time, and I drove us farther than ever before, to the Black Water in the mountains of Arcadia, where the River Styx begins its descent into the underworld. Psyche shivered beside me, as much from the dropping temperature as from rising fear.

I lifted my hand, and a crystal goblet materialized between my fingers. "Take this cup and fill it. For I am quite parched."

She studied the gushing waterfall before her, the steep rocks made slippery with hateful water and grime, and her despair permeated the ether between us. The odds that Psyche would miraculously reach the source and retrieve a cup of water were slim at best. And if she did accomplish that part of the task, she would almost certainly slip on her return, either to be crushed by the cascade or scooped up by the current and dropped into the underworld.

"As always," I purred, "you have until morning."

Once again, I walked away, but this time I hid closer, for I needed to know how she was achieving these feats. Tucked behind a fir tree, I watched, utterly astonished, as an eagle flew from out of nowhere to perch beside Psyche. I could not hear what was said, but the bird clasped the goblet in its talons, flew directly to the waterfall, and returned to Psyche with a full cup, not spilling a drop.

No ordinary eagle, to say the least.

I stormed from my hiding place and the eagle screamed, taking rapid flight.

"Such blatant treachery!" I cried. "You thought you could deceive me? Who comes to your aid, girl?"

Psyche's lips clamped shut.

"You weren't so loyal when it came to your husband!" I sneered. "Tell me, or I give my word that you will never see Eros again in your lifetime."

I could sense the moral struggle within her. Would she betray her savior to gain my trust? Finally, Psyche sighed, relenting. "Hestia sent an army of ants to help me sort the grain and seed. Artemis's voice came to me as a river reed and advised me to collect wool from the thicket of briars where the sheep slept." She shrugged. "And the eagle was Athena's."

Hestia, Artemis, and Athena. The three maiden goddesses of Olympus. Did they interfere out of support for Psyche and Eros or their aversion to me? Oh, Alexandros, sometimes I felt that everyone was against me.

"I was going to release you after this," I lied, "but now I must add a fourth and final task, one that cannot be subverted." I took the crystal goblet, dumped out the water, and changed it into a platinum box, with a shine and surface so perfect, the sunlight refracted against it in blinding rays. "Take this to the underworld and ask its queen to fill it with some of her vivacity. You may say I am in sore need after administering to my despondent and debilitated son."

Besides Hermes, no Olympians were permitted in the realm of the dead. This time, there would be no divine assistance, and Persephone hated me even more than the immortal virgins did. After Adonis's death, she would never consent to part with her beauty on my account. But Psyche knew none of this history and had no choice in the matter. She accepted the box and the mission with the same dogged resilience I had come to expect from her.

"And if I do this, you will return me to my husband?"

"Yes, but I cannot promise he will love you again."

"All I need is a chance."

I figured it was over. For all intents and purposes, Psyche was dead. Even if she survived the journey to Hades's palace—Charon, the ferryman, and the three-headed dog Cerberus—Persephone would smite her down the moment Psyche mentioned my name.

With only the tiniest of misgivings, I returned to Olympus and my son.

I BARELY MADE IT through the front door of my palace before Apollo was grabbing my arm and pulling me back outside.

"Where is the girl, Aphrodite? What have you done with her?"

"I hardly know what you mean," I bluffed. "There are so very many girls."

Apollo's face hardened with condescension. "I've searched everywhere for Psyche, and she cannot be found. I know you've done something."

I scoffed. "Don't tell me you are infatuated with her, too?"

"Your son is woebegone, or have you failed to notice?"

"Of course I noticed that *my* son is hurt! He is the only child I have left."

"And this is how you treat him?" My friend raised his arms incredulously. "He loves her."

"She shattered his heart!"

"Yes, but hearts can heal. They could recover, but you deny them the chance."

"He is recuperating quite well here with me."

Apollo shook his head, lips curled. "I know what this is. Eros can't have Psyche because you can't have Ares."

Apollo might be upset with my behavior, but I was furious with his assessment. My hands clenched into fists. "Remove yourself from my house and my life. Immediately!"

"Gladly. But should my Aphrodite—the one who can be irreverent and frustrating but believes in love above all else—return, let her know I called."

I slammed the door in his face.

ALEXANDROS, HAVE YOU already been told how this story ends?

That persistent little gnat of a human passed through all the underworld's horrors and reached the queen of the dead's residence. Persephone, recognizing Psyche's arrival as an opportunity for revenge, filled the box with sleep, not effervescence. She assumed I would open it, expecting a boost to my vanity, and would instead fall unconscious, only to awake once somebody who truly loved me kissed me back to life.

Persephone, the spiteful bitch, figured there was nobody who did.

But Psyche, whether by accident or curiosity, opened the box before she could deliver it to me, and immediately collapsed into a coma that none could wake her from.

If I had known, I would have moved her body somewhere remote and left her for the moss and mushrooms, but as it was, Zephyrus discovered her first, and he raced straight to his friend Eros. Of course, my son was unaware of Psyche's hardships; all throughout his convalescence, he had assumed she'd returned home to her family and had moved on, possibly with a human prince. I never corrected him.

His conversation with Zephyrus was enlightening to say the least.

Eros leapt from his bed and flew to Psyche's side. He did not kiss only her lips, but her forehead and cheeks, her eyelids, the parting of her hair. After missing her so ardently, regretting deeply how he had cast her out, he was moved to tears by the trials she had willingly endured to win back his favor.

"I love you, Psyche."

Even before her eyes opened, Psyche smiled.

They held each other, expressed their remorse, and composed new vows. Psyche confirmed Zephyrus's report of my actions, and my son, livid with me, brought his wife straight to Olympus, to Zeus himself, and petitioned for Psyche's immortality.

"Please, my king, Psyche has proven herself a true hero, and with her steady presence, I will cause far less trouble for our kind."

Zeus, tickled by the opportunity to defame and thwart me, quickly threw his favor behind my son. "Eros, your mother's behavior has always been deplorable, but I never thought she would deceive her own child." He motioned to an attendant. "Bring Aphrodite here, immediately, to witness my decree, that there will be no question of Psyche's protection."

I arrived at the spectacle shortly after, to Eros's glare and Zeus's oafish grin. I sighed heavily.

"Your persecution of this innocent ends today, Aphrodite."

"She consented to my challenges. This was not persecution."

"You sent her to the underworld!"

I gaped, placed a hand over my heart. "And it's my fault Persephone played a vicious trick?"

Zeus's brows drew together. "Do not shift the blame."

"You could have killed her, Mother!"

I flinched. Eros never called me *Mother*, always *Mama*.

"I—"

"I was tested, yes," interrupted Psyche, and all heads spun in her direction. "Any mother deserves to know the merit—and mettle—of one who wishes to share her child." She walked to the center of our triangle, regarding us all with her arms lowered, palms upturned. "I sought out Aphrodite, and hasn't she granted my wish? I am reunited with my husband, in more love and with more appreciation than ever."

Psyche came toward me and bowed her head. "Thank you."

I glanced at Eros. His glower softened into a frown, suspicious, still, but his foul temper assuaged. Psyche had spared me, saved me from my son's ire and Zeus's plans for my public humiliation after everything I had put her through. Oh, I was truly wretched.

When Psyche looked up, our eyes met. I found in hers no resentment, only hope.

"You are . . . most welcome," I replied, somewhat stiffly.

She beamed.

"Psyche," pronounced Zeus, holding up a goblet. "Drink of this ambrosia and join our ranks as the goddess of soul."

Psyche accepted the drink, and as she sipped, a butterfly flitted inside the hall and lit upon her shoulder. Thin, almost transparent wings sprouted from Psyche's spine. She flapped them once, twice, full of joy, as Eros watched proudly.

And that, Alexandros, is how I received a daughter-in-law.

If I am honest, I've grown past tolerating Psyche. I like the girl—even her annoyingly incessant optimism. She makes my son incandescent with happiness, and she gave me a granddaughter, Hedone, who is even more unruly than her father was in his heyday. If I have to share my son with someone, it might as well be her.

I was outmaneuvered. It doesn't happen often, so respect is due.

23

ATHENS

I HAD BUILT A life around my son, and now he was building one with his wife and daughter. It's a common trope, older generations ceding their place to the new, but I was hardly an elder. Still beautiful, still full of dreams. I was bored, a bit lonely, and seeking pleasure again.

I began to travel, engaging in a quest to visit all my temples and shrines. It was an exciting time, an era of great passions and escapades. Chariots raced toward the sun; Heracles labored. Kings heard prophecies that threatened their reign and sent their children to distant lands or hid them in golden boxes. Mortals challenged Olympians to contests of skill. Horses flew, and Gorgon heads fell.

And, oh, how the city-states fought! Argos versus Sparta. Athens versus Sparta. Minos versus Athens. The seven champions against Thebes. I wondered how Ares managed . . .

It had been so long since he'd seen eternity in my lavender eyes.

I am sure I sound half-mad, but sometimes I thought I heard his voice, in the wind, in the lull—that gasp—just before sleep. No message, just my name.

"Ares," I'd whisper back.

These strange encounters made me restless. Perhaps that's why I roamed so frequently during this time; I was looking for him.

Of all the human cities, no place shone brighter than Athens, the central diamond in the mortal crown. I spent little time there, however, because Athena was the city's patron. She and I were diametrically opposed in every respect—she liked administration and chastity; I preferred to enjoy myself. As Zeus's favorite child, Athena held prestige. Those of us who refused to feign or flatter did well to avoid her.

Poseidon also struggled with his niece, for he'd wanted Athens as his own, but lost the patronage to Athena in a humiliating contest. I mention Poseidon because I encountered him there once, as I visited a construction built in my honor by King Aegeus. Athena might not want me in her city, but its people still did, and so my temple was raised on a hill west of the agora, a short walk away from Athena's massive monument to herself on the Acropolis.

By my request, the priests and priestesses had departed for the night, and I stood alone among the marble and hard blue limestone, savoring a serene moment in this otherwise spirited city.

"Finally, some fun arrives in Athens."

I whipped around. Zeus's brother stood in the doorway, wearing none of his regalia. Without it, I noticed details I'd previously missed: the arch of his eyebrows, the one overly sharp canine, slightly crooked.

I always found Poseidon the handsomest of the three brothers.

"Athena knows as much about fun as a fish knows about flying."

He laughed. It was a nice one, when it didn't come from spite or snark. "We are all quite aware."

"Are you here to see my new place? Or just to share our mutual dislike of Athena?"

"Both, if it would please you."

I slid my arm into his. "Come along."

I showed him my favorite mosaics, pointed out the style of pillars, and he provided the obligatory compliments, as if I had anything to do with the labor or skill required for their completion. We paused on a balcony, and I gestured to the sun setting over the western agora.

"The Athenians are building a temple to Hephaestus right there. I'll be able to see it from nearly every window."

"Under Athena's orders?"

"Naturally."

"My niece is vituperative and underhanded," he related, gazing into the dusk with grim acceptance.

"I refuse to let it bother me."

"Good." He nodded, pleased by my response. "She wanted to be goddess of war, you know."

I perked up. Poseidon noted my interest and continued.

"Oh yes, Zeus denied her request, perhaps the only time he has done so, for though Athena possesses a keen strategic mind, nobody, mortal or immortal, can fight like Ares."

"So I have heard."

"You've never seen him in battle?" Poseidon was shocked.

"I haven't seen him in years," I replied tightly.

"Not many of us have," admitted Poseidon. "But Zeus tells me that Ares has been fucking and fighting his way across Greece."

My hands, in need of something to grab, clasped together. "Charming," I managed to say.

"He was a fool to let you go," murmured Poseidon.

And I was a fool, too, allowing Poseidon's flirtation to soothe my aching heart, but I needed a reminder that I was desirable. Alexandros, sometimes a woman just wants to feel good.

"In his defense," I quipped, "he takes many blows to the head in his line of work."

Poseidon laughed again. "Clearly!"

My hands unclasped, and one reached for Poseidon's.

"The men on Rhodes," I began. "Your sons. Maybe I overreacted."

He shrugged. "They were rude to you."

"Did you ever dig them up?"

"I moved them to a cave. They cause me less trouble now."

Poseidon and I ended up at the fountain house, a separate building to the side of the temple, where frescoes of nude, cavorting lovers covered the walls. As the braziers were still lit, the warm water sent steam rising from its surface in a scented, unmistakably seductive fog.

Perhaps too much inhalation explains what I did next.

"I never thanked you," I told Poseidon, "for paying the adulterer's penalty."

The tip of his tongue grazed his lower lip. "Is that why you brought me in here?"

Had it always been my intention? I think we both knew it, both felt that something laced the air between us, like the earthy smell before and after a thunderstorm.

"I'd like to experience the god of the sea in water." Still clothed, I walked down the steps into the bath. My dress clung to my body. "If you'd like to accept that as gratitude, so be it."

Poseidon removed his tunic and followed. The waters swirled around us. Hot and wet, we made a part of Athena's city our own.

SOON AFTER, I was called to Athens again. Not by Poseidon, but by my forever foe, his unbearable brother.

"Zeus has summoned all the Olympians to court in Athens," announced Hermes, the faithful messenger, dropping into my refuge on Cyprus.

"Why Athens?"

"It is the scene of the crime."

I hesitated, just for a moment, wondering if Zeus knew about my tryst with Poseidon, who was married. I dreaded another scandal.

"This is all very cryptic," I said dryly, "and ostensibly meant to be exciting, but I'd rather know now what is afoot."

"I'm not at liberty to say."

I rolled my eyes. "Then I'm not at liberty to attend. Tell Zeus I have plans to wash my hair today."

"Put it in a braid."

"I'd rather not take fashion advice from you, Hermes."

"Aphrodite," he exclaimed, "out of respect for our history together—"

"We have no history together," I corrected.

"Our *brief* history together, I think you should reconsider."

I shook my head, took a pointed seat on my couch, and folded my arms across my chest, but Hermes leaned forward and yanked me up by my arm.

"How dare you!" I exclaimed, slapping him away.

"Enough with the antics!" he cried, nostrils flaring, and I admittedly enjoyed his exasperation. "I'm doing you a favor!"

"Ha."

"If you do not come with me now, Aphrodite, your voice will not be heard."

"Nobody listens to me anyway," I snipped.

"I don't know why I care, but I do. You need to come with me." Hermes's typically playful mouth straightened into a hard line. "Ares is on trial for murder."

MURDER. MURDEROUS. MURDERER.

Ares had told me once how he despised all variations, all implications, of the word.

"Soldiers kill on the battlefield, but they do not commit murder. Death in war is expected under the rules of engagement. Both sides understand the stakes."

"Then what is 'murder'?" I pressed.

"A killing, off the battle grounds, out of malice."

We lay beside each other in the bed of my old Cyprus home. "But how can soldiers kill if they carry no ill will?"

"They are following orders. They fight for their king, their kin, their city."

"Yes, and they fight against an enemy, whom they hate," I argued.

Ares rolled away from me. "This is why I'll never take you with me."

"Ares!" I cried, pulling him back. "I'm only trying to understand."

"I have accepted being a killer, Aphrodite, don't make me a murderer, too."

It was this conversation I recalled the day Adonis died, when I called Ares a murderer.

Had Ares killed another mortal in an unfair duel? Would I defend him if he had?

Or was I needed to offer evidence against him? If so, would I?

Too many questions when I needed to move.

I left with Hermes, grabbing only a favored seafoam-green shawl. Though I nagged relentlessly for more information, he refused. "I've already said too much."

"Then why tell me anything?"

Hermes stared ahead. "Because while it probably meant nothing to you, that night after Harmonia's wedding was one of the best I've ever had."

I did not pester him again.

The Olympians convened in no building, but beneath the sky, on a large outcropping south of the agora. Zeus had re-created the Hall of the Gods on the flat top of rock: All our ridiculously embellished chairs were present in their traditional arrangement. Only one was empty.

Ares knelt in the dirt at the center of our congregation, chained at the ankles, wrists clamped in manacles behind his back—I recognized Hephaestus's work immediately. Blood, which I doubted belonged to Ares, splattered his tunic. He'd grown out his hair since I'd last seen him; it fell below his chin in deep brown waves. And he'd shaved. I'd never seen his face so exposed before.

Who was this man, who could be so familiar and so strange at the same time?

And why did his presence continue to galvanize me?

Do not react, I reminded myself. *Give nothing away.*

As I took my seat, my eyes wandered over our disaster of a family, all connected through some sort of bloodline—some looser than others—but also by generations of betrayals and alliances. Would Ares, regardless of what he had done, receive a fair trial? Zeus and his brothers and sisters would surely vote in concordance; it was the next generation—and me—that mattered.

Though Eros was not a part of the court, I did have family here now, someone I hadn't before. Before he took his own seat, Dionysus approached me and kissed my cheek.

"I will follow your lead," he murmured in my ear, and I squeezed his arm. He lifted the jug of wine in his hand, head cocked to the side in question, but I declined. I enjoy a strong drink, but today required sobriety.

Zeus cleared his throat, and any stragglers rushed to their positions. Side conversations ceased.

"Today is a sorry one in our Olympian history," he said solemnly. "Since the overthrow of the brutes who came before us, I have tried to cultivate an existence based upon civility and nobility. Behavior appropriate to our prestige."

If I had accepted Dionysus's wine, surely I would have spit it out right then.

"Imagine, then, the anguish I experienced when my brother calls upon me, aggrieved, for my own son has killed his. Not by accident, not in an ordained combat, but with cold, malicious intent." Zeus performed a mock show of grief, clutching at the neck of his tunic as if he would tear it—which he wouldn't; it was far too splendid a material. "Justice must be served, but even a king cannot choose between the demands of his brother and the defense of his son. I have no choice but to invoke the assistance of my court."

Ares did not flinch. His spine remained as straight as an arrow, even on his knees, and though he made eye contact with no one, he did not lower his head.

"Father," began Athena, "your wisdom commends you, and I welcome you all to my city, the unfortunate site of this most wretched event. This tribunal, in its intent to be virtuous and ensure a fair result, must hear testimony. Otherwise, we vote for condemnation or acquittal based on gossip and previous bias."

"Wise words from my wisest child," commended Zeus, and in a mock display of humility, Athena closed her eyes.

Apollo rolled his.

"I will speak first," fumed Poseidon, pointing at Ares. "That animal slaughtered my son! Your wild dog has gone unchecked for too long, Zeus! Put a collar on him or I will!"

The crowd broke out in tittering, histrionic gasps, and clucked tongues, forcing Zeus to raise his hands in a useless demand for peace. I said nothing but bristled. The "Ares is an animal" discourse was wearisome. Unlike Zeus, Ares had never had sex with a woman as a bull.

"Enough," interceded Hades in his phlegmatic way. "Provide facts, Poseidon, not theatrics."

Poseidon scowled at his brother but steadied himself. "Yesterday, Ares entered this city, sword in hand, and decapitated my son, Halirrhothios."

Hestia squealed; Hera scowled. Demeter tsked and shook her head.

"Unfathomable!" they murmured. "Unconscionable!"

"Demonic!"

"Disgusting!"

My own stomach turned over, imagining the force of hate required to slice a head from a body, but I was far more bothered by the posturing of my peers.

"My sincerest condolences to dear Amphitrite," I needled, cutting through the noise. "A mother outliving her child is a mother come undone."

An awkward, uncomfortable pause ensued, for everyone heard

what I left unsaid: Amphitrite was not Halirrhothios's mother. This child was born of one of Poseidon's many affairs, another nymph. Poseidon had a thing for them.

Poseidon regarded me with a slightly dropped jaw, and I returned his disbelief with a shrug. Did he truly think our one night in a hot bath was so life-changing as to forever earn my loyalty?

Men are so delicate.

"Ares," said Athena, redirecting the conversation. "You have heard Poseidon's accusation. Can you offer a defense?"

"No."

Appalled murmurs followed. *Oh, Ares,* I thought miserably, but also proudly. *You obstinate ass.*

"Then you entered Athens with the explicit purpose of killing Halirrhothios?"

"Yes."

Poseidon slammed both fists against the arms of his throne. "This trial is unnecessary. He admits to murder. Punish him accordingly!"

More exclamations followed, gods and goddesses all shouting over one another. Hestia broke into tears.

"Ares," said Apollo, a touch imploringly, "there must be a reason for your actions. Make sense of this for us."

Of those assembled, only I spoke the language of Ares's body, and I read his emotions in every clenched muscle, every twitch of jaw or brow. Ares was not afraid of retribution; he was still fuming.

"I removed his head from his body because he might survive if I only removed the part I came for."

Hermes slapped a hand over his mouth, but everyone heard him giggle.

"You call me an animal, fine. But it was a monster that raped my daughter Alcippe."

Was I more jarred to hear Ares had a daughter or that he'd uttered the word so few dared to speak?

Rape.

The gods in the tribunal stiffened in outrage, but also in defense. Olympians are fluent in euphemisms, and the obsequious poets—almost entirely male—have followed that lead. *He took her* is the norm, repeated over hearth fires and etched in print. *He plucked her.*

"She bled for days," spit Ares, "nearly dying from her wounds. If she had perished, would we be here? Would anyone care? I killed the bastard and have no regrets. I would kill him again."

Ares loves this girl. The cracks in my own character deepened with jealousy. Who was her mother? Was it a great love affair? A fling? When did they meet? Where? My mind spiraled, and I needed to pay attention.

"Is Poseidon's child more important than Ares's?" questioned Athena. "Because one is a man and the other a woman?"

"There is no proof!" shouted Poseidon. "And Halirrhothios is not here to defend himself against some loose girl's defamation!"

Chains clanked and strained as Ares lunged at Poseidon—Hestia shrieked—but Hephaestus's work held true. Poseidon laughed and shot me a hard look. "My nephew has a soft spot for whores."

"Is that directed at me, Poseidon?" I snapped back. "If you'd like to call me a 'whore,' by all means, go ahead." I leaned forward in my seat. "But Alcippe is a survivor."

Lightning cracked above our heads, followed immediately by a subsequent roll of thunder. Zeus stood in the space between his son and his brother. "We did not meet today for a vocabulary lesson!" He appealed to his favorite. "Athena, summarize our findings for this assembly."

She cleared her throat. "Poseidon claims that Ares killed his son Halirrhothios, deliberately and without mercy. Ares himself professes guilt. However, he counterclaims that Halirrhothios . . ." Athena stumbled here, unsure of how her diction might betray her loyalties. "Lay with his daughter Alcippe against her will—allegedly—and Ares's actions were just."

Poseidon snorted.

"I cannot vote," proclaimed Zeus, "but I will hear yours now. My fine Olympians, consider these accounts and tell me: Do you condemn Ares for murder, to which he has readily confessed, and demand his immediate exile from our number? Or do you acquit him of the charge?"

"I vote to condemn," replied Poseidon, so quickly that spittle flew from his mouth. "Send Ares to some distant, less civilized land that better appreciates his violent nature."

"As the aggrieved," interceded Athena, "you cannot vote. It's unethical. Neither can Ares."

Poseidon appealed to Zeus with incredulous exasperation, but Zeus acceded to his daughter's point. "Athena speaks rationally, as always."

Hades, the dutiful brother, quickly picked up Poseidon's proverbial trident. "Then I will cast the first *official* vote for Ares's guilt."

And so, down the line, each Olympian voted almost exactly as I predicted. Hestia, Demeter, and Hephaestus all in favor of Ares's exile. Apollo, Artemis, and Athena in support of his acquittal.

"Ares killed Halirrhothios, but it was righteous," rationalized Athena. "It was not murder."

Alexandros, you may wonder at Athena's decision, but despite my tense relationship with her, she and her half brother shared a martial mind. There was a mutual respect there. And remember, her hatred for Poseidon was long-lasting and far-reaching. Sometimes a mutual enemy creates a stronger bond than an actual relationship.

Let me tell you the surprises.

First, Hera.

"I, too, am torn between a brother and a son, but unlike Zeus, I must choose." Hera's hands were held firmly together in her lap. "My son has broken the bonds of family. I cast my vote for his exile."

My lip curled in disgust. There is nothing Eros could do that would turn me away from him. Nothing. Maybe that makes me evil, I don't care. I am his mother, always.

But perhaps it was Hera's callous display that turned Hermes, for he voted in Ares's favor.

"He's a little beast, but he's *our* little beast," quipped the messenger god. "Ares is innocent."

Dionysus, without even waiting for my signal, agreed.

"It is five for permanent exile and five against," announced Zeus, stating the obvious. All heads turned in my direction. "How do you proceed, Aphrodite?"

Poseidon's eyes bored into me, demanding I recognize him. To vote against him now would create a true enemy. I already knew Ares would never appeal to me. He would sooner accept punishment than beg. And a solitary life away would not destroy him. The stain on his honor might.

Ares, I hate you. For the death of Adonis, I called you "murderer." For abandoning me after our affair was revealed, for accusing me of using my power against you. I hate that you lie in other beds, sire other children. That you cherish this mortal daughter more than the one I bore.

But I still loved him, right or wrong.

"Ares is guilty"—Athena gasped, Poseidon grinned—"of loving his daughter too much. If every girl were so lucky, this world would be a significantly safer place. I am the goddess of love, and a woman who hemorrhages for days was not loved but assaulted. I vote for Ares's acquittal."

Poseidon was livid. I could not tell if Zeus was relieved or disappointed by the outcome, but he clapped once and announced the trial concluded. He signaled to Hermes, who brought forth a jug, and to Hephaestus, who, with much grumbling, unlocked the chains. Free at last, Ares rubbed his wrists.

"Put forth your hands, Ares, and we will wash them clean."

Zeus poured the jug over Ares's outstretched fingers, and water splattered in the dirt, sending up dust.

"This trial is closed."

Those who had spoken against Ares huddled near Poseidon or

made a quick, offended exit. The rest loitered, unsure of what to say. *Congratulations? I'm happy for you?* Both fell flat considering the gruesome circumstances.

Dionysus found me first. "Dinner?" he asked. "I know a wonderful spot in town for music and wine. I already sent word to Eros and Psyche."

I murmured something, but my attention was elsewhere. Ares stood alone at the edge of the hilltop. If I joined him, would he push me over?

As you well know by now, I've always been one to take a risk.

I abandoned Dionysus in the middle of our conversation and walked to Ares's side. The city of Athens spread below us in all its human complexity, where, at that same moment, other lovers might be coming together or breaking apart, where some families were fighting while others laughed. We were a microcosm of them, not the other way around.

"He broke her nose," said Ares, gazing into the horizon, "and her teeth. She fought back, used the moves I had taught her because I saw how small and appealing she was, and I feared this might happen. Halirrhothios beat her and raped her repeatedly, enamored of his own brutality."

"Shall we journey to the underworld and behead him again?"

Ares turned his head toward me, his mouth curving upward the barest bit.

"I am so tired, Aphrodite. I only wish to lay my head on your chest and sleep."

"And I only wish to feel your weight on my heart."

I laced my fingers into his, and he let me.

The other Olympians gradually departed, baffled, as always, by love and war, hand in hand.

We stood silently, in our mutual understanding of the world's misunderstanding. They would never get what we were.

24

MILOS

Second Century BCE

ALEXANDROS HAS LONG since abandoned his stylus. His sketch lies forgotten on the table.

"Did you . . . ?" he asks.

She laughs. "Did we fuck each other senseless on the mountaintop?"

The artist blushes.

"No, I had dinner plans with my family." Aphrodite turns the beehive over in her hand. "The animosity between Ares and me had ebbed. That was enough."

"Ebbed, but not over."

She nods.

"Once, when he was a child, Eros wandered too close to a hive in a hollowed-out tree. He was stung, and ran to me crying, his chubby finger swollen. 'It was a snake with wings!' he cried as I removed the stinger." She sets the hive on the floor. "Tell me who you love, Alexandros. Is it sweet or does it sting?"

He sighs. Is he obligated to share since she has told him so much? Does he want to?

Yes. The goddess of love herself sits before him, expressing interest in his common life. Only an ingrate would bypass such an opportunity.

"Since I left Antioch, there has been one person most dear to me. His name is Timon."

She smiles and leans forward. "Timon," Aphrodite echoes warmly, like it's the most exquisite name to ever grace her lips.

He likes hearing her speak it, for it is his favorite name, after all. "Timon is a fisherman, like his father and his grandfather and so on. And my father and grandfather and so on, albeit on the other side of the sea. We come from the same stock, but I . . . differed."

"You were called to art."

"Yes. But it can be difficult for others to appreciate. Timon understands hard work, for fishermen rise early in the morning, but Timon also enjoys the afterward. He loves the tavern, the camaraderie of others. He wants me there with him, but I am preoccupied. I cannot leave a piece when it needs me. For me, the job is not over when the sun has set."

She nods, understanding, and so he keeps talking.

"Timon wants more of me. He does not relate to my moods. He cannot comprehend the demands of what I do. When I am creating, I do not care about meals or sleep. I forget to bathe . . ." His voice drifts off; he is embarrassed.

Aphrodite rises and takes an apple from a basket. Alexandros isn't sure it was there before. With a knife he also does not recognize, she slices the fruit in half and holds it up for him to see. There is the shape of a star flower at its center.

"Creation," she says, "begins with a seed. Creation is its own kind of love. To nurture a seed into fruit takes devotion."

"Yes," he agrees. "Yes. My art needs my time and my energy."

Her mouth twists: She is thinking. Then she lifts the apple in a pose. "Maybe this is what I hold, Alexandros, for this apple also comes into the next part of my story."

Alexandros retrieves his stylus.

"I want to talk to you about creation and love. And I want you to listen closely."

"I am," he promises. "I will."

Part IV

A HALVED APPLE

Aphrodite Genetyllis, mother
Aphrodite Pandemos, for all
Aphrodite Epistrophia, of the return

25

BOEOTIA AND CYPRUS

HEARTBREAK REVEALS YOUR depth.

Healing illuminates your boundaries.

After Ares's trial, I felt strong. Secure. When my vote mattered, I made the correct choice. I was proud of how I'd acted, and grateful to be at peace with Ares. I saw myself with greater clarity and understood, better than ever, the dynamic range of my own emotions, of what I would—or wouldn't—accept from others. It must be so difficult for you mortals with only one lifetime in which to understand yourself! I required dozens.

My profane hunger to demonstrate my power was sated, and I found myself almost averse to retribution. I wasn't remorseful, per se, but I had seen enough—caused enough—wicked justice and vowed myself to more philanthropic endeavors.

"I am entering a new era," I announced to Apollo. "An age of almsgiving."

He raised an eyebrow.

"Bring me the unrequited loves, the heartsick, the lonely, and I shall heal the world!"

"Are you well, Aphrodite?"

"I am in my prime!"

And to prove it, I went in search of projects.

I helped Hippomenes marry the huntress Atalanta, and bestowed beauty on a giant's daughters. I saved an Argonaut from the Sirens, and gifted Ariadne one of my most fabulous crowns.

"Apollo!" I called, entering his home on Olympus. "Come congratulate me on my charity! Perhaps you could compose a paean to my altruism?"

I listed all my accomplishments, but he scoffed. "None of those required great skill or effort."

I pursed my lips, then set forth to find a more dire situation in need of my guidance.

His name was Pygmalion, an artist like yourself, from Cyprus, my own dear island. He chose celibacy for two reasons. The first being his overriding passion for art, and the second, his dislike of women.

Alexandros, you do not desire women, yet you do not despise them. Pygmalion proclaimed his distaste to all who would listen, and many who would rather not. He monitored the female Cypriots like a hen, nipping and clucking, fussy with judgment and reprimand. The girl children were too tumultuous, too messy. The teenage ones too volatile. And grown women? Too domineering in their role as mothers—creators who rival the artisans. Prostitutes—both the pornai and the hetairai—left him scarlet-faced and speechless.

But Pygmalion lied to himself. He didn't hate women; he was obsessed with them.

As I watched this misguided man, I realized that his discomfort originated in overwhelming desire. He was terrified of women, petrified of rejection, and thus he never tried to engage. Sometimes it is easier to be the first to hate, the first to say no. Then nobody will laugh when you fail.

He would be my greatest challenge yet.

At this time, Pygmalion was working on a grand commission, a statue of a woman to place in an aristocrat's andrōn, which I may have played a hand in arranging; Pygmalion had yet to carve the female form from stone. He almost turned the offer down, but the price offered could not be so easily ignored. The money would allow him years of freedom to work on whatever he liked. Pygmalion accepted. At night, as he worked in a studio much like this one, I whispered in his ears an assortment of observations.

Look, Pygmalion, at all the ways she is special!

Her hips, so important, for the womb they support and the toddlers they will carry.

Hands, for comforting and healing, for soothing.

Lips for conversation, but also for connection.

Eyes that will see you, notice you in return.

Legs for walking by your side.

Pygmalion worked feverishly on the project, which was typical, but he also began to bring his piece little offerings, which was very strange. First a flower in bloom, plucked from a nearby meadow, then a shawl he purchased at the agora. Jugs of water and wine. When he cooked his meals, he put together a second plate and laid it on a small table at her side. He spoke to her, of his childhood, his own abusive parents, the teasing and name-calling. He asked her questions, frustratingly rhetorical, for he wanted to know her in return.

It was a type of madness, certainly, but at its core was care.

What had begun as devotion to a project, an object, had transcended.

And because he loved her, he gave her a name, not a title.

Galatea.

She was complete, but Pygmalion stalled, making false apologies to his benefactor and threadbare excuses for the delay. He tore his hair, and when the warm summer months brought the Aphrodisia festival, he surrendered.

I wonder what it took for him to step inside my temple that day. To offer milk and honey upon my altar, to fall to his knees and pray.

"Generous Aphrodite, I have avoided you even longer than the truth. And in that sorry time, I have made countless mistakes, speaking and acting with the meanest of minds. Looking back, I see more to reproach than commend." Tears spilled over onto his cheeks. "Is it too late for me to change?"

"That depends," I sang, my voice emanating from the stone before him. "Can you forgive yourself?"

"I can," he insisted. "I can definitely try."

"Then anything is possible."

He cleared his throat, wet his lips; his fumbling made me smile.

"My dormant heart has awoken, Aphrodite," he finally stuttered. "And it beats for the possibility of one wish."

Then Pygmalion whispered to me what I already knew.

It takes a strong man to admit fault, and an even stronger one to start again. I blew one precious kiss upon the wind to his home. It entered through the open window and settled into the marble, slowly, steadily permeating.

When Pygmalion awoke the next morning, Galatea stood before him.

"Galatea?" he asked, shaking like a leaf.

"Good morning."

She spoke hesitantly, walked hesitantly, so he jumped to his feet and guided her tenderly to the table. Over a breakfast he prepared, Galatea took her first bite of sweet bread, drank her first sip of water. And they were not strangers to each other. She answered all the questions he had posed during her sculpting, for she was an excellent listener. Pygmalion sat, unspeaking and ignoring his food, amazed by her every reply.

"I have not always been a good man," he admitted. "I want you to know everything before you make any decisions about me."

He omitted nothing, not the slurs he used, the snide asides he made aloud and in his mind. Pygmalion told Galatea of the women he snubbed on the streets. She seemed bewildered and sad.

"I have only known you as you are in this studio, yet I trust what you tell me. For how would it benefit you to lie?" She laid her open hand on the center of the tabletop between them. "Can you bring that considerate, compassionate artist to the man? Can they be one?"

Pygmalion had to think. He had created her, and now here she was, asking him to re-create himself.

"With love, yes," he said at last, placing his hand in hers. "And you will stay? While I try?"

"When I came alive, I could have walked out the door while you slept." She smiled, and he thought it might be a masterpiece. "Yet, I remained, and I *will* remain, but thank you for asking."

And they were happy together, bearing children—a son named Paphos, in my honor—and inspiring more art. Pygmalion's most prolific work yet to come.

For the best art originates in life.

Aphrodite, Again, in Direct Address

NOW WE MUST speak on art and beauty, of love and life and time, for they overlap and entangle in limitless ways. And I like you, Alexandros. If you will listen to my licentious stories, then you can also hear my advice.

I have lived longer than you can fathom, and I know this much is true:

The pursuit of perfection can be destructive. The idea of an ideal breaks us. And this kind of immaculate beauty does not necessarily engender love. I have seen gorgeous men and women who are vain and stupid and unloved.

And yet, love almost always creates beauty. When two souls connect, the physical defects disappear. A good heart radiates from the core; a great love transforms. And this beauty, the one that comes from love, makes us feel the most alive. This is art.

Alexandros, you love your work, and this passion creates art. Sometimes that art is beautiful, but it doesn't need to be. Art isn't always nice or even understandable. It should make you feel.

You must feel, too.

Inspiration does not always come from the Muses, delightful as they are, but from real life. Why do you turn Timon away? Bring him here, into your workshop. Invite his fishermen friends over to drink.

Share in all that you do. Let them connect to you and your art, and their love will magnify its beauty. I promise.

Love, not just *for* art, but with art.

For at the end of time, there will be chaos, and everything will collapse. Art and beauty, love and life and time, will prove their impermanence.

So enjoy them now.

Do not separate what must be experienced together.

I WILL CEASE my lecturing. I see the effect on you—please don't hide your tears! Never, not with me! I will surely cry before we are through, for we are hardly finished with this apple.

Let me tell you how it turned my world upside down yet again.

26

MOUNT PELION

BACK ON OLYMPUS, I reposed in my garden, admiring all the new pieces I'd acquired in Pygmalion's tribute. Apollo, who had a better eye than me, helped arrange them so that the trees and flowers perfectly complemented each sculpture. Truly, Apollo had become my closest confidant. I was forever offering to help in his many disastrous relationships, but he always resisted.

"I seek truth above all else."

That was a sentiment I could well understand.

But on the day I speak of, I was alone, admiring a statue of my son Eros, when a barking dog interrupted my reverie.

I stood, mystified, only to be greeted by Graegus, hideous as ever and dripping water. He rubbed himself against my legs, leaving stray hairs and streaks across my expensive dress.

"You hopeless, horrendous demon," I cooed, kissing his nose. "I'll have you skinned and made into a rug."

I swear he smiled.

When Ares entered the garden, Graegus raced away to heel at his master's side.

"I didn't steal him," I announced, raising my hands in innocence. "He came of his own accord, and under no spells."

"I know."

"Why is he so wet?"

"I bathed him."

I could hardly register my shock. "With soap?"

Ares shuddered. "Stars, no. He's a dog."

Man and beast walked toward me, joining me on the bench. Ares had cut his hair; his beard had grown out. He looked mine.

"I haven't been here in so long," he mused, looking around. "It is different."

"I've become quite the art curator."

"I recognize many faces among these works, yet I do not see your likeness."

I lifted my shoulder, tilted my head. "Who alive could do me justice?"

The side of his mouth quirked upward, and then he leaned forward, propping his elbows upon his knees. "I wanted to be the first to tell you," Ares began. "There's going to be a wedding."

"Oh."

And that easily, my heart disintegrated into a billion grains of sand and fell through my chest. I felt it pile in the pit of my stomach.

But Ares was still speaking.

". . . and I wondered if you would attend."

"Your wedding? Ares, be serious."

"*My* wedding?"

We stared at each other, in mutual confusion, annoyance growing. He scowled. I frowned.

"Why is everything so difficult with you?" he fumed.

My eyes widened. "Ares, I am very committed to being less reactionary, but I would sooner lick Zeus's feet than celebrate your marriage."

"Thetis's wedding, Aphrodite!"

"Oh."

Thetis the sea nymph, sister of Amphitrite and Nerites.

A smile spread slowly across my face. "Are you inviting me to accompany you?"

"I thought that was clear."

"It wasn't, you barbarian. Ask me again. Beg me." I fluttered my lashes.

He got to his feet and snapped for Graegus, too frustrated to speak. "It's tomorrow," he grunted. "And please don't mention my father's feet. Ever again."

He left with his dog, and the grains of my heart reassembled into something overlarge and pulsing, threatening to burst from sheer force.

I had not been so excited in such a long while.

UNSURPRISINGLY, I DRESSED for the wedding as if it were my own, with utmost attention, retrieving every compliment Ares had ever given me—which were few, but treasured. Recalling colors, his hands in my hair, revived the giddiness of our earliest days. I painted no color over my lips, just a light oil, enough to make them moist, a visceral—lascivious—reminder.

I even salvaged the girdle from the back of my wardrobe.

Despite the poignant words we'd exchanged after the trial, Ares and I had not seen each other. I'd been occupied with my campaign of kindness, and content simply to know that he and I were no longer at odds. His invitation was unexpected, not just because of our thorny past, but because we would be appearing in public.

In my darkest moments, I sometimes wondered if Ares was ashamed of me, of our history, but his asking me to join him today proved otherwise.

When Ares's chariot pulled in front of my palace, I was ready but made him wait regardless. From my window, I watched his four fire-breathing horses stomp and snort, smoky mist emanating from their nostrils. And Ares adjusted his own tunic, fastidiously checked his belt and sword and bracelets. I bit down upon my grin.

I didn't press my advantage for too long—there was a decent

chance Ares would leave without me—and I threw open the doors, emerging at last in a specific aroma of rose petals and vanilla.

And despite his best attempts to hamper any reaction, I noted, as his eyes took me in, the simultaneous stiffening and loosening of his defenses. Ares wouldn't praise me, but he didn't need to. I knew.

I boarded the chariot. Though he held the reins, I wove one arm through his, nestling closer.

"Do you know where we are going?" he asked.

"I don't even know who Thetis is marrying," I replied happily.

He cast me a sideways glance, brows slightly knitted. "You make a habit of boarding chariots, with armed and dangerous men, unsure of where you are going or what you are doing?"

"Not a habit, no." And then I slipped. "I suppose I still trust you."

After that admission, we spoke only of small things.

The wedding, I learned, was between Thetis and Peleus, a mortal king of Thessaly—which was where we headed, to a northern mountaintop on a peninsula between gulf and sea. The cavalcade of Olympian arrivals followed a specific order: first Zeus and Hera, followed by Poseidon and his long-suffering wife, Amphitrite; Hades and Persephone; and then . . . us.

Aphrodite and Ares, presented together for the first time.

I heard whispers on the winds, the susurration of shock and scintillating scandal, but I didn't need to affect any airs. I was genuinely unbothered. No insults could infiltrate my high spirits.

All the usual festivities commenced: ceremony and feast. Weddings can be so droll. I picked at my food, preferring wine, enjoying the light mood, the easy laughter. Ares and I leaned together, consuming each other instead of the meal. I'd missed his intense attention, the way he shuttered everything else out besides me.

I barely felt Poseidon's raking glare.

As the dishes were cleared and desserts were distributed, Athena came toward us with some urgency. "Ares, there's been a commotion with your horses. Can you calm them?"

"What happened?"

"A groom lost control and Phlogios burned the crossties."

"Did he bolt?"

Athena's arms crossed over her chest. "Obviously. Or I wouldn't be disturbing"—she tipped her head toward me—"this."

Reluctantly, Ares sighed and rose from the table. Once he left, and we were alone, Athena narrowed those icy petrel eyes of hers.

"I don't like you for my brother."

I grinned. "Do you like me without your brother?"

She ignored the question, which was as good as acceding to my point. "There are acts in motion you wouldn't understand. Ares will be needed soon."

"Magnificent."

Athena and I stared at each other, her in frustration, me with amusement.

"Ares is a weapon," she articulated, her impatience evident, "and you diminish him. He becomes a blunt sword."

"I assure you, around me his sword is almost never blunt."

Athena grimaced. "How does Ares stomach your crudeness?"

"With the same patience he stomachs your prudishness, I suppose."

I saw the pulse hammering in her throat and chided myself. Coming to blows with Ares's sister would win me no favors.

"I am his companion this one night, Athena, I wouldn't get ahead of yourself."

"No," she replied, almost ruefully. "I know Ares too well. He's looking at you that same way. He's yours again."

Mine.

I sipped my drink evenly, hand as steady as stone despite my rollicking emotions.

"You two are unreasonable as individuals, even more so as a pair. It makes no sense, and I do not support it," she concluded.

"Coincidentally, I did not ask for, nor do I need, your support."

Athena opened her mouth and lifted a hand, response at the ready, but Ares returned, shaking his head. "Phlogios was in the paddock. I couldn't find the groom."

"Interesting," responded Athena brusquely. "Perhaps I heard wrong." And to me: "Enjoy this one night."

"Thankfully it's a long one." I winked.

Her cheeks burned a piqued shade of pink, and Ares frowned, bewildered, as his uptight sister spun and strode away.

"I do not care if your horses burn the entire mountain to ash," I told him, pulling him back down beside me. "Don't you dare leave me lonely again."

His forehead grazed mine. "Are you ever lonely for long?"

"Are either of us?"

So many bodies lay between us, but had any of those lovers eased the ache for each other? Mine certainly hadn't.

"I make love, Aphrodite, but I don't feel it." His voice was so low, I had to lean forward. "But—"

"Attention, everyone!" bellowed Zeus in his impossibly loud voice. "This is the first dance!"

King Peleus and his willowy wife assumed the center of our crowd, and Apollo produced his lyre. Accompanied by a chorus of Muses and the Graces, my friend began to play. The bride and groom circled and spun, and we clapped.

Other guests joined the dance. Though Ares resisted, I lured him forward.

"You've been waiting all night to touch me," I teased, placing my hands in his and pulling him toward me and the music.

"To touch you properly requires more privacy."

I wrapped my arms around his neck. He was a warrior, not a dancer, but obliged me in his way, following my movements with a stiff, self-conscious obedience. And I didn't require much, just an uncomplicated sway. The proximity, the beat, and the wine in my head had me nearly swooning.

Imagine it, Alexandros! The bruised and battered goddess of love made faint by the scent of a man!

But when an apple flew over the crowd, crashing to the floor and rolling to a stop before the newlyweds, Apollo and his chorus abruptly stopped, final note hanging awkwardly in the air. Ares stiffened and pulled me into his chest with one arm while his free hand unsheathed the knife he kept on his belt.

The crowd murmured.

"What happened?"

"Was a weapon thrown?"

"An arrow? A spear?"

King Peleus, behaving as if the apple might explode, stepped cautiously forward and examined the tiny invader. His brow furrowed as he brought it closer, and then, with a glance at Zeus, he read the inscription aloud:

"'For the fairest.'"

Where had such an apple originated? Who would dare?

There are some silences so heavy you can hold them, so loud you can hear them. In this one, I caught every breath catch, every exchanged look, all the anticipation and opinion, greed and envy.

Poor mortal man to carry such a weight! Wisely, he passed the apple to Zeus.

"My king, the honor is yours."

Peleus could not return to his wife fast enough.

But Zeus did not appear so honored. I saw him swallow, fumble the apple in his hand, nearly dropping it. From her place at the table, Hera gazed at him with such sharp anticipation, I'm certain it stabbed him. He cleared his throat. We waited. And then, surprising us all, Athena presented herself.

"It is mine, Father."

Hermes let loose a low whistle.

Though I dislike Athena immensely, I can objectively agree that she is quite pretty. In a silvery way, like winter. But when Zeus did not immediately pass her the apple, Hera stood.

"My husband," she pronounced, chin lifted. "As your queen, I believe myself to be the intended recipient."

Everyone noticed Zeus's struggle, caught literally and figuratively between his favorite daughter and his wife. I pulled my bottom lip between my teeth, considering, my toes tapping in their sandals.

"Don't," murmured Ares in my ear, standing behind me. "You already know."

I leaned backward into him. Turning my head, I purred upward, "And if an apple inscribed with 'To the bravest' entered the room, you would let Hermes take it?"

"Only over my dismembered body."

I grinned and entered the fray.

"Zeus, darling, I'll accept my apple now."

I sauntered, I spun, I let my hips swing and kept my shoulders back, displaying my body at its best from every angle.

This was my arena, and I was its favorite gladiator.

But Zeus did not bequeath me the apple either.

"I cannot choose between wife, daughter, and sister."

My bright smile faded. I was nobody's sister.

And in a characteristically cowardly move, Zeus deferred. "I will hold this apple in my possession until I find one of keen judgment to provide resolution."

The crowd groaned but quickly applauded once Zeus's bad temper became apparent.

"So wise, our king!"

"The wisest!"

"Well said, well thought!"

So many powerful men are overgrown babies. Zeus was no better than a hissy child you spoil with treats and toys so their tantrums don't ruin the day.

Back with Ares, I released a theatrical sigh. "Alas, my moment of glory is hindered."

"You don't need a stupid apple, Aphrodite," he said, almost gruffly. "You're the most beautiful creature that's ever walked upon this ugly world, and that's only a piece of who you truly are."

I didn't know how to respond, and I didn't want to. I wanted to hold those words inside me for a moment. With my eyes closed, I laid my cheek upon his chest. His arms circled me.

"Take me away, Ares."

"Yes. I tire of watching simple men ogle you."

We left the immortals to their chaos, believing—incorrectly—that it would never affect us. Ares guided his chariot away from the wedding, past Chiron's cave, to a remote point over the sea. Together, we dropped the pole and unyoked the horses, letting them graze unbridled. Ares removed his armor, then leaned back against the chariot's carriage.

"Come here."

The sun was setting, but I was flushed. I went to him, and we pressed our hips together, navels meeting through fabric, as he took my chin in his hand.

"Your vote saved me from exile."

My lips curved upward. "You're welcome."

"You could have been free of me, of all this."

"Distance would have changed little," I demurred. "You're always here." I brought his hand to my breast, and his thumb began to stroke me in small circles. My knees wobbled, but Ares held me steady.

"I think, Aphrodite, I was not fated for war, but for loving you."

Soldiers can be poets, too.

Our mouths met, our urgent tongues, then Ares spun me around and lifted my dress. I bent forward and welcomed his possession, his fingers in every right place, as the night deepened and the sun and I both fell.

27

MOUNT OLYMPUS

IN THE BLISSFUL days that followed, I waded through the ripple effects of the wedding, smiling serenely, partially hearing, as if from a watery distance, of tensions and preoccupations, of a golden fruit, now called the Apple of Discord. It had been thrown by Eris, the goddess of such, in retribution for not receiving an invitation. Goddesses can be as easily offended as their fussy male counterparts. But Eris's schemes meant little to me. While Athena and Hera continued their campaign for "fairest," I hummed to myself and glided about my garden, cooing to the doves.

Because Ares's sandals rested beside mine at the doorway.

We were together. Committed. Open and honest, no secrets, no shame. I could kiss him in the Hall of the Gods, and he could walk through my house in broad daylight, free of clothes and guilt.

Some days we never rose from bed, but remained in our robes, sharing ourselves, asking the questions that plagued us—ones without simple answers, for that was the point. I hungered for his perspective in the same way I yearned for his body. And we were compensating for time lost. There was so much to cover.

He especially loved stories of Eros in his childhood. In return, I heard of Phobos and Deimos.

"They are inseparable and fearless—devastatingly so. I've never seen their like behind a chariot. They have a trick where they drive the horses rapidly across the plain to create a dark cloud of dust. The enemy loses sight of them, hearing only their war whoops, and then comes the charge."

I grinned, imagining it. "What did you think when the Graces brought them to you?"

He remembers, and answers seriously, "That caring for them was both my penance for deserting you and a gift."

"A gift?" I scoffed. "Those boys were impossible."

"Yes, and a piece of you I got to keep." Ares's hand found my face; his thumb traced my cheekbone. "Thankfully they got my brown eyes. If they had yours, I might have come undone."

In all our centuries, we rarely experienced the extravagance of sleeping beside each other. Now, Ares lay with me every night, his arm slung across my body. Even someone as timeless as me yearns to be held. I learned his sleep patterns, the rhythm of his breath. When he thrashed, I knew nightmares plagued him, and I kissed his forehead, one hand rubbing circles on his chest, until they passed.

His absence from Olympus, and the night terrors, shared the same cause: war. One lifetime on the battlefields is more than enough to destroy a man's mind, and my love lived the horrors over and over again. Memories tortured him, even as he was being pulled into new frays. It was an all-encompassing trauma: his past, present, and future.

"Sometimes I doubt, Aphrodite, that anything alive can be inherently good."

I laid a finger over his lips. "No."

"It is kill or be killed."

"Zeus asks too much of you. One god cannot bear it all." I sat up, recalling a conversation with Poseidon. "If Athena wants to wear a helmet and carry an aegis, then she can go fight."

"Athena understands only politics. For her, battle is a map, a piece of parchment in a game."

"Then educate her."

"No, Aphrodite." His expression hardened, his eyes screwed shut. "I don't want her to have to learn. I will keep war away from all of you if I can."

Ares was called away from the mountain, away from me, with greater frequency as the mortal cities invented new reasons to fight one another. I did not worry about where he laid his head at night. No mortal woman threatened me, no immortal either. But I wished I could accompany him, to stand by his side, defending his heart and mind from those intrusive battle-weary thoughts with my lips and hands.

He would not permit it, and his adamant refusal led to many heated arguments.

"A spear cannot kill me, Ares."

"You could be hurt."

"I'll stay behind, in the tent."

"On the battlefield, my word is absolute. Disobedience means death. And I cannot trust you to behave."

I nibbled his ears, and he flipped me over onto my back, all hazy eyes and lazy smiles.

"Besides, returning to you is my motivation."

And so I stayed. Because I loved him.

"But before you go," I begged, "say something sweet to me."

"When things are perfect," he replied, lowering his face into me, "nothing needs to be said."

WITH ALL OF this happiness, I was in a mood to be generous.

So, when Hera arrived at my front door, I accepted her and the proffered gift basket with magnanimity.

"This is a surprise," I remarked as she sped inside, clearly worried somebody would catch her in my presence.

I ignored the slight.

I led her to my favorite room for receiving guests, the one with the most exquisite chairs and low divans. Servants brought a plate of cheese and fruit, amphorae of wine and lemon water. I put out the candies I found in the basket.

Hera did not even pretend to eat, keeping her hands clutched tightly in her lap, knuckles white at the strain. As immortals, our physical appearances do not much change, but the queen of the gods seemed gaunt and tired.

Neither she nor I was the type for platitudes, so I waited patiently. When she was ready to speak, she would.

"He didn't choose me."

I admit, I was temporarily perplexed, but then I remembered Zeus's humiliating indecision with the apple at the wedding.

"Ah."

I allowed myself a moment of empathy. How would it feel to be married to someone who didn't pick you, in front of everyone who mattered, when appearances were your everything? Her pain, even just in fantasy, did affect me.

But Hera had caused plenty of that herself. Blaming me for Zeus's prurience. Voting for her own son's exile, tossing an infant from a balcony when he wasn't born to her exact expectations. Stealing Harmonia.

The last one still burned.

I chose my words carefully. "He didn't pick anyone."

"A devoted husband would call his wife the fairest even if she wasn't, just because she belongs to him." Hera's face twitched. "He is not proud of me."

I softened. "You are very beautiful, Hera."

She shook her head. "But not enough. Never enough. You couldn't understand, with your purple eyes and implausible lashes. Even when we were first wed, I did not hold his attention. For all these years I have suffered his . . ." She swallowed tightly. "Indiscretions. I am forced to sit beside his lovers, his bastard children." Hera reached for the wine jug on the table before us, but her hands trembled and I intervened, pouring each of us a glass. She drank hers quickly, gulping, staining her mouth red. "My life is a compilation of embarrassments."

"Those are his embarrassments, not yours."

"A girl is pregnant," Hera continued, "an Aetolian princess with barely two decades to her name. Yet another maiden with ebony hair and ivory skin." She cackled, a laugh that cracked, without soul. "He . . . lay with her . . . as a swan, for he knew I kept watch."

I grimaced and set down my wine. It paired horribly with the unctuous disgust at the pit of my stomach.

"This Leda lost her virginity to a lusty bird. Zeus would rather change himself into an animal than stop. He goes to them as eagles, ants, even a shower of gold. He's addicted to . . . intercourse."

I let her keep her euphemisms, though they irked me. And I revealed nothing of what I knew. Apollo had also informed me that Zeus approached mortal women in the guise of their own husbands. These wretched women would share the most intimate acts with the person they trusted most, only to be deceived. I found it difficult to grasp how anyone could be so sinister.

"What would you have me do, Hera? A debilitating rash across his cock would be quite straightforward. Or maybe blistering sores upon his mouth?"

Though I had declared myself closed to the business of vengeance, for Zeus I would make an exception.

Hera had something else in mind.

"Hephaestus told me once that he constructed a girdle of a unique design that can make its wearer irresistible." Hera wet her chapped lips; her bloodshot eyes met mine. "Might I borrow it?"

Her request wasn't at all what I expected, but my answer was clear.

"Yes."

THAT DAY, I dressed Hera myself. First adjusting the girdle to best accentuate her body, then draping her in one of my gowns—a red one, which suited her coloring. I lent her gold earrings and bracelets. At her neck I dabbed a perfume of ambergris, my most elusive scent, for it is gathered from the inside of a whale. I brushed her hair until it shone, rubbed olive oil on her hands and feet until they were as a soft as a child's.

I whispered a few of my trade secrets in her ear, and Hera did not squirm. She nodded, resolute.

"And one more thing."

Hera gazed up at me, as serious as any soldier before their commander.

"Before you give him what he wants, get what you want. When he's at the edge, he will grant you anything. That is your moment, Hera. Hold it."

"Yes. This is sage advice, Aphrodite."

I wondered if I should offer her a magical assist—I would not do so without her permission—but the way Hera regarded herself in the mirror settled any debate. The queen of the gods had never sparkled so brightly, not just in her decor but in her demeanor. How long had it been since she'd last felt this good about herself? I would not interfere, would not cause her any doubt.

When she came around the next morning to return the girdle, she was further changed—in posture and spirit, shoulders thrown back and anxiety nonexistent.

"Well?" I demanded, bringing her inside like we were old acquaintances.

In my private rooms, she told me everything.

"When I had him in my throes, I extracted a promise on the River Styx that he would never again lie with a mortal woman."

I raised my eyebrows, mouth falling slightly open in appreciation of a well-played move. "And?"

"I wouldn't let him finish until I had his word."

I did not hug Hera, but I shook her hand.

We were not friends, never would be, but for one day and night, we were something better. Allies.

I would be punished for this, too.

28

MOUNT IDA

AFTER RECONNECTING WITH Ares and forging somewhat of a truce with Hera, I made myself consider which of my other relationships required reparations. There were those effortless to maintain—Apollo, Eros, Dionysus—but where had I erred? Who deserved more?

It's probably obvious to you, Alexandros, but I can be oblivious when I want to be.

We come, of course, to the Graces.

Since the earliest days in Cyprus, the sisters catered to my every mood and whim and need. How they continued to treat me with any kindness after all my mercurial drama was a mystery. Our entire history together was erected upon an unbalanced platform, with an unfair sharing of duty and affection. I could be better. I wanted to reciprocate, to tip the scales, for once, in their favor.

I invited Euphrosyne and Thalia to a picnic at the Enipeas Gorge at the foot of Olympus. There, beside the meandering river and its resplendent waterfalls, we ate and drank, and I presented them with gifts—a silver flute for Euphrosyne and a rare potted vine for Thalia. They were delighted, but I knew these were superficial, uncomplicated gestures. I wanted to hear their dreams.

It was so long overdue.

Euphrosyne longed to travel beyond the lands Olympus held dominion—specifically to Kemet, with its north-flowing river and rich, dark soil.

Thalia wanted to train as a midwife.

I was surprised—and impressed—by their aspirations, and eager to help. Already, my mind spun with plans. I would speak to Hermes about properly equipping Euphrosyne for a journey, and I would ask Eileithyia, the goddess of childbirth, to consider Thalia as an apprentice.

"What would mean most, however," offered Thalia slyly, "is for you and Aglaia to make amends."

I sighed. I had barely spoken to Aglaia since her wedding to Hephaestus, which I did not attend. Our social interactions were limited to cursory nods or brief kisses to the cheek.

"She willingly married my former husband," I pointed out, cringing at the whine in my tone.

"And?" countered Thalia. "Did you still want him?"

I gave her a withering look.

"This all happened so long ago," added Euphrosyne. "They have four daughters now!"

"It is uncomfortable for both of you, remember that."

Inviting Aglaia to my home was the more comfortable option, but for a true attempt at resolution, I needed to return to Hephaestus's palace, the origin of my trauma. I had lived there with Harmonia, in the bittersweet period she was mine. It was the location of my forced marriage, the scene of my humiliating entrapment. I couldn't think about that place without succumbing to bitter rage, and I wanted to let that go.

I needed to let it all go.

Aglaia greeted me in the entrance hall wearing elaborate clothes, adorned in custom-made jewelry. An automaton scuttled forward on its spidery legs and took my cloak, as disturbing as ever.

"Please, come in," she said.

Walking through those rooms felt surreal, overwhelming. I mentally cataloged every similarity and difference. The vases I used to fill with fennel-stalk torches had moved. Instead, spring foliage filled every room, and the windows were open. The women's suites were now painted a cloudy shade of blue. They had been red before, Hephaestus's favorite, which I'd never bothered to change. I assumed he wouldn't let me, but I was beginning to wonder whether that belief arose mostly from my bias against him, my laziness and refusal to actively participate in our married life.

Could I have made this place my own, too?

Aglaia and I chatted of simple things, shared pleasant memories of drunken nights laughing and dancing in Cyprus. But my former relationship with her husband was always present, lurking beneath our innocuous words, recognized without being acknowledged.

Until Aglaia spoke of it.

"Hephaestus was a poor match for you, Aphrodite, but he is a steadfast husband to me."

I nodded but did not comment, sensing that if I left an opening, she would elaborate.

And she did.

"I think—I *know*—he became obsessed with being enough for you."

I straightened. "His behavior is not my fault."

"No"—Aglaia tilted her head—"but you did prove his worst fears were grounded."

"I am not proud of hurting him," I admitted, "but I will never consider what I did a sin."

"But you think I do. You've never forgiven me, Aphrodite, not for marrying Hephaestus, but for telling Zeus about Ares."

Oh, the accuracy, even if I wished it were otherwise!

"Bemoaning the past is for the malcontent. Have you ever known me to snivel?"

Her mouth lifted into a half smile. "Snivel? No. But complain?"

My laughter broke the tension.

"Being your friend is a constant frustration," Aglaia chided, "but I respect how you honor your heart. I always have."

"And your heart?" I asked. "How does it fare?"

"Once I might have desired someone else, something different and impossible, but I have four daughters." Her face glowed. "I am excellent at being a mother."

"Oh, I don't doubt that at all. You took care of me for centuries."

"It was the finest practice."

We left on the best of terms, promising not to let time and space grow between us again, and I clutched her in a tight embrace.

"Aglaia," I replied, overcome, "I want to do something nice for you."

She gestured to the opulent home behind her. "I desire nothing, Aphrodite." But she paused, considering. "Actually, there is something."

"Anything."

"Can you love yourself, Aphrodite? Without the defenses and the jests, regardless of Eros or Ares. Love yourself, fight for yourself, just as you are?"

And wasn't my initial reaction to toss back a joke?

Aglaia knew it. She held up a hand, halting me. "Don't say a word," she reprimanded.

I walked home, mind spinning, for my domain continued to confound me. How could self-love feel maudlin but also deeply discomfiting? I thought I was confident in who I was, but did I truly love that person?

No, not entirely. I struggled with my jealousy, my shame, my temper. And vanity wasn't love, either.

Do I love what I do more than who I am?

Yes.

I, who had given my heart to so many, found giving it to myself incomprehensible.

A SERVANT I RECOGNIZED from Zeus's retinue presented himself one day with a message from Ares.

"The war god, currently occupied with the disputes between Troy and Phrygia, asks for you to join him in the Troad below Mount Ida," announced the attendant with clipped formality and a ramrod posture.

I reeled. "When?"

"Immediately."

Nothing about this was expected, and that should have aroused my suspicion—why would Ares send word through Zeus?—but I was love blind, invincible.

Stupid.

He told me how to find Ares's retreat in the foothills.

"It is a simple shepherd's cottage, otherwise unremarkable, but situated beside the largest oak tree you've ever seen."

I thanked the servant so effusively, you would have thought I'd been invited to a seaside villa or aboard a pleasure barge. To be included in Ares's world, I would toss all my preferences aside. If I'd camped for Adonis, what wouldn't I endure for Ares?

Finally, I would experience the front. When war was discussed, I could share genuine insight, I would relate.

As I said, Alexandros, I was stupid.

I flew my chariot over a land that was still foreign to me, past the walled city and the Scamander River, to mountains carved in white limestone ridges, covered in forest of pine, cedar, and juniper. The monstrous dimensions of the oak tree were impressive even from the sky, its branches spreading and sweeping, down and then back up again, in a twisting, turning testament to resilience.

I spotted the hut, sheep and cattle milled in the nearby meadow, and I smiled in delight. Nobody would suspect the god of war hid in this pastoral refuge, or that he was visited by his sweetheart. I landed my chariot and summoned rosebushes from the earth as camouflage.

Light gray tendrils of smoke rose from a hole in the roof, so I knew Ares waited inside. I adjusted my dress, my hair, and approached the hut, but something strange happened at the doorway. As my hand breached the threshold, a jolt ran through my body, from my toes to the crown of my head, causing me to lurch, barely holding myself upright. When I glanced down at my palms, my stomach, and legs, I could have sworn that I shimmered—only for a breath, and then it was gone.

Was that real or imagined?

Slightly afrown, I shook off the odd sensation, surmising that Ares had laid a safeguard over the hideaway. It would have been a sensible protection.

Inside, Ares stood before a table, poring over a map, and he, too, seemed to momentarily glimmer. His head swiveled at my arrival, and he seemed confused, but quickly smiled.

"I did not think you would come."

"I never thought you would invite me."

He gestured to the scant, simple furniture, the single room. "This is rough living."

"It has been ages since we shared a bed so small," I agreed, "but it might make for a creative night."

A crimson flush crept up his neck.

"Are you embarrassed?" I exclaimed. "I thought it impossible!"

Ares stiffened. "You are in quite a mood today."

"And you are not, I gather." I sighed and took a seat at the table. "Do plans for battle consume you?"

"Unfortunately, yes."

"Tell me."

And he spoke of maritime and overland trade routes, of allies and enemies. I basked in the details, for typically when Ares was with me, he avoided such conversation. We were a couple based on banter and theory, not minutiae, but I listened. I evaluated and posed questions.

"I wonder why Greece has yet to attack Troy," I mused, pointing to the map. "This access to the east could bring in immeasurable wealth."

A jug of wine sat on the table, and Ares poured two cups.

"They only need an excuse." He took a long pull, then lowered his cup, almost hesitantly, as he stared at it. "Did you bring this? I don't remember it being here."

I shook my head. "No."

I tried the wine. The taste was unusual, but I suspected it was more watered down than the vintages I preferred. Unsurprisingly, I like my drinks strong.

But it was late. Ares shrugged, and we both paid the wine no more heed. I took his hand and led him away from his troubles. We came together on that small bed, and I remember that Ares was especially restrained that night. Almost forbearing.

It took me much longer than him to relax. Something was off, something I couldn't identify. Then the explanation came to me: *Graegus is missing!* Where was that damned dog? Ares never traveled without him.

I should have woken Ares then, but instead, I listened to the breeze, which carried the soft sounds of sheep. Their nocturnal moments, their sighs and shuffling. I moved to the window. The night was cold enough that I could smell the flirtation of frost upon the grass, and above, I noticed a faint, fuzzy oval of light. Could that smudge in the distance be another world, another set of worlds, where other lovers and fighters grappled with sleep?

Returning to bed, I wrapped Ares's arms around me, wearing his warmth like a blanket, and eventually, I, too, found rest.

I AWOKE TO CHAOS, furniture toppling, yelling and swearing. Rubbing my weary eyes, I sat up.

"Good morning to you, too," I groaned crossly, for I have never been my finest in the mornings. Only it wasn't Ares gaping at me across the room, but a wan and wide-eyed stranger. I shrieked and pulled the linens up over my bare chest. "Who are you?"

"Who am I? I'm Anchises, and you *were* my betrothed! Where is she? What witchcraft is this?"

I don't find the "witch" label particularly insulting, but his insinuations that I would lower myself to play tricks on a man whose name I'd never heard in my life definitely rankled.

"I am Aphrodite," I commanded, rising from the bed, holding myself with a regalness belied by the blanket draped across my nudity, "sea-born and eternal, physical manifestation of love and beauty, and you will take more care when you speak to me."

Anchises collapsed to his knees, lowering his head and begging apology.

I gathered my actual dress from the floor and slipped it back on while he cowered. "I cannot explain what happened here, but we are both victims of some fiendish plot."

He raised his head a fraction, peering up at me. "Who did you believe me to be?"

"Ares."

Anchises blanched. "You thought *I* was the god of war?"

"You thought I was some mortal girl?"

"Eriopis," he corrected defensively. "And she is precious to me."

"Yes, yes, of course she is," I replied, waving a hand, for my mind was racked with revelations.

I had been tricked by someone with immense power and slept with a stranger.

But more than that. I had just betrayed Ares.

He would never forgive me.

My hand rose to my mouth, holding back the burgeoning sickness.

Anchises walked to the table and collapsed into a chair. He leaned forward, elbows propped upon his careful map as he massaged his temples.

"It was an honest mistake," he murmured, more to himself than me. "And nobody has to know." He gazed at me hopefully. "This can remain a secret, yes?"

I began to nod, but then my stomach lurched.

It wasn't the first time. I know my immortal body and how it functions. Oh, Alexandros, I longed to cry, but what would that accomplish?

"Not for long. Already our child stirs within me."

"So soon!" he cried.

I swallowed my irritation. "Need I remind you I am a goddess? But rest assured, I will get rid of it."

"You will do nothing of the sort, Aphrodite."

The door to the hut swung open.

Zeus.

Of course this was Zeus. How had I been so oblivious? The messenger, the glimmer. Even the damned oak tree, his sacred species.

"That child belongs to the royal family of Troy."

"You are a king?" I asked Anchises.

"A prince of Dardania. My cousin is Priam, king of Troy," he admitted.

My living nightmare deepened and darkened.

Zeus stared at me; his eyes sparkled with smug victory. Oh, I would wring his fat neck. It would require the combined might of Olympus to pry my nails from his body.

"Since Aphrodite has proven yourself, time and time again, to be an unfit mother, I've already made arrangements. Once born, the boy will be raised by mountain nymphs, and when of age, join his father in the Trojan court."

I wasn't even sure I wanted this pregnancy, but I would not allow Zeus to tell me what I would or wouldn't do with my body.

"Anchises and I will discuss this privately. And it might be a girl," I snapped.

"Aphrodite, I will no longer remind you that I am your king!"

His stentorian voice shook the cottage walls. Anchises covered his ears, and mine rung.

"Troy is a favored city of mine, and they will need men with divinity in their blood for the future."

Anchises had gone speechless; negotiations fell to me. "Zeus," I cajoled, concealing my panic and disdain beneath calm clearheadedness. "Shall we cut a deal? If I bear this child and bring him—or her—to the mountain, we can keep this . . . misunderstanding . . . between us?"

Zeus chuckled. "It's too late for discretion, Aphrodite. I already sent Hermes ahead to deliver your joyous news."

How could Zeus have known I would fall pregnant? Awareness dawned on me like a dreaded day. "What was in the wine?"

"A concoction of Hera's, to ready the womb for conception." Zeus stepped closer, glowering down upon me. "By now, Ares knows you carry another man's child. I cannot imagine he will take it well."

"You are a monster," I fumed.

Zeus lowered his voice. "It doesn't feel so nice when others meddle in your relationships, does it?"

This was about Hera, then.

"Because I loaned your queen a girdle?"

"Because you empowered her to manipulate me! Yes, Aphrodite, I made her tell me everything, all your little suggestions. You used my wife to punish me."

I laughed. "I did no such thing! She begged me for help controlling your filthy cock."

I felt his electric energy collect inside the cabin as his stormy anger coalesced power. I thought he might strike me, but because Anchises bore witness, Zeus tempered himself, regained control.

"You are a small man," I hissed.

"I am the king of kings, and you are fortunate I do not put you on trial for treason." The lightning surrounding him sizzled out. "When the boy is born, bring it to the Oreads of this mountain. They will nurse him until he is ready to reunite with his father in Troy."

Zeus then addressed Anchises. "You were the hapless victim here, noble Anchises, but this child will be a credit to your name. Let that console you." He squeezed the mortal prince's shoulder. "And it will be a legendary story, told in every tavern: the night you bedded Aphrodite."

Anchises did not smile. I felt dangerously close to tears.

After Zeus departed, Anchises and I sat in solemn reticence. We had everything to say to each other and nothing.

Eventually, I left without a word. I would need all of them for what I was about to face.

29

MOUNT OLYMPUS

I FLEW MY CHARIOT straight from Mount Ida to Mount Olympus. My poor swans squawked in protest at the relentless pace.

The doors to Ares's palace were open wide as servants moved his belongings outside and into a series of carts. I found him in his bedroom, oiling the wood of a spear, dressed for travel.

"I can smell him on you," he said, without looking up.

I should have stopped to bathe.

"Then Hermes has been here."

"Yes, to tell me with great glee, how you've been unfaithful." He made a pointed glance at my belly. I placed my hands over my navel, and he sneered. "Now she covers up."

"Stop it, Ares. Don't be cruel."

He hurled the spear he'd been so carefully cleaning into the wall. It shattered the stone, sending dust and rocks to the floor. I flinched. "You would lecture me on cruelty?"

"Zeus had us entranced! Our appearances were altered. I didn't know!"

"You should have. Maybe he looked like me, Aphrodite, but did he speak like me, act like me?" Ares prowled closer, his head dropping lower. "Did he fuck like me?"

I swallowed. "No."

He snorted. "Men are all the same to you."

"You are nothing like the others!" I protested. "This is ridiculous!"

"You don't get to say that!" he roared. "You don't get to say this is nothing to you when it could be everything to me!"

"Ares, I was seduced, magicked, and you are being unfair."

"And you would forgive me if roles were reversed?"

"If you were under a spell, yes!"

"No, Aphrodite. You would find the girl and curse her."

I reeled, stunned as if slapped. He knew how hard I had worked to change.

"I would still forgive you, Ares. Because I love you even when you leave me, even when you are mean. I still love you every morning after."

He wouldn't look at me; he continued to pack, shoving tunics and a leather cuirass into an open sack. "I don't know if I trust you."

"Because of Anchises?" I sputtered, incredulous.

"Because of him and because of Hermes. Because of Poseidon." I'm certain I did not breathe, and Ares nodded with grim satisfaction at my reaction. "Yes, Athena also called today. She bore messages, as well."

"That was before, when you were with Aurora and Alcippe's mother and so many I care not consider." I shoved away his pack and held his face firmly between my palms, though he tried to resist. "I know those women weren't the same as me, why can't you extend me that grace?"

"My existence is difficult enough without you," he said, and he slowly pulled down my hands. "You make me weak."

A blunt sword.

Oh, yes, Athena had been here and had much to say.

"Love is neither fault nor flaw, Ares, and it cannot be controlled. You cannot break it like a horse or corner it in battle. You can go, but this"—I closed a fist over my chest—"us, me, will follow you."

Ares retrieved his spear, yanking it from the wall, and added it the collection of weaponry laid across his bed.

"Forgiveness demands bravery," I continued, "and you are such a coward. You can lead the vanguard in every battle, yet you cannot be strong enough for me. Why must you always surrender? Why can't you fight for us?"

"We have tried this too many times. Love and war do not belong together."

I would never believe it, no matter how many times I was told.

"Where will you go?" I asked, trembling.

"To Themyscira. The Amazons have need of me."

"It's only women there," I quipped. "I'm sure they do."

He glared at me then, and I saw in the depths of his eyes the depths of his pain. I had hurt him too badly; this damage was irrevocable.

"I have to leave, Aphrodite, for as long as I love you, you can still break my heart."

He abandoned me standing in his own rooms, the ones we'd come to share. I picked up a jug and hurled it at the wall. It shattered, spilled water. I found another one and another. I went from room to room breaking Ares's possessions, screaming, until Aglaia arrived, arms open, and I fell into her chest and the dam within me broke.

I cried.

I REMEMBER VERY LITTLE of my pregnancy.

I recall a dark room, my room, the windows covered in drapes. And Psyche forcing me to eat. I think Thalia and Euphrosyne took turns singing, Apollo played his lyre. Dionysus tempted me with wine, Eros brought my doves inside, but very little could draw me from my bed. I had already cried myself raw, wept tears of blood. Now I would sleep, and I would escape. I would dream things better.

This unbearable grief was the cost of my happiness, hurting far more than the first time Ares left, because this time, we had given our relationship the respect it deserved. We weren't escaping to each other but building something solid, together. I was so confident that we were doing it right, that we would last, but once again, it failed. Why? Was it, as I suspected, all my fault?

Were Ares and I just another cycle of life, like the stars or seasons?

Should I finally snip the circle and let it end?

In my waking hours, I begged my friends for word of Ares. They told me reluctantly and only after I made outrageous threats.

"He has not returned to Olympus."

"He has become the favorite of the Amazonian queen Otrera."

Ares had already found another woman, a warrior who could better share his burdens and understand his work, while I lay cocooned in blankets and misery, growing a child I did not want.

I mourned him and his joy.

When the time came, Thalia assisted in the delivery, for she had mastered this art in her time with Eileithyia.

"It is a boy," she cooed. "A sweet, healthy mortal boy."

My fifth child, my fourth son, and somehow, I knew, my last. I would never bear another.

I kept the baby for one day and one night before delivering him to the mountain nymphs as ordained. In that time, I nursed him, I sang to him in my voice, that he might recognize it one day. I did not tell him he was an accident or a mistake, but I did apologize.

"I am so sorry, little prince, that I cannot care for you. It isn't that I don't love you enough, it is because you deserve a normal life, and you would not get that with me. You will join your father soon, and he will teach you how to be a righteous mortal man."

I had flirted with the idea of defying Zeus and running away with the child but decided against it. Maybe Zeus spoke the truth, and I was an insufficient mother, or maybe I was wise. The sadness infecting my soul needed to be cured before I became responsible for another life. One day, when I was myself again—when I loved myself as

Aglaia wished—I would make amends. Hopefully my son would understand my decision.

"I already named him," I told the nymphs as I passed him into their arms. "Do not change it."

They nodded.

"He is Aeneas, and he will be praised."

30

MOUNT PELION, ONCE MORE

THE GREAT LOSS of a great love pushed me into solitude, and after giving up my son, nothing seemed important. I entered a period of numbness. I did not cry or rage; I did very little of anything. Visitors came and went; I responded to the requisite demands at the temples, received their offerings. I moved like one of Hephaestus's unfeeling automatons.

Insular years passed. I kept my companions tight and close around me and did not seek love.

If ever my mind started to slip backward, I slapped it back into the present.

When Zeus summoned Hera, Athena, and me to Mount Pelion, I assumed I headed toward another round of public shaming. It hardly mattered; I was half-asleep. It never occurred to me that he was settling our competition for "fairest" at last, for I had long forgotten about the wedding and the apple. The Aphrodite of before may have delighted in small-minded rivalries and frivolous competition, but this one lacked the strength to even pretend.

Zeus selected Paris, a young Trojan prince and cousin to my Aeneas, to finalize the matter. Had he truly been searching for someone all this time? Who cared so much? Had Athena been plaguing her father for an answer, or Hera?

The five of us convened on the mountaintop, four Olympians and one innocent mortal, and Zeus explained his rationale: "You have wondered at my delay, at my reticence to respond"—I hadn't—"but you cannot fathom the breadth of my responsibilities. In addition to my demands as king of Olympus, the lightning bearer and most powerful, I had to choose an arbitrator for this most notable dispute. Which goddess is the fairest? My own heart, too biased by love, demanded I recuse myself."

It would be far more notable if I made it through this speech without rolling my eyes.

"But in Paris, I found an independent mind, someone who could settle the matter without partiality or previous entanglement. He can be neutral."

To me, Paris looked like a boy. A handsome one, but a boy nonetheless. How much experience could he possibly have? And he seemed more nervous than honored. Pity for him stirred my inert heart.

I suppose, in a way, I began to wake up.

Zeus revealed the fruit, hidden in his toga, where he'd kept it dramatically hidden. "This apple, 'For the fairest,' was thrown by the goddess of discord to sow enmity among my Olympians. Today, the matter will be settled, and we may continue to live and do our work in camaraderie."

"Paris," announced Athena, "when you choose me, I will establish you as the most distinguished military leader of your time. To you will go the spoils of war and to your name the title of hero."

Zeus clapped, delighted by the plot twist. This was all for his entertainment. The most willing to perform for Zeus, of course, was Athena. Her father's pet.

Hera, too, understood her role. "And when you select me, fair Paris, I will provide you a preeminent nation to rule. You will be a king remembered for generations to come."

Zeus cheered, and I wondered if he had scripted this entire farce. Had he rehearsed lines with Hera and Athena, all so I would lose?

It was something he would do.

Which begged two questions: Would I play my part in this theater, and if so, what would I offer the boy? Candidly, Alexandros, I did not require a trophy to prove my beauty. I could've withdrawn my bid right then and walked away from it all.

Think how many lives I might have saved.

But my anger was returning, shattering the emptiness and detachment I had cultivated.

I hated Zeus for his impunity, Hera for her latent misogyny. I despised Athena's puffed-up pride.

And I was so very tired of everyone's condescension and interference.

Quips and flirtations had always been my way to defend myself. But with some armor, if you wear it long enough, it sticks. Mine had melded into my person. My personality wasn't just for protection anymore; it was the me I loved.

Was this an epiphany? I wasn't sure I'd had one before, so it was difficult to determine. But consciousness had returned with vivid clarity: I was Aphrodite, goddess of love and beauty, and I wanted to win.

"Paris," I said, in a voice like silk. "I cannot cede knowledge of warfare or government, for I have none to give. My peers may chuckle at my prowess, diminish what I offer, but those who underestimate my gifts most often do so to their inevitable distress."

"What do you present?" snapped Zeus, impatient. "Baby birds and a bed?"

Athena snorted.

"The love of the most beautiful woman in the world."

Zeus's jaw dropped.

"Helen of Sparta," replied Paris immediately. "But she is already married to King Menelaus."

I shrugged a shoulder. "That's never stopped me before."

Hera and Athena both broke out in protest, hurling insults in my direction. I smiled coyly.

Zeus slammed his scepter into the ground, causing the mountain to shake. "Silence!" he bellowed. "You have all pled your cases. Paris must decide."

Though Paris appeared to deliberate, it was finished. The others knew it, too. The twinkle in his eye at Helen's name continued to shine. When Paris presented me with the apple, I feigned surprise and kissed him gratefully, with an open mouth. Athena leaned her head back and groaned.

Hera approached Paris and me, as indignant as I have ever seen her. "You cannot simply walk into a mortal palace and steal its queen. This is a crime against matrimony!"

"I will find the king another suitable bride."

"You never change," she admonished. "You undermine everything we hold sacred with your irresponsibility and irreverence."

"Relationships end all the time," I replied bitterly.

"She might love her husband," argued Athena.

"And she might not! Give Paris a chance. What is the worst that can happen?"

But, as you well know, the worst did happen.

And I would be blamed for that, too.

Endless accounts have been written of the Trojan prince. Poets and philosophers struggle to define him and often contradict one another. Was he a playboy, a villain? Coward or betrayer? Men like to classify, but even in those days, Paris resisted any easy, ubiquitous identification. Labels are clear and sturdy and comfortable. A worn chair to rest upon, an order in the chaos. Those of us who resist definition cause aggravation, become pariahs.

Paris and I shared much in common. He, too, placed love and beauty on the highest altar, and pursued both without fear of consequence.

"I would rather devote my short mortal life to love than ambition," he told me. "I've never aspired to the throne. I don't need more wealth."

Alexandros, I liked him.

On our ocean journey to Sparta, he spoke to me of Helen, whom he first met long before her marriage to Menelaus.

"As children, we were both in Athens at the same time. I visited in the retinue of Theseus's best friend, who lived near me on Mount Pelion. Helen had been taken there by order of Theseus, on a mad contest to collect daughters of Zeus."

I frowned. "Helen is . . . ?"

"The child of Zeus and Leda."

Ah, yes, the infamous swan.

"We were both homesick and found reassurance in each other." And Paris was both with me telling the story and somewhere in the past. His eyes glazed over, reminiscing. "She kissed me, and we promised ourselves to each other, for a future day when we were grown. But before I came of age and could propose myself as a suitor, her father, King Tyndareus, sold his daughter to the highest bidder."

We stood on board the long ship, an oared galley. I sighed and laid my hand atop his on the rail. "It is a familiar tale, I'm afraid."

The wind lifted his fine black hair. "Can first love be real? Is it childish to think the first hand I held could be the one I will hold until the end of days?"

His earnestness reminded me of Adonis, though my lover had been far more pragmatic. Paris was an idealist, perhaps to his detriment.

"I believe a first love can be a forever love," I responded in truth. "But only if you believe in each other's intentions rather than condemn each other's mistakes."

"My brother Hector and my cousin Aeneas are devoted husbands. I will be the same to Helen."

My ears perked up at the mention of my son. "Tell me more of Aeneas."

"He is the best of us."

"In what way?"

Paris gave me a half smile. "For one, he would never plot to steal a married woman from her husband."

I waved a hand. "Some women want to be stolen."

"Aeneas is loyal to his wife and kind to his child, but he worships his father. Anchises is blessed to have such a son."

I paused, insecure. "Does he ever mention his mother?"

Paris answered carefully. "He knows who she is, yes."

I wondered at the stories he had undoubtedly heard, tales of wantonness and vengeance. Was he too mortified to claim me? Did he resent my neglect? Both would be fair, but they hurt, nonetheless. I had never met Aeneas, had no claim upon this boy—this man—but maybe I was ready to rectify that, and maybe he would accept me.

We pulled into the seaport of Gytheio, then traveled the remainder of the distance on horseback—well, Paris did. I was carried in a litter. At the gates of the Spartan palace, I announced our names and guards tripped over themselves to prepare our arrival.

"Do you want a love spell?" I murmured privately to Paris.

He shook his head, mouth set and firm, eyes bright. "No, I only want a chance. Give me a night alone with her, and if she should accept me, a path for our escape."

I smiled.

31

MILOS
Second Century BCE

APHRODITE PAUSES, EXAMINING the halved fruit she still holds. "I started the Trojan War as surely as Paris did. For I was the seed." She sighs and drops the apple to the floor. "Or maybe it was Zeus's fault, for bringing an unequipped mortal into our immortal games."

"Or Eris's fault for riling the goddesses. Or Thetis and Peleus for not inviting her."

"The chain of responsibility is neither straight nor singular; you cannot always trace it back to one source."

He considers. "Most people my age were taught to blame Helen."

"Men do not go to war for love of others, but for love of themselves. The same is true for gods. The Trojan War was never about Helen."

"Did she leave with Paris willingly, or did he abduct her?" It is wild, he thinks, how comfortable he has become discussing the most famous event in history with one who was present. Should he share this experience one day, will anyone believe him?

Maybe Timon.

"Theirs was a true romance," the goddess answers. "She ran away with him, hand in hand."

"Did you accompany them on their journey?"

"No, once I saw them safely in the walled city, I returned to Olympus."

The artist senses an ending, and he is rueful. "Everything changes now, doesn't it?"

"What happened during those terrible years would bring all the immortals together, onto sides, pulled by lovers, siblings, children. The monstrous mess we created over generations came back to confront us. None of us emerged the same."

He fears that her story is nearly over, and he does not want their night to finish.

A white swan enters the artist's hut and strides toward its mistress.

"Dawn nears," she muses, petting the top of its head, "and when it does, I must depart."

"But we have not yet chosen a pose or a prop."

Aphrodite stands and unties an elaborate knot at her shoulder. Her dress falls open, baring her chest.

"Is it possible to reclaim my body after others have taken it, twisted it? Put stories on it? Sometimes it hardly feels mine."

"In this story, the one we will tell in stone, yes."

He kneels before her, draping the dress around her hips, covering her from the waist down. "We will not give them everything, though."

A white feather lies on the floor beside him; he picks it up and hands it to her.

"Have you ever heard a swan die?" she asks.

"No."

"They are silent, all their lives, yet right before their death, they unleash the most mournful song." Aphrodite brings the feather to her cheek, closes her eyes at the delicate, delineated softness. "This, then, is my swan song."

The swan bites into the apple.

Part V

THE SWAN'S FEATHER

Aphrodite Enoplios, armed
Aphrodite Areia, warlike
Magna Mater, mother of the Romans

32

MOUNT OLYMPUS

I HAVE HEARD AN expression in the tongue across the sea: *Dulce bellum inexpertis* (war is sweet to those who have never fought). I'm not certain I ever considered war to be sweet, but I am guilty of romanticization. Even after all the nights holding Ares through his night terrors, I still imagined handsome men in armor. Clean, noble deaths. Hale and hearty horses. Shining swords and windswept capes.

It embarrasses me that I ever entertained such misguided thoughts.

Greece mobilized almost immediately after Helen and Paris fled. "A thousand ships" convened to avenge Menelaus's honor and retrieve his stolen wife, for the cuckolded king of Sparta was also the brother of Agamemnon, high king and commander.

As I have already suggested, the Greeks came not for one errant woman but for trade routes to the east. Agamemnon used his brother's pain as a political ploy. It's always about money, Alexandros. For any question, follow the gold and you'll locate your answer.

And wasn't this what Zeus and Athena always wanted? The ultimate competition. A great game played with great heroes. All those generations building cities and infiltrating bloodlines came down to this siege. Olympians chose sides in support of our respective chosen ones, sharing updates and reports with callous casualness. But this despicable farce could not last. Not when the bodies began to amass and the funeral pyres burned day and night and children starved and women were passed around while men who would never receive any gold butchered one another, never understanding why.

This tale has been told many times before, and often far better than I ever could. But I have never been asked for my experience. This is it, and you might be the first to hear it.

Because of Paris and Aeneas, my allegiance belonged to Troy. Even my dear island Cyprus, which promised fifty ships to the Greek cause, sent only one in deference to me. Apollo also joined the Trojan cause. To some extent, so did his sister, Artemis. She held a long grudge against Agamemnon for slaying one of her sacred deer, and I respected her umbrage. I hated the bastard, too. The king of all Greeks was pompous and crude. Violent. Greedy. Insatiable.

Similar to another king in my life . . .

On the Greek side stood Hera and Poseidon as well as the nymph Thetis, mother of the hero Achilles, and Hephaestus, who cast his famous armor.

Some Olympians preferred neutrality. As war is no place for mischief or revels, neither Hermes nor Dionysus felt compelled to action, and with a steady army of souls marching into the underworld, Hades and Persephone were far too busy managing their domain to participate in the aboveground conflict. Demeter, who always followed her daughter's lead, similarly removed herself from the fray.

Athena began on the Trojan side, but would change mid-war, and as perfectly befits his character, Zeus did not choose, preferring chaos to commitment.

Our disastrous Olympian family in disastrous disarray, as always.

But there is one name I have yet to mention, as I am sure you've noticed.

Ares.

As lord of war, both sides claimed him as their own.

One day, the Greeks would sacrifice an ox to him, and Ares would fight in their ranks. But at the next dawn, the Trojans would behead a flock of roosters, and he would answer their war cry. He did not rest, battling constantly, wiping Greek blood from his sword, pulling his spear from Trojan bodies. Phobos and Deimos spread panic—the urge to flee—and deep, paralyzing fear among both camps, crippling the minds of even the most stalwart soldiers. They also maintained Ares's chariot.

I had no plans to descend upon the city, until Apollo barged into my home and begged.

"I think I am in love," he proclaimed, slumping into a chair.

I raised an eyebrow. "With . . . ?"

He groaned. "Prince Hector."

"Isn't he married to a woman?"

"You, above all, should know that love is as fluid as the sea," Apollo snapped defensively.

"Well, what should we do about it?"

At my use of the word *we*, Apollo's spirits lifted. He sat up straighter. "He is Troy's finest fighter. That places him in the gravest danger."

My heart sank for my dear friend. To love a warrior, especially a mortal one, is an exercise in anguish.

"Come with me, Aphrodite, to the front. If I am there, I can keep him safe."

"What use would I be?" I raised my hands, palms out, and shook my head. "Nobody wants me there."

"Aeneas might."

Poor, motherless Aeneas, born of deceit. He tugged at me in a way Phobos and Deimos never did. Maybe it was because he was my last, my youngest. Or perhaps it was due to his mortality. Is that why I sent him to the nymphs so obediently? Yes, I had been depressed, but also, what did I know of raising a human boy?

"He will fight, too," added Apollo.

Aeneas, my child who would die, and with the outbreak of war, that day might be soon. If I didn't go to Troy now, I might never get a chance to meet my son as an adult.

Anchises would be there. Ares, somewhere, as well.

"Apollo?" I asked, voice catching. "Am I strong enough?"

He came to me and kissed my forehead. "Like a diamond."

BEFORE I LEFT for Troy, Eros tried to dissuade me.

"Mama, you don't even know how to hold a bow," he argued.

"I hardly think that will be necessary."

He rubbed at his temples. "I know you feel responsible for Paris, but what do you think you will accomplish there?"

I continued packing, ignoring his perfectly valid points. Eros examined the inside of my trunk and exclaimed: "Pearl bracelets? Saffron?"

"I'm only bringing what I need," I sniffed.

My son closed the trunk and sat on it. "Be honest, if not with me, at least with yourself: Is this all because you hope to see Ares again?"

I froze for only a breath, then blinked. "I think that is quite done."

"Psyche doesn't think so."

"Your wife is prone to the sentimental, and I find it quite sickening." Eros's eyes rolled heavenward, and I softened. "But we will need her good cheer in the days ahead. Hold her tightly while I'm away, Eros."

He opened his arms, and I welcomed his embrace, kissing the top of his head, the smell of his skin through his curls so achingly familiar.

My son did not tell me to be careful; he understood it would be a waste of breath.

33

TROY

THE GREEKS BEACHED their ships at the mouth of the Scamander River and built a wooden encampment, filled beyond capacity, with tents and men and violent virility. Across the plains, on a rising hill, sat Troy, well fortified and wealthy.

I stayed with Apollo in his temple sanctuary at Thymbra, a city in the Troad southeast of Troy, but I also kept my own elaborate tent raised on the Callicolone hill over the valley. While Apollo regularly counseled with Hector and the other Trojan generals in the city proper, I remained on the periphery of the action, waiting.

But for what?

I couldn't properly address my own inaction.

On our nights together, Apollo and I slept in his bed, fully clothed, often talking until morning.

"You do not smile anymore," my friend told me as we lay on our sides facing each other.

"What if he dies before I meet him?" I whispered back.

"Then why delay?"

I struggled to explain myself. "Apollo, describe your mother to me, as if I had never met her."

He considered. "Well, Leto is a Titan of Coeus and Phoebe. She lives on Delos, and—"

"No, what does she *do*?"

"She protects mothers and their young." His eyes shone in the candlelight as he spoke of her. "She is demure, so modest that she wears a veil, even at home."

"Your mother is exceptional," I concluded. "You are proud to belong to her."

"Aphrodite, I understand what you are trying to say and—"

"Do not dare tell me that Aeneas finds comfort in my reputation as a whore. I will not listen."

Apollo was ruminative. "I was going to say that you and my mother are more alike than you think."

"Ha."

"After Zeus raped her," continued Apollo, ignoring my sarcasm, "and Leto became pregnant, Hera instructed every land to deny her entrance. She had nowhere to go, but she persevered, moving constantly with no rest, from one place to the next, until she found her floating isle, tied to no land. It is the same way you continue, loving with your stalwart heart, no matter how many times it has been broken."

"My heart is just pieces, Apollo."

"And yet, your pieced-together heart is more whole than any other."

Tears pricked at my eyes, but they were good ones. Apollo reached forward and brushed the hair from my face, then grabbed a strand and tugged, just enough to be interesting. "Do you ever wonder about us?"

His voice was tender, curious, and yes, I examined the handsome face of my friend and wondered. I moved forward, gave him a slight nod, and took his lips in mine.

There was no fault in his kiss. He had style; he tasted sweet.

I released him, feeling . . .

Nothing.

Apollo wrinkled his nose. "No?"

"No," I agreed. But then he began to laugh, and I joined him in that breathless laughter, and those tears that had threatened now poured down my cheeks.

"I love you," I told him, thrilled at how uncomplicated it could be to say such. And mean it.

"And I love you." He lay on his back and whistled. "If you had been a man though, things between us might have been different."

"My cock would be enormous."

He grinned. "Obscene."

"How would I walk? Would I be able to ride a horse?"

We continued to ruminate on my hypothetical manhood, hands clasped, until cozy, congenial quiet settled between us, and we retreated into our separate thoughts and anxieties, without ever leaving the other's side.

AFTER THE GREEKS sent ambassadors to negotiate for Helen's return, and King Priam refused, their hero Achilles led relentless attacks upon the Trojan walls. But the towered, impenetrable city stood firm. The Greek army pivoted and changed their strategy, assaulting Troy's closest allies instead, destroying any opportunities for the besieged city to receive aid.

Hector and his forces, empowered by horses of notorious acclaim, kept the Greek soldiers from moving up the plain, but were unable to fully force them back into the sea. As neither side made progress, resolution—and peace—became increasingly elusive.

Eventually, a gentleman's duel was called, not between the two most acclaimed heroes, Achilles and Hector, but between Menelaus and Paris, the spurned husband and chosen consort, to decide Helen's fate and end the conflict.

I worried for Paris against the weathered Spartan king. Paris was younger, inexperienced. Menelaus fought for pride, Paris for love. Which would prove stronger? And then there was Helen, who had no voice or hand in the matter.

On the day of the face-off, I joined her in the Trojan palace while the men assembled below. She and I found a place on the rampart where we could watch privately, draped in dark cloaks to disguise ourselves.

Helen, with her lovely face gone pale as a plant without sun, and eyes haunted but dry, remained stoic.

I thought of my own failed marriage. What if a similar duel had been called? Hephaestus had always controlled the arena in his interactions with Ares, luring Ares to his forge, then to his bedroom, but on an open plain like this, the outcome would have been wildly different. Ares would have destroyed him.

"Has Paris prepared?" I asked.

"Hector sparred with him last night. They talked him through countless scenarios." Helen inhaled deeply, fortifying herself to relay the truth. "But Paris is an archer. He is no combat fighter."

Down below us, the men on both sides cheered, banging shields and stomping feet, as Paris and Menelaus, carrying spears, entered a drawn circle. Hector and Odysseus, the officiators, drew lots from a bronze helmet, and Paris's name was selected. He would throw first.

Beside me, Helen reached out and gripped the wall's ledge.

To the Greek army's amusement, Paris's spear bounced off Menelaus's shield. I swore, wishing Helen could not hear the taunts. Menelaus's spear followed, shooting through Paris's shield but only slicing the end of his tunic.

"He has survived the first round," I told Helen, for her eyes had closed.

Hector and Odysseus passed out swords, and the second round commenced. Menelaus moved on Paris with immediate aggression, slamming his sword into Paris's helmet. The Greeks were uproarious, cheering their hero. Paris, overwhelmed, faltered, but did not cede. Each time Menelaus thrust him down into the dirt, he scrambled back to his feet.

By this time, spectators on the wall had recognized Helen. Insults hurled our way.

"There she stands, the harlot of Greece!"

"Paris's dog."

"Hell-to-men Helen."

"Troy hates her."

"Give her back."

"Shove her off the ramparts and end this now."

I spoke over them, hoping my own message could drown out theirs: "Never listen to the herd. They only understand one way to handle fear—to defend what they know and attack what they don't."

"It's not just the men," she murmured. "The women can be even worse. They do not know me, but they hate me."

Hera. Athena. The virgin goddesses. Hadn't I said the same once?

"Yes, Helen, there are women who hate women. It's how they manifest their hurt."

And then a shrill voice yelled: *"Only a whore abandons her daughter for a new cock!"*

Helen's lips tightened into a straight line. "Menelaus used to choke me," she said with an austere calm. "That's how he got me to gasp in bed." Her hands found her own throat, massaging, mimicking her trauma. "Sometimes I would pass out and he would finish while I lay there."

I did not boil with disgust; I burned with anger. I could have scorched the earth, left nothing behind.

So much violence in the false name of pleasure, in the false idea of property, in the false pursuit of honor.

We were all unworthy souls.

But down below, the battle continued, unaffected by the onslaught Helen endured.

The next time Paris hit the ground, Menelaus grabbed him by the helmet and dragged him toward the Greek army. When the chin strap broke, Paris scurried away. Enraged, Menelaus hurled the helmet into the crowd and roared into the sky.

"Zeus above! How does this snake keep slithering from my grasp?"

A fellow Greek soldier tossed Menelaus another spear, and the Spartan spun on his heel, running at Paris with his full force.

Helen screamed—for her lover, but also for herself.

Alexandros, I did not want Paris to die, but more than that, I could not stand by and watch another woman return to her captor. Marriage should not be a trap or a leash.

I flew into the battle, riding upon a sea mist, and reached Paris before Menelaus. I clutched the wounded prince in my arms, enshrouding us in divinity, and we rose from the ring, hidden and protected. Menelaus's frustration and the jeering soldiers chased us as we floated away, up and over the Trojan walls, and through a balcony into the safety of Paris's rooms.

To everyone who bore witness, Paris disappeared into shimmery air, but the Olympians who watched knew better.

I laid him, dirty as he was, upon the bed.

"Aphrodite, you shouldn't have done that," Paris moaned, "but I am grateful."

I stroked his forehead.

"Today, at least, love wins."

Moments later, Helen rushed through the door, flinging herself at his side.

"Paris," she cried, repeating his name over and over as he brought her to his chest.

"Thank you," said Helen, looking back at me. No longer emotionally stolid, she let her tears fall freely.

I nodded, heart aching, and left them.

Though Agamemnon claimed Menelaus the victor, Helen remained in Troy. Paris and I would both face the repercussions of that day, but my intervention gave the lovers more time. I would never regret it.

34

TROY

I DREAMED OF ARES that night, so vividly.

Too vividly.

I walked across the fields of battle, cutting a path through the bodies. Vultures circled, appearing and disappearing as the smoke shifted. Wisps from fiery arrows, heat rising from the split bodies, the steaming viscera. Separated limbs, teeth, and tongues. A landscape in sordid fragments, everything tinted gray and umber.

He stood amid the carnage, arms bare and dropped to his sides, one hand still gripping a grimy sword. All his exposed skin was filthy, painted in mud and blood. So much blood: some brown and dried, some bright and dripping. A fresh cut ran down through his eyebrow to the top of his cheek. But there was no fury in him, only the grim solemnity of one whose time has come. The executioner and the man about to die.

"You should carry a weapon."

His voice rasped as though his throat had been burned.

"I wouldn't know how to use it," I replied.

"You have driven a dagger into me more than once."

"Our battles feel trivial while men are dying, Ares."

Somewhere an injured horse screamed. I shuddered.

"I watched Paris's duel. I know you intervened."

"I hid myself."

His eyes flickered, remembering. "I smelled you. A scent like the sea."

I pursed my lips. "I smell like roses."

"You perfume yourself with roses, Aphrodite, but the ocean runs in your veins."

Something fluttered in my chest, but I said, "I only gave Paris and Helen a bit more time."

"Haven't I told you that war is hate? This is no place for a beauty such as yours."

"Well, I have never been a good listener."

He rubbed his face with both hands in frustration. "I am the only Olympian who comprehends the extent of this brutality. I answer every call for help, massacring the same men I aided the day before. Greece needs me, Troy needs me. If this continues, I will kill everyone."

"We could leave," I implored. "Let me take you away from here."

"Still my dreamer, I see."

I opened my arms to him. "Love is superior to reason."

Ares charged over the corpses and gripped me by my upper arms. I lifted my face to him, and the winds whipped my hair behind me.

"You must leave. I can hardly think straight for fear that you will be hurt."

"Then don't think."

And he kissed me.

We were still us, even at the end of the world. I would have kissed him for as long as he let me, but I woke, chest heaving. Shaking fingers found my lips, and when I lowered them, I saw they were coated in dirt and blood.

THAT MORNING, I stole a cloak and horse from Apollo and headed for the Dardanian plain. I'd recognized the location in my dream. Aeneas led the Dardanians. If Ares fought for the Greeks, my son was in danger.

And if Ares killed Aeneas . . .

I could not imagine what might follow.

I rode the horse through camp after camp of Trojan allies, searching for Ares and leaving quite a commotion in my wake.

"Aphrodite rides!"

"She is here!"

"The goddess of love blesses the Trojans."

And more than one lewd comment I will not repeat.

I asked a boy, far too young to be a soldier, where I could find the god of war. Dumbfounded, he merely pointed to a black tent raised at the farthest edge of the periphery.

I hobbled my horse and entered, hoping to find no woman warming his bed.

But Ares was alone, washing his hands and arms at a basin, unarmored and wearing a short linen tunic. Somebody had crudely stitched together the gash in his eyebrow, but the wound existed, nonetheless. He did not seem surprised to see me.

"I told you to carry a weapon; you do not even bear a shield."

My chest expanded, spirits lifting. I knew it wasn't a dream.

"It would ruin my outfit."

He grunted. "Be serious, Aphrodite. This is war."

"And I come with a serious plea."

Ares flung out the droplets from his hands and wiped what remained on a rag. "Yes?"

"Pledge your fealty to Troy."

He chuckled. "So many appeals of late."

"That was only one, but—"

"You are too late. Athena and I spoke yesterday on the banks of the Scamander. She has asked me to join her and the Greeks."

"What is her reasoning?"

"She believes if I combine my abilities with Odysseus, her Ithacan champion, we might be able to end this engagement."

"Don't! To side with Athena, you also side with Hera and Poseidon. After the trial, how could you?"

Ares shrugged. "It isn't the gods I care about, but the real human men, on both sides, who are lost and terrified. I fight for the soldiers. An expedient conclusion to this war is best for them."

"Then I will beg." I lifted clasped, pleading hands above my heart. "My son Aeneas leads a Trojan battalion. Do not let your hatred for his father make him a target. Please, Ares, he is my last child. Do not kill him."

"I do not hate his father."

"Oh."

"I do not *like* his father, but . . ." Ares hesitated, "Soon I, too, will have a child in this war."

Just like that, my chest—filled with hope—collapsed inward.

"I have a daughter." Ares brought my prayerful hands down. "With Otrera."

"The Amazon," I whispered.

"Yes . . ." As his voice trailed off, a muscle in his jaw twitched. He seemed unsure, conflicted. Something was wrong; I knew him too well.

"What is it? What are you not telling me?"

Ares took a deep breath. "Otrera is not only the mother of my daughter . . . she is my wife."

I stumbled backward, one word repeating, pounding like fists, like a battering ram, against the walls of my skull.

Wife.

"I cannot breathe." Unstable, I sank onto the edge of his cot. Never once, even in the direst hours, when I tortured myself with images of Ares's hands on another, had I ever considered him married.

"But . . . you kissed me only last night."

"In a dream, Aphrodite."

"A dream we shared." I looked up at him. "Do you dream with her, too?"

I watched as his expression closed up; his eyes dimmed. "The Amazons received me on Themyscira and allowed me to begin again."

"So you married their queen?"

"She built me a temple."

I couldn't swallow my laughter, it spilled out of me, a torrent of hilarity, until Ares held up an angry, warning hand. "Aphrodite, stop."

"Oh, I did not worship you properly! You wanted me to raise a memorial in stone, and there I was, down on my knees!"

"I cannot do this with you." Ares rubbed his face with a hand. "If I pledge myself to King Priam, will you return to Olympus or Cyprus?"

"Yes," I lied. "But you must promise the Amazon forces, as well. Doesn't marrying their queen make you king?"

He sighed. I waited.

"From henceforth, I fight solely for Troy."

"And . . . ?"

"And the Amazons, as well."

I did not thank him, but remained sitting, unsettled.

"Where is Graegus?" I asked.

"In Thrace."

"Not with your wife?"

Ares's nostrils flared slightly, the only evidence of his discontent. "He has not taken to Themyscira's . . . climate."

Good boy.

I nodded and rose from his cot with renascent strength. At the tent's exit, his voice stopped me.

"That's not your cloak."

"No, it isn't."

But I offered up no name, only tightening it around my shoulders. Let him wonder.

I RODE BACK TO Apollo's to return his horse and cloak, but did not stay. I needed privacy to sort through my turbulent emotions. I hiked up the hill to my own encampment and, though it was the middle of the day, crawled into bed and pulled the blankets to my chin.

My body curled up, and my mind turned inward.

Athena had attempted to recruit Ares for the Greeks.

I fantasized about entombing her in an unbreakable box and throwing her out to sea. Maybe this Amazonian queen could join her.

Otrera called Ares "husband," something I had never done. They shared a family—a grown child on her way here.

But I had a son of my own.

I had tarried long enough. I would enter the city and meet Aeneas.

Tonight.

35

TROY

EACH DAY, THE fighting between Greeks and Trojans concluded at dusk. Once the sun set, both sides' warriors returned to their homes of leather or stone, to the fires where women and the enslaved prepared and served hot meals with increasingly scavenged supplies. Some washed their bodies or tended their wounds; some drank. Some couldn't stop fighting, starting quarrels and throwing fists. The lust of war, the frustrated, macabre monotony of facing death day after day, is not so easily shrugged off in the after hours.

And the women did their best to survive it.

I entered the walled city, clandestine and disguised, and headed straight for the home of Anchises. Apollo had explained its location, and I'd asked him to go over the directions with me multiple times in my nervousness.

"You cannot miss it, Aphrodite. There is a golden bough painted above the door."

As a member of the royal family, Anchises lived on the edges of the inner limestone citadel, where the Trojan elite crammed together behind a second set of walls. His home was smaller than most, only one floor, and I paused outside to consider the tree branch. I reached up to touch the golden leaves and wondered who painted it. Was it Anchises, or was it my son?

I did not knock but opened the door and slipped inside. Anchises sat at a wooden table, and a younger man stood beside him, setting down food. When I lowered my hood, the man dropped a platter. It shattered against the floor.

Anchises broke the awkward stillness with a chuckle. "I have aged terribly these twenty years, I wonder if you recognize me."

I smiled. "Good evening, Anchises."

He did look different than I remembered, but I'd spent mere moments with his true face. The man I recalled was distraught and wan, and this one was weathered by sun, lined by life.

"Please, Aphrodite, come join us."

He stood and pulled out a chair for me. I accepted it, staring at Aeneas all the while, unable to force my eyes away. He and Anchises were so similar. Unlike Eros and Harmonia, when I investigated Aeneas's face, I found none of myself. Maybe that was a blessing.

"Aeneas, make Aphro—your mother—a plate."

"No," I demurred. "That is unnecessary. I do not hunger."

A partial truth, but I would not steal food from their stomachs. Not when both men's bones stretched taut their skin.

"My wife made it," offered Aeneas politely. "I bring my father food when his back bothers him."

"I broke it, many years ago, during a terrible storm," Anchises explained.

"The pain is worse when he does not rest, and he does not listen to me."

"I must go to the palace when Priam requires it!"

"Yes, but you also visit the wounded, the widowed. You go to the orphanages. You are on your feet all day."

Anchises tossed up his hands. "Ah, well. There is much to do."

"But you did not come here to watch us bicker." Aeneas regarded me across the table. Yes, he was foreign to me but so handsome. Gray eyed, with an auburn beard and the build of an athlete. I was mesmerized. "What can we do for you, Aphrodite?"

He did not call me *Mother,* and I felt relief. It would have ruined the integrity of the moment.

"I came, not to speak of war, but to meet you. I . . ." I'd rarely felt so discomposed, never stumbled over my words with such clumsiness. "I came because . . . I'm sure you wonder why I would visit, after all this time, but I—"

Aeneas cut me off. "I am simply glad you are here now."

I shook my head. "Aeneas, you have every right to be mad at me."

"Perhaps." He shrugged. "But we live in a time of war. I might die tomorrow. I would not spend what could be my final night on this earth throwing my mother out of a house."

Anchises said nothing but proudly patted his son's forearm.

"You remind me of my other son's wife," I finally said. "She, too, speaks and acts with grace."

"I would like to hear of her. And him. Of all your—our—family."

I regaled him with my better stories, ones that made him and Anchises laugh but also showed me in a more flattering light. Like Aeneas said, this was wartime. Nobody wanted to spend living, waking hours discussing the morbid and miserable. And my son didn't need to hear all my mistakes.

"You have entertained us tonight!" exclaimed Anchises as I took a long drink of water. "I haven't smiled so much in a long time."

Aeneas agreed. "It is our turn. What can we share with you?"

"I would enjoy hearing about your son."

Aeneas grinned. "Ascanius is a four-year-old boy in all the best four-year-old ways."

He and Anchises took turns regaling me with anecdotes about this much-adored boy. I marveled at their solidarity, the way they spoke in conjunction, adding and emphasizing, to build a narrative. Their closeness, their direct and obvious care for each other, was everything an Olympian family was not. I was glad I gave my son this life.

As the night progressed, I noticed Anchises shift in his seat, and his face paled, sweat beaded on his brow. The pain in his spine must torment him, and I would not be the one to delay his respite, even if I would have gladly remained in their company until morning.

"I will depart," I announced, rueful, and I'd like to think Aeneas might have shared a fraction of my disappointment. "The war will not stop for our reunion."

"But Troy can count on your support?" asked Aeneas, then scowled at himself. "Not that meeting you, at last, wasn't enough. I only—"

"I understand, Aeneas. And I promise all the power I possess to you and yours."

Anchises made to stand, but I held up a hand. "Please, do not get up for me."

"I must. I will."

With a hand from Aeneas, Anchises rose to his feet and stiffly escorted me to the door. I slowed my own pace to match his. "What Zeus did to us was cruel," he said, "but our son is my joy. Thank you for letting me have him." He lowered his voice. "I know he looks like me, but when he is happy, his eyes flash lavender."

As I kissed Anchises's cheek, I said something I do not say often. "Thank you."

THE NEWS OF Ares's commitment to the Trojans raced among the camps, eliciting cheers from one side and curses among the other. At the same time, Athena's spies sent word to their mistress of my visit to Ares's tent just before his decision. The goddess descended upon the beach, enraged by my success and ready to retaliate. All she required was a proxy, and she marched through the Greek camps searching for one hotheaded enough to accept.

She found her warrior in Diomedes, the cunning Argive prince. Within the secrecy of his tent, Athena commenced negotiations.

"I will provide you preternatural strength and skill to turn the tides of this war."

"Yes, but what do you want in return?"

"I want you to kill Aeneas."

Diomedes snorted. "He is one of Troy's finest, bested only by Hector, and protected by his divine mother."

"Then I will offer the same deal to Ajax or Achilles. Already their reputations precede yours." Her forehead furrowed. "I wonder, with so many Greeks on their hero's journey, will Diomedes be remembered?"

He considered her point; in his silence, he conceded the truth. "And when Aphrodite intervenes?"

"Attack."

Athena passed him a spear, its tip glowing with an eerie green luminescence. A strange, dark magic. Diomedes accepted it with an amoral thrill.

"While, unfortunately, this cannot kill her, it will cause grievous harm."

"Permanently?"

The goddess smiled without showing her teeth. "Perhaps."

"But what of Ares?" he asked, examining the weapon with shrewd appreciation.

"I will shield you from his wrath," Athena promised. And then, leaning closer, she whispered the words his heart most fervidly yearned to hear: "And you will be a legend."

Then Athena held her hands over the young Greek, imbuing him with magic, fulfilling both her promise and her own revenge fantasy.

Diomedes reentered the fray, thrice empowered.

36

TROY

DIOMEDES, IMPATIENT TO demonstrate his power—and not one to press his luck—unleashed a murderous rampage upon the Trojans with no delay. His infamy reached the walled city and the temples beyond, his name repeating with exponential fear.

"Diomedes fights like a new man."

"The Argive has become unstoppable!"

"He kills with the ferocity of three men!"

Apollo panicked, but I did not.

"The tides are turning against our Trojans," he fretted, pacing the length of his temple.

"Not while Ares fights."

"He cannot protect everyone, Aphrodite."

"No, but Diomedes is only a man." I took a fig from a basket of offerings on Apollo's altar and bit into it. "Ares will stop him."

"Is Diomedes only a man? I'm no longer certain."

"He is no match for Hector, Apollo."

But my friend, unable to relax until he saw Hector alive and standing with his own two eyes, left for the front. I did not accompany him. Per the deal I struck with Ares, I was not supposed to be in Troy. Obviously, I was always going to do what I wanted, but I had no intention of angering him yet. For now, I would keep my presence discreet.

Despite my separation, the battle cries reached me. I heard them first as a distant murmur, but they grew to a roar that became impossible to ignore, especially once I realized it wasn't just noise but one name, three syllables, cantillating from the plain.

Aeneas. Aeneas. Aeneas.

I grabbed the nearest servant. "Why do they chant the prince's name?"

"The crazed man from Argos demands Aeneas's blood."

The Aeneas I met, the one who brought dinner to his father each night, even after a full day of fighting, would meet Diomedes. His actions were dictated by honor; he would never permit others to die in his place. I spurred into action.

"Armor, my goddess!" exclaimed a priest.

"No time!"

But I did arrange my hair.

I entered the fray on the Trojan side, rushing through the lines of Trojan soldiers like a madwoman, searching for my son.

"He took a chariot with Pandarus," answered a man emerging from a healer's tent with a bandaged shoulder. "To the front."

"And the war god? Ares?"

"He was sent to the beach, I think," said the weary healer. "Nobody has seen him today."

This was inauspicious. Too much so. There was something odd about the timing of Diomedes's sudden prowess and Ares's absence. I did not trust it.

Apollo's earlier trepidation was merited, and once again, I was the fool.

I continued running, filled with horror that I would arrive at the skirmish too late to save my son.

Aeneas! Aeneas! Aeneas!

The chorus cried, louder and with more exigency, as I moved closer. Nobody seemed to recognize me as I pushed my way toward the commotion. A few men even shoved me backward, and I slipped in a pool of blood. My dress tore, the combs fell from my hair. I pulled myself up, wiped the dust from my eyes, and continued, but it was nearly impossible to see anything over the shoulders and helmets and horses.

Before, Helen and I watched the battle from above, from behind the safety of a stone wall. Today was nothing like that. I could smell the piss and bile, feel the violent vibrations of earth through the soles of my feet. This was the battlefront, what Ares had spent centuries keeping me from, and it was insane and awful.

I wanted to go home.

But not without Aeneas. I wouldn't abandon him a second time.

I knew I had found him when I saw soldiers on both sides giving a wide berth. The chariot carrying Aeneas and Pandarus, a Lycian aristocrat, raced toward a solitary warrior on foot, Diomedes. I watched as Pandarus shot arrow after arrow at the Greek. Each one missed its mark.

The Trojan horses were without equal, speedy and bravehearted, and Aeneas could handle them better than most. Pandarus was an accomplished archer. Diomedes should be dead by now.

And yet, he was very much alive.

Diomedes hefted a spear above his shoulder and hurled it toward the moving chariot. It flew like a peregrine falcon, diving straight into Pandarus's eye, slicing through his face—teeth and tongue—before jutting out below his jawbone. My hands flew over my mouth, covering nothing. I couldn't make a sound, couldn't enunciate my horror. Pandarus toppled from the chariot, and Aeneas brought his galloping horses to a halt. He leapt out to collect his comrade's body, which was precisely what Diomedes wanted.

Just as Aeneas reached his friend, the Greek hefted a massive boulder and hurled it toward Aeneas.

That's when I found my voice; I screamed.

The rock hit Aeneas in the joint between leg and hip, shattering bone, and sending Aeneas into immediate collapse. He lay in the dust beside Pandarus.

Diomedes pounded his chest, roaring in triumph, like a beast.

"Down with Troy!" he cried. "Death to all Trojans!"

Frantic and terrified, I pushed past the onlookers and entered the scene, unarmed and without any defenses, thinking only of my son. When I reached him, his eyes were closed but his clenching fists shook. Still alive.

"Thank you, thank you, thank you," I murmured.

Dropping to my knees, I lifted him the best I could, dragging his torso into my lap. Aeneas's face puckered with pain.

"Mother," he moaned.

I would not let that be his last word.

Around me was mayhem. Bodies slammed against one another; bits of rock and metal flew indiscriminately. I bent myself over Aeneas, hoping to protect his head and chest with my own back as my overwrought mind sought an exit. Pandarus was dead, but I could still save Aeneas. I should have spirited him away as I did Paris, but I hesitated. His bones were in pieces, and I was petrified of hurting him.

Meanwhile, a Greek soldier made an opportune dash for Aeneas's abandoned chariot.

I lifted my arm—to stop him? Summon magic? Call for help? I can't be exactly sure—but Diomedes, who monitored my every move, seized his opportunity. He pulled a dagger from his belt. He threw it.

The dagger entered the back of my outstretched hand, piercing me with iron, and slammed my arm downward, pinning me to the ground.

My body convulsed; I bled ichor into the Trojan soil.

"Take this wound as a warning from Athena, Aphrodite!" bellowed Diomedes, eyes red with bloodlust. "Stay out of this war!"

"It is you who have crossed the line," I hissed back. "A fool who fights immortals is a fool who does not live long."

These were brave words, for in truth, I had never felt such pain besides childbirth. My free hand slid out from under Aeneas, who was barely conscious, and I moved it, trembling, toward the one stabbed into the ground. I needed to remove the dagger so I could muster enough power to get us out of this ghastly place.

Alexandros, I was so scared, of all of it. The blade through my palm, Diomedes's mad quest, my moribund son. The chaos continuing to circle me, tightening its hold. I felt trapped in place, without an exit, and on my own.

But then came a voice I would know anywhere.

"You will eat that dagger before this day is through, Diomedes."

My head jerked up as my heart leapt into my throat; he had come.

"Ares is here!" screamed the Greeks. "The war god fights!"

Diomedes fled from my view.

Easily a dozen soldiers stood between Ares and me, but he spun through them as only he could. Thrusting kicks and headbutting, his sword twirling and slashing faster than I could see. Blood sprayed, bodies spliced.

A spear whistled his way, but Ares caught it in midair, spun it, then hurled it back to its sender with such force, it pierced the Greek soldier and sent him flying backward.

And then Ares was crouching before me, shielding me from the din with his body.

Our eyes met. His brow was slightly creased as he locked onto me with insistency, imploring, demanding my attention.

"Do you remember where we went after Hebe married Heracles?"

"The Hall of the Gods," I whispered.

"You straddled me on Zeus's throne," he said, "and bit the backrest to keep from screaming."

"I left teeth marks in the gold."

A memory so vivid, I could almost relive the pleasure. And as my pulse raced, Ares extracted the dagger.

It sliced my hand open anew as it exited the wound, but I muffled a yell into my shoulder.

"Do not move, Aphrodite. I am going to dismember Diomedes, then get you out of here."

But behind Ares, I saw Aeneas's chariot speeding toward us. No driver held the reins, though they were lifted in midair, and beside this spectral conductor stood Diomedes, spear raised, a drunken look on his face. The point of his weapon, gleaming an otherworldly green, seemed trained on my throat. Ares noted my horror and instinctively turned, screening me from Diomedes as the spear shot through the air.

It hit Ares in the side, at the break in his armor, between the chest and backplate, and the agony that issued from his body rocked the field. Soldiers covered their ears, clutched their heads. But even with a spear shaft lodged in his torso, Ares charged after the chariot on foot, sword slashing, cutting down everyone in his path, until the god of war keeled over.

"Apollo!" I screamed. "Help us!"

My friend materialized, appearing beside me with a shimmering lasso. He threw the rope wide, binding Aeneas, Ares, and me together, and we escaped into his magic.

37

TROY

WE REAPPEARED IN Apollo's sanctuary at Thymbra. The priests helped us move my son to a couch, and Apollo tipped a sleeping draft down his throat while I lifted Aeneas's head. Within breaths, he was asleep. I kissed his face as I hadn't since I relinquished him to the Oreads.

"His bones are badly broken, but I can heal them," Apollo began, pouring himself a cup of water. "I will send a message to Hector that Aeneas is here and stable."

"Then he will not die?"

"Not today."

Ares, on the other hand, stumbled wildly about the temple, crashing into pillars and votives, knocking over candles. He had snapped off the protruding spear shaft, but the tip remained embedded in his body.

"There's something strange happening to him," remarked Apollo. "He needs to stop moving so I can inspect the injury."

I tried to get Ares to sit, but he backed away from me, pointing at Apollo. "If he comes near me, I'll smash his face in! Where is my sword?"

"Don't be an ass!" I scolded. "Apollo won't hurt you."

"That's not Apollo." The whites of Ares's eyes had gone viridescent; his pupils were dilated.

A brave—or perhaps masochistic—priest stepped forward, arms above his head in a gesture of goodwill, but Ares backhanded him into the nearest wall.

"Ares, no!" I cried as the man slithered to the floor.

"He's not of sound mind," Apollo declared. "We need to restrain him."

But that would only inflame Ares more. I needed to get him away from the other men.

"I'll take him back to my tent."

Apollo shook his head. "You cannot be alone with him. It's unsafe."

"I can handle my own safety, thank you very much. I simply need assistance getting him there." Apollo wasn't convinced. I placed a hand on each side of his concerned face. "Stay here, watch Aeneas, and wait for Hector. Please."

He sighed but nodded.

It took six of Apollo's most robust priests to corral Ares up the hill and settle him upon my bed. All the while, he thrashed and moaned.

"We can stay," offered one, as the others exchanged alarmed glances.

"He will not hurt me."

At that moment, Ares's chest lurched upward, his back arched, and he howled. One of the priests began chanting a prayer, and I forced a smile. "He is fine. We are fine."

I led the men to the exit and practically shoved them from my tent, sealing it closed with my power. Then I returned to Ares, crawling up onto the bed next to him. "Hush," I soothed, running my hands across his forehead and over his chest and shoulders until his body slowly settled. When, at last, his breath became more measured, I adjusted the pillow beneath his head and whispered, "You saved me. I no longer believed you cared."

"I would crawl my broken, battered body across every field of war to reach you," he rasped.

Then Ares fell unconscious.

Just as well, I thought, for the work ahead would not be pleasant. I wrapped my own wounded hand the best I could in a shawl and pulled my hair up into a roll at the top of my head. Then I undressed him, both his armor and the tunic beneath, mumbling disingenuous apologies to Queen Otrera.

The spearpoint was stuck in his side, directly above his hip bone and parallel to his navel. I stuck two fingers into the wet, oozing wound, cringing as they passed through layers of ravaged flesh, but though I could just grasp the spear's end, my grip kept slipping.

I would need my whole hand to pull it out.

I retrieved a single-edged blade from my trunk. I had never used it before, but I placed the tip at the edge of the opening and sliced a straight line through Ares's skin. Green blood spilled outward onto his abdomen.

What poison coated this spear? Some kind of serpent blood?

This was dark magic.

Girding myself, I stuck one hand inside the large slit I'd made, wrapped all my fingers around the hard, leaf-shaped bronze spearhead, and yanked.

It popped out.

Disgusted, I tossed the gore-coated object onto the floor.

Realizing that I would need to stitch the wound closed, I groaned. I could barely sew. I hated needlework.

Meanwhile, Ares had begun to pant. I wiped my hands upon my dress, then felt his forehead, inhaling sharply through my teeth, for he burned to my touch. I dragged a large basin of water to the bedside and poured ladle after ladle over his head. As the water streamed down his face, it steamed.

The fever persisted. I could not banish it from his body, and when its heated mania entered his mind, Ares roused into semi-awareness, eyes open but seeing invisible enemies instead of me. He struggled against my ministrations, hallucinating himself into some hellscape. One moment, he claimed he was in Tartarus, the next he was burning in Hephaestus's forge.

"No more," he moaned. "Brother, no more."

I did my best to placate him. I hummed. I summoned lavender, a flower that has always provided me serenity. But still he convulsed. Worried I would be pummeled by his fists and feet while I stitched, I considered binding him to the bed.

It wouldn't be the first time.

"Where is Aphrodite?"

"Here," I reassured him. "Ares, I am here."

"I need her. I need Aphrodite."

"She is on her way."

His head on the side, he murmured into the blankets, "She is my only happiness."

Deep night embraced the hill, and I lit oil lamps inside the tent. By their light I could see Ares's skin turning yellow as the green magic advanced through his veins. What if this poisoned blood entered his heart? Would he transform, fall into a trance? Could he die? Anything felt possible in this upside-down world of war.

I had to remove every trace of it from his body before I stitched him closed, but how?

Memory came to my aid, specifically my time in the forest with Adonis. A meadow viper bit his forearm.

He sucked the venom out.

Damn it all to Hades.

I knelt at the side of my bed, facing Ares's wound, and after a deep breath, put my mouth to it. I sucked his blood as hard as I could until my mouth was full, and I spit the liquid into an empty basin.

I inspected the contents. Fully green.

And so I continued, all through the night, pulling the blood from Ares's body, pulling it back toward the site of the wound, out the way it came in, and keeping it from reaching his heart. Sucking and spitting, sucking and spitting.

"There is a joke here," I told Ares dryly. "But I'm not sure I find the humor in it at the moment."

Ares mumbled incoherently above me.

The taste was vile, a bitter mixture of copper and fire and fish. I gagged, my own bile joining the venom at the bottom of the basin. Once it filled, I took it outside and dumped it into the soil. Immediately, the grass withered, and the ground went black. I did this a dozen times at least, and gradually, the blood I took from Ares's body became more gold than green, and his natural ichor returned. I did not stop until I'd removed every hint of poison and Ares's skin resumed its natural color, his fever finally abated. Then I scrubbed my tongue and gums, rinsed my mouth with the strongest wine I had.

Exhaustion threatened to break me, but the hole in his side still needed to be sewn. I splashed some wine from my bottle across Ares's abdomen, then used a needle and string of catgut to stitch a haphazard line through the nauseating mess of muscle and skin.

I was no healer, no seamstress, but I did my best that night.

At long last, Ares dozed. I yanked away the blood-soaked blankets around him and covered him with one clean and dry, placing it carefully over his body, up to his chest.

Then, upon the servant's cot I'd placed beside my own bed, I collapsed into dreamless sleep.

WHEN I WOKE only a few hours later, in that one breath of bliss between away and aware, I felt . . . warm. Sheltered.

Ares was on my cot, arms around me, sound asleep.

How had he gotten here? He must have moved himself.

I wiggled a hand free to test his forehead. No fever. Relief pricked the backs of my eyes.

Nearly two decades had passed since we'd last held each other, but it might have been yesterday. Ares was home for me. Alexandros, is this how mortals feel when returning to the place they were raised, as if they never left?

"Where are my clothes?"

His eyes were tender, not alarmed to wake, naked, in bed with me, but accepting. A recognition. The inevitability of us.

"Many things happened last night—but not that." I softened my voice. "What do you remember?"

"Horror."

The showdown between Diomedes and Aeneas. Pandarus's skewered skull.

"War is . . . not what I expected."

"I don't refer to the war, Aphrodite, but to you. To how I felt when I heard you had thrown yourself into battle."

Ares told me how he'd been called to the coast that morning, warned of some serious offense underway, only to discover it was all an exaggeration. But Ares maintained his own network of spies within the camps. One came running, gasping, with a dire message: *Diomedes has challenged Aeneas. Aphrodite has arrived at the front.* Ares left the beach immediately.

"I have never, in my entire life, experienced such dread. And then I found you and you were hurt. And the fact that you had suffered even a moment of physical pain, that someone had dared to desecrate this sacred body . . ." His eyes scrunched close. "I went insane."

My mind retrieved the image of Ares cutting through men like he was scything wheat.

"You weren't insane, Ares, you were—"

"I was," he countered, cutting me off. "I never fight with emotion. No anger, no anxiety. You cannot win that way."

"And yet, despite that lapse, we are here. Still whole."

"Are we, Aphrodite?"

Lying upon that narrow cot, facing each other, I thought we might be.

"Let me see your hand."

I slid it up into the breath of space between us, and Ares brought it to his mouth, resting his lips against the shoddy bandage.

"It hurts you?"

"Not right now," I whispered.

His attraction to me persisted. I felt it, insistent, pressing into my thigh.

"I did not believe you would look at me as you are," he said, "after seeing me the way everyone else does. As an animal."

"Enough with that, Ares. Animal. Human. God." I shook my head slightly. "The longer I live, the more arbitrary these words seem."

But Ares only sighed and rolled over onto his back. "What am I doing here? I must return to my men."

"You are barely healed! You are many things, but not stupid."

One of his arms snaked underneath and around me, and he curled me into his chest. "Oh, I am made the fool by you, time and time again."

I nestled against his bare skin, and my fingers traced the muscular lines of his stomach. "That chariot did not drive itself. Someone like us held the reins. And that same someone poisoned the spear."

"My sister."

I nodded. "I think so, too. But it was intended for me. She would never hurt you."

"As if poisoning you wouldn't?"

My eyes closed, remained dry, but I allowed my heart to weep for us.

"Yet you will remain faithful to . . . the Amazon?" I could not say her name.

"Our daughter arrives soon. I need . . ." His hands played with my hair; I felt his knuckles brush against my lower back. *Say me,* I thought. *Say you need me.*

"Time."

ARES FOUND HIS bloody tunic on the floor and pulled it over his body. I helped him don his armor. At the tent's door, his hand reached for my face, and I pressed my cheek into the warm, calloused palm I knew so well.

"Where do we go from here?" he wondered.

"I don't know."

No witty retort, only honesty.

"And how long before the entire army knows I spent the night in your tent?"

"I'm sure they already know. So you better appear satisfied on your walk back." I forced a small smile. "I have a reputation to protect."

38

TROY

THE WAR WAS far from over, and it made no sense to me who lived and who died. The Trojan women prayed to Athena for mercy, but her hawkish ways remained stalwart. Hector and Aeneas continued to lead the Trojan defenses, the Greeks carried on their plotting and looting and infighting. Achilles deserted over a girl he didn't even love.

Helen wished she had never been born.

Another duel was called between the great warriors, Hector and Ajax, but it ended in a draw. Another attempt at a truce foiled.

At this point, Zeus called an emergency counsel of the Olympians on Mount Ida. He descended upon us in full splendor, wearing polished armor and riding the winged white horse, Pegasus.

"This war has dragged on too long!" he complained as he dismounted and handed his steed's reins to Ares. "When they aren't killing each other, the mortals are starving to death. The fields are fallow, crops decimated by pests. Livestock are neglected. Our temples mourn from lack of offering; our powers deplete. This is not sustainable!" Zeus removed his immaculate helmet and tossed it at us. Hestia and Demeter flinched. "I forbid any further interference. No more plagues, no more sea storms. We are done with disguises and subterfuge. Let the humans end this their way."

"Then you damn the Greeks," protested Athena. "They are losing!"

"So be it."

But Athena would not acquiesce. "Providing counsel is not interference," she argued.

"It is what I say it is!" roared Zeus. "Any of you who disobey my orders shall be sent to Hades for an indeterminate sentence."

Poseidon cleared his throat. "My wife's sister Thetis begs me to remind you of her son, Achilles. How is a mother supposed to sit back and watch a massacre?"

My mouth opened, but before I could retort, Zeus spoke: "Thetis is not special. I have children in this battle, too."

Helen.

I watched a cold front pass over Hera's face like ominous clouds. No wonder she favored the Greeks. But after all she'd done to me, I would extend her no sympathy.

"But Achilles is the greatest warrior of his age!"

Zeus glared at his brother. "If you want me to say Thetis's child is more valuable than anyone else's, I refuse."

Dionysus looked my way with wide eyes. It was a magnanimity we weren't accustomed to hearing from our noble king. I wondered if Zeus, who had once thought a great war would be good fun, had changed his mind. *He is frightened*, I realized. *He knows he's losing control of his humans, of his Olympians, as well.*

I loathed him as surely as ever, but I empathized with his fear, with his awareness that he might have made a mistake. I understood, too well, how it feels to lose everything.

But temper your expectations, Alexandros. My esteem did not last for long.

A rough throne thrust up from the ground, composed of rock and branch, and Zeus sat. "I will remain in Troy and monitor the war from this mountaintop. Should one of you intercede, I will lay punishment without trial."

By no mistake, his eyes landed on Ares.

Because Zeus did not formally dismiss us, nobody dared to leave. Instead, we beckoned seats from materials of the mountain, arranging ourselves like a dysfunctional family at dinner. Athena and I would rather pluck our eyes out with oyster shells than acknowledge each other. Hera chewed her bottom lip until it bled. Hermes and Dionysus got drunk. On the periphery, Ares glowered.

At this height, we had a panoramic view of the movements below, but after experiencing combat firsthand, I could not stomach spectating. To sit idly while my son fought, possibly to his death, was an assault on decency.

Not to mention the hypocrisy.

For Zeus played favorites, too. Multiple times that day he shot lightning bolts at Diomedes's chariot to stop him attacking Hector. Nobody said a word until, finally, Hera walked to her husband's side and whispered in his ear. Whatever she said had its intended effect, for Zeus sent an eagle to fly over Agamemnon, a sign of his love for the Greeks, as well.

Hera and Athena exchanged small smiles.

I watched it all with rampant disgust.

Though Zeus favored the Trojans overall, he wanted the worship of both nations. He would never commit to one side or the other, because he was too afraid of not being adored. No matter the munificent speeches, he stood only for himself.

And I could stand no more.

I offered no excuses as I made to depart.

"Aphrodite!" Zeus thundered. "I command you to stay!"

"Oh, let her leave, Father," groused Athena. "She's a glorified camp follower, slinking around from one man's tent to another. She has no purpose here."

I laughed. "Athena, I consider my lack of purpose in this nightmare to be the greatest compliment you've given me." And to Zeus, I said, "You commanded me to abstain from battle, and I will, but I will do so away from those who love the game more than they love the living."

I was the first, but not the last of us, to go.

A FEW DAYS PASSED before Apollo appeared on the Callicolone hill with news. Over a shared plate of cheese and grapes, he told me how Hera and Athena had continued their small but defiant acts of collusion until Zeus threatened to throw his favorite daughter from her chariot and infect her with untreatable wounds for ten years if she did not obey his orders.

That made me smile.

Hera found a replacement ally in Poseidon. After she laced Zeus's wine with a powerful sedative and her husband rose in a drowsy cloud, Poseidon was able to reassemble—and reinvigorate—the Greek armies and charge the Trojans, giving Ajax the opportunity to injure Hector.

When Zeus awoke, he threatened to whip Hera and hang her from the sky if she did not return to Olympus at once. But after she departed, the cataclysmic fight between brothers threatened to topple the mountain. Because Poseidon believed them to be equals, Zeus was forced to remind him who was king.

"The only consolation," concluded Apollo, "was that after all the trickery on behalf of the Greeks, Zeus allowed me to heal Hector."

"What of Diomedes?" I asked, my lip curled in disdain.

"Unfortunately, that lunatic is still alive."

I wrinkled my nose "Who will win, Apollo? Tell me what you truly believe."

My friend rubbed a grape between his finger and thumb as he gathered his thoughts. "I think we speak too much of Achilles and Diomedes and underestimate the ruthless genius of Odysseus. There is a reason he is Athena's favorite. But the Trojans have made it this long. There is still a possibility that both Hector and Aeneas will survive this ordeal."

A possibility.

Apollo and I could break Zeus's decree and spirit our loved ones away, but to remove them from their homeland in its crisis would be inconceivable to both. They would never abandon their city or their people, and they wouldn't forgive us if we stole them away regardless.

In my heart, I knew we neared the terminus. After ten years, there was an unmistakable sense of fragility. Something was about to break, something central, and when it did, the rest would fall.

I was proven correct when Hector accidentally killed Patroclus, the lover of Achilles. Olympians rushed toward both sides to control the damage, but Thetis's son was a man half-crazy with grief, half-mad with revenge. There was no stopping him. And when he massacred Hector, he broke Apollo's heart.

EVERYONE KNOWS THIS part of the tragedy, for it is disturbed. And dreadful. Is that why people relish it? Or is it simply harder to forget? I hope it is the latter, but I have my doubts.

I speak of Hector's death.

As Hector lay dying, he begged Achilles for an honorable end, one worthy of the dignified prince and warrior he sought to be, but Achilles refused. He stabbed Hector through the throat, then invited the Greek army to mutilate the corpse with their own blades. The men took turns unleashing their resentment at this ridiculous war on a dead man whose brother fell in love with a married woman. They urinated on him, mocked him, desecrated Troy's noble warrior beyond salvation. Then, Achilles tied Hector's body to the back of his chariot and dragged it around the tomb of Patroclus, symbolically avenging his lover, and before the gates of Troy, taunting a grieving King Priam.

Achilles would not release Hector for burial.

It was profane. Grotesque.

I met Apollo in the lowland between Thymbra and the Callicolone hill, for he was coming to me as I was going to him. I clutched Apollo tightly as he sobbed into my shoulder.

"Oh, my darling," I murmured.

"In his last words, he mentioned two people, Aphrodite." Apollo wiped his tears with the back of his hand. "His brother Paris and me."

"What can I do to help?"

"Remove my heart."

"Apollo . . ."

"I do not jest. Curse me if you must, but I cannot love again."

I stepped back, shocked.

"Apollo, I—"

"I know you have the power!" he yelled. "You said you would help, now do it!"

He, too, blames love, I thought. *My dearest friend sees me as the cause of his misery.*

But I tempered my reaction—I would not make his suffering about me—and I chose my responding words with precision.

"Do you remember the rocks at Leukas?" I asked. "And how I couldn't jump? If I forgot how Ares betrayed me, I would also lose how he loved me. And what would I be without those moments of joy? If I take your heart, you will no longer hurt, but you will no longer be my Apollo."

"That's exactly what I ask!"

"The world might need your music and medicine, but I need *you*." I placed my hand at the center of his chest. "This is you, Apollo. This feeling, forgiving organ. Without it, would you have carried my daughter out of Hephaestus's bedroom? Would you have braved my wrath to help Eros and Psyche? Without it, what becomes of Leto's beloved son, of Artemis's better half?"

His precious face contorted in misery. "I can no longer hold any hope. My heart is shattered, Aphrodite."

"Never. I feel its beat. And I hear its message."

"What does it say?" he rasped.

I tapped my finger against his breastbone to the syllables of one word. "Onward."

He shrugged off my touch and walked away from me, but I waited, and soon enough, he returned. His cheeks were wan, stained by tears, but he seemed resolute. "You must help me protect what's left of him."

"I would never let you do so alone."

Achilles maintained his macabre parade for twelve interminable days, and every night, while the bereaved man slept, Apollo and I stood guard over Hector's corpse. I fought off vultures and hyenas with magical shields, but also stones and sticks. Apollo repaired the damage to skin and bone with the expertise of a healer and the tenderness of a lover. Together, we kept the Trojan prince's body in the most decent form we could, until Zeus intervened and sent Thetis to speak sense to her son.

Weeping at all he had suffered and done, Achilles finally returned the body to the Trojan royal family.

For ten days, until the smoke of Hector's funeral pyre dissipated, there was no bloodshed between Greece and Troy.

AFTER THE LOSS of their beloved prince, it was no surprise that the beleaguered Trojan army received the Amazonian arrival like a boon from the ancestors. I stood beside Aeneas on the beach, watching as the ship from Themyscira cast anchor. Onlookers cheered as rowboats lowered and came ashore, depositing wave after wave of women warriors upon the sand.

The Amazonian tribe was renowned for their skills at archery and horsemanship, but I marveled at the beauty of their bodies—their muscled arms and thighs, stomachs that could take punches and ride bareback. I felt so soft and useless in comparison, so unexpectedly self-conscious.

To anyone who asked, I was there to support Aeneas, but that was only a partial truth. Curiosity was eating me alive.

For standing in the helm of the last rowboat was the princess Penthesilea, Ares's daughter. As she came into view, my hawklike eyes landed on every detail of her being. From her bearing, she seemed proud. In the battle-ax strapped to her back, the bronze belt at her waist, she seemed strong. I saw Ares in her height and in the helmet she wore over black curls, a near replica of his own. But beneath the armor was a woman's body. Were those curves the same as her mother's?

"Father," she cried, leaping effortlessly over the side of the boat and splashing through seawater to reach him.

Ares met her in the surf, greeting his daughter with a warmth he did not often display before witnesses. He smiled as they clutched each other's forearms.

Yes, I was profoundly jealous.

I could not overhear their conversation, particularly when the legendary Amazonian horses started swimming from the anchored ship. The wet mares and stallions met dry land, rearing and bucking, so overjoyed to be free of their cramped and rocking berth, then broke into gallops so fierce they sent biting bits of sand in every direction. I covered my face. The Amazons whooped and cheered as they ran toward their horses with swinging ropes. Aeneas, a devout equestrian, joined their corralling with enthusiasm, leaving me alone and awkward, unsure of my place, and increasingly aware that it was not here. Certainly not on this beach, and probably not in Troy at all.

Disheartened, I turned to leave, but Ares's voice stopped me. "Aphrodite, come meet Penthesilea." When I did not immediately respond, he added, "Please."

Ares was always courteous to Aeneas; I could do the same.

Enjoining both dignity and compassion, I approached my former lover and his daughter. Penthesilea bowed before me. "It is an honor," she said.

Ares regarded me keenly, perhaps wondering if he was about to regret this decision.

"Majestic Penthesilea," I replied, "it is warriors such as yourself who deserve honor on these banks."

"My mother, the queen, believes Troy must stand to preserve fair trade between east and west. And my father never chooses the wrong fight." Penthesilea had impeccable posture, standing as straight as a cypress tree. She was not pretty in the traditional sense, but all young people are so gorgeous. "I am proud to lead my forces alongside the Trojans."

Ares placed a hand on her shoulder. "Aphrodite saved me on the field from terrible injury."

Did the girl want to know more? Was she privy to our past? For a moment, I thought I saw indecision flash across her face. But Penthesilea held herself with the poise of either a true royal or a good daughter. Maybe both.

"The Amazons will forever be in your debt."

"Keep Aeneas alive and I will call us settled."

The princess nodded. "To protect is the Amazonian way."

I did not linger. It was enough to speak with her face-to-face. I did not need to hear more of her queen mother or analyze Ares's every word and gesture. And I might be tempted to say ugly things that could hurt this alliance the Trojans so desperately needed. Things like:

He has never loved your mother like he loves me.

Nobody will ever know him like I do.

Besides, there was strategy to discuss between the Trojan and Amazonian elite, horses to be grazed, camps to erect. Ares, Aeneas, Penthesilea, even Apollo, they all spoke the language of battle fluently. Whether the banal necessities of war were below me, or I below them, remained to be determined, but either way, I was never invited. Nor did I participate.

I was overwhelmed with a need for my own family, so I did not return to my tent on the hill that day. Instead, I flew to Olympus, to Eros and Psyche and Hedone, and I stayed with them for many weeks. I checked on my doves, met with the Graces, and pretended at peace to moderate success.

Until I heard word of Penthesilea's death.

She and her gallant horse, felled by the mighty ash spear of Achilles.

39

TROY

PERHAPS IT WAS regret for the way he had defiled Hector's corpse, perhaps it was fear of Ares, but Achilles returned Penthesilea's body to the Trojans and Amazons with marked reverence, unharmed, for a prompt and proper burial.

I did not attend the service; I did not even return to Troy. I gave Ares the space to mourn his daughter with their people.

What can a goddess of love and beauty do when those who matter most to her grieve? I would not manipulate them with my magic, would never excise their hearts as Apollo had begged, but I did send both my lover and my friend reminders of love. Whispers and wishes with the wind.

Ares, remember her childhood. Her little hands. The bend in her neck as she gazed up at you.

Apollo, do not forget that companionship. Those long nights in trusting conversation. How he honored your advice and protection.

The beautiful moments of love are the best solace—perhaps the only solace—when a soul is tormented by loss. And with the persistence of memory, no one you love is ever truly dead.

After so many years of fighting, of one side moving a bit forward and the other side pushing back, ten years of no real progress either way, events began to escalate with near-dizzying speed. Hermes relayed updates from the front to Olympus, and for the first time in our combined existence, I looked forward to seeing him.

First Paris killed Achilles, a lucky shot to his heel.

Then Philoctetes killed Paris, with Heracles's famed bow.

I recalled Paris as he was over a decade ago, on our trip to Sparta. *Can first love be real?* he had asked me. *Is it childish to think the first hand I held could be the one I will hold until the end of days?*

Oh, dear boy. Look what we've done.

Without Paris or Hector to defend her, I worried for Helen. Nobody was going to honor her heartbreak as they sought retribution. What wouldn't the men on both sides do to her, an attractive woman they considered the cause of their suffering? Did Helen possess the abilities to save herself? The guile or the skills? My faith in men wavered; I couldn't trust that King Priam would speak for her, or that her own father, Zeus, would intercede.

So I met her in a dream.

In it, Helen stood at a balcony's edge, staring outward.

"I will jump before I let them push me," she said, without turning around.

"You could, I won't stop you," I replied, approaching her. "Or you could survive."

She faced me then, and her sunken cheeks, her swollen eyes, spoke to her devastation. "I loved Paris. Nobody approved, no one understood."

Didn't I though?

"You cannot wait for them to forgive you or love you. Helen, all women—but especially ones like you and me—must bear our own weight."

"But it's so heavy," she protested, voice breaking, "and I am so tired."

"We cannot change them," I reiterated. "We can only"—*Oh. Oh, dear, I finally understand*—"love ourselves."

She scoffed. For Helen was in the throes of her self-hatred, precisely where I had been after half of Olympus witnessed my affair.

"I'm not offering platitudes," I insisted. "I'm trying to save you."

"Then leave me a knife."

I would leave her something better. I brought my hands together, and as I slowly drew them apart, I focused on clouds, the low-lying ones that form above the sea. My palms glowed blue, like the bioluminescent tide at night, and Helen watched in reluctant awe as I laid my hands upon her heart, one on top of the other.

"Remember Paris's duel? I offer you the same escape. One flight, to wherever you wish." And I whispered in her ear, "Do not fall, child. Soar."

We did not embrace before I vanished from her dream.

It was difficult to keep track of her after the war. Some say she never left Troy, that she died there, but most believe she returned to Sparta with Menelaus. I heard she was eventually stoned or hanged by the queen of Rhodes, a war widow.

But there is another rumor, lesser known, in which Menelaus loses his wife again—this time, she disappeares into a magical cloud, never to be seen in Greece or Troy again.

In this telling, she reappears in Egypt, landing on her own two feet.

I like this version best, don't you?

WHILE WE ALL existed in this state of torpor, in war weariness, Athena unveiled her master plan, one she and her wily protégé, Odysseus, had long in the making.

I was at dinner on Olympus when I heard.

"The war may be over," Eros announced, pouring himself another glass of wine. "The Greek army packed up and departed Troy."

"Impossible," I rejoined. "Menelaus would not depart Troy

without Helen, and Agamemnon would not leave without the city in ruins."

"And yet, both seem to have happened. All that remains of their camp is a massive wooden horse."

"How strange!" remarked Psyche.

"Indeed. The Trojans believe it a peace offering. They brought it into the city."

A peace offering? White fear, both icy and hot, permeated my body.

"When did this occur?" I demanded.

"Hermes told me just this evening." Eros frowned. He set down his goblet. "Mama, what is wrong with you? This is excellent news for your Trojans!"

I pushed my chair away from the table, preparing to leave. "Did he say where the Greek ships are now?"

"Moored at Tenedos."

This confirmed my worst suspicions. I knew the map; I'd lived it. Tenedos was an island just off the western coast. The Greeks weren't preparing to cross the sea home; they were conveniently hiding. Only biding time, until they could sail up the Dardanelles, the narrow strait, and enter Troy from behind.

Their departure was a ruse.

I was no military mastermind; nobody had ever sought my advice. But this must be obvious to the others, as well. Anchises and Aeneas would not be so gullible. Ares or Apollo would warn them.

But why, then, was Eros speaking as if the war were over?

I, who had been tricked and trapped more than any of the other Olympians, saw Athena's icy handprints all over this.

"They are all going to die," I declared, voice shaking though I stood on firm legs.

Psyche's brows knitted. "Who?"

"The Trojans."

Eros jumped up from his seat. "Mama, wait—!"

But I was already gone, rushing for the royal stables. I wished for the speed of Hermes's sandals or Phaethon's chariot, but I would have to do with what I had. As I had always done.

But as I collected my silver swans, I heard a snort, spied a flash of white, and an audacious, brilliant idea entered my mind.

Pegasus.

I closed the bird paddock and moved to his stall.

"You don't know me," I told the horse, feeling slightly absurd, "but we are both beautiful and motherless and have been abused by men with dreams of grandeur. Will you fly me to Troy so I can save my son?"

It was a noble request, considering he was a horse, but when Pegasus neighed, I figured he understood.

And hoped that meant yes.

With no idea how to saddle a creature with wings, I was forced to mount him bareback. I held tight with my thighs, laced my fingers through his mane, and clucked my tongue once.

We shot into the air like an arrow on fire.

Alexandros, you are the first mortal to ever hear this story. I stole Zeus's prize steed and rode him to Troy like the Amazonian warrior I would never be.

But somebody had to be the hero that night. Might as well be Olympus's whore.

My body recalled everything Ares had taught me. How to guide with my legs, how to lean into my seat. That gorgeous animal and I were one, united in flight and our mission, a comet of white and rose gold streaking through the night. By the time I arrived over Troy, the Greek ships had abandoned Tenedos and cast anchor up the Dardanian strait, in the exact place I expected, and their soldiers were jogging down the Troad toward the unsuspecting city.

Even from a distance, the wooden horse stood prominent amid the cramped and congested streets, and as Pegasus and I descended, I spotted the trap door hanging open at the bottom of its stomach.

Whoever had hidden in its bowels had already descended and was, without any doubt, opening the gates.

The full Greek army was en route, and assassins had already infiltrated the walls—no doubt headed for the most important homes, where the most important Trojan men laid their weary heads. Everywhere I looked, Trojans lay sprawled and sleeping, slumped against the streets, exhausted and drunk from a night of celebrating the Greeks' supposed retreat.

This was an unmitigated catastrophe, and if I did nothing, it was going to be a bloodbath.

"Trojans, wake!"

I've been told I have an overly feminine voice, not a formidable one, but I yelled from the pit of my stomach, scalding my throat.

"The war is not over! Retrieve your swords!"

Someone cursed at me; another told me to shut my slut mouth.

With my heels, I urged Pegasus faster, guiding him to the place where Aeneas slept with his wife and son. Pegasus landed with considerable grace, considering my sloppy handling, and I stroked his muzzle, leaning my forehead against his. "Thank you, dear one. Now rise and fly far from this danger before you are hurt."

He nickered and took off with a loping leap, his wings breaking the night sky, a shooting star in pursuit of oblivion.

I did not knock at Aeneas's door, but barged inside, calling my son's name. He met me in the atrium, rubbing sleep from his eyes.

"Mother?"

"Hurry, Aeneas," I begged. "The Greeks will arrive any moment!"

He blanched. "But the ships . . . ?"

"Have returned. The wooden horse was a ploy, Aeneas."

Awareness washed away the shock and sleep from his face. He whirled into action. "I need my armor. My sword."

I grabbed his arm. "No. The time for battle is over. You must flee with your son, preserve our bloodline."

A woman appeared at the other side of the room, petite and pale, eyes wet. His wife, Creusa.

"I cannot leave Troy," she keened.

"You can and you will." I strode toward the woman and placed my hand on her cheek. "Pack only what you can carry and Ascanius." To Aeneas, I said, "Collect your father and leave. Now!"

He hesitated. "But these are our people . . ."

"I will tell as many as I can to meet you at Mount Ida. You must survive, Aeneas. For Troy."

Just as he relented, we heard the first scream. Creusa dropped to her knees, covering her mouth.

Flames illuminated the window, casting demonic shadows on the opposite wall.

"Aeneas, *run*."

ALEXANDROS, WHAT HAPPENED next is unspeakable and indescribable, but I will relay what I can. Even an immortal can feel restricted by language because there are some things too unconscionable to be named.

The city burned is an inadequate description, for the people burned, too.

The beloved shops and livelihoods, sometimes passed down through generations, other times the hard work of individual dreams, the market where friends met and rivals side-eyed. The alleyways where young lovers first kissed, hiding from their parents.

All on fire.

The elderly burned. Grandmothers with cataracts from years of watching, arthritis from years of weaving. The grandfathers with bad backs and sore knees, with missing teeth but epic smiles.

Ash.

The cradles that once held the most beloved became kindling.

The stray dogs ran down dead ends. Litters of kittens, confused and scared, mewed for help that never came.

Everything green was fed to the indiscriminate flames. Plants tended with love and persistence, herbs for food, for healing. Even the weeds.

The conflagration entered houses and temples, torching altars and mementos. Jewels and dried flowers and children's toys.

The greedy burned, the miserly, and the lonely. The drunks and the temperate. And those untouched by fire were met with iron. People were slaughtered in their homes, in their beds, in their temples. By sword and dagger, but also by fists and feet, wooden clubs.

Bashed skulls. Thrown infants.

And so many women raped. Girls. Mothers. Their mothers. Priestesses and princesses.

I heard them yell for Helen, the harlot who started it. The bitch who ruined a decade of lives. They were hungry for her.

We were all Helen to them, that night.

Troy, as we knew it, collapsed, and Greece won its trade routes to the east.

AENEAS LOST CREUSA in the crowd, but he continued, carrying both his father and son on his back and in his arms. He made it to the mountain and waited as the survivors trickled over. Standing stoically, standing in the reality of his dead wife, his slaughtered people. I carried the word for as long as I could be heard, for as long as I could dodge the flames, urging Trojans to find their prince at the mountain.

And then I, too, went to Ida.

"Bring the survivors to the city of Antandros," I instructed Aeneas, feeling as if I'd swallowed fire myself. "I will provide you enough pine tree lumber for twenty ships, and then I want you to sail away from this place and never look back."

Dry-eyed and halfway dead, he managed to nod. I kissed his forehead. "Just live, Aeneas. And forgive yourself. Not today, but one day."

"We will be runaways."

"No, my love. Seekers. Dreamers."

He did not respond.

You know what happens to him, Alexandros, don't you? Aeneas wanders over sea and land for seven years until he sails up the Tiber River to his destiny. There, he marries the Latin princess Lavinia and fathers a second son, mixing their blood with ours, a heritage passed down through generations to Rhea Silvia, who will give birth to Romulus and Remus on the seven hills.

Which, of course, changes everything.

But that is many lifetimes ahead.

Throughout that long night, while Anchises clutched his little grandson, Aeneas attended to the bleeding, immediate injuries of his countrymen. The other wounds, the ones weeping behind empty eyes, would have to wait. I pulled fruit trees from the ground, and the people fed on quince and apples. "More," they begged. "More." And I pushed those poor trees into maturity over and over as those poor people filled their sacks and mouths again and again.

When the sun rose on the Trojan wasteland, I left the mountain, dazed and numb, and walked to Apollo's temple, crawling the last length to his altar. My friend was not there. Nobody was there.

The Trojan War was over.

Sobbing on the floor, arms held tightly around myself, I prayed to nothing.

40

CYPRUS AND THRACE

ALEXANDROS, I HAVE started and ended my story with war. Will the history of all time be similarly bookended? I would like to think otherwise. I would like to think everything won't end on the battlefield.

But it might.

From chaos to chaos.

And in between, immortality. An eternal stillness. We artificially create elements of time by taking lovers, making marriages, bearing children. We watch the seasons, believe in the concept of years. Maybe it is a survival instinct, or perhaps it comes from our love of storytelling, that need to force narrative structure onto existence.

And I think maybe life isn't about the beginning or the end, though both can be noteworthy, but more about the in-between and what you make of it.

When the Titans clashed with Zeus, it didn't affect me. For I had no relationships, no strings tugging me into the fray. But with Troy, I was entangled, even before it began. And then later, only more so. Maybe strings aren't the appropriate metaphor, Alexandros. Roots might be better. Continually branching off as I met more people and shared more moments. When Troy crashed down, so did I.

Upended and overturned, I returned to Cyprus to swim, as if there were enough seawater on this earth to wash away my experience. If the wind hit the precise angle, I could still smell smoke in my hair. I bore a scar through my left hand from where Diomedes's dagger pierced me. You found it, Alexandros, the moment we met. The other scars were less obvious.

One war and never again.

My son made it through; how many mothers could say the same? I mourned these women and their empty arms.

Ten years of young men dying for the whims of the old. Trojans defending a home they lost anyway. Greeks returning to sons and daughters who'd forgotten them, wives who resented them, farms and fields gone to waste. In the battle of greed and pride, does anyone truly win? What was settled?

Very little.

How did Ares's soul survive war after war? If he continued this way eternally, what would remain of him?

Once, at a spring where a dead dragon lay buried, Ares had warned me that wars would change from something bad to even worse, and he was correct. Could our souls save us, if they could change, too? What if we remade ourselves better?

If not, I worried we were doomed to infinite repetition.

For a decade, my powers had waned. In times of great strife, the altars of love and beauty are the first to go cold. Not many prioritize romance over starving children and brothers dying overseas. But in the tenuous afterward, my candles were relit. The garlands and wreaths returned. People called to me once more, but for a different type of passion. They craved connection to recover from all they had lost and missed. People needed to commune, to know that others had beaten the unbearable, too, and it was possible to continue living.

I did what I could.

And then Hermes was landing on my beach, as he had done ages ago. "Zeus wants us all in the Hall of the Gods."

No snark, no smirks. From either of us. I simply nodded and

accepted his arm. This time, the hall was not full of attendants. There was no banquet, no decor. Just us, in our assigned seats. I took mine, beside Artemis, as we awaited Zeus's arrival.

Across from me, Ares's throne sat empty.

"Shall we bet on it?" I heard Apollo ask his sister half-heartedly, but she shook her head. There was little point; my heart knew Ares would not come. Perhaps Artemis did, too, but I think she just couldn't find the fun in guessing anymore.

I surveyed the faces of my fellow Olympians. Hades's exhaustion colored the skin below his eyes, tugged at the corners of his mouth. My great-grandson Dionysus was already in his cups, shaking one foot, impatient to leave. Hera seemed distant, her eyes far away.

And Athena and Poseidon, who had gone from enmity to unlikely allies, were at odds once more. It had something to do with that Ithacan and a giant—the details failed to interest me—but I did find mild enjoyment watching them trade glowers.

It was already quiet when Zeus entered, no need to hush.

"It has been hundreds of years since I first called you here, so full of excitement and pride, so eager to build a new world. We did it together, and we did it well."

Murmurs within our small audience. Many nods. I did neither.

"And then Troy happened. The war doesn't end for us, only the bodies left behind on that plain. We are still here." Zeus wet his lips, brow furrowed, then continued. "I wish I could say otherwise but cannot compromise the truth: This situation split us, and if our legacy is to continue, we must seal the divide."

Athena crossed her arms over her chest. Poseidon scoffed.

"Can we forgive each other?" Zeus asked. "Is it possible to erase the tally marks, forget the score? I do not require an oracle to know this is the only way to move forward with any success."

He was no less robust than he'd ever been, still barrel-chested and large, but his back seemed bowed. There was a new lean to him, a break in posture, that showed the weight of governing. This would never go away.

Poseidon was the first to protest, jabbing an accusatory finger in Athena's direction. "Her Odysseus blinded my Polyphemus."

"Yes, he took an eye but left your brute—yet another one born off a nymph—alive!"

"He is a giant," snapped the sea god, "not a brute."

Athena slammed her ceremonial spear into the floor. "Polyphemus eats human flesh!"

"ENOUGH!"

Never, in all the decades of Zeus's tantrums, had I heard his voice reach such a deafening crescendo. Even in all his anger toward me. Both Hestia and Demeter winced, and even Athena paled, looking abashed.

"I will never give up on Olympus," stated Zeus. "When this mountain crashes, so do I, and it will not stand without all of us."

Nobody spoke. And as much as the ungenerous part of me thrilled to observe Zeus squirm, there were feelings inside me, transforming into words, that sought release.

So I let them loose.

"Zeus," I said. "I forgive you. I forgive all of you, actually, and harbor no hate for anyone here. And I apologize that being who I am caused pain. But I love myself, and I will continue to love myself regardless."

I didn't do it for them, Alexandros, I did it for me. And it felt wonderful.

Apollo winked.

I paused a moment, giving the others an opportunity to follow my admission, but nobody spoke.

"Thank you, Aphrodite," Zeus replied, and though his voice was gruff, his eyes shone with some emotion akin to gratitude.

I nodded. "Now, if you'll excuse me, I must return to Cyprus."

"What? No! We aren't finished here—Aphrodite, APHRODITE!"

I had almost reached the massive gates before a hauntingly familiar beat reached me: *One, two, three, one, two, three*—a waltz I never danced to. And a different voice calling my name.

"Aphrodite! Wait!"

It was Hephaestus with his walking stick, out of breath and beet red.

"I made the armor for Diomedes, but I never knew . . . I never would have . . . I wouldn't have done it if I'd known what he'd do. To you . . . and Ares."

I had never considered any of this—that my former husband constructed the metal panoply of heroes, that he might, subsequently, feel responsible for their actions. And I was surprised by the solicitude that flooded my heart.

"I do not blame you, Hephaestus."

"Yes," he replied, as awkward as ever. "Well, good."

"Your wife is a treasure," I added.

"Yes. She is."

We did not exchange farewells but gave each other a half smile.

Once I asked Pygmalion if he could forgive himself. Once Aglaia asked me if I could love myself. These are interdependent forces. Necessarily symbiotic.

I wasn't forgiving the world so I could maintain my power, but so I could fall in love with Aphrodite again.

I set her—like my words, like my forgiveness—free.

OLYMPUS WAS NEVER the same. After a war so catastrophic, the world we made had broken and rebuilt itself—this time, perhaps, in its own image. Not ours. Human civilization expanded, ideas were shared, innovations arrived without our sponsorship. The mortals had learned not to rely upon us. Who would trust a god that let Troy burn? Zeus mellowed into the immortal equivalent of human midlife. The Hall of the Gods convened less and less often.

I didn't miss it.

For here is what I've learned of empires: Though they all believe themselves eternal, each one crumbles eventually. Different locations, different stone and wood, different distribution of responsibility, but the same inevitable result. The only part that remains universal is the souls within—the oppressors and the complicit, the artists, the rebels.

The lovers.

For I had a dream around this time, inviting me to Thrace, with images for directions.

I had an inkling of what I might find there but couldn't be sure. I was just as likely walking into a trap. My enemies were as numerous as ever. But, Alexandros, you know me well enough by now.

My curiosity is stronger than an aegis, and my instincts for self-preservation are dismal.

I arranged my hair. I donned my best dress.

I flew my chariot north over the sea, eventually emerging upon a rich woodland of rolling hills, thick with oak and pine. Birds of prey soared beside me—hawks and eagles, vultures and falcons—as if they were my escort. When the terrain began to resemble that of my dream, I landed the chariot and released my swans, preferring to walk the remainder of the journey.

When I came to a modest limestone estate hidden in a thick grove of sycamore, I knew I'd found it. Outside the door bloomed a flower I'd never encountered, lush and fluffy with pink and white petals. I placed my hand beneath its bloom, and lowered myself to inhale the sweet, alluring aroma. I did not pick it, could not bear to break the stem.

"It is called a peony."

Ares emerged from the house wearing a simple tunic. No armor, no blade in sight.

"I love it."

"I grew them from seeds." He crouched down, inspecting his plant, adjusting the soil, then dusting off his hands. "I was told they bring healing. And a happy life."

"That's a mighty ask of such a little flower."

Ares nodded. "It is. But I am selfish. Especially when it comes to her."

I pulled my cloak farther up my shoulders. "It is cold here, will she survive?"

He lifted a brow. "If I keep her warm."

Ares opened the door and led me inside.

"What is this place?" I wondered.

"My escape. Something I've been building for ages."

"I didn't know." I spun in a slow circle. The minimal decor was comparable to his Olympian palace with one major exception: I did not spy a single weapon.

"Nobody does, so nobody has ever visited."

My eyes shifted from the furniture to him. "Until now."

"Until you."

"And you've had this, all this time?"

"Since you married Hephaestus."

A commotion rose from the back of the house, pounding footsteps followed, and then, there was Graegus, leaping up, his front paws smearing mud into my dress. More gray than brown colored his mottled, matted fur, the tip of one ear was gone, and a horrific scar traversed a path down an eye. Here was a creature that had been to war and back, a hundredfold.

"Oh, you are even more awful than I remembered!" I exclaimed, bringing my nose to his, and, Alexandros, I'll admit it to you: wiping away a tear.

"Down!" commanded Ares.

As obedient to his master as ever, Graegus dropped to all fours.

"As mean as ever, isn't he?" I cooed, and I scratched the top of Graegus's head.

Ares and I sat at a table, and the old dog curled around my feet. A plate of nectarines lay at its center, which neither of us touched.

The things we did not say filled the space between us.

Finally, I asked, "Where did you go, after . . . ?" There was no need to finish the sentence; he understood what I meant.

"To Themyscira."

"Ah."

"Otrera deserved to hear of Penthesilea's death . . . and other things . . . from me."

I fiddled with my bracelets, my rings, anything to keep my hands busy. "That cannot have been an easy conversation."

"It wasn't." Ares looked away for a moment, brow furrowing. "I ended our marriage."

I stiffened. "Why?"

"Because I am still in love with you, Aphrodite."

"Ah."

Ares cleared his throat. "Aeneas is well?"

"Yes. Sailing toward Latium."

"He will do well there." Ares paused. "Is it true you stole Pegasus and rode through Troy to warn them of the invasion?"

"Why? Does that surprise you?"

"Not in the slightest. I've never doubted your courage."

Then Ares left his chair and came before me on his knees.

"I do not love you because you are beautiful"—he grinned—"or because you're an absolute beast in bed, but because of who you are and have been and will be."

"And I do not love you for your strength or your sword. I love all of you, Ares." My voice lowered, trembling with joy. "I am so happy you exist."

This love of ours was not static, but dynamic. A continuous process of discovery toward an infinite. If there could be an end, it wouldn't be possession, but interdependence. For Ares could sweep me up, sweep me away even, but not from myself. Never again. We were two souls, knotted together, made stronger by our individual freedoms.

"Are you fighting for us, Ares?" I mused, leaning forward and stroking the side of his face. "After all this time?"

"I have struggled to feel worthy of the love you give, Aphrodite.

Lesser is easier. But you have met me in war, now I must meet you on your terms."

My chest lifted. "Unconditional love?"

He shrugged a shoulder. "More or less."

I opened my legs to invite him closer, and he accepted. My thighs grazed his hips, and then my hands were in his, his hands were in mine.

"Would you like to stay here?" he asked quietly, seriously. "For a while?"

"There will be more conflict, Ares, and we will be in demand."

"I said 'a while.'"

I gazed out the window just as a dove landed in a sycamore. I held my lower lip—and my smile—between my teeth. "I will need a fur of some sort."

"Yes."

"Something decadent and hard to come by."

"Naturally."

"Maybe an albino wolf or—"

The words were still leaving my lips when Ares kissed me.

He kissed me as if my mouth alone might redeem him, and I kissed him back, both savior and saved. I knew now that I could live without him, had done so for centuries, but our lives were made more beautiful by this very real love.

We would try again. And again.

Upsetting each other, arguing, almost walking away, but fighting to stay.

Always.

Together, hands intertwined, we remain the paradox, the polarizing duality in every soul. The capacity for both tenderness and terror, love and war. The same energy transferred back and forth until the last breath extinguishes upon this earth.

A puff, a sigh, then nothing.

41

MILOS
Second Century BCE

THE ARTIST STARES at the goddess, mouth open.

"But that was a long time ago; how does it end between you and him?"

A corner of her mouth curves upward. "It never does."

"You are together, then? Even now?"

"No. He has been fighting in the Macedonian Wars for decades."

She sets the feather down upon the table and picks up a bronze mirror. "At Delphi, Apollo's priestess demands, 'Know thyself!' I never need to check my reflection. I already know I look perfect." Instead, she turns it outward, toward Alexandros. "But what do you see? For when you look at me, you are also looking at yourself. I am love and beauty, but I am also whatever you make me."

That's it, he thinks. *We have found it.*

For, as an artist, he knows beauty is not just about what a person sees, but what they need it to be—what they reimagine it to be.

Outside, the shades of blue brighten, lightening the colors in the studio, casting the goddess in pink and gold. For a moment, she glows, but then she frowns and steps away from the window. "I still despise the dawn."

"I do today, for it means you must leave."

She regards him warmly, indulgently. "You've viewed me from every angle tonight."

They share a look.

It is enough, she seems to say.

It is enough, he knows.

"I will not return until it's finished," she adds. "I don't want to plague you, and I want to be surprised."

Alexandros rises from his chair. Should he shake her hand? He fumbles with his body and his speech. "How will I get word to you?"

She smiled. "Sweet boy, I will know."

AFTER SHE LEAVES, Alexandros examines the mess of shells and flowers, fruit and feathers. Symbolic detritus of a life well lived, still living. He examines his sketches.

And then he sets to work.

For his type of art, he creates shape and texture. Color is inconsequential. But with Aphrodite, he sees every shade and shimmer in her form. He must carve her with this vibrancy of depth and richness. It is euphoria, to begin a new project with fresh inspiration.

She has changed the way he sees.

He barely sleeps those first days. The work is too important.

And yet, despite the numinous nature of his commission, he remains a mere mortal whose body demands rest and sustenance. Just as his physical energy drops to its nadir, he receives a timely, though unexpected, visitor.

Timon is in the doorway, holding a basket filled to the brim with bread and cheese, wine and fish. Figs, pomegranates.

And a peony.

Alexandros steps back, shaken, surreptitiously smelling himself. He imagines how he appears, covered in dust, eyes undoubtedly swollen from lack of sleep. When has he last scrubbed his teeth? Timon only smiles. "It is good to see you," he says.

"Is it? I mean, thank you. I mean, why are you here?" Alexandros curses his stupid rambling mouth.

"I was told to bring this to you."

"By whom?"

Timon shrugs. "It was all quite strange. A woman met me at the dock as my boat came in. She wore her cloak over her face. I caught only her lips and a flash of purple in her eyes."

Alexandros accepts the heavy gift.

They stand at the threshold. Finally, the artist asks what his heart wants: "Will you come in?"

Timon beams. "Yes."

"It's a bit of a disaster; I've begun a new commission."

With a sense of the surreal, Alexandros watches his former lover enter his home for the first time in years. Timon heads straight to the worktable and investigates the sketches. "This is different than your other work."

"It's a strange story."

"I'd like to hear it."

They share the food and speak of the goddess. When he finishes, Alexandros asks, "Do you believe me?"

Timon takes a pomegranate seed between his teeth. "Do I believe Aphrodite picked you, of all the mortal artists that have existed these thousand years, to compose her portrait in stone?"

Alexandros flinches. It sounds ludicrous coming from another's mouth.

But Timon grins. "Of course I do."

The artist is so tired, but this meal, this visit, revitalizes the heart he neglected for his mind. "I miss you," he confesses. "And I am sorry. I thought I knew what was important, but I was wrong."

"Thank you," Timon replies.

"It was an apology, not a compliment."

"It was both."

Alexandros becomes increasingly rattled, increasingly convinced he is bad at people, bad at love, but he tries again. "There are better compliments I could give you, Timon. Besides being the most handsome man on Milos, you make people feel good and seen. I like myself better when I'm around you. I like the world better."

"I have missed you, too, Alexandros."

There is happiness between them. And hope. Like a white butterfly landing on his shoulder.

"Would you like to stay for a while?"

TIMON NEVER LEAVES.

Only in the mornings, when he rises for work. But then, instead of stopping at the tavern, he invites his fishermen friends back to the home he shares with Alexandros. The men bring a selection from their daily catch and jugs of cheap wine, and Alexandros sets down his chisel to join them as they share news and laughter. And Alexandros begins to allow them into his process. He speaks of his struggles with the marble, his fears for the piece, and these rough men share their opinions, offer their support.

Meanwhile, Aphrodite slowly emerges from the stone, and she is beautiful, but he does not fall in love with her. He is no Pygmalion. He falls in love with his own life, the one she reminds him to make.

Seasons pass as seasons always do. From the wet spring of the goddess's arrival to the brutal heat of summer. Sometimes he breaks early and meets Timon at the port. They walk together to their favorite beach and swim until nightfall, lying on the rocks as their bodies dry and cool. The men bring mussels home and boil them with fresh garlic over the fire. Afterward, Timon crushes their shells and lays them in the garden—the most impressive one on the island. In the cold, slumbering months, Alexandros rises early. With shorter daylight hours he must prioritize the good light. Wrapped in blankets, they share warm water with honey before Timon leaves for the sea.

And then one rainy day Alexandros finishes. To touch it any more may ruin it.

He sets down his tools, pulls a chair before his goddess, and looks at her. It isn't easy to be objective about his own work, but he knows it is good and right.

Much like love.

Love, he now knows, is real, but it isn't an objective reality. It's a subjective affirmation that yes, he exists, and a confirmation that yes, this life is worth it.

"Is it done?" Timon asks excitedly, coming in later that day and finding Alexandros still on the stool, staring.

"I think so."

He has re-created every detail, even the extended length of her second toe. Torso bare, dress draped across the lower half of her body. Focused straight ahead, not gazing to the left as that fool Praxiteles had done. She wears a headband, not a crown, and no shoes. She is serene, but surprisingly complex.

Everything in harmonious proportion.

"She will come soon?"

Alexandros nods.

"Are you scared?"

The artist leans back. His head meets his lover's stomach, and he closes his eyes as arms wrap around his shoulders and neck.

"Not anymore."

SHE ARRIVES IN the middle of the night, while the men sleep. Whether it is her distinctive smell or the tinkling of her jewelry as she moves, Alexandros's senses alert him to her presence. He shoots up, flushing at his nudity, but she waves a dismissive hand.

"Don't be so embarrassed. It is nothing I haven't seen before."

He grabs a tunic from the floor and pulls it over his head anyway, then joins her before the statue. Her fingers wiggle and the lamps alight.

It is the strangest reveal of his work that he has ever, will ever, experience.

"Look how tall I am!" she exclaims. "Like an Amazon."

She circles the marble and Alexandros reels, stumbling in the strangeness of art and inspiration, object and subject, flesh and stone, in conjunction. Worlds colliding.

"The hands . . ." she muses, and this has been his most major concern, that she will not approve of his decision. The sculpture's left arm extends outward, holding a handled mirror.

"The reflection faces outward," he explains, "but on the back . . ."

She reads the inscription: "'Love thyself.'"

The right arm hangs at the statue's side, the hand slightly curled.

"You are keeping space for what you hold most dear," Alexandros clarifies. He licks his lips, nervous. "For him."

Aphrodite's inserts her own soft hand into her marble incarnation's. She breathes, "Perfect."

Timon joins them. He who is typically so gregarious struggles for words in Aphrodite's presence, but she brightens at his arrival. "My sweet boy's sweetheart! At long last!" She winks. "You are so handsome; I might keep you for myself."

Her charm banishes his discomfort.

"She—you—has become such a part of our life. I think Alexandros will weep when she leaves!"

The artist nudges his lover, hard, in the unspoken language of intimacy.

"Will you take it to your palace on Olympus or your home in Paphos?" wonders Alexandros, redirecting the conversation to less vulnerable places.

"I have no plans to take it anywhere," she replies. "It belongs to you, and I want it to be seen. *This* is how I want to be seen."

He was not expecting such a response, but nothing about this commission has been conventional.

"Should I donate it to your temple here?"

Aphrodite nearly levels him with a diamond-hard look. "Stop giving, Alexandros. Demand what you deserve. Know your worth."

"Love thyself," agrees Timon.

"Sell it, Alexandros," instructs Aphrodite. "Claim your gold and spend it on something beautiful." Her gaze pointedly shifts to Timon. "Or someone."

He can keep her likeness for another night at least, but he doubts he will see the goddess again. Despite how much she means to him, he is but a tiny detail in her deathless design. His purpose—the sculpture—is fulfilled.

"Where will you go from here?" he asks.

"I am called to Thessaly."

A look of horror crosses Timon's face. "But they are at war!"

She shares a furtive smile with Alexandros. "Precisely."

Her body prepares to leave, arms lowering, palms turning out. She tilts her head back slightly, evoking and accepting the energy that powers her. The goddess starts to vanish in sparkles like stars twinkling out.

"It's magnificent," sings her voice. "You are magnificent."

For a long time after she is gone, they stand together in quietude.

"I like her more than I thought I would," Timon admits.

Aphrodite would not care, Alexandros thinks, *But I do.* He wanted Timon to like her, and he is happy they've met. One night with the goddess of love and beauty, a lifetime with his fisherman, in momentary eclipse.

REGARDLESS OF APHRODITE'S command, Alexandros does not immediately search for a buyer. He loiters and lingers, makes excuses, but eventually, Timon intervenes. One evening he brings home interest with the local catch.

"Alexandros, this is Kostas. He owns the gymnasium."

A burly man nods.

Alexandros mumbles his excuses and pulls Timon inside angrily. "I'm not ready!"

"She takes up too much room in our home. If you don't let her go, you won't be able to start something new."

Timon crosses his arms over his chest. He is stubborn; he is right. Slowly, Alexandros's pulse steadies and the panic subsides. He is able to return to the discussion of sale, reluctant but resigned.

"Why do you want her?" And his question sounds like a demand, but he does not care.

"Isn't it obvious?" returns Kostas with a shrug. "With Aphrodite watching, my men will train harder."

This rationale puzzles Alexandros, but he's not an athlete. Neither is he attracted to or motivated by women. Regardless, he gives Kostas an exorbitant price, no negotiation.

"I'll take it."

Everything moves quickly after that.

Days later, Kostas returns with his business partner and a crew of enslaved men. Alexandros cannot watch as they maneuver the statue onto a cart, but he hears the men talking.

"I don't understand the mirror."

"Pretty girls like to look at themselves."

"I like to look at their tits."

In their crude chortles, Alexandros understands the life he's condemned his girl to. Will the men in the gymnasium leering at her bared chest answer the mirror's question? *What does the way you look at her reveal about yourself?*

He worries his message will not be delivered, lost en route.

Alexandros stands on the dirt road until his eyes can no longer track the cart.

"How will I ever perform such a feat again?" he wonders aloud. "How will I outdo myself?"

But Timon is by his side and answers, "Stop trying to be better, just do something different."

Different. Yes, it might be nice to try something different.

Alexandros grabs Timon's face and kisses him hard on the lips. "With all this coin, we should travel. A trip to Naxos?"

"Yes!" Timon is radiant. "And then Crete and Rhodes."

"Cyprus?"

"Alexandria!"

"But first, bed."

"I am not tired."

The artist reaches for his lover's waist. "Not to sleep, my love, not yet."

A LIFE PASSES. ONE in marble, but also one in destinations, dinner, red wine, white wine, old friends, strangers, arguments, love—fierce love, quiescent love—times of budget and others of excess. Alexandros and Timon expand their home, keeping the studio in its middle, but adding more rooms for guests, for the many people they meet on their many journeys who come to visit.

The artist creates again, but nothing surpasses his Aphrodite. If he did not have Timon, it would trouble him, but his life is full. His subsequent pieces are well received but never make him rich. The trajectory does not always need to rise; he does not always need to be better.

Milos aligns with the powerful Roman Republic and enters a period of peaceful prosperity. With the incoming wealth from the mineral trade, artistic projects expand. The people build a marmoreal amphitheater beside the sea. The temple to Dionysus boasts a mosaiced floor of unprecedented proportion and mastery.

Alexandros appreciates these innovations. He is grateful to see them in his lifetime, and he dreams of all that might arise from the bottomless depths of imagination. As long as there exists a human experience, there will be real art. But then an illness in his chest lingers longer than normal. Years of inhaling dust. A persistent cough that begets blood. His appetite wanes to nothing but so, too, does his need to create. This is when Timon knows to worry. Alexandros prefers to be outside in the rose garden than in the studio. Wrapped in a thick blanket, despite the heat, he admires the world, the one that was transformed for him through attention and love.

That he can still feel wonder at such an age feels a great gift.

But before the difficult breathing becomes impossible, there is one final task.

"Timon, I need you to help me."

Dear Timon, still spry in his old age! Though he hasn't gone to sea in years, he still spends each morning on the dock with the fishermen, wishing them a safe trip and bountiful nets.

Timon, sitting in the grass, lays his head in Alexandros's lap. "Whatever you ask, my love."

Under nocturnal cover, they leave their home. Alexandros, with his hammer and chisel, rides a donkey that Timon leads by hand. They arrive at the gymnasium, long since closed for the night. While Timon monitors the entrance, Alexandros sneaks inside and vandalizes his own work.

When he joins Timon, holding his stolen loot, he stands taller than he has in months.

"You haven't asked me if I'm sure about this," he chides his lover.

"I do not doubt. I trust you."

But on their return home, Aphrodite waits, standing on the empty path, blocking their way, just as Alexandros suspected she might. She is upset.

"You stole my arms!" she cries.

"I did."

Her eyes burn like the lavender flame of driftwood. "I deserve an explanation."

"You do."

With considerable pain, Alexandros slides down the donkey's side. He brings Aphrodite her pieces.

"I tried to teach a lesson with your statue, but its viewers weren't ready to learn. Instead, they misinterpret—you, what you did, what you stand for. By removing her hands, I have made her as perfectly imperfect as the real you."

"But I do have hands!" Aphrodite bemoans. "And she is broken." Nevertheless, she accepts the marble offerings.

"She is a mystery," Alexandros corrects. The pain in his chest is an agony but he continues, for this might be the greatest speech of his life. "And because of that, she will transcend time and place. Don't you see? I put the answer before the question! As long as something remains unknown, it retains the possibility of forever. Art only lasts if we continue to ask questions, if we continue to believe in the mystery. If humanity stops thinking, we take it all for granted." He pauses to recover his breath. "Aphrodite, we cannot give them all the answers. Let them, in all the ages to come, continue to discuss love and beauty."

She works through her anger. Might she smite him on the spot? There is fear in the way Timon's hands shake on the donkey's rope, but Alexandros, so close to the end already, is unafraid.

"I will keep them guessing," she repeats slowly, and then she beams. "Dear boy"—though he hasn't been a boy in so many decades—"Athena herself would envy your cunning!"

He enters a deep, inordinate peace. A sense of completion. This is his masterpiece, all of it. The statue and the goddess. The man beside him, leading a pack animal. The years it took to get here, on this insignificant dirt road in the dead of night.

She clutches marble arms within her flesh ones, and the image sears into his soul. He will hold it forever.

Timon helps lift him back upon the donkey.

Before she leaves, he calls out the question that has plagued him.

"Will it hurt?"

Aphrodite knows what he means and offers a rueful smile. "I don't know, but I will be with you if you'd like."

"Yes. Please."

AND WHEN DEATH comes for him months later, it is scented with flowers. He sighs and releases himself into the overwhelming rose light.

There is no pain, only love.

Part VI

IN PIECES

Aphrodite, Venus
Inanna, Ishtar, Astarte
Eve, Jezebel, Salome
Helen of Troy, Cleopatra
Guinevere
Madame Bovary, Anna Karenina
Liz, Marilyn, Pamela, Britney
Me
You

42

MILOS
The Roman Period

Alexandros,

You have been gone for enough decades that you would not recognize this world. The Ptolemies are no longer. Athens has fallen—so has Egypt—as all power shifts to Rome, which is no longer a republic but an empire.

The Greeks are not as they were.

We are being absorbed.

The Romans call me by a different name. To them, I am Venus. That is fine, I suppose. I've been associated with other names for far longer: Inanna, Ishtar. Astarte.

And Ares has become Mars. The Greeks never particularly liked Ares, not unless they needed him, but the Romans worship him above all others. Obsession is a perversion of love, and they have manipulated his image into something dark and different. As their empire conquers the continent, they do not just call for him but demand him.

There is so much greed.

In their capital, they have a colosseum where they kill one another for entertainment. A gentle soul like you could not fathom such carnality. They pit gladiators, athletes in the brutal blood sport of death, against elephants and tigers, bears and bulls. Even crocodiles! They fight with chariots and nets, curved blades and tridents, producing hundreds of thousands of corpses.

And yet, it is a treasured institution.

There is more to share. Alexandros, they have armed me! A new sculpture of "Venus" was recently debuted, and I am naked holding a sword. Eros—whom they now call Cupid—is a toddler, resting at my feet, wearing an oversized helmet.

Who would go to war without clothes? Who would bring their baby?

Because you know everything about me, you know I have never held a sword in my life. I have never won a duel. I've yet to shoot an arrow that actually strikes anything. Still, I have become the causa belli, the cause of the greatest war. Paris gave me the apple; I gave him Helen. Excess love leads to excess killing.

I am no harbinger of war, nor am I anyone's camp wife.

All the emperors and generals claim to have lain with me. To say so has become a rite of passage. If you've slept with me, then you are Ares—excuse me, Mars—incarnate, and I have blessed your campaign. As if I give a damn about expansion.

As if I would allow any of them to touch me.

Ares and I are often imitated: Hadrian and Antinous. Augustus and Livia. Marc Antony and Cleopatra. (Antony even gifted her Cyprus. My island. The audacity!) But they are not our proxies, no matter how many poets claim otherwise.

Maybe people no longer listen to the old stories, for in those days, nobody wanted love and war anywhere near each other.

I enjoy returning to Milos, though I don't do it often. I like walking the path from the beach to your hill, to the house where I posed for the first and only time. And I like talking to you in this garden, the one I made for you, where you and Timon are buried. I have continued to add flowers and trees. I think you would enjoy the textures.

Somebody keeps trying to replace the arms on my statue, always with that cursed Apple of Discord. It's strange, but those shoddily constructed arms continue to fall off.

I wonder who would do such a thing.

Alexandros,

When I last visited Milos, I did not mention the Christians, who follow the teachings of a gentle man from the eastern desert. I like some of their stories, especially the ones where the Messiah is kind to prostitutes. I did not think their movement would last, yet its message persists. Now even the emperor of Rome has proclaimed them as his own, and Christianity is the official religion of the empire.

Only one way to believe? It is unfathomable!

And Constantine, this emperor, has moved the capital from the seven hills, where my son Aeneas's line reigned for so many generations, to Byzantium, which is now called Constantinople.

On Milos the followers of the Christ built a series of caves, of catacombs, into the volcanic rock belowground. They store their dead down there, with prayers and strange rituals.

The people do not visit my statue as often anymore, but when they do, they yell at me. They blame me for their heartache, which I am accustomed to, but they want to hurt me because of it.

They smash my lesser idols, burn them, destroy them with glee.

Harlot, they call me. Concubine. Profane. Unclean. Abomination. Whore.

I still do not understand how they attribute such harsh language to that peaceful, long-haired man, but they idolize a virgin version of his mother—one who was herself immaculately conceived. In a world where the divine feminine is sexless, I am their original temptress. They call me Eve or Jezebel or Salome. I am wicked or foolish or both.

Even Hera would find this sterile standard for women impractical and oppressive. Not that I talk to her much anymore.

Oh, Alexandros. I do worry for the mortal women and everyone who loves differently. How are they expected to live like this?

43

MILOS
The Byzantine Period

Alexandros,

Your dear island is neither Greek nor Roman. It was Turkish, then Venetian, and now it is Turkish again. Milos passes from empire to empire with the speed of plague or sensational gossip. I've never understood land as a possession. How can you own earth? It's like owning air.

It is mayhem.

There are pirate raids. Earthquakes.

The old gymnasium was destroyed, and my statue within. I was yanked from the rubble in pieces but claimed by nobody. Left to die in a graveyard of stone. Other bricks have been confiscated and repurposed. But I remain. Halved and waiting— For what? Discovery? Recognition?

Rebirth.

I do not think I will visit as much anymore. It hurts to be here.

Constantinople has fallen to the Ottomans. Christianity battles with Islam, another religion with only one god. They do not seem to see the similarities in each other.

Humanity continues to confound me.

The world changes again, not in essence, but in how they name things. How they define and delineate.

Before it left Greece, I went to see the Praxiteles statue of me on Knidos. Remember how we spoke of it when we first met? In it, I am fully nude, my right hand reaching for my pubic area. A man has ejaculated onto it so many times he has permanently stained the marble of my thigh.

You had no need to fear it, Alexandros. Yours is so much better.

Alexandros,

I am famous again.

Sandro Botticelli, an artist from the Roman land of Italy (what you and I once called Latium), has painted me with oils on canvas. This impressive piece depicts my birth. Many elements are correct, like the color of my hair and the shell, the proportions of my face. But others are wrong. The Graces waited to greet me at Cyprus, not the Horae, and I did not sail upon winds, but swam like my very existence depended upon it. I did not arrive on that island floating and dry; I was wet and exhausted. Bedraggled.

In Botticelli's version, I am covering myself with my hands and hair. Not to create mystery but because I must be modest. It is the proper way of women. Likewise, men of learning call a winged Zephyrus "angel."

What is an angel?

They refer to me as "Eve before the Fall"!

To these men, once my bare feet touch Cypriot land, I become every sin.

Sin is such a popular word now.

Overall, it is very beautiful work, the colors are lovely. It has become another piece of my image and story, even if it's part fantasy.

Very different from your sculpture.

The painting was not commissioned by me, but for a powerful man. A Medici, which means nothing to you but so much to others. They have said all women should look like me if they want to be beautiful. How is that possible when they have none of my power? It does not seem fair. Why shouldn't all men look like Apollo, then?

I see beauty in every woman, in those who are similar to how I look and in those who are nothing like me. Women with hard bodies and soft ones, with no hair and abundant hair. Eyes in all shapes and colors. I think elderly women to be the most stunning. All that life they hold in them! I am jealous that I do not get to age in such a way, that I do not reflect my acquired wisdom in my body.

Perfect women are created by men, they say. Like Pygmalion made Galatea. But I made her.

Love did that.

44

MILOS
The Ottoman Period

A FRENCHMAN NAMED OLIVIER Voutier is stationed on Milos, a sailor in the French navy, fighting alongside the Greeks in their war for independence. Olivier does not enjoy battle, he does not dream of naval formations and gunpowder, but of art. Of history and myth. He loves antiquity, the old, ever-beating heart at the core of civilization.

It is April of 1821, spring. His ship is at port, and he is hiking through the rocky hillsides. And thinking, always thinking. He likes to imagine how the island would have appeared in its ancient glory, when ideas and stories were traded like currency, and people believed an Olympian immortal could show up at your door any moment.

"You romanticize the past!" his father says. "None of that is real. In the olden days, nobody had teeth, and everyone died young!"

But what does his father truly know? The man prefers accounting logs to books.

A local farmer, Yorgos, is schooling Olivier in Greek conversation, and Olivier heads in the farm's direction. He is curious about the pronunciation of *siniditopíisi*, a feminine noun that means "realization."

As he approaches, he senses a disturbance in the ether, something amiss in the fields. Ahead, his friend Yorgos and his father, Theodoros, are standing upon their plot of land. He reads revelation, perhaps excitement, in their body language. They beckon Olivier forward. Because he is French and a foreigner, they believe him to be more worldly than them.

Perhaps they romanticize him.

"Look! Look! Olivier, come! A discovery!"

Olivier runs, knowing somehow that his life is about to change.

In the ground, in a crudely dug hole, sit large pieces of carved marble.

"Please, allow me!" exclaims Olivier. He takes the shovel from the elder and then he and Yorgos continue to dig.

Word travels down the hill, to the beach and around the island. More locals arrive. More French soldiers, too. Together, they unearth a statue of a partially nude woman, broken in half, an arm holding an apple, and a plinth.

"The Apple of Discord!" shouts an onlooker, pointing.

"Is it Eve?" wonders a puzzled Frenchman. He is Catholic and confuses Eris's apple with the one from Eden.

"No, no. This is Aphrodite."

Olivier briefly explains the onset of the Trojan War to those who never took a classics course. A woman with a pinched face crosses herself. She spits.

"Trollop," she says, in her native tongue, as she walks away.

The sculpture, even in its current state, is coveted by many men, but she belongs to Yorgos and his father. The family, devoutly Orthodox, decides to sell the piece to their priest.

Olivier, when he hears, is beside himself. He nearly runs to Yorgos's home.

"Your priest is sending it to Constantinople as a gift to the Ottoman court!"

Yorgos shrugs.

"But they are your enemy!" argues Olivier in his limited Greek. "When the *Aphrodite of Knidos* went to Constantinople, it was lost in a fire!"

"I am a God-fearing Christian man. I do not want this naked thing. It does not matter who takes it."

"But this is your history, Yorgos! She may come from the Hellenistic—even the classical—age!"

The farmer shakes his head. "A whore is a whore in any age."

Frustrated and frantic, Olivier reaches out to his superior offices but meets only resistance. "What do we want with a massive marble statue of unknown provenance?"

But maybe the Moirai, the Fates, are on Olivier's side.

The *Chevrette*, a French ship on a hydrographic survey of the Greek archipelago, docks at Milos, and Olivier's message makes its way to the bridge. Though the captain refuses to take it on board, citing insufficient space, an amateur classicist, Jules Dumont d'Urville, agrees with Olivier and seeks help through a more immediate channel: He writes directly to the French ambassador, pleading for assistance with this remarkable find.

This letter arrives upon the desk of the ambitious Marquis de Rivière, who recognizes an opportunity.

Five years earlier, France lost the Napoleonic Wars and the country is still an embarrassment within the European community. A Greek statue from the Hellenistic period, in excellent condition and never debuted, might regain their standing.

And, thinks the marquis smugly, *owning the statue means you own beauty itself.*

Beauty is a commodity, and it belongs to the French.

Eventually, the sculpture makes its way across multiple seas and numerous countries to Paris, to join the royal collection in the Louvre.

But before her formal presentation to King Louis XVIII, classical experts clean and analyze the piece, quickly acknowledging the arm with the apple as a forgery. It is too rough-hewn, not of the same Parian marble as the rest.

"Probably added on later by another artist," hypothesizes one scholar.

"Then what happened to her arms?"

"A group of illiterate farmers handled the site," sniffs another. "They either missed the arms or stole them."

The plinth is similarly cast aside.

"Who is Alexandros of Antioch on the Maeander?"

"Nobody."

Aphrodite's name is changed to the more fashionable Latin name *Venus de Milo.*

"She is more beautiful than any of the Praxiteles copies!" people murmur.

"And she is *ours.*"

"Our reputation is restored!"

However, the monarch, Louis XVIII, will not see the statue for another year. His obesity and gout keep him restricted to the palace.

Alexandros,

They found me. They took me.
What does this mean?
Where do I go from here?

45

PARIS
Twenty-First Century

A STYLISH WOMAN STANDS before the *Venus de Milo* in the sixteenth gallery of the Louvre's Sully wing. She wears black Celine sunglasses, even inside.

A tour group of bumbling and sweaty yet eager Americans stumbles to a halt beside her. Though their feet go still, their fingers remain frenzied, typing and swiping on their phones as their French guide addresses them in fluent English.

"Here, of course, stands the *Venus de Milo*, arguably the most famous statue in the world, seen by over seven million people a year and up to twenty thousand people a day. She is the inspiration for poetry and fine art, essays and criticism, advertising—even the actresses of the golden age of Hollywood."

"I like the winged statue better," complains one bored little boy.

"At least this one has a head," retorts an older child, probably the big sister.

"She has outlasted wars, traveled the world. During the Nazi occupation in World War II, the museum smuggled her out of Paris for safety. And in the 1960s, she was shipped to Japan on temporary loan. Thousands waited upon the dock just to see her ship arrive. Earlier in that century," continues the museum docent, "two East Coast American universities held a *Venus de Milo* contest where women submitted their measurements, hoping to match hers."

"She's not even that hot," jokes a college-aged man to his friend.

"Boobs are too small."

"And she's got a pooch."

Beauty might be immortal, but its standards are not unchanging. The girls and women of this age quantify beauty in the number of heart-shaped affirmations tapped upon a screen. The *Venus* is not their Venus. Another ideal has emerged, one produced in med spas and doctor's offices, perfected by camera editing. The modern woman has proportions even an immortal could not achieve. Overly prominent lips and immaculate brows. The same nose and jaw, repeated ad nauseam.

The tour guide ignores the comments. She has heard them all before.

"The statue is modeled, of course, on the goddess of love and beauty. Venus, as she was known in Rome, or Aphrodite in Greece."

"I always thought she was the worst goddess," mutters a woman to her partner. "She doesn't do anything cool."

"She's a symbol of our oppression. I hate her."

The docent takes off her glasses, wipes them on her blazer, then puts them back on. "The most common question I receive is 'What happened to her arms?' In truth, we do not know. Maybe war, maybe an earthquake. Or perhaps those in charge of her safekeeping just did not do an adequate job."

"Do you know anything about her hands? What did she hold?" asks a curious visitor at the rear of the group.

"There is so much speculation. The most prominent theory is that one hand clutched the edge of her tunic, to keep it from slipping down her hip, and the other held an apple." The tour guide pauses; her mouth twists. "I don't know though. I spend a lot of time with her, and that's never felt right to me."

"I bet she had a dagger," says the boy, and his sister rolls her eyes. "What? That would be cooler than something stupid like a rose."

The girl steps past him. "I would hold your hand," she whispers, just under her breath so that her family cannot hear and tease her.

The woman in Celine shades remains quiet. She would stay longer, just to eavesdrop, but she has an appointment she cannot miss across the Seine. As she leaves the exhibit, her hand brushes against the girl's back, and the girl's mind fills with images: seeds and stars and shells and swans. Ideas, too, about permanence and identity. The child gasps at the wonder of it all and will later credit this exact moment in the novel she writes about love and beauty, art and time.

The stylish woman crosses the bridge into Saint-Germain, unbothered by the height of her heels on the cobbled roads. It takes her less than fifteen minutes, but she is still late.

She is not known for her punctuality.

He is, however, and is already seated at a table for two outside, deep in a newspaper. He still reads the paper copies, even with all the technology available.

Before her empty seat waits an espresso and a glass of champagne.

He knows her order.

Only when she sits does he finally look up, and that smile, one that doesn't show teeth but fills his eyes, still undoes her.

"You went and saw it?" he asks. There is a slight unidentifiable accent to his voice.

She nods.

"And?"

"I am still magnificent."

He shakes his head. "You and your museums."

"They are my photo albums."

They are mandatory stops on her travels, a way to remember where she came from without living too much in the past. Yesterday she took a quick train north to view Raphael's *Three Graces* at the Musée Condé in Chantilly. And there are so many pieces in America now.

Peter Paul Rubens's *The Wedding of Peleus and Thetis* in Chicago. Gérôme's *Pygmalion and Galatea* and Rubens's *Venus and Adonis* at the Met. She likes to watch the visitors consider them, and ask questions.

She takes a sip of her espresso. "There is an oil painting in Brussels you would find of interest. It's called *Mars Being Disarmed by Venus*."

He scoffs and she smiles.

The waiter takes their food order, and the man and woman discuss their work. He is a member of the United Nations Secretariat and has worked with the Blue Berets, in various peacekeeping roles. She is a human rights lawyer who specializes in prosecuting acts of violence against women, most notably by high-profile men. They are very busy, but that is nothing new.

Still, they make time to see each other. Not as often as they would like, but in places all over the world.

A piano bar in Casablanca.

On the sands of the Halona Beach Cove.

An ice palace in Russia.

A balcony in Verona.

A houseboat in Seattle.

For they are present in every romance.

As for the others like them, some adapted and thus survived, while others did not. Some kept in contact, and others willingly disappeared. To continue requires change, a flexibility not everyone who has held power can accept. It requires imagination.

In every world, in every age, existence requires sacrifice.

The stories help, for immortality depends upon belief. Their names printed in hardcovers and paperbacks, repeated in classrooms, enables some magic, but when formal worship waned, so did their power. Without the temples and the offerings, none of them are transforming into animals or flying chariots anymore.

Athena transitions easiest of all, wielding the authority she always coveted as CEO of a major corporation. Capitalism, she learned, was the surest way to control the government. Apollo maintains an esoteric life, conducting symphonies in Central Europe. Hermes developed a messaging application that landed him on the cover of *Wired*, a baseball cap replacing his helmet of invisibility. Hephaestus builds innovative cars that attract women who would otherwise ignore him.

But these are the exceptions. Most of the others fade away. The Graces and their simple elegance, their courteous goodwill, become less and less appreciated as crude cruelty gains popular acceptance. And as computers colonize art and language and history is deemed fake, the Muses wilt. While Eros remains hale, his darling wife Psyche, the representative of the soul, wavers in the divisive digital age.

And Zeus? He struggles most of all. For thunder and lightning inspire little awe in a world where nuclear bombs can decimate entire nations.

The woman in the sunglasses understands that to exist within this terrible world, you must still believe in its beauty. You must love it, regardless. So you find a way to make it a little bit more bearable.

For her, that means litigation. Legislation. She will never relent in removing the violence from sex, particularly when power dynamics are manipulated against women.

Her companion engages with war on his terms, finding solutions, supporting civilians. A truly wise warrior avoids conflict.

It is the work of several lifetimes.

At this café in the sixth arrondissement, her name is Brigitte. He is Oskar.

"I have something for you," he says. "I found it in Brazil."

From his pocket, he removes something small, something purple, and he passes it to her hand. A stone of lavender quartz.

"I have searched for . . . well, a long time . . . to find the exact color of your eyes."

She turns the stone over. In the style of his own hand, a word is etched.

αἰών

Eternity.

His gifts are few and far between. And this one is perfect.

"I brought nothing for you." She tucks the stone into her pocket. "I should buy you a dog."

"I travel too often."

"A small one, then. A bichon frise."

"I would have fed those to Graegus as treats."

Before she can comment, they are recognized.

"You!" accuses a stranger, staring at Brigitte. "You're that lawyer bitch for the Hollywood sluts! You're the one ruining all the movies!"

Oskar lights a cigarette and brings it to his mouth, a ghost of a grin haunts his lips. "I suggest apologizing immediately."

"Or what?"

The angry stranger is so predictable, it bores the woman. She finishes her espresso as the men lock eyes. What the stranger sees leaves him pale, trembling. The paper cup of coffee in his hand crashes to the ground.

The god of war continues smoking.

"I am so sorry," the stranger stutters. "I should never have insulted your wife."

"Oh, I'm not his wife." She drinks from her champagne glass. "But he never pays, so I guess I'm not his whore either."

The goddess of love and beauty beams.

And the flustered stranger walks away.

"That was fun," she says. "Now, about this puppy . . ."

"A night with you at Le Meurice is the only gift I require."

Her favorite hotel, the most expensive, the most exquisite. She had booked their stay when they'd arranged to meet in Paris.

She raises an eyebrow. "One night never used to be sufficient."

"I'm getting old, Aphrodite."

She loves when he says her true name in the old language. Something inside her tightens and tingles. She is ethereal, arising from the sea again. Breathless.

"Ours is still a young love, despite being the oldest one."

She rises, leaving him the bill, and kisses his temple, where the hints of gray have entered his hair. He still keeps his hair and beard tightly clipped.

He reaches for her hand and brings it to his mouth. Kissing her, smelling her, with eyes closed. A murmur, a promise.

"I have one more chore in the city, but I'll meet you by dinner."

"Oysters?"

She gestures to her empty coupe. "And another bottle of that."

HER ERRAND BRINGS her to the Banque de France.

She is discreetly welcomed into a private room, where she waits while her safe-deposit box is retrieved from the subterranean vault. Supposedly a moat surrounds it. She adores the drama of it all. A man returns, hefting a dark wooden box onto the table, and bows.

"Merci," she replies.

After he departs, the door's lock clicks into position, and she lifts the lid. Inside are her treasures, surely worth a record-breaking amount at any Sotheby's auction. She lets herself see them only every century or so. And every time she touches them, it is an emotional reunion.

Two stone arms.

One holding a mirror, turned outward. Its hand has a thin, traceable scar on both the outside and the palm, from where a dagger once rested. And the other arm—her favorite of the pair—with its hand in mid-grip, fingers curved and apart, holding space for its beloved.

She holds hands with herself, feels the marble, and remembers. The artist and his studio. Telling her story for the first and only time.

One day she might place them somewhere to be discovered, if the finder is particularly worthy. But she is loath to part with them. Alexandros was right—the sculpture is better without them.

But there wouldn't be a statue if she and he hadn't spoken of hands. Of poses and portrayal. Of all that she held.

And the one hand that she will never let go.

A man who waits for her now, perhaps by the open window of their upper-floor room, considering the neighborhood below. Here, in this modern city with an aged heart, where treaties ending war have been signed and nascent lovers stroll through parks in the early dusk.

Aphrodite will return the box and meet him, slipping out of her clothes and into his arms, into their bed.

Into infinity.

Him and her, until the world ends.

Author's Note

Misunderstood women are my muses. I'm forever inspired by the intersection of the world that was and the world that is. My novels are a patchwork quilt of research and imagination, primary sources and modern influence. To compose my reimagining of Aphrodite, I listened to many voices.

Aphrodite originally came to Greece from the east, probably an evolution of the Sumerian goddesses Inanna and Ishtar and the Assyrian goddess Astarte. The primary sources offer different accounts of Aphrodite's birth and parentage. I used the version found in Hesiod's *Theogony*. Homer's *Odyssey* (Book 8) details her forced marriage to Hephaestus and her affair with Ares. Apollodorus, in the *Bibliotheca*, describes Aphrodite cursing Eos* for lying with her sweetheart, Ares. The myth of Psyche and Eros comes from Book 4 of *The Golden Ass*, an ancient Roman novel by Apuleius. The story of Pygmalion is told in Ovid's *Metamorphoses*. In the "Homeric Hymn to Aphrodite," Zeus causes Aphrodite to fall in love with Anchises as retribution for her meddling. Most of her adventures during the Trojan War are found in Homer's *Iliad*.

---

* I changed Eos's name to the Roman version, Aurora, to avoid confusion with Eros and Eris.

Besides the classics, I read *Love, Pamela*, Pamela Anderson's memoir, and immersed myself in the golden age of Hollywood—in particular, the many interviews of Elizabeth Taylor (and Richard Burton), Marilyn Monroe, and Mae West. I drew a lot of Aphrodite's character from these legendary women.

Lastly, Rodin's essay on the *Venus de Milo* helped me comprehend the enormity of its mastery. As Enobarbus declares in act 2, scene 2 of Shakespeare's *Antony and Cleopatra*, "Age cannot wither her."

Acknowledgments

Anne, you are an alchemist, taking my rough, raggedy drafts and purifying them with your input and insight. Together, I think we create something golden. Thank you for everything. All the Graegus scenes are for you! And thank you to Alyssa, for your work in getting this book done and on time.

Jane, a legendary woman with legendary advice. You always make me feel like I matter and that I can do this, so I had to put some of your wisdom in this story. As Aphrodite tells Apollo—onward!

The copy editors and production team at Ace/Berkley who tolerate my incessant corrections with patience and professionalism. You are the best! And can we take a moment to acknowledge this cover? Jill De Haan, you are a genius. Pop art *Venus de Milo* fabulousness. Alison Cnockaert, you made Aphrodite proud with this beautiful layout.

The PR and publicity dream team, Jessica and Chelsea at Ace/Berkley, thank you for all the support and the tireless work you do to get my books into the world.

And in the UK, Elora and Charlotte at Titan Books. It's an honor and pleasure to work with you both. What a dream to have my books in your capable hands!

To the friends (my girls!) and family who buy too many copies of my books and come to all my events and deal with me when I'm on deadline and celebrate when I'm done. Thank you for the love, the check-ins, and the cocktails when I need them most.

To Dan Bear and our cubs, my whole heart. My children keep me laughing and my husband keeps me fed; without either, I could not do this work. Babies, I'm sorry, but you cannot read this book until you are much older. DB, I'm so happy you exist.

To the booksellers who have boosted my career and recommended my work, and the incredible authors who read early versions of this novel and offered their kind words. To the Bookstagrammers and BookTokers that have spread the good word. Readers are my people, and I owe many of you a box of tissues. Thank you for sticking with me.